Death 2 My Past

About the Author

Angelia Bailey is a full-time single mother. When she isn't tucked away writing, you can find her on a beach in sunny central Florida or in the country side of southern Ohio. If you'd like to connect with the author, follow her on Twitter @AWritersLifeTBC. Keep up to date on all bookish news at www.AngeliaNBailey.com

Death 2 My Past

Angelia N. Bailey

2020

Copyright © 2020 by Angelia N. Bailey

All rights reserved. This book or any portion thereof may not be reproduced or used in any manner whatsoever without the express written permission of the publisher except for the use of brief quotations in a book review or scholarly journal.

First Printing: 2020

This is a work of fiction. Names, characters, places, and incidents either are the product of the author's imagination or are used fictitiously. Any resemblance to actual persons, living or dead, event, or locales is entirely coincidental.

The Cataloging-in-Publication Data is on file at Library of Congress.

ISBN 978-1-090-13036-5

Book design by Angelia N. Bailey
Cover designed by Angelia N. Bailey
Cover image © https://placeit.net/

Ordering Information:

Special discounts are available on quantity purchases by corporations, associations, educators, and others. For details, contact the publisher at the below listed address.

U.S. trade bookstores and wholesalers: Please contact Angelia Bailey Tel: +1 (614) 369-7477 or email authorANB@AngeliaNBailey.com.

Printed in the United States of America

For my 'Lucas'

I'll forever be grateful for the lessons you taught me.
Thank you.

Acknowledgements

First and foremost, thank you to my patient and talented editor Justine Manzano. She's a god send! I'm constantly thanking the saints for her pristine editing skills. She took Abigail's story and helped make it soar. You rock Justine!

To my very first reader, when *Death 2 My Past* was just a short story, Kristin Hough. She gave me the confidence to take a seven-page story and turn it into an entire novel.

Kristen, I still remember going on walks with you to the church by grandma's house. You used to read the pages under the street lamp. I'll never forget the monumental impact you made on, what I can now proudly call, my writing career. Thank you!

I owe a depth of gratitude to Mariah Estep, my wonderfully patient best friend. She's been my main supporter, confidant, and this book's cheerleader. Without her, I'd have given up a long time ago.

Riah, I'm more thankful for you than you'll ever know. You've endured draft after draft with this book and my ramblings nonstop about the story. There isn't enough room in this entire book to go through every reason I'm thankful for how you've helped with this dream. I hope one simple 'thank you' will suffice.

So, **THANK YOUUUU!**

A *massive* thanks goes to the beautifully abundant writing community on Twitter. I've learned so much through them and the opportunity of meeting so many talented writers has been a blessing. A few of those writers' tips and feedback has helped this book along. A hundred thanks to all of you!

I especially need to take a moment to give a special thanks to Zohra Amimi, my friend across the pond. Your help has been so valuable. Being able to get first-hand information about Rouen has been so crucial to ensuring I respect the French culture. Thank you for taking the time to read the early draft and for your continued encouragement!

In addition to her, I'd also like to thank the Owners of La Couronne whom have been beyond helpful in my endeavor to include their remarkable establishment in Abigail's story. I can't wait to visit one day!

This special bit has its own meaning and it's not so much a thank you. More of a recognition for how these two people changed my life. They inspired me a long time ago, when I was 9-years-old, to keep writing. This book would've never happened if it had not been for one particular day.

On that day, I meshed together a poem, my very first piece of writing. First, Uncle Bud, you were happy to read it, but ended up crying. You never cry. And you were so mad at the person and the place of pain that poem came from.

Then, Aunt Val, you couldn't understand what was wrong. Uncle Bud handed you the poem and the moment you read it, you wrapped me in the tightest hug while crying too.

Their reactions inspired me to keep writing poems until one day, I got the courage to write an entire novel. And now I'm crying while typing this! Ah, hell. I know I said this wasn't a thanks, but how can I not thank them for that! So, *THANK YOU!*

To all my friends and family who endured all my "Hey. What do you think about this?" or "Hey. Can I get your opinion on something?" messages, THANK YOU! I hope after reading, you find it all worth it and the memory annoys you a little less.

To all four of my parents, hey you created/raised me so of course I'm going to mention you.

There. You were mentioned.

Kidding! **Stow the lectures.**

Mom & James – Thank you guys for not sending me off to boarding school.

Momma – Ah, hell. You're the beez neez! Thanks for giving me a little sister so I wasn't the only girl out of six kids. It helps that she's not the worst.

Dad – You weren't always around growing up, but I've never stopped wanting to make you proud. That helped me strive for the best and never give up. I have to recognize that because it's helped me push myself when writing got daunting. I love you. Thank you for being here *today* because that's all that matters. I appreciate everything you've done for me.

R.I.H. Grandma. I wish you could be here to see this. ***Love you!***

Grandma Sue, you sparked my creativity at a young age. I always wanted to be an artist just like you. I love you.

Maw Maw, even when you were really hard on me, I knew it came from a place of love. I know you want to see me strive for the best. I hope I've made you proud :)

Shane. Oh, my love. You've instilled me with strength I thought to be long gone. You've reinforced my confidence in myself and my abilities. The light inside my heart was very frail, but then you came along and doused it with your love. You really don't know how much you saved me. So, thank you. From the bottom of my heart. There aren't enough words to describe how you've helped me grow and healed me. I love you.

A small reminder:
If I did not name you above, it isn't saying you aren't important. This section is intended for anyone who helped me with my writing or writing career in some way. And there are too many aunts, uncles, siblings, cousins, – especially cousins – and other people to name every single person.

Death 2 My Past

1

The couple ogling each other at one of my tables is pissing me off.

I slam a stack of dirty dishes from table four down into the soapy water, nearly breaking a plate. *Merde.* Stuff like that—happy couples, acts of love, and all things romance—are part of the reason why I'd rather hole up in my bedroom. This sappy crap doesn't have anything on my night terrors.

I can't believe I actually used to fascinate over having my first long-term boyfriend. Naïve fifteen-year-old me thought it'd be all sappy and romantic. Love, romance, and all that lovey-dovey relationship stuff is as mythological as unicorns. It all eventually ends in heartbreak and disappointment.

Out of habit, I steal a glance outside the front door of La Couronne as I leave the kitchen to take the customer's order at table one. I breathe in relief at the sight of the clear blue skies scattered with a cloud here or there. Stupid astraphobia. Stupid night terrors for causing this phobia that sounds more like a ridiculous fear of space.

I break my gaze from the window, readying my notepad to take the customer's order.

"Hello. Welcome to La Couronne. Have you found anything to your liking?" I ask, plastering on my best customer service smile.

He keeps flipping through the menu and saying "Uhm" every five seconds like I have nothing else to do except stand here to wait the rest of my shift for him. I click my pen anxiously until he finally announces he needs more time to decide. Obviously.

I storm away, yanking my burgundy apron off. Crap like this makes me have mixed feelings about starting my therapist's idea for exposure therapy. But hell, it's worth something since it's gotten me this far. As of today, I've officially worked seven straight days as a waitress, which means I've officially completed my first fear ladder. Sure, there's probably at least a dozen more to go, but it's still more progress than I ever thought I'd make.

The grin spreading on my face deepens as I hand over my tables to my co-worker and clock out. They're his problem now, including Mr. Uhmm at table one. My shift is finally over. Thank the saints.

My feet rejoice as I sink into one of the patio chairs outside La Couronne while I wait for Erianne. Aw well if it's only Monday. I accomplished a huge milestone in my mental health recovery. Like hell if I'm not celebrating this.

My leg won't stop bouncing and wringing my hands isn't doing anything to calm the frizzled electricity running through my limbs. The little hand on my phone's analog clock ticks forward. It's been twenty minutes already. Erianne needs to hurry up. The wind is starting to pick up. And that's usually a sign a storm is going to start.

A gust brushes my face and sends my pulse skyrocketing. Recognizing the minor change in the weather any other sane person wouldn't sends blood rushing to my ears. If it wasn't for this stupid phobia of mine, I might be able to ignore or shrug of these things like a normal person. Fighting against the urge to check the sky is useless. It's calming blue from earlier has shifted now that gloomy gray sheets of clouds are rolling in. *Merde.*

Click. Click. Click. Click.

The familiar tapping of high heels against the pavement rings through my ears, pulling me out of my panic. Erianne is the only girl I know brave enough to strut around in those things she calls shoes while serving tables all day. But even in school, she'd have some kind of high heels on. It's her trademark. I guess it'd be weirder if she *wasn't* wearing them.

She sashays gracefully out of the restaurant, her hips swaying with each step she takes. Her usual bright 'life-is-so-perfect' smile is plastered across her face. Most people would envy her slender figure and the way she has petite curves framing her perfect body, but not me. I love my thicker figure. It's her confidence I envy. She never walks into a room, or goes anywhere, really, without looking like she's in charge. Americans on this TV show I've been watching would call her a "boss bitch".

"You ready, Abby?"

She beams brighter as she walks past me, slipping on her pea coat.

"Where are we going?"

I jog to catch up. Those mile-long legs of hers always make it hard for my short stubby ones to keep up. Tiny wet specs are splattering the ground by her feet. No. Everywhere on the ground. My throat tightens. The roar of thunder comes from far away, but it's like a siren right next to me.

One foot after the other, it's that easy. Repeating my mother's words in my helps, but it's not keeping me from wanting to turn back. No, I can't let my phobia win. This is *my* body. I'm in control. I have to concentrate on breathing, running through the calming techniques my therapist taught me: In, hold, count down from five, then let it out. *In—five, four, three, two, one—and out.*

"A favorite place of mine is about a ten-minute walk from here. You'll like it," she says.

I shake my head, realizing what seemed like an eternity to calm myself was barely a second. Stealing a glimpse at the darkening sky, I squeeze my hands together. *In—five, four, three, two, one—and out.*

"Sounds good to me." I smile up at her.

The faster we get there, the better. Erianne wraps her scarf around her neck as we turn the corner down Place de la Pucelle.

"So why La Couronne?" She asks.

"Huh?"

Her random question that makes no sense tears my attention away from the weather.

"I mean of all the places in France you could work, why La Couronne?"

I stare down at the sidewalk, watching my feet tap the pavement. I don't even know how to answer that question. The reason I stay working there, even when I don't have to now that I've completed the last step of my fear ladder for therapy, is because La Couronne is unique. Being one of the oldest business' in all of France, I have respect for the way it sticks out and stays true to its roots compared to all these other places trying to 'modernize'. La Couronne reflects Old France, a time when technology and social media didn't control everyone's life.

I tuck my hands in my pockets, getting a bitter taste in my mouth when my hand grazes the cell Mama picked up for me despite my strong protest and even after I threw the last one out my bedroom window.

But that's stuff I happened to fall in love with along the way. It's not the reason I started working there. I think because I was mindlessly going through the motions when Mama and my therapist suggested getting the job, I did it without really thinking about it. The alternative—hiding away in my room for months on end—wasn't working. And it's not like I had any real solutions.

Erianne shakes her head. "Sorry, I don't mean to pry. I just—"

I cut her off. "No, it's okay. I just got sick of sitting in the house all day, I guess," I say, sparing her all the personal details.

She knows I'm in therapy and vague reasons why, but nothing too deep. She witnessed a few of my panic attacks when I first started. Instead of thinking I'd gone mad, she did everything to help me. So, we've become close over the past week since working together, but not *that* close.

She nods, but the distant look on her face tells me she's thinking about something else.

"What about you? Why did you start working there?" I ask, hoping to get her out of her own head.

A hint of a smile breaks at the corner of her mouth. "Well, my mum used to work there and so did her mother." She scoffs. For a moment, darkness flashes in her eyes. "Tradition, I guess. My mum wouldn't have it if I tried to work anywhere else. I am forever destined to be chained to the wretched place." She curtsies playfully.

I shake my head. "That's awful, though."

She shoots me a sideways glance. "My Ma would never see it that way."

I'm ready to run with my curiosity when Erianne stops in front of a small pub. O'Kallaghan's is displayed in big, golden letters above the door of the green bar front. To the left, signs displaying the menu hang in the windows, accompanied by a drawing of a man with red hair drinking the foam as it spills over the side of a beer bottle.

"It's an Irish pub." Erianne grins wickedly, like the sight of it alone comforts her. "Come on, let's go get that drink."

We cross the threshold and the stagnant odor of beer sears my nostrils. Erianne's lips move, forming words, but I can't hear crap. A melody of Irish music is fighting its way over a mixture of heartfelt and obnoxious drunken laughter echoing off the walls. I squeeze through the only small walkway to the bar top with Erianne. All the wooden tables, six chairs to each, are taken. For a Monday night, that's surprising. The Irish sure know how to party.

Erianne stops to greet someone she knows every few tables. It's like walking down the aisle at a wedding ceremony. One small step, smile and greet someone. Another small step, greet a few more people. She wasn't kidding when she said this is her favorite place.

We finally reach the bar but before we can even slide onto a bar stool, she's already flagged down the bartender.

"Que buvez-vous les lassies?"

The bartender's terrible attempt at an Irish accent makes me cringe.

"I'll have a beer," Erianne yells over all the commotion. "What about you, Abby?"

I could order liquor. I have no problem passing for being eighteen and it's not like they'd ID me anyway. Half of the business for all pubs and clubs is people my age. On the other hand, getting wasted my first time out with her isn't the best idea. I've known her since school, but we never really hung out then.

"I'll just have a beer," I shout to the bartender.

He pours our drinks into mugs and slides them down the bar to us, not missing a beat while he continues taking other orders.

Erianne smiles. "Today is a day to celebrate. For seven days straight, you've handled your recovery like a boss! Tonight will be fun."

I swallow a lump forming in my throat. No. I won't let myself cry. Not anymore. *Merde*.

Erianne grabs my hand. "You okay?"

I bite down on my quivering lip. "…I'm not sure."

Her smile falters as she places a hand on my shoulder, softening her tone as if she's a preschool teacher talking to a crying toddler on the playground. "Look. I know this is a big step, but I've got your back. You'll do great."

Moments like this remind me I'm like a recipe for emotional stability gone wrong. But I'm here. It's taken a lot of therapy sessions to get me here, so as much as I hate it, I have to admit...Erianne's right. I can't back out now. Today is a day to celebrate. I'll be fine. *In—five, four, three, two, one—and out.*

I swallow hard and push past the ache in my chest. "Let's do this."

Erianne presses her palms together, bouncing on her heels. "Come, there's people I want you to meet."

I nod, an uneasiness gnawing at the pit of my stomach. I grab my drink just in time as she tows me over to a group of people chatting and clinking their glasses together at one of the tables. I recognize a couple of them from our graduation ceremony, but I don't think I've ever taken classes with any of them. Not that I'd remember much of anyone from school considering I was absent half of my terminale year. Depression is a fickle bitch.

"Everyone, I want you to meet my friend, Abigail," Erianne chirps proudly as she takes a seat next to another girl with rusty orange ringlets cascading down to her shoulders.

A silence falls over the group as they stare at me expectantly. I wave, and with my voice a weak whisper, say, "Hi."

I didn't think it would be this hard—being around people, making friends. Blood rushes to my cheeks as the four strangers keep staring.

"We don't bite. You can sit down." One man's voice, velvet and smooth as a fine, red wine, cuts through the silence.

I turn to follow the voice in hopes of seeing an equally attractive face, but another man wearing a beige turtle-neck sweater stands, drawing my attention to him instead.

"My name is Mathieu. It's nice to meet you, Abigail." He extends his hand. "Any friend of Erianne's is a friend of ours."

His smile is warm, gentle even, like that of a big brother meeting his little sister's friend for the first time. He's kind of cute with his tousled strawberry blonde hair and freckled cheeks. I take his hand, attempting to shake it. Instead, his pale pink lips brush my knuckles and sends a shiver down my spine. My cheeks are blazing like they're on fire. I guarantee they're as red as Erianne's hair.

Erianne swats his hand away, glaring at him. "Mathieu quit messing with her. Abigail, have a seat." She pats the chair next to her, the twinkle alight in her eyes again.

Mathieu laughs, sitting back in his chair and eyeing me from across the table.

"I can't help it she's beautiful," he says, raising his glass, "Cheers."

Okay, meeting new people is one thing, but having the spotlight on me like this is an entirely different level of nerve-wracking. *In—five, four, three, two, one—and out.* I'm in control. Screw this. I grab my mug with shaky hands and take a drink to hide my face. The bite of beer coating my tongue and the crisp oak flavor it leaves behind helps sooth my frayed nerves. Woah. This beer is good, better than any I've ever tried.

I dart my eyes from one person to the next as Erianne rattles off their names, but I'd rather know more about the one person she doesn't bother introducing. He definitely didn't go to my school. I'd remember seeing him and those icy-blue eyes. Not a single wrinkle or sign of aging is present against his smooth olive skin, which tells me he's around my age. A slight stubble runs along his jaw and the dark hair on his head is slicked back like something out of a shampoo commercial. My throat goes dry as I notice the curves of his muscles stressing the fabric of his black button up shirt.

His whole calm, cool 'I don't give a crap' attitude doesn't fit with everyone else at the table. The others are laughing, upbeat, and none of their smiles have faltered, even for a second. But not this guy. He's so intense. Something dark is hiding behind that annoying cocky grin plastered on his face. It's probably an ego the size of Normandy. Guys like him with more good looks than brains, never have a good personality to match.

There's something familiar about him though. I know him from *somewhere*, but my memory isn't the most reliable thing to count on. *Ugh.* This is bugging the crap out of me.

"What about you Abigail?" Mathieu asks.

My cheeks enflame all over again. *Oh, hell.* I've been gawking at this guy for who knows how long. I'm tempted to let my agoraphobia take over and lead me straight back to the comforting isolation of my room.

Mathieu flashes a lopsided grin. "The Royal Princess cruise ship is coming to France. And all of us were just saying how cool it would be to take a trip on it."

Erianne interrupts him. "Uh, no. *You* were saying how cool it would be. I don't think so. I'd rather go back to Ireland than get on any flying or sea-based form of travel. My feet are staying firmly planted on the ground in France." She downs a shot in one flick of her wrist.

"I think it would be fascinating. It would be like an adventure. To live the American Dream, move to New York!" The pale girl sitting next to Erianne chimes in with way too much enthusiasm.

"I've never been outside of the country." I shrug.

The overly cheerful girl leans forward with eyes wide. "You mean you've really never left France? Your whole life?"

I nod. "Yeah. I don't mind though. I like it here."

She gawks at me. "Have you at least been outside of Rouen?"

"Well, yeah. But I just convinced my mama three years ago to stay here after moving around every year for as long as I can remember. No way am I leaving now." I grip the handle of my mug. I'm actually talking to a stranger. Without freaking out. *Stay calm. Stay calm. In—five, four, three, two, one—and out.* I've got this.

The guy with the shampoo commercial hair scoffs. "No good things have been said about America anyway. So, I'm not sure why anyone would *want* to go there."

Erianne nods. "And the drinking age isn't eighteen like it is here. I've been counting down the days until I can have my first legal drink. I am *not* adding another three years to that."

I smile. "Me either. I only have six months left to go now."

Mathieu chuckles. "Erianne, like you need more reasons to drink."

She grins and chugs half her beer.

"Cheers to traveling to the Americas!" Mathieu shouts, raising his glass for a toast.

Every person at the table raises their glasses to meet his—every person but one. Shampoo hair guy's devilish blue eyes are fixated on the petite blonde at the table next to us. Her crop top might as well be a sports bra with how tightly it's hugging her chest. He saunters over to her, slyly placing a hand on her back as he whispers something in her ear. She laughs like it's the funniest thing she's ever heard. *Oh, give me a break.*

He subtly places a hand on her thigh. She hops up from her chair, following him over to our table. He subtly turns to wink at a brunette waving at him from the nearby table. *Really?* This guy is definitely a womanizer. Guys like him are assholes. I roll my eyes as her obnoxious laugh pierces my ears. The two of them together are nauseating and make want to gag. But I still want to know how I know this asshat.

By the end of the night, everyone has talked about the cruise ship until the mention of it alone became as annoying as the laughter coming from the blonde sitting on that guy's lap. Hardly anyone at the table pays attention to their sloppy drunken make-out sessions because they're all just as wasted.

"Come on, bébé, let's take a selfie for InstaGamma." The blonde presses her face against shampoo hair guy's and snaps a pic.

I'm so glad I deleted all my social media accounts months ago. It's pointless and not like I have any friends or family anyway. Mathieu hasn't stopped hitting on me. At this point, it's hard to even understand half of what he's saying because he keeps slurring.

Being sober. Around drunk people. *Bad. Idea.* So much for 'celebrating'.

"It's getting late guys, and I gotta walk Abigail here back to her place." Erianne stands from the table, slipping on her coat and bringing my attention back to the group.

"Whyduncha lemme take er home." Mathieu surprisingly manages to mutter a semi-complete sentence.

He hasn't had too much to drink. No, not *at all*.

"Absolutely not." Erianne's tone is ferociously protective.

His bottom lip pushes outward. "B-but wuh not?"

Erianne rolls her eyes. His pouting isn't working on her, but I'd seriously pity the girl it did work on. Erianne makes her way around the table, hugging everyone and saying goodbye. I wave to them as she grips my wrist, dragging me with her toward the exit. *Oh, hell.* I never got around to asking shampoo hair guy if we know each other somehow.

Sneaking a peek back, I notice he's gone. Erianne releases me as she steps outside. I scan the bar for him, but there's no sign of him or the girl he had with him.

Shaking my head, I catch up with Erianne. She stumbles as she peels her heels off, but surprisingly manages to stay upright. Glimpsing at my phone, 12:19AM gleams back at me. All warmth drains from my face. Mama is going to have a heart attack, if she hasn't already. I've never come home late and especially not around midnight. It's a rule, one of many for as long as I can remember. Be home before 10:00PM. I'm seventeen and I still have a curfew. I hate it. No other kids my age have a curfew.

"What's wrong? Didn't you have fun?" Erianne tilts her head to the side, her heels slung over her shoulder.

"Oh no, I'm fine." I force a smile to reassure her. "I just don't usually stay out this late. My mama is probably going to have a meltdown."

"I'm sorry if I kept you out too late." Her dramatic lopsided smile makes it hard to take her serious and is like ice over a wound to my worrying.

I chuckle. "No, it's okay! I really did have fun. I haven't got to do anything like that in a long time."

Not really true, but I'd rather not scare away the only real friend I've had in a long time by being rude.

She loops her arm through mine. "Good. We definitely need to hang out more. Maybe we can even find you a cute guy."

The over exaggerated mischievous grin on her face as she struggles with trying to waggle her brows makes me double over. She makes it so easy to let go of things I'm anxious about and live in the moment. It's one of the reasons I've clung to her like glue this past week.

I nudge her side. "Speaking of guys…who was the one sitting next to Mathieu?"

She skids to a stop, all joy from earlier a distant memory. "Abigail…" She grabs my arm with each finger gripping so tight her nails dig into my skin. "Don't go messing around with him. He's trouble and not the good kind. He's dangerous. Y-you can't."

A hallow ache fills my gut. "No, I just didn't get his name, that's all."

I'm not lying to her, but I guess I'm not exactly telling the truth either. I want to know who he is. It's not going to stop bothering me until I figure out where I know him from. And what the hell. If he's so bad, why was he there hanging out with them tonight.

She shakes her head, her voice barely a whisper, "Believe me, you're better off not even knowing his name. You don't deserve any of this."

Huh? What does she mean? I don't deserve any of what? She mumbles something I can't understand and stumbles over her own feet. It's probably nothing. She's had too much to drink… It wouldn't hurt to ask her about it when she's sober again, though. But a change of subject is needed right now. Anything to break this tense silence that's fallen over us. I'm definitely making a mental note to never bring him up to her again.

"Hey, who was the other red-head sitting with us at the pub?" I ask, not really knowing what else to say. She didn't seem like the usual kind of person Erianne would hang out with.

Erianne scrunches her nose, dropping my arm. "That faux dyed hair you call red should be burned. Then maybe it would actually look red." The disgusts laced in her words catches me off guard, but is freaking hilarious. Touchy, touchy.

"Woah!" Throwing my hands up, I playfully back away.

She shakes her head. "Anyway. Her name is Clarissa. She's a girl I met through my mother. Our mothers are best friends."

"Well, then are you two?" I bite my lip, trying to suppress my grin. By the way she just talked about her, I know they aren't friends at all. But getting her all worked up is hilarious. It's like poking a hibernating bear for fun to see what happens.

She jerks her head to the side, staring at me like I grew a third eye. "What? Her and I? Best friends? You're joking right? *Ní cinnte.* You and I are going to be the bestest of best friends there ever was! No one can be better bestest friends than us!"

A laugh escapes my lips as I catch some words in a completely different language. "Erianne, I think you've had too much to drink."

Her face contorts into some unnatural mixture of confusion and excitement. "Yeah, you might be right."

"We're here." I say as we reach *Rue Verte*, my street.

She leans down, pulling me into an embrace. "Alright. You be safe! I'll see you later."

Apparently, drunk Erianne is a hugger. If she did decide to go to the Americas, she'd fit right in. I hear they're all big on hugging each other, which is so weird. The only person I hug is my mama.

I wave her off as she skips down the sidewalk, singing an Irish melody. As interesting as this night has been, I need some sleep in my life. But first, I have to face my mama.

2

"Abigail Karline Halsey!"

My mother's stern voice echoes off the walls of our two-story flat. I wince, easing the front door shut. All my sneaky efforts are pointless. I'm caught.

"Where have you been? I have been worried sick about you! You live under *my* roof and will abide by *my* rules. When I say no staying out past 10:00PM, I mean it!" The lines on her forehead crease as her brows knit together.

I'm tired, and all I can think about right now is climbing into my soft, cushy bed. I don't like upsetting her though. My mama is the most important person in my life. She's helped me through so much and is always here for me when I need her. She's also the only family I have. As exhausted as I am right now, I should explain and reassure her. This is my fault anyway. I could have called or texted.

I hold my hands up. "I went out with a friend from work, Mama. Her name is Erianne. You'd like her."

"Why didn't you call? Or you could have texted me! You may be turning eighteen in December, but that doesn't mean you can start doing whatever you want!" She points a finger at me.

I sigh. "I know. I'm sorry. Can you please stop lecturing me now? Aren't you happy I went somewhere besides work? Today makes seven days mama…"

Her shoulders drop and her expression visibly relaxes. Walking toward me, she grabs my face in her hands. "Abigail, I love you. You can't just take off without telling me where you're going. I'm very happy you're doing so well. That's all I want. The storm earlier didn't bother you too bad?"

Storm? What storm? Jolting upright, my awareness snaps back to me like a boomerang.

"There was a storm earlier?" It never fully hit. It was just a little rain.

"Yes. Around the time you got off work. I thought maybe you waited it out in the church across from your work. But when you still hadn't come home after eleven..." My mother scans my face. "*Ma chérie*, is everything alright?"

"Mama. I didn't know there was a storm. I've been with Erianne since I left work." My brain is on high alert right now. How did I not hear the thunder when it was overhead?

My mother's frown rises into a proud smile, helping me to relax again. "I told you that job would be good for you."

I sigh, my level of exhaustion growing by the second. "Can I go to bed now?"

"Of course, dear. Go, get to bed. No more staying out this late though! I love you." She hugs me as if it's the last time she ever will before heading to bed herself.

Instead of falling right to sleep like I would *love* to right now, my mind is swarming. Thunderstorms scare the crap out of me, and one doesn't pass without triggering a panic attack. But I didn't even realize the one that started earlier did. It's so odd. Is the astraphobia almost gone now? I squeal like a toddler being handed a piece of their favorite candy. Maybe hanging out with Erianne had something to do with it. Maybe I can even get a full night of sleep without my night terrors haunting me. They used to only be triggered by thunderstorms. But ever since my ex dumped me for someone else, they've been every night.

  A tale tall scattered tapping against my window rings through my ears like a siren. No… It's a storm. My hands tremble. And here I thought I was free of this crap. Stealing a glimpse outside my bedroom window, even though I know I shouldn't, my fingers grip my blanket at the sight that sends my stomach plummeting.

  Low, ominous clouds have spread a dark blanket over the night sky, engulfing the stars and stealing the safety of their light. My chest heaves when the roaring of the wind seeps through the seal of my window, whistling into the corners of my conscience. As the first crack of lightning illuminates the vast blackness, I curl my body up into a ball on my bed, bracing myself for what's to follow. *In—five, four, three, two, one—and out.*

  But no matter how tight I squeeze my knees against myself, there's no escape—from the storm or the shaking in my hands and body. The frantic pattering of raindrops striking the glass fall like buckets now and match the drops pouring down my face. I bury my head in the sheets, a pointless attempt to sooth the empty burning in my lungs. My heart is beating so hard and fast, it's making me dizzy.

BOOM! Thunder reverberates through the air, rattling all the windows in my flat and roaring like an angry lion.

"*You're safe. You're inside. You're home. You're safe. You're inside. You're home. Home. Mason. S-Safe.*" Repeating the mantra over and over aloud eases the sobs that have taken over my body as the memories begin to seep past the wall in my conscious.

The man's voice booming off the walls. My mother hysterically crying, begging the man to stop, her tears painted a hint of red as blood seeps from an open cut on her face. The man takes a menacing step toward her, fist raised above his head, ready to strike again.

"No!" A scream involuntarily escapes my lips, leaving my voice hoarse.

The pattering of footsteps in the hallway pulls me out of the memory.

"Abigail!" My mother's voice rings like a sweet song from the other side of my bedroom door through my ears.

The seconds it takes for her to reach my room pass like minutes. "Oh! My sweet girl!" Her hands fly up to cover her mouth.

Mama glances out the window then back to me lying in the fetal position on my bed, shaking uncontrollably. I can't speak. She was so proud of me earlier. Now look at me.

She hastily approaches my bedside. "Scoot."

Rolling over, giving her enough room, she climbs into my bed enveloping me in her arms. Little by little, the shaking eases, the throbbing pain slowly slips into a dull ache, and the memory fades back into the darkest corner of my mind it crawled out of.

"I-I'm s-sorry if I woke you up." I stutter.

"Nonsense! *Mon trésor*, I'm your mother. This is what I'm here for." A light caress of her hand runs down my hair. "Now, get some sleep. I'm not going anywhere."

The chaos from the storm is drowned out by the calming, sweet rhythmic tune she whistles while gently sweeping her hand in a repetitive motion down my hair. As sleep beckons, I'm faced with a devastating realization... I'm not free at all.

3

Blinding rays from the rising sun peek through the ivory curtains covering our kitchen window. I have to squint to be able to see the food laid out on the table. Mama got breakfast before I even got out of bed. It's weird because she doesn't normally go all out in the mornings like this. The most I'd see prepared on the table is a few pieces of tartine: slices of baguette with a heaping spread of salted butter and peach jam. She's up to something. I eye her suspiciously while she slices a loaf of tradition baguette, same as she *always* picks up from the bakery on the corner of our street. It's baked fresh every morning.

I get a whiff of its fresh baked goodness as she lays the slices on a serving platter. It catapults me into the memory of the mornings I'd walk with her to carry the loaf home. It would still be warm from being just removed from the baker's oven. But I ruined that. A bittersweet ache weighs on my chest as a gawk at the table crowded with food.

Aside from the normal tartine, croissants and *pain au chocolat* are nesting in a basket, still glistening from the melted butter on top. She must have picked them up from the bakery too. *Pain au chocolat* is my favorite cubed-shaped pastry. Not only is there two pieces of dark chocolate stuffed in, it's the perfect combo of crunchy on the outside and soft on the inside. It's like a dreamy square slice of sanity I can eat.

I lick my slips. She's *really* up to something. All of my favorites are laid out: blueberry yogurt, a bowl filled with fresh assorted berries, and she's just finished pain Perdu—slices of old bread soaked in egg bash and milk then grilled on a pan. *Oh, sweet saints.* Is that crepes filled with sweet, nutty Nutella she's pulling out of the fridge? Mama's pastry dough made from scratch and stuffed with fresh locally made hazelnut spread…okay, who cares about the reason, I'm starving, and my mouth is watering.

She sets two cups of coffee on the placemats and quietly sits down at the table to join me. No breakfast, or morning, would be right, no matter how extravagant, without my *café crème*. Mama likes her coffee plain and strong. It's gross. And should be illegal.

"Mama, what's all this for?" I ask, not able to help my curiosity.

Maybe I do care, just a little.

"Can't I make my daughter breakfast on her day off?" She places her hand over her chest dramatically.

I grin, recognizing the same sarcastic humor I got from her as I take a big gulp of my coffee.

"Yes, you can… Every morning actually. It's about time I get the royal treatment I deserve."

She scowls. "Very funny."

I chuckle and load up my plate like I'm at a buffet. No more talkie. I pop a raspberry in my mouth as she reaches across the table, grasping my hand.

"I am just so happy you're doing so well."

"You don't have to worry about me, Mama. I'll be alright." I squeeze her hand gently.

"I know you will be." Her lips stretch into a soft, genuinely sweet smile only a mother is capable of. Warmth spreads through me.

"Thank you for breakfast," I say, loading my plate and trying not to drool over everything.

"You're welcome." She grins, not caring to hide how proud of herself she is.

She's so goofy. It's a freaking relief compared to most adults who have sticks up their asses. I shove a forkful of pain Perdu into my mouth. As the light, fluffy cloud of maple-flavor greets my tongue, I melt like butter. For the sake of my future husband, I hope I can cook even remotely close to as great as her. If not, I'll be surviving on cheddar *fromage* and baguettes.

"Have you heard from any of your friends since they went off to University?" Mama asks, setting her coffee mug down.

My bliss created by the delicious food evaporates like steam. "No. Because they aren't my friends."

Gritting my teeth, I run through Dr. Carrere's psychotherapy talk. Something about channeling the hatred, the anger, into positivity. Well, I absolutely *hate* those people she still calls my friends and I *hate* when she brings them up. I'm *positive* pigs will fly before they ever get to be called my friend again. Oh. And I'm *positive* William deserves to fall from the highest point of the Eiffel tower. Or be ran over by a car. *In—five, four, three, two, one—and out.*

There. Now I feel better.

Mama sighs, not meeting my eyes. "All that matters now is getting you better. I do love you, Abigail, and that means I'll always worry about you."

I roll my eyes. "I know. I love you too, Mama."

She opens her mouth, prepared to say something else, but a buzzing followed by several loud beeps interrupts her. Pulling the black pager from its clip holstered to her belt, she silences it as she reads the message running across the rectangular screen.

That thing is so ancient. I can't believe her boss makes her carry it around. He needs to get with the times. No one carries pagers anymore. And he needs to let her enjoy a day off. Since I *finally* completed my terminale school year and graduated, I plan to spend my summer waitressing to help with the bills. So far, it's been enough that she's backed off a little on working so many hours at Bouldarez Realty. But her boss still has her on call when she's supposed to be 'taking the day off'.

Slouching back in her chair, Mama's shoulders drop. "Sorry, Abby. I have to run into work. One of the homeowners we were supposed to sign with today is wanting to back out. It seems my boss can't figure out how to do his own job." Her words are laced with the same vehemence that makes me want to punch her boss right in his face.

"It's okay, Mama." My smile doesn't quite reach my eyes.

I hate when she gets called into work like this. Today was supposed to be our day to spend together. Her boss might as well sign the realty company over to her because she spends more time working than he does.

On the other hand, this is the perfect opportunity to get some answers from Erianne about that guy—non-alcohol induced answers at least.

"I won't be too long, I promise." Mama has already cleared her plate, slipped on her coat, and is headed for the door. "Don't forget your appointment with Dr. Carrere today at one."

Covering my mouth with a napkin, I swivel quickly in my chair to face her. "Well, I was actually going to see if Erianne was free today."

"You can do that and make your appointment, Abigail." Mama narrows her eyes, pointing one slender finger at me.

She never lets me miss an appointment. And if I even try to skip it, Dr. Carrere will show up here. Then I'll be forced to do those annoying worksheets to remind me why therapy is important. I graduated high school last month. Homework is supposed to be long gone, but my therapist has a sadistic sense of humor. *Ugh.*

"Abby." Mama's glare could make the most masculine guy shrink down.

I throw my hands up. "Okay, okay! You win, I will."

"Are you sure you'll be alright today?" She pauses a moment at the door, her hand resting on the brass knob.

"*Oui*, go ahead. I'm done with my breakfast. I'm just going to get dressed and leave too." My leg bounces at the thought of *why* I'm going to meet up with Erianne.

A slight smile forms at the corner of her mouth. "Good. I will see you back home tonight. No later than seven for dinner!"

Once the familiar click of the door follows behind her, I can't get up the stairs fast enough. One goal for today is steady in my mind: at least learn the name of this annoyingly hot guy.

Throwing my hair in a bun, I can barely keep my hands steady. Only minutes now before this gnawing on my curiosity is put to rest. Erianne was dead set on not spilling anything last night. Hopefully I'll have better luck now that she's sober.

My favorite short-sleeve lime green off-shoulder tee seems perfect for today. Nothing says 'luck' like green. And I need all the luck I can get. I slip on a pair of white high waisted cotton shorts and my beige sandals. As I'm heading out the door, I could face palm myself. I don't even know where Erianne is. *Real smart Abigail.* Well, no better place to start then our job.

Peeking in through the windows of La Couronne, Erianne is nowhere in sight. I really don't want to go inside because running into Delano Bowman, my boss who's also the manager and only eyesore in the entire place, would be the lowest point of my day. Good thing we have tables out front and waiters who serve those tables. All I have to do is stand innocently by until one comes out.

As if having read my mind, the chime of the bell on the restaurant's door rings. Out comes a man I don't recognize at all, but that burgundy button up dress shirt tells me all I need to know.

It helps that he's also wearing an apron and carrying a tray of food.

I approach him. "Excuse me."

"Yes?" The waiter snarls.

Trying to ignore the snippy tone in his voice, I plaster on my best polite smile. "Have you seen Erianne around?"

"Erianne? The Irish girl? Oh, she called in sick this morning. She picked up a later shift." The waiter saunters off without giving me a chance to even thank him.

He's kind of rude. I'm glad I don't know him. And I hope I never have to work a shift with him. But something he said stuck with me: Erianne is Irish. That explains a few things. No wonder she likes O'Kallaghan's so much. Maybe I'll find her there, hanging around.

As I walk toward the sidewalk, a chill brushes against my cheek. The wind whistles, making my breath hitch. Crap. If I don't turn around, head home now, I'll risk getting caught in a storm. The beating of my heart hums in my ears. *Breath. I'm in control. In—five, four, three, two, one—out.*

When I was with Erianne last night, I didn't pay attention to the weather. Maybe being around her is enough of a distraction. Maybe if I can get to her fast enough, there won't be anything to worry about. But if I don't… No. I'll make it.

Heading off toward the pub, to Erianne, as if she's a lighthouse acting as my beacon, I make sure to keep my head down. One glimpse at the clouds and I'll start to panic. I can't. No, I *won't* do that.

It's like Dr. Carrere says, "*The more you allow yourself–*"

Oof! Colliding into a solid, hard surface, I fall flat on my butt. Oh, my saints, I didn't just run into a wall, did I?

"Woah, there!" A man's soft voice calls out.

Nope. Definitely not a wall. Peering up through my lashes, heat rises in my cheeks. The dark silhouette of a tall lanky man is standing over me. The glare from the sun stings my eyes as I stare up at him. He reaches a hand down, offering to help me up.

"Thank you." I shield my eyes from the rays, able to make out his face better. I recognize that strawberry blonde turtle-neck-sweater-wearing Casanova.

"Oh, don't worry mademoiselle." The corner of his mouth hitches, his eyes forming small slits. "You're Abigail, no?"

"*Oui*, I am. I remember you. You were at the pub. Mathieu?" This guy again. It takes so much effort to resist the urge to roll my eyes at him.

"That's me." He grins. "Erianne told me you two work together. You about to head in?"

I shake my head. "Not until later. I was just looking for Erianne."

His lips set into a firm line as he glares past me, studying the restaurant. The gentle, casual aura about him from last night–and just two minutes ago–is gone. Standing in front of me now, he's radiating an intensity I'd never guess he's even capable of. It makes me pause and see him in a different light. If it weren't for the constant annoying flirting he does, I might actually find him attractive.

"She isn't here?" He glances down at me, "We were supposed to hang out today."

"No, she called off." My stomach churns when I notice the existence of his muscles. "It's probably because she isn't feeling well after how much she had to drink last night."

He smiles. "You're probably right. Why were you looking for her?"

The hairs on the back of my neck stand to attention as he shortens the distance between us. "Oh. I-I uhm... I just had something to ask her."

Mathieu raises an eyebrow, stepping away. "This is about Lucas, isn't it?"

"Lucas?" I ask, tilting my head.

That name. The memory I've been scratching my brain for is so close, as if it's banging on a door, desperate to be free.

He scoffs. "He was sitting next to me last night at O'Kallaghan's. Tall guy with muscles. Hair so perfect it could have its own brand. He was staring at you all night. I'm surprised you didn't notice."

Oh, I noticed alright. My curiosity burns bright again, flames erupting in my gut. So, he's tall too? I'm suddenly a little more interested than before. But the image of him with Ms. Crop-top kills my interests. That's probably a regular thing for him.

"So, his name is Lucas? Are you friends?" I ask, trying not to get carried away with myself. I still want to know who he is.

Mathieu's face contorts, his mouth melting downward. "You're into him, aren't you? I guess I'm not surprised. Every woman he comes across falls all over him."

What the hell. I'm not falling all over *Lucas*. I don't fall all over any guy. I'm offended he thinks I'm that kind of girl.

I fold my arms. "That's not even what I wanted to talk to Erianne about."

Entirely not true, but he doesn't need to know that.

Mathieu sighs, pinching the bridge of his nose. "Look, Abigail, don't go getting involved with him. He's dangerous, and it's best you stay away."

"That's the same thing Erianne told me last night."

Two times now, I've been told this guy, Lucas, is dangerous; that I should stay away. Why, though?

The weight of his hand lands on my shoulder, sending a shiver through my side. "And you would do good to listen to us. We know what we're talking about."

His demeanor softens as if he's talking to someone younger than himself instead of his equal in age. No flirting, no fierce protectiveness that's kind of hot. Just a genuine concern and playfulness. I'm starting to wonder if maybe he should come to my psychologist appointment with me.

I shift from one foot to the other. "If that's how you and Erianne feel then, why are you friends with him?"

Mathieu shakes his head with pinched lips, shoving his hands into his pockets. "This isn't the place to talk about this." His eyes dart around quickly from the patio tables to the sidewalk. "Why don't you come with me? There's a cafe a couple blocks away. We could talk there." Mathieu's grip on my shoulder tightens, an urgency rising in him.

Yeah, because that's how every serial killer gets you into their murder van. Except his knowledge is like the perfect form of candy to lure me in. A knot forms at the back of my throat.

I put my hand on my hip. "But weren't you just warning me about him?"

Mathieu's gentle smile returns. "I can tell that you're not going to let this go. I'd rather set you straight than send you off and take the chance of you asking the wrong person about him. Getting to take a beautiful girl like yourself for coffee is an added bonus." He waggles his brows.

I bite my lip and try to ignore my stomach doing somersaults. "...I don't know."

Mathieu chuckles. "You're safe with me, Abigail."

This *need* eating relentlessly at my insides isn't going away unless I get *some* answers. And this is my opportunity.

"Fine."

He hooks his arm with mine, walking me to a nearby ruby red car parked a few feet away. "It will be faster if we drive there."

Okay, so it's a far stretch from a murder van, but this *is* the 21st century. Serial killers might be 'modernizing' too. Mathieu opens the passenger side door, gesturing for me to get in.

Half of my brain is screaming *Don't get in the car.* The other half is telling me to get in the car, give in to my curiosity, and take a chance. So, I climb in.

4

It doesn't take long before we reach the small café. It's squeezed between the other shops and businesses on the street, with '*Des Carmes*' in big, bold golden letters above the door. The seating area out front is larger than the entire café. As I take a seat at an umbrella table, a mixture of fresh baked breads fills my nostrils. I can already pinpoint a few. From the mouthwatering sting of cinnamon wafting off classic *pain aux raisins*, fresh baked baguettes reminding me of a warm summer day, to a variety of light and flaky croissants. Not to mention the sweet aroma of fresh ground coffee beans floating in the air around us. This is paradise.

Mathieu disappears into the café, leaving me alone with my thoughts. Sitting here, internally I'm freaking out. My stomach is in knots and my mind is swirling with the hundreds of questions I want to ask about that arrogant womanizing shampoo hair guy from last night.

I know his name is Lucas, but why are his friends trying to make me scared of him? And why have I been told twice now that he's dangerous? He didn't seem dangerous or scary at the pub. I'd also like to know what's with the hair. Is he some model by day then secret agent by night? *Agent Hot Stuff reporting for duty, monsieur!* Now, *that* would be interesting.

As I'm fidgeting with my hands, I realize Mathieu has been inside the café for a long time. He only went in to get a few coffees. It's not busy so he should have been back by now.

Not a second later, Mathieu takes a seat across from me, setting two beige cups, filled to the brim with coffee, on the table. Taking a slow, deliberate sip, I try to be as patient as possible. I'm on the edge of my seat though. And patience isn't really my thing.

"Okay, before I tell you anything, Abigail, you need to agree to something for me..." Mathieu furtively glances around before leaning forward, resting his arms on the table. "You have to let this go. I'll tell you anything you want to know, but once I do, you put any thoughts about Lucas behind you. Do we have a deal?" A smirk stretches across his mouth, void of any trace of humor. Something about it tells me his intentions aren't genuine. No surprise there.

I roll my eyes. "Deal."

Mathieu sits back in his chair, a look of arrogant satisfaction etching his face. "Good. What would you like to know?"

"Uhm, O-kay." I can't stop wringing my hands. "Well, why did you say he's dangerous?"

He lowers his voice so much I have to strain to hear him, "His name is Lucas Danforth. I'm sure you've heard of him."

What the shit. Lucas Danforth? *The* Lucas Danforth? Holy... I was sitting at a table with *The* Lucas Danforth? No wonder he's so familiar. I can't count the number of times I've seen that asshat's name in the news, accused of hundreds of crimes, but never convicted. There's been articles in the papers written about him, too. And the crimes he's been accused of? It makes me sick just thinking about it. No wonder he's so damn arrogant. He can do whatever he wants and get away with it.

But it still doesn't explain what their deal with him is. Clearly, he can't be that bad if they hang around him.

"I have heard of him, but he's just some delinquent 19-year-old kid. What's the big deal?" I ask.

Mathieu's mouth pops open as he sits back in his seat. "You really don't know? Abigail, he's the son of Dominick Vitale. Lucas only got lucky by getting his mother's last name so he wouldn't be immediately associated with anything his father does. Not that it matters. But I guess that's why you didn't put two and two together there."

I can't believe it either that I didn't put that together in my head. *In—five, four, three, two, one—out.* This is not for real. *Merde. Breath, Abigail, breathe.* I was sitting across the table from Lucas and what's even worse is that I didn't even realize it. How stupid am I?

I shake my head. "I've heard of Dominick before, of course, but there isn't a single soul in Normandy that hasn't heard of the Vitale family. They showed up one day a few years ago. Now, Dominick pretty much runs the city, along with half of Normandy. And everyone practically bows at his feet." It's ridiculous, if you ask me.

Mathieu crosses his arms. "Awfully brave of you to say something like that when you know how dangerous he is."

I scoff and sit back in my chair. "Well, that doesn't mean Lucas is dangerous. His father is, but maybe not him."

I will my heart to return to a slow and steady pace. I'm not sure if I'm trying to convince him or myself.

"Abigail, listen to me. Erianne and I have known Lucas since we were kids, ever since his family moved here. Sure, if you asked me about ten years ago if he was dangerous, I would have probably laughed at you. He was different then, and I couldn't have imagined him hurting a soul. But when his mother passed..." Mathieu hesitates as if he's choosing his words carefully, "It changed him. He's done things, horrific things to hurt people and I get the feeling he enjoys it."

"Wow... well, what happened to his mother?" I ask, disregarding Mathieu's reaction.

"The news said it was a car wreck that caused her death, but a lot of people are saying it wasn't an accident. She was the one person that kept Lucas away from his father's lifestyle." Mathieu shakes his head.

I place my hand over his on the table. "You seem like you really care about him. Is that why you and Erianne still hang around?"

Mathieu sighs, a small smile reaching the corner of his mouth as he grasps my hand. "*Oui*. He's our best friend and we still worry about him."

I gently squeeze his hand back. "I'm sorry. Maybe he'll turn around one day."

As hard as I'm trying to focus, my mind is still reeling from all of this.

He nods, raising his coffee cup. "All we can do is hope."

Mathieu is a really good guy to be that understanding. I smile and take a sip of my own coffee. Its heavenly goodness gives me all the warm and fuzzies.

"Well, thank you. I just wanted to know who he was. I'm sorry if I asked too much." I say, tracing the rim of my cup.

"I think it's better if you know. Now you know to stay clear of him." He purses his lips.

I sigh. "I will. I don't need to get involved in that mess."

He throws his hands up, his arrogance unwavering. "Great! Trust me, it's for the best."

His victorious grin makes me chuckle. That goofiness is kind of growing on me.

He glances down at his watch and stands from his chair. "It's getting late. Why don't I take you home?"

His hand presses against the small of my back as he escorts me to the ruby red car parked a few feet away. Peeking up at him through my lashes, a warm smile greets my face. He's not a bad guy at all. I got all worried for nothing.

He's actually kind of funny and I like how easily he can break the tension. I thought our conversation was going to be awkward, but it turned out okay. I got the answers I wanted, and it wasn't all bad spending some time with him. He's quirky and a little odd, but really, who isn't?

"Why don't you let me take you for a real meal?" His thumb runs circles on my back as he opens the passenger door.

Oh, hell. I almost forgot about my appointment with my therapist. There's no way I'm letting him take me there.

I step back. "I can't."

He drops his hand to his side as his smile falls, making my heart hurt for him.

"I just mean, I can't because I almost forgot I have a doctor's appointment."

His smile returns. "I can take you. I don't mind."

I laugh and shake my head. "No, it's okay. I'm fine with walking."

"Well, what are you doing after?" He grabs my hand, enclosing it within his.

I would like to go out with him. He seems nice. But he also seems easily offended. A guy has to have some seriously thick skin to deal with me.

"I have to work." I say.

His frown deepens, making me feel bad. *Ugh.*

I force a smile. "But rain check? Maybe tonight at eight? You can pick me up from work."

He beams, pressing his lips against my knuckles. "Definitely. I'll see you then." With one last pointed look, he walks away.

As he pulls away from the curb, I watch until his car is out of sight. As soon as it disappears behind a building, a wet droplet plops on my arm. *No, no, no. Not now. Please not now.* I take off in a full sprint down the sidewalk in front of *Des Carmes*, doing a series of zigzags down some streets to try to find my way.

A familiar burning fills my lungs. *In—five, four, three, two, one—out. In—five, four, three, two, one—out. Merde.* This isn't working.

Taking deep breaths, I check for nearby street signs. There's a furniture store, a toy store–wait. I recognize that toy store. Mama use to take me there all the time as a kid. I'm not far from my lycée. I guess high school can be good for something other than drama and boring students to death.

I know exactly where I am. *Oh, sweet Joan of Arc.* Relief floods through me. Only a couple more blocks to get to my psychologist. I'll make it before it starts raining. I *have* to make it. Dr. Carrere I hope you're ready for me. Because here I come.

5

"Tell me how that made you feel?"

Dr. Carrere is sitting in her usual black, leather pleated chair. With one elbow resting on the arm, she peers up over the top of her glasses at me.

"Okay. You know how much I hate it when you ask me that, right?" I'm not even trying to hide how annoyed I am. It's not like there's any point. She'll just use that psychologist wit to see right through me.

She purses her lips. "Maybe if I ask you enough, you'll stop hating it."

I scrunch my face. "That's... not how it works."

Her mirthful laughter puts me even more at ease. Dr. Carrere isn't like the therapist you'd see in movies. She doesn't ever blatantly psychoanalyze me; despite that being her job. And every time I come all the problems that bring me here don't seem so important anymore. Talking to her is so easy. But it never used to be.

She flips a paper in my file over and I chuckle as I catch a glimpse of the extensive list of my diagnoses.

Carrere Therapy Solutions LLC
Patient: Abigail K. Halsey
Start of service: 02/06/2017

Diagnosis: Depression, Agoraphobia, Anxiety, Astraphobia, Night Terrors stemming from PTSD, and mild amnesia from age 10 and below caused by repression of childhood memories also stemmed from the PTSD.

That list used to control my life. But, with the good doctor's help, it doesn't anymore.

"Any memories come back?" She asks, not looking up from my file.

I spread my arms out over the back of the back of her black leather sofa. "Nope. Still the poster child for mental instability."

She laughs. "Haven't we talked about thinking of yourself in a more positive way? Suppression of childhood memories is quite common when they're as traumatic as I believe yours are. It's your subconscious' way of helping you deal with what you went through."

Out of all the medical jargon she throws at me, that makes the most sense because I don't remember anything from before I was ten. And thanks to my new best friend, Google, I understand a lot of the things I have better.

I wring my hands. "I know. I know. But none of this would be this bad if it weren't for William."

She shakes her head, scribbling something in her notepad. "You can't blame your ex for how you dealt with the breakup," I open my mouth to argue, but she holds her hand up, "no matter how he handled it. And to be frank, I think the way he left you triggered your subconscious because it's similar to what happened in your past. But I know you aren't ready to discuss that yet."

My voice cracks. "Maybe he needs to be in therapy! Who leaves their girlfriend of two years on her birthday? A sadistic crazy person."

Dr. Carrere presses her lips firmly together, giving me that same look my mother does when I'm pushing my luck. "Abby," she says sternly.

Tears roll down my cheeks. "No! Don't *Abby* me. When our two-year relationship terminated six months ago it broke something inside me. Why didn't he break, too? Why should he get to live his life just dandily, while I'm here? Why does he deserve to be happy and... and I don't?"

I swipe the tears off my face. That idiot doesn't deserve shit, especially not the tears I'm crying over him. I grab the plush pillow off the couch and hug it tightly against my burning chest. Damn exes and stupid breakups. I swallow hard, fighting back the tears pooling in my eyes, but the more I think about what he did, it's impossible.

"I wish his existence would have been terminated, too. I was doing fine until he came along. Now, I don't even know who I am anymore. How is that fair? I *hate* him, Dr. Carrere. I hate him s-so much. I-I wish I'd never met him." I shove my face into the pillow sobbing.

She sighs. "Oh, Abby. I know. He was your first love. Those are the hardest. Remember, he doesn't control you. Who is in control here?"

I inhale deeply and exhale a stuttering breath, pushing the tears away. I hug my knees to my burning chest and stare up at her.

"Me." I croak.

She smiles proudly and her eyes crinkle at the corners. "Good. Give me your hands. Let's run through your breathing technique together."

I flop my legs off the couch and scoot forward, taking her outstretched hands. With one reassuring squeeze, she soothes some of my anxiety. *In—five, four, three, two, one—out*. I close my eyes and repeat the steps a few more times, holding onto her hands like they're an anchor keeping my grounded.

It's crazy how easily she can calm me down. But I'd seriously question what my mom is paying her for if she couldn't. I release her hands and try to ignore how hot my cheeks feel. I hate when I get like this over that loser. The day I see him again, I'll show him a fraction of the hurt he's made me feel with my fist and his face.

Dr. Carrere sits back in her chair, flipping to the front of my file as I snatch a tissue off the table next to me. She moves on from my… episode like it never happened. I love that. Less mortifying this way. The soft tissue is like sandpaper over my swollen, tender eyes.

"How are you doing with your fear ladder?" She peers up over her glasses.

I shrug. "Well, I made a friend at work. We went for drinks and I actually mingled with a small group of people. It was just a few though."

She sets her pen down on the notebook in her lap, grinning proudly. "That's amazing! See, you're making real progress. And that means you've completed your first fear ladder."

I let a small smile break at the corner of my mouth.

She grins and readies her pen. "Anything else new going on you want to share?"

"Well," I wring my hands, taking a deep breath, "I have a date after my shift tonight."

Her smile broadens, baring her teeth. "Look at you, kicking butt with your fear ladder."

"I guess." Lying down on her sofa, I prop my hands behind my head.

She shuffles through the file under her notebook, pulling out a single piece of paper. "Why don't we use this date tonight as an opportunity to start your next fear ladder?"

I roll my eyes. "Sure, doc."

So much for wanting to enjoy the date without thinking about anything else, especially not worrying about facing a new fear. This date is going to get a whole lot more interesting. I rub my eyes. Maybe facing this fear won't make me have a panic attack and pass out like before.

"Let's start out small. If it starts to rain, I want you to stand outdoors for five consecutive minutes during a light sprinkle. If it begins to feel like too much, remember your calming techniques." Dr. Carrere pushes her brown rectangular-framed glasses back as they slide down her nose. "You think you can manage that?"

I take a deep breath, my skin crawling at the thought of it. "I'll try but consider this a fear rating of four out of ten."

Yep. I'm going to pass right the f—

"Great! I'll jot that down as your first step." She starts scratching away on her notebook. "So, what's your plan for when you have to stop seeing me?"

"What? Who said that?" My voice raises an octave as I beam at her.

It's taken a lot for me to be this comfortable with her. I don't want to see anyone else. The thought of it makes my stomach do flips. There's no way in hell I'm baring my soul to someone else like I have with her.

"Abigail. You know once you turn eighteen in December, I can't see you anymore." A lock of her chestnut hair breaks free from behind her ear. She tucks it back into place as she removes her glasses, blinking her gentle hazel eyes rapidly for a moment.

Sitting up from lying on her sofa, I swivel my legs around to face her, grinning wildly. "That's what fake ID's are made for! And hey, I'm a working woman now. How's an extra ten a week sound? You'll be rich."

She shakes her head, chuckling. "I'll miss you. You are definitely one of my more difficult patients."

"Can't miss me if I don't go anywhere." I wink.

She stands, smoothing her gray plaid dress. "Alright, you. Time's up. I'll see you same time next week."

"I'll be here." Flashing a genuine smile, I give her a sideways hug. She's an American transplant who brought her hugging ways with her.

She calls her next patient as I make my exit, "Mr. Cusey. Right this way."

This job is supposed to be a major step forward...

But I'm probably going to get fired for being fifteen minutes late. The rain slowed me down, but my boss doesn't give a crap about my mental health. I could break both of my legs and he'd still expect me to come into work.

Fresh lemon from polished oak mixed with a distinct, horrid odor of clams and mushrooms smacks me in the face as I pull open the door to La Couronne, bringing me to a halt in the entryway. *Ugh. So, gross.* I try breathing through my mouth until the horrifying stench passes—or until my nose at least adjust to it enough that I don't have to hold my breath. It's sad to have such a disgusting smell floating around such a beautiful place.

The precisely placed solid oak tables and matching green upholstered chairs fit with the inn's medieval atmosphere. Droplets of water cascade down my arms and drip from my hair onto the dated carpet.

Delano catches sight of me standing in the doorway as he enters the dining area. He abruptly stands stock still, his dark brows arched and nose flaring. His fists clench at his sides, knuckles blooming a ghostly white. Yep. I'm getting fired.

Maybe I should try to explain myself. Nah. I don't think I'll manage to stop shivering long enough to mutter a complete sentence. And I'm in no hurry to have my sinuses assaulted by that cheap cologne he reeks of. It's like sniffing musky sandpaper. Lowering my head, I make a beeline for the bathrooms. I'll worry about him later. First thing's first: my uniform. There's not a single dry spot anywhere in sight. So much for changing at Dr. Carrere's office to save time.

Casting a hasty glance into the kitchen, a set of inquisitive emerald eyes meet mine. Erianne's gaze follows me as I sling the restroom door open.

Yanking paper towels from the holder, I start wringing my clothes out. The bathroom door creaks ajar, and the very same emerald eyes stare back at me as Erianne peeks her head from behind the door cautiously as her red locks fall over her shoulder. The fluorescent light reflects off them, showing off a tint of orange. Her mouth parts like she's going to speak, but then closes again when I go back to sopping my clothes with the paper towels.

"Hey." She raises her hand, waving her long-manicured fingers. "You alright?"

"*Oui*." I say, still trying to wring the water out of my skirt.

Her smile beams, showing off her porcelain teeth. "Have you met Victor, yet? I was thinking about inviting him to the pub tonight. He's so hot!"

Everything about her screams, 'I'm perfect'. It's kind of annoying. No one should be that perfect. Even her face is shaped just right, with her petite, freckled nose set perfectly against her smooth, almost translucent, complexion.

I snort. "I haven't had a chance to meet anyone here except you and Delano. All he does is bark orders at me all day like a drill Sargent."

Erianne swats the air. "He rides all the new people's asses. Don't let it get to you," she pauses, "We better head back to work. I have an extra uniform in the back if you want to borrow it. And a scrunchie." Her nose scrunches as she points at the knotted mess on my head.

"Really? You don't have to do that." *But please do.*

"Eh, don't worry about it. It's nothing." She smiles and beckons for me to follow her.

Positivity should be her middle name.

I'll take it, though as long as I get to change. Not only am I freezing, but there's no way I'm working in a sopping wet uniform all day with a bird's nest for hair. I'm already in enough trouble for being late.

Erianne reaches into a colorful, woven tote bag resting on a chair in the corner of the room, pulling out the same burgundy button up blouse and white skirt every female has to wear. The guys have the privilege of wearing whatever pants they want. I think it's a little ridiculous, but it's Delano's rule. He made the asinine dress code.

"Thank you. You're a lifesaver." I wring my hands together as she sifts through her bag.

"It's nothing. I can't let my new best friend work in wet clothes. And I don't think you'd want Delano even more on your ass all day. I'm sure he'd love a reason to be." She hands the outfit over, waggling her eyebrows suggestively.

Her 'new best friend' comment reminds me of the conversation with her a couple nights ago. I wonder if she remembers everything. Maybe now I can ask her about the weird, ominous comment she made.

"What's going on back here?" The low grumble of Delano's voice barks as he storms into the break room, stealing my chance to ask Erianne anything. His mouth sets into a firm line and his focus rests on me.

Erianne whispers into my ear, "Speak of the devil…"

I bite my lip to stifle the laugh threatening to escape. "Nothing. Erianne was just giving me a change of clothes. I got caught in the rain."

Delano's mouth parts slightly, his tongue gliding over his lips, dampening them. "Yeah, I noticed." His gaze rakes hungrily over my body from head to toe, making me fold my arms protectively over my chest where his beady eyes land. "Get back to work." He winks as he's leaving, walking back down the hallway.

Erianne gags. "That man creeps me out."

"Me too." My stomach churns.

I take the uniform from her hand and head for the bathroom to change. My clothes are already sticking to me.

I'm dancing internally thinking about going out with Mathieu. Sneakily taking a peek at my phone, I check the time. Only ten more minutes left in my shift. Everything lately has been getting better. Aside from being a flirt, Mathieu's a great guy. And he's safe. Safe is good.

Delano storms out of the kitchen, fists balled up at his sides. Someone should make him an anger management ladder. Step one: take a chill pill.

His face is blooming red and if steam could come out of his ears, it would. I can't help the laughter bubbling up as he stands in front of me. I should be worried that all this pint-sized rage is directed at me, but it's kind of hard to take him serious. He's such a short, pudgy guy it's like watching an Oompa Loompa get angry. He doesn't even stand eye level with all 64 inches of me. His honey brown hair is sticking up in some places, like he's raked his finger through it a hundred times.

"Would you like to explain to me why I have a customer asking for a refund?" He growls.

I restrain from rolling my eyes. "I'm not sure. Did they say what happened?"

Maybe it's the cook you hired that wouldn't know what fine dining is if it smacked him in the face. Or it could be that you're constantly yelling across the restaurant like a buffoon. I don't know what it is with Americans and all their yelling all the time.

He scoffs. "Yeah, you and your poor service! Keep this up and you can kiss your job goodbye!"

I force a weak smile. "Yes, monsieur."

He stomps off back into the kitchen. I peer up to the heavens, thanking the saints that he's left me alone. And, even better, my shift is officially over. Thanks for burning up my last ten minutes, Delano.

I rush to the break room to change out of my uniform. I can never manage to keep a spare in my locker, but always keep a change of normal clothes. Totally ass backwards, like me.

I slip into my favorite white loose crop tee and dark blue jeans. This is why I love flats. I can wear them with a dress, my work uniform, or even a crop tee with jeans.

After stashing my uniform in my locker, I dart out of the break room, keeping my head low so I don't draw Delano's attention. He can kiss my butt goodbye.

I make it through the dining area and yank the front door open, but stop like I've ran into a brick wall. *Merde.* The ground is still wet from the rain. My ears ring as blood rushes to them. I squeeze my eyes shut. *In—five, four, three, two, one—and out.*

Having a panic attack in the middle of a five-star gourmet restaurant would not earn me any points with Delano. I think if that ever happened, I'd be happy to lose even more memories.

Squeezing my fist until my nails bite my palm, I will my feet to step outside. Mathieu is leaning against the side of his car, grinning wildly as I walk to him. I get a whiff of his cologne as he meets me halfway. It's like the vanilla candle mama burns on her lazy Sundays, if it were sitting in the middle of a lavender field. He got all dressed up for the date in a navy-blue suit. I'm impressed, but I definitely didn't think we'd be going anywhere fancy.

"Am I under dressed?" I ask, glancing from his neatly pressed dress slacks to my comfy crop tee.

He waggles his brows. "Maybe not under dressed enough."

My cheeks burn as if a fire has been lit on them. I roll my eyes. Of course, it wouldn't be Mathieu if he didn't shamelessly flirt with no boundaries.

He chuckles. "You're fine. With that face, you could wear a brown paper bag and look ravishing in it." His finger skims lightly along my jaw.

"Thanks." I smile politely and walk around him. If he keeps laying it on thick like this all night, I'm going to hurl.

Mathieu rushes over, swatting my hand away from the door handle. "What kind of man would I be if I didn't hold your door open for you? After all, chivalry isn't dead."

Touch my hand like that again and you will be.

I glare at him, but still climb in. I don't mind him being a gentleman. It's cute, but I can get my own door. There's a difference from grabbing it when he's already in front of me and shoving me out of the way to open the thing. It's not that serious.

Mathieu fumbles with the keys as he tries to start the car. Furrowing my brow, I notice a slight shake in his hands. Is he nervous? *Awe.* That's adorable. This boy, who seems so confident and sure of everything, especially women, is nervous. I'd never peg him as the nervous nelly type.

"So, I, uh, I thought you might like this." Mathieu taps the screen on the dash, pulling up Speckify.

A girly pop song fills the car speakers, making me cringe. Not Dustin Fiever. Okay, I'll take his obnoxious flirting over this. Leaping out of the car is an option if he doesn't turn it off. But, he's already nervous. *Ugh.* I sway my head to the music and try to enjoy it anyway.

"You don't like it do you?" He peeks over at me as the car slows to a stop at a red light.

"No! I do. Really." I force a smile.

He laughs. "I just thought you might because most girls fall all over the Fiever."

I roll my eyes. "Do I seem like the type to fall all over anyone like that? Just because I'm a girl, doesn't mean I like boy bands."

His eyes alight as the corners of his mouth slowly turn upward. The light turns green and Mathieu keeps staring at me, admiring like I'm a shooting star in the night sky. A honk from the car behind us breaks him out of his daze. He shakes his head and puts his eyes back on the road, a smile still constant on his face.

"My favorite singer is Post Malone. You probably don't have him though. You know, because most guys don't listen to emotional stuff." I grin.

He laughs and flips to a different playlist. Post Malone's '*I Fall Apart*' cuts off that Fiever crap playing. The music floats through the car in soothing waves. His music is deep. Especially this song. And it's one of my favorite songs of his next to '*Enemies*'.

"*She told me that I'm not enough…And she left me with a broken heart…She fooled me twice and it's all my fault,…She cut too deep, now she left me scarred…Now there's too many thoughts goin' through my brain…And now I'm takin' these shots like it's novacane…Ooh, I fall apart,*" I stare at the window, singing along to the chorus under my breath.

The car rolls to a stop in front of a store. There's an assortment of wedding gowns in the display window. Okay… What are we doing here? PRONUPTIA is printed in bold dark blue above the window display. I think I've seen a commercial about this place before.

"Why are we at a bridal shop?" I ask as he steps out of the car.

He flashes a mischievous grin and walks around to open my door. What if he's one of those guys that's completely bonkers and proposes to girls on the first date. Mama used to watch reruns of an American TV show called Prank'd, or something like that. Am I being pranked right now? I couldn't be because that show plays pranks on celebrities. I'm far from famous. But Mathieu could still be playing a joke on me.

Mathieu leads me by my hand inside and past an entire section lined with wedding gowns. Thank the saints we pass it right up. Okay, I can breathe a little easier now, but I still don't know what the hell we're doing here. He leads me to the other side of the shop. Every rack is filled with evening gowns and cocktail dresses in all colors and lengths.

"I thought I'd show you how a real man is supposed to pamper you." He stares at me triumphantly with his nose pointed up.

Oh. My. Saints.

I bite my lower lip to hold back my laughter. "A real man?"

He scrunches his forehead. "Yes. I'm eighteen. Technically, I'm your elder. So, you're supposed to do whatever I say."

I release my lip and laugh my ass off. "Is that so? You're lucky you're adorable. And even luckier I know you're not being serious."

"Well, what do you say? Want to let me pamper you?" He asks and hold out his hand.

I take it, rolling my eyes. "Sure."

Mathieu's slick. I'll give him that. Two hours later and I look like I belong on the red carpet. The sheer form-fitting fabric of my powder pink, floor length evening gown is comfortable and the open back helps so it's not too constricting. I wouldn't be able to sit down in the seat of his car if this was any tighter. Me and too-tight clothing don't mix any better than too loose clothing.

I run my hand down the beading on either side of the waist. They match the transparent beads that create a tattoo-style design over my shoulders. Pulling out the pale pink heels he pointed out as the car slows to a stop, I slip them on. Not bad. And they match my dress.

It feels weird to be dressed up like I'm some kind of barbie doll. I loved barbies when I was little and have nothing against them. But I'm not some toy. I know he doesn't mean anything bad by it, but I hope this isn't how he shows he cares. I don't want to be bought.

"Where are we going now?" I ask as he puts the car in park.

He flashes a lop-sided grin, steps out of the car, and walks around to my side. He's really persistent about this door thing. I step out and my stomach flips. We're at *Gill*. This isn't just any restaurant. It received two Michelin stars and was featured on an episode of Fine Living. This place is the epitome of fancy. I guess it's a good thing I'm not wearing jeans anymore.

Mathieu places his hand on the small of my back, leading me inside as the Valet pulls away with his car. He gives the host his name and she escorts us to a table in a dimly lit corner.

"I hope you don't mind. When I made the reservation, I requested the 7-course meal of Gill Tournadre's specialties." He says as the waiter pours wine into the empty glasses on the table.

I force a smile. "That's okay."

But it's not. I wish I could have ordered my own food. I can already tell how this date is about to go. And I have a feeling I'm going to regret coming.

Seven courses later and I'm stuffed like a duck at Christmas dinner. Seven whole courses. I'm talking a parmesan cheese tart, pan fried langoustine, artichoke charlotte, a seared beef fillet, a cheese platter, and a toutain souffle. Even though the portions were miniature, it's *so* much food. Just staring at the piece of chocolate tucked in a fancy gold wrapper the waiter brought when he refilled our wine glasses is making me queasy.

All this stuff is great and all, but it's just stuff. We haven't had any meaningful conversations, unless his random flirting counts. But even then, less than five words have been said between the both of us. It's so awkward. This date did *not* go how I thought it would. I pick at the chocolate wrapper. My skin is crawling. I want to go home and peel myself out of this dress. He's a fun person, a great guy, but maybe better off as just a friend. This stuff isn't me.

6

It's been days since I talked to Mathieu. I haven't seen him at all since our date. Erianne has even been avoiding me like the plague. If he's going to be such a cry baby over me only wanting to be friends and if she's going to stop talking to me over it, to hell with the both of them. I don't want to talk to them anyway if that's their problem.

Lucas has taken permanent residence in my brain with the absence of Mathieu and Erianne. I've been thinking about what Mathieu told me and a lot of it doesn't make sense.

Lucas' mother passing couldn't have been easy on him and let's be honest, everyone deals with grief in their own way. I'm not saying that him turning into a mafia prince is exactly the answer, but how bad could he be if they still choose to be around him? It doesn't make sense. *Ugh.* And here I am thinking about him while I'm supposed to be working.

I clear my tables and pick up all my tips. Once everything is taken down, ready to be put back up tomorrow, I punch out before Delano can find an excuse to keep me.

"Hey, Abigail! Wait a minute!" I recognize that voice instantly.

As I turn down the sidewalk, pretending to not hear her, the tell-tale sound of heels clicking across the pavement gets closer.

Looking back, I catch a glimpse of Erianne as she's jogging out of the restaurant. How she runs in those things, I have no idea.

"Hey," I say, but keep walking.

She rolls her eyes, sighing heavily. "Okay, look. I'm sorry I've being so distant with you. I caught up with Mathieu after your date. He told me everything you guys talked about at Des Carmes."

"Of course, he did," I mumble under my breath.

"What?" She snaps.

I shake my head, gesturing for her to continue. If she snaps at me again, I'll end this conversation quicker than she can say, "Au revoir."

"Anyway, I kind of pried it out of him. He said you two went on a date." She smirks.

I'd love to dish out all the not-so-wonderful details of my date, but I'm still pissed at her. And Mathieu for that matter.

I roll my eyes and snap right back. "Erianne, it's cold. Is there something you wanted to talk to me about? I mean, are we even friends? Because it's hard to tell."

"Yes! Of course, we're friends Abigail! Why would you think like that?" She asks.

My blood boils. Oh, *really*? She is not asking me that. It's totally normal for a 'friend' to avoid you for a week then act like there's nothing wrong. *Not*. My sanity is in decent shape compared to her, Mathieu, and Lucas.

I whip around to face her, almost making her collide into me. "How couldn't I think that Erianne? You have been avoiding me for the past week and haven't said two words to me!" I say louder than I meant to.

She rubs her forehead, and her mouth creases downward. "Can I walk you home? We can talk on the way."

"Whatever." I scoff and throw my hands up as I turn on my heels down the sidewalk without another word.

She quickly catches up. "Abby, I have been distant, and I know that. You have to understand why though. Before you say anything, just hear me out!"

Looking up to meet her eyes, I wait for her to keep talking. If I open my mouth, she won't like what I have to say.

"Asking questions about Lucas is not good. It scared me when I heard you were. The last thing I want is to see you get hurt." She says and smiles like that makes everything dandy.

I stare at her in disbelief. "How exactly does staying away keep *me* from getting hurt? That sounds like you wanted to keep *yourself* safe." And here I thought Ms. Perfect is a selfless, model example of a good person. "And how would asking about Lucas get me hurt? Huh? Can you answer that?"

Screw this. I don't give a damn if I'm losing my patience. I just got off work. I am *so* exhausted and so am *not* doing this right now. I should be curled up on the sofa with Mama, watching her soap opera with her, not arguing with Erianne.

"You just proved my point right there! Abigail, if I had talked to you right after you talked to Mathieu, all you would have done is hound me with questions next." She rests her hands on her hips, her lips pressed firmly together.

I open my mouth, ready to argue my point, but the words die on my lips. What the hell. She has a point. Before Delano barged into the breakroom, that's exactly what I was going to do.

I cross my arms, watching my feet as I walk. "Okay, I probably would have, but what's the big deal?"

She scoffs. "Probably, my ass! Can you just drop this? Please?"

I roll my eyes. "Sure, on one condition."

"Anything!" A sparkle gleams in her eyes.

I grin. "You have to do my dish duty at work for the next month."

I'm ruthless.

Erianne laughs with me, and the tension between us gradually lifts. "Deal."

I step up to the front door of my flat. "Well, this is me. You want to come inside? I'm sure my mama has the entire dining table filled with a bunch of different things she's cooked for dinner."

She smiles warmly. "How could I turn down home cooking?"

I laugh, shaking my head at her as we walk inside.

"Abigail, *mon trésor* you're home! Good because I just got done with the *coq au vin*. I was just about to get the–" My mother stops abruptly when she notices Erianne standing next to me. Her face brightens like a kid's on Christmas morning.

"I hope I'm not intruding, Ms. Halsey," Erianne says, noticing Mama's sudden silence.

Mama's eyes widen. "Oh darling! No, not at all! Please, call me Carla. You must be Erianne?"

"That's me." Erianne smiles politely.

Mama gawks silently at her like she's starstruck. Great. Let's make it *so* obvious I never bring friends over. That won't weird Erianne out.

I wave my hand. "Mama..."

Her hand flies to cover her mouth. "Oh! Where are my manners? Come! Both of you sit! I'll get the plates!" She rushes off into the kitchen.

Coq au vin is one of my favorites. There's no going wrong with chicken and vegetables.

Erianne cautiously peers down at me, her brow furrowed. "Is she okay?"

I chuckle. "Come on, let's eat before my mama drags us in there herself."

The mix of spices coming from everything Mama has cooked has my mouth watering. This is what dreams are made of. I take a seat at the table, already knowing whatever she's cooked is going to be fan-freaking-tastic.

A full loaf of fresh baked brioche is already sliced and laid on the table. An entire serving dish full of niçoise salad next to it, the sauce seeping in from the middle, is calling my name. And no anchovies on top. I know it's how it's supposed to be made, but anchovies are disgusting. They should be banned right along with plain coffee.

Mama scoops the *coq au vin* onto our plates, pouring a spoonful of her homemade chicken gravy over next. Erianne is following her movements like she's in some sort of trance. It's absolutely priceless. There's almost a childlike happiness to her as she watches the food being served on her plate. She's practically drooling.

My shoulders shake as I laugh. "Erianne. Are *you* okay?"

She scrunches her nose. "What? It looks *so* good!"

"I am so glad Abigail is making new friends. She's had a tough year. I trust you'll be good to my little girl." Mama says as she takes a seat at the table, smiling adoringly at Erianne.

I glare at her, but she intentionally ignores me. I'm almost an adult and yet she still finds ways to embarrass me.

Erianne picks up her fork. "I promise, Carla. Your daughter is safe in my hands."

Mama has to work a late shift tonight. She clears the table and gives me a hug, making sure to thank Erianne profusely for coming before heading out the door. Erianne and I plop onto the ugly brown sofa in the sitting room. There's nothing like spending a Saturday night channel surfing.

Hardly anything is on. Flipping to one of Mama's shows–a soap opera about a couple who fall in love–it makes me think of how

I want to find love. Not one that quickly burns bright because that fire always dies out just as quickly. I want the love that withstands every test, every trial, and every obstacle put in its path. Not the stuff in fairy tales, because that's not anywhere near realistic. It's mythological as shit. But the kind that leaves its mark on you forever. And not the way William left his mark on me either. Cheating bastard.

Erianne switches off the TV. "Why don't we do something."

"Hey, I was watching that!" I playfully nudge her.

She throws her hands up in the air. "Abby, come on! It's a Saturday night, and we're sitting in your house watching a really bad soap opera. Let's go somewhere or do something!"

I raise an eyebrow at her and smirk. "Alright."

She jumps up. "Thank. God!"

"Let's go. I don't know where, though." I walk to the door but stop short as I realize she hasn't moved an inch.

"You are *not* trying to go out wearing *that*, are you?" She snarls her nose and points at my clothes.

Looking down, I notice I'm still wearing my work uniform. "What? It's totes *chic*. Burgundy waitress uniform is the new black… *Okay*, I should probably change." I laugh.

"I was hoping you'd say that." Her eyes narrow, a wicked smile creeping over her lips.

I eye her suspiciously. "What's that look for?"

She cackles before dragging me by the hand upstairs. "Where's your room? We need to get you ready!"

"I don't know about this." I wring my hands. "Why can't I be cute and comfortable? There's nothing wrong with simple. I like simple."

She glares at me, folding her arms. *Merde*. I'm so not arguing with her, seeing how determined she is. No way in hell would I win even if I did try.

"Oh, alright!" I throw my hands up, leading the way.

"Are you ready?" Erianne asks, bouncing on her heels like she's a freaking bunny.

I sigh. "Sure."

It only takes Erianne about an hour to pick out an outfit for me and cake on twenty layers of makeup on my face. I somehow squeezed into the impossibly tight black halter dress she plucked from the depths of my closet. I haven't wore this thing since the fundraiser dance my terminale year in lycée. I have to keep pulling down because I'm afraid my butt is going to pop out. She snuck a pair of black heels from Mama's closet. And if we get caught, I'm absolutely throwing her under the bus. Every girl for themselves when it comes to my mama's wrath.

She's holding my mirror in her hand, waiting for me to give her the okay to turn it around and bouncing on her heels like a bunny again. I should nickname her Bunny. She'd kill me.

"Can we go now?" Patience: zero.

These shoes are already making my feet hurt. She flips the mirror over and... *woah...*

I *cannot* believe my eyes. That's my reflection facing me. I touch the glass to make sure I'm not hallucinating. I wouldn't be surprised if my brain didn't up the ante with that next. I don't look anything like myself. This feels weird.

The dress is smoothing out my body. Hell, did I always have shapely curves like this? I thought the makeup was too much. It still feels like it, but I look *fire*. My glossy sandy brown hair is flowing in perfect curls past my shoulders. *Wow.* I'm like a boy talking to a girl for the first time as I stare back at my reflection. Thinking back, I used to feel like this all the time... before William. Ah, hell.

Erianne sets the mirror down and rushes to me as a tear streaks my makeup. "What's wrong? Do you not like it?"

I strain to force a smile on my face. "Erianne! I love it!"

I'm ready to burst into full blown sobs, but screw that. I plop on my bed behind us as Erianne grabs some tissues and carefully dabs my eyes with them.

"Then what is with the tears?" she asks, as if I'm fragile.

I chuckle. "It's nothing. I look hot. Haven't felt this good in a long time. It caught me off guard."

She must think I'm ridiculous. Or crazy. Both accurate assumptions.

She simply nods as to say, *"I understand"* and jumps up, extending her hand out to me. "Come on. I know exactly where we need to go."

7

I insisted we take Erianne's car because there was no way in hell I'm walking in this dress or these heels.

I never pegged her as the sports car type, but here we are, driving down the road in her Bugatti Veyron. The sleek, glossy black paint with a single crimson stripe down the side suits her. I can't help wondering how she's even able to afford it. We both work the same jobs and I can't even afford a used 1997 Renault Safrane, which is practically the cheapest used car there is.

Erianne parks at the end of *Rue Saint-Etienne des Tonneliers*. Stepping out, I follow her up the street to the front of a building with one single illuminated sign blinking '*La Luna.*' It's a wall painted black with off white letters displaying, '*La LUNA*'. A red crescent moon is painted underneath with the same name in red cursive on the inside. I stare at her dumbstruck because there's no door.

She laughs. "The entrance is through here." She pushes open the door of a rusted green gate leading into an alley.

"Erianne, where are you taking me?" I ask, picturing all the warnings for not following anyone down a dark alley at night.

"Just come on!" She rolls her eyes and walks through the gate without me.

I follow her around the side of the building and through a set of green double doors with a bouncer on each side. Both nod at Erianne like they know her and let us through. Walking down a set of winding spiral steps, I stop at the bottom as the scenery unfolds.

La Luna is a busy club filled with bright lights of blue, pink, red, and green. Upbeat dance music blares from speakers set up in every corner and the place is packed. My jaw drops when I notice a woman dancing in a circular, barred cage. She's dressed in nothing but high heels, stockings, and some type of lingerie. All of the women here are hardly wearing any clothing, if that's what you would even call it. And now I feel overdressed.

Erianne's glowing as she scopes the scenery proudly. "Let's get drinks!"

Before I know it, she's dragging me to the bar. I have a feeling I'm going to need to get used to her pulling me everywhere.

"Two shots of Cointreau!" Erianne shouts to the bartender.

I gape at her in horror when her order registers in my brain. "Are you crazy?"

She turns, flashing a wolfish grin.

Cointreau is a strong liquor; like strong as in I'll be wasted within minutes of drinking just one shot of that gasoline. I've been to loads of parties with my ex, but I never really drank. Erianne is going to kill me.

She whisks our shots off the bar top and grabs my hand. "Come on, let's dance." She bustles through the crowd with the two shots in hand like a pro. As soon as we reach the dance floor, she hands me my drink. "Bottoms up!" She downs hers in one swoop.

Sniffing mine first, my nose curls up at the stench of it. I seriously don't know about this. "Bottoms up, I guess." I cough as the liquor burns my throat all the way down. "Are you trying to kill me?" I ask her, still trying to brace myself. It's like chugging gasoline. What the shit.

She's already dancing, her hips swaying to the beat of the music. She grabs my hand, making me dance with her. Letting the music work its magic, I start to just relax, falling in sync with Erianne. She playfully spins me around.

Getting lost in tune to the rhythm I spin back around but stumble, nearly falling on my butt. Just as I regain my balance, I lock onto a pair of familiar glacier blue eyes following my every move, like a hawk having cornered its prey. My heart sinks to the pit of my stomach. There, behind a red velvet rope, sits Lucas himself. Oh, f—

Seconds, maybe minutes, pass. Lucas doesn't seem to care at all. I mean, how could he though? Aside from one other man, the entire section is filled with about a dozen half-naked women. Color me surprised. The women fawn all over him like he's some kind of celebrity and he eats it up. As if that ego of his needs anymore stroking. It's ridiculous. What do they even see in him?

A hand grabs my arm, pulling me back and I find myself facing Erianne who doesn't look so vibrant anymore. A bead of sweat forms on her temple as she stares right at him, straight through me.

She grabs my arm and shields me from his view. She's never been so fiercely protective.

With her grip stuck on my wrist like glue, she drags me to the other side of the club and through a distinct set of doors out onto a patio. The night air sends chills down my spine. The patio, enclosed entirely by a wooden privacy fence, is nearly empty. Maybe a dozen people are scattered throughout. She yanks my arm nearly out of socket, pulling me to an empty corner. *Newsflash. I'm not a rag doll. Kay. Thanks.*

"We need to leave. I don't like the way he looked at us," she says, her hand still gripping my arm. She isn't even looking at me. Her eyes are locked on the back door, watching it like it's going to grow legs and morph into Lucas himself.

"What do you mean Erianne?" I ask, my head throbbing.

I don't know what's going on, but pure dread is pumping through my veins. I idolize her confidence, but it's no where in her. He scares her *that* much. Like a ripple effect, it horrifies me.

Erianne averts her eyes from the doors. "I told you to stop asking questions, Abigail. We need to get out of here. Now." She doesn't wait for me to speak as she starts scanning the patio for an exit. "There. Let's go." She pulls me toward a wooden fence door.

And now she's calling me by my full name, which she never does. Yep. We're screwed.

The green metal doors leading back into the club swing open. A man in a black suit and red dress shirt stands in the doorway and spots us easily. I instantly recognize him. He was sitting with Lucas.

His bald scalp reflects the moon light as he pushes through the crowd with precise determination. All the blood drains from my face, my heart thumping wildly in my chest.

Erianne, near breathless, glances over her shoulder, her eyes falling on the man and widening. Her grip on my arm tightens excruciatingly, cutting my circulation. She yanks me harder, ready to take off in a full sprint. I can hardly keep up in these heels. My feet are throbbing, aching. Only a few more steps away from the gate. By all saints, we have to make it. I can't even imagine what that man is going to do once he catches us. He doesn't look like the friendly *'let's talk it out'* type. More like *'let's break bones. Rawr.'*

I quickly glance over my shoulder, instantly regretting it the moment my heel catches on a break in the cement. Losing my balance despite the vice-like grip Erianne has on my arm, I brace myself for the impact of my face smacking the pavement. But someone else grabs ahold of my right arm. Using the opportunity to regain my balance, I get my back on my feet.

All hope of being able to make a break for it vanishes as I stare back at the man holding my arm. Erianne is gawking at him wide-eyed, paler than a ghost. She hasn't released my other arm either.

A nervous laugh bubbles up and escape my mouth. Here I am, standing in-between Erianne and this man whom I'm sure is ready to break my kneecaps or something. I can't help finding it sort of funny. Maybe that's just the nerves, but whatever it is, I can't stop laughing now as I slump my shoulders. The man furrows his brow at me as if

I've lost my mind. Buddy, you're late to this train. My sanity bounced on me a long time ago.

"Mr. Danforth would like a word with Ms. Halsey." The man says, glancing from me to Erianne. "It is not a request."

She hesitantly releases me. My laughs stop. She mouths '*Sorry*' as a tear rolls down her cheek. Why is she crying? What's happening? Not funny anymore. *Mama.*

This brute drags me back into the club. The crowd parts for him as he pulls me up to the velvet-roped section where Lucas is. All the women that surrounded him are gone. He's sitting on the pale pink leather sofa like a king on his throne. I've got three words for him. Get. Over. Yourself.

"Abigail." Lucas says, a cocky grin plastered on his face.

I'm at a loss for words. Kind of like when you see your idol or favorite celebrity mixed with seeing the most terrifying, but equally interesting thing you could imagine, like a politician, all for the first time. *Merde.* I can't stand here and fangirl over his dangerous, arrogant, annoying, womanizing... a lot of bad, no-no thing self... He'd actually make a perfect politician.

Lucas nods at the man standing next to me. "Jimmy, you can leave us."

Jimmy releases my arm and quickly disappears into the crowd.

"Sit down." Lucas gestures for me to sit next to him.

My eyes strain as I resist the urge to roll them at him. It's annoying that he thinks he can just order me around. I'm not one of his goons. I press my lips firmly together to keep my thoughts from spewing out.

He chuckles and shrugs. "Or stand there. I don't really care."

He leans forward, grabbing his glass filled a quarter of the way with a light brown liquid. As he swirls it, the stench of liquor greets my nostrils. After that shot Erianne gave me earlier, I have a new hatred for alcohol. I wring my hands as those blue eyes remain fixated on me.

"You know I'm not going to hurt you, right?" He flashes a mischievous grin. "I'm sure you're wondering why I sent Jimmy to ask you to come talk to me."

Him talking about his brute dragging me without a choice breaks my silence.

"He didn't *ask* anything…" I mutter as I rub my arm where Erianne's grip left a yellowing bruise.

His knuckles bloom a ghastly white that's visible even in this dimly lit V.I.P. section as he grips the glass in his hand. I wouldn't be surprised if it shattered any second now. He glares at the spot on my arm I'm rubbing.

"I'll have a talk with him. It won't happen again." He says, his jaw clenching.

I force a smile. But I can't shake the way he said that. I hope I didn't get Jimmy in trouble. Or his kneecaps busted.

Lucas sets his glass down. "I hear you've been asking about me."

My eyes widen as my heart skips a beat. "*Oui*. I-I was just…"

Lucas chuckles. "Abigail. Relax."

I sigh. "It was just that when I first met you that night at O'Kallaghan's, you seemed so familiar. I couldn't remember where I knew you from and Erianne wouldn't even talk about you. I tried asking her but…" Recalling her weird cryptic comment that day sends a chill throughout my body. *"You don't deserve any of this."*

"What did she do?" He furrows his brow.

"Nothing." I shake my head. "Are you going to kill me?" I blurt the words out before I can stop myself. I wring my trembling hands. *Merde.*

Even in this dim lighting, I can visibly see the color pooling in his cheeks, his jaw flexing. "No."

I try to ask something else to change the subject, but my voice gets caught in my throat. He's so damn intimidating. *Get it together, Abigail. In—five, four, three, two, one—and out.* I guess it's a good thing to know I'm not his next target. That thought helps me breathe a little easier.

I swallow hard. "Why are people so scared of you?"

Lucas' eyes relax, his lips forming a tight smile. "I had no idea anyone feared me."

Oh, the arrogance. This guy is intimidating one minute, then infuriating the next. His mouth begins forming a word, but quickly melts into a firm line as a figure approaches the velvet ropes. Standing perfectly still, aside from her hands shaking ever so slightly at her sides, is Erianne.

"I had to know you were okay." She glances hastily from me to Lucas.

Lucas throw his hands up. "There you are! I was beginning to wonder where you'd run off to. How's *work*?"

The loathing at the end of his sentence catches my attention. What throws me even more off guard is the way she's frantically looking between us more than before. Why does that bother her so much? All he did was ask how work was going. We work at a restaurant. What's the big deal with that?

"I'm not going to hurt the girl. My saints! Would you relax already? Some of us know how to do our job. *Correctly*." Lucas sprawls his arms across the back of the pale pink leather sofa, glaring at Erianne.

His prickly, brash attitude toward her and the way he keeps mentioning her job is making my head spin. What is he talking about? And why is it so easily bothering Erianne? She hasn't said a word. More importantly, why is she so scared of him? I have so many *more* questions.

A deafening, awkward silence has blanketed the area around us. Rubbing my temple, I try to think of a way to defuse this silent dispute between the two of them. I have no idea what it's even about, but this staring contest going on has got to stop at some point.

I cough, not so subtly, to get their attention. "I'm okay, Erianne. We were just talking."

As if being pulled out of a trance, Erianne shakes her head briefly. "Well, we should get going, Abbs. It's getting late."

I almost don't want to leave now. I thought I'd be just as scared as…well…as Erianne is right now. But I'm not. My lungs struggling to keep up with my racing heart are light as a feather. With my nerves on edge, I'm ready to burst at the seems like a primary school girl.

Biting my lower lip, I dare ask, "Can't we stay a little while longer?"

If looks could kill, I'd be cold as stone right now.

"Fine. But I will be right at the bar." She hesitates, glaring daggers at me before walking over to the bar top.

"She cares about you," Lucas blurts.

"You think so?" I smile as Erianne takes a seat on a barstool, a warmth spreading through my chest.

Lucas sits forward abruptly. "Do you want to get some air?"

Unable to hide the ear-splitting grin on my face, I meet his eyes. "Yes, please."

He laughs, shaking his head before placing his hand on the small of my back and guiding me out of the V.I.P. area. I've been crawling in my skin since I got here. This isn't my scene and it's so packed. On the plus side though, I think I've kicked my fear ladder's ass.

Walking into the club left me gob smacked but walking out on Lucas' arm is like I'm walking out with a celebrity–or royalty. Everyone around us is whispering, their eyes only briefly darting at his hand pressed firmly against my back. My stomach is in knots and the more I scan the crowd, the more I realize something is off. Making a path as we approach, not a single person has actually looked directly at Lucas nor myself. In fact, I think they're intentionally averting their gazes.

What the hell is that about?

Surprisingly enough, like a pure gentleman, Lucas walks a few steps ahead to grab the door. Standing with poise, he ushers me outside. This guy is something else. After taking a moment to admire the show of chivalry, I walk briskly past him out into the chill of the night.

Billions of stars glistening down, accompanied by a full moon, illuminate the blackened sky. A warm, yellow glow coming from a streetlamp in the parking lot outlines the silhouette of a man leaning against a single black sedan. Lucas joins me at my side. The man standing by the sedan abruptly opens the rear door. Lucas makes eye contact with him and nods ever so slightly.

Like some sort of silent language, the man nods back, shuts the rear door, and climbs in the front seat. Squinting, I can make out a few details of the man's suit just before he shuts the car door; like the red button up. Jimmy. The exchange between Jimmy and Lucas leaves me wanting to ask what it's about. But I know I shouldn't. This is becoming a never-ending trail of questions. And I'm getting antsy for some answers.

Lucas gazes up into the night sky, placing his hands in his pockets. "I asked Erianne about you."

I jerk my head up in his direction, my eyebrows knitting together. "You did?"

It hadn't dawned on me just how tall he is until now. And I definitely underestimated his height when Mathieu told me. I have to bend my neck just to get a glimpse of him.

He grins. "Yes. She said you're a good person. Are you?"

I gaze up at the night sky. "I think so. I try to be, at least."

Lucas' smile broadens.

I look back to him. "Why did you ask Erianne about me?"

An upturn of his mouth, baring teeth, crinkles the corners of his vibrant crystalline eyes. "I heard you went out with Mathieu."

My cheeks burn bright as the lights in the club. An unfamiliar knot squeezes my chest. The urge to look at anything but him surges through me. How does he know about that?

"I wonder how my shoes are holding up. The poor things have been dragged through a crap ton of messes tonight." I kick my leg up to get a better look at my heels, having found an excuse to change the subject.

He chuckles. "What do you like about him anyway?"

"Huh? Why do you ask?" I drop my foot.

Lucas shrugs. "He just doesn't seem like your type."

Like he knows my type. I don't even have one. *Ugh.* And I bet he's going to tell me he's my type. Mr. Ego with the ridiculously styled hair who makes a habit of surrounding himself with women all the time. Yeah, right.

I roll my eyes. "You're wrong. He's a good guy who's funny and kind and… and…"

I press my mouth shut tight. I don't know if it's his arrogance pissing me off or that I can't think of anything else I actually like about Mathieu. He's not right.

I scoff and fold my arms over my chest. "Well, we just met. So, I don't know everything about him. Not that it's any of your business, but I do like him. And if after several more dates, he asked me to be his girlfriend, I'd say yes."

Not true, but I won't give him the satisfaction of being right.

Lucas turns to face me. Tipping my head up by my chin, leaving me nowhere to look other than directly up at him, into his eyes. Their vibrant light dims, a deep sorrow filtering through. His smile has dissipated, leaving only a flat line in its place. The fleeting, light caress of his hand glides across my cheek, but is gone all too quickly. A sudden, unexpected hollow ache follows. *Woah.* Oh, he's *good*. And it just pisses me off even more.

He grins. "I bet if you went on a date with me, you wouldn't think twice about him."

My heart is pounding against my chest. A million thoughts flit through my mind as I consider all the possibilities. Someone needs to take his ego down a notch. Maybe I should do it. It's not like everything in me isn't screaming *say yes*, though. If only to shut him up and prove him wrong.

I nod. "Okay. You're on. But on one condition."

A hint of a smile plays across Lucas' lips. "What's that?"

I grin. "You have to answer any question I ask you. Honestly!"

His wickedly mischievous grin makes me regret this already. "Deal. What are your plans tomorrow?"

I sigh. "I have to work until seven."

"I'll pick you up after work then."

The warmth of his lips presses against my knuckles just long enough to make heat pool in my cheeks. Leaving me standing in a mess of my own thoughts, Lucas climbs into the waiting sedan. As I watch the car pull off onto the street, the thought of going on a date with *the* Lucas Danforth causes my breath to catch in my throat. It's stupid and dangerous. But someone has to shut his arrogant self up.

The doors to the club fly open, metal crashing into brick with a thud. Practically jumping out of my skin, I whirl around.

"What the hell is wrong with you?"

Oh, hell. I forgot about Erianne.

8

I'm in deep shit.

"We are leaving!" Erianne shouts, making me flinch as she storms off into the alley, toward the gate we entered through.

"But…" I try to protest, to explain myself.

"Now!" Her voice bellows into the night as she holds the gate open for me.

I scurry along without another word—not that she'll let me get a single one in anyway. I've never seen her so mad. The worst part is I have no idea *why*. It's not like she heard my conversation with Lucas. We climb into the car and the tension is thick, nearly suffocating. She whips her car out of the parking spot. My heart would bust through my ribcage right now if it could.

The screeching of tires echoes across *Rue Jacques Lelieur*. Gripping the arm rest, I'm thrown back into the seat as she speeds off into traffic. *In—five, four, three, two, one—and out*. The speedometer keeps climbing higher and higher. *In—five, four, three, two, one—and out*. It's not working. I swallow hard as sweat beads on my forehead.

"Erianne, slow down!" I yell.

"To hell with that! Have you lost your damn mind?" she screams.

Her hands squeeze the steering wheel tighter until her knuckles bloom white. My grip on the seat loosens as I lean away and against the door like a frightened child. Why is my mouth so dry? *In—five, four, three, two, one—and out. Merde.* It's not working. I can't breathe.

A red glow from the traffic signal illuminates the street about a mile ahead. As we approach, she doesn't let up off the gas at all. Her hands wind around the steering wheel. Shit. *Red means stop, Erianne.* I press my body firmly against the back of the seat, bracing myself on the dash and at the same time she slams on the brakes. The car skids to a halt just before the intersection, tires squealing against the pavement. She releases her deathly grip on the steering wheel, heaving a single deep breath as she rubs her hands over her face.

Her voice is barely a whisper, "I'm sorry."

Breathless, I gawk at her. "Screw your *sorry*!"

Her hands drop from her face, smacking her thighs. "What?" she hisses.

I grip my chest. "You just nearly killed me!"

A sharp, stinging in my throat makes it harder to breathe. My lip is quivering, and my head is throbbing. The space in the car suddenly feels so small, so confining as everything starts to close in on me. *In—five, four, three, two, one—and out.* Hot tears sear my cheeks. I can't. My breathing won't slow down. The car is shrinking.

I press my palm over my heart like this will slow it down. So many thoughts swirl around in my head, but I can't focus on one. My ribs are crushing into me, caving in like the weight of a ten-story building rests on them, brick after brick. Getting heavier and heavier. It's too much. This is all too much.

Fumbling, I reach for the door handle. *I have to get out. I need to get out.*

My trembling fingers slip, leaving the handle out my reach. *No, no, no. I need out.* Knots tear at the depths of my stomach. *Escape.* My breathing exercise isn't working. I'm not in control. Not me. Someone else. My head is so light. Everything is so blurry. Out. I need out. I need to be safe. Away. In control. The faint chirp of Erianne's voice floats through my ears, but her words drown out as images flash in my head.

The man from my dreams, his teeth baring through that evil snarl. Mama is sprawled across the cold tile, lifeless. He's coming for me now. My body feels so small. Why do I feel so small? I can't escape. There's no escape. A cackle resonates through my ears. My face dampening, eyes burning. He's only inches from me now. The man's husky voice repeating my name like a song: Abigail. Abigail. Ab-i-gail. Abby.

The image melts into an empty street in front of me past the windshield of Erianne's car. I blink. One. Twice. Over and over until the man's words contort, twists. Erianne's sweet, soothing voice mixes with his. Erianne? *Erianne.*

"Abigail!" Erianne's screams ring through my ears as I float back out of the memory.

Merde. Merde. Merde. A sharp, splintering pain is shooting through my hands from underneath each of my nails pressed tightly into my palms. One by one, I flex my fingers, noticing the burning and crimson tint they leave behind.

Erianne gasps sharply. "Oh my god! Abigail!"

"What… happened?" I ask.

It's not real. None of that was real. I dug my nails so deep into the palms of my hands… I… didn't realize. I didn't know. Four perfect arches are indented in the palms of my hands, each glistening with blood.

Erianne gawks at my hands. "I could ask you the same thing. What the hell? Are you okay?"

She places a comforting hand on my shoulder, but I jerk it away. I don't know why, but the touch sends chills all over my body. I'm going to hurl. I need the hell out of this damn car. Willing my arms to obey, I grip the door handle and send the car door flying open. Stumbling as my feet hit the pavement, my body is pulled by gravity like it's for the first time. The night air smacks my face like little specks of ice. *Air*. Inhaling to fill my lungs with the cold, to soothe the burning lingering in them, I squeeze my eyes shut and scream until my throat hurts.

"Abigail…" Erianne's baby steps toward me anchor me back to the here and now.

Lifting my head, my voice sounds so small, "…Erianne."

She sprints to me, wrapping her arms around my torso as I sink to the pavement, sobs wracking my body.

"I-I'm sorry! I'm so sorry!" I shove the words out of my mouth.

I don't know why I'm sorry though. For freaking out? For waking all of Rouen? For being a mess? I'm not sure.

"Shh. Don't be sorry. It's okay." Her frail hands glide soothingly up and down my back.

Acting as my personal lighthouse guiding me out of the darkness and back into the light, Erianne filters all the bad out. My body is cocooned by the warmth of her embrace.

I pull away from her, sitting back on my heels. She glances behind me, closing her eyes briefly and shaking her head from side to side. I follow in the direction she's staring, but no one is there. When I look back into her emerald eyes, her full attention is on me again. My curiosity creeps in like an itch I can't scratch.

Everything is back to normal.

"I'm sorry. You probably think I'm looney." I wipe away a stray tear.

"It's okay." Her slight smile just barely curves at the corner of her mouth. She presses up on her heels to stand, reaching out her hand. "We need to talk."

9

I smile at the clear sky glistening with millions of stars as I pull my bedroom curtains shut. No storm tonight. Thank the freaking saints. I've had enough excitement for tonight.

"Why don't you sit down?" Erianne asks.

She's across the room, sitting in the black swivel chair at my cherry oak computer desk. I twist the lock on my doorknob and shuffle over to plop down on my queen-sized bed.

"You wanted to talk. So, talk."

She takes a deep breath. "There's some things I need to explain to you. I need you to be patient and just sit there. Just... listen and let me explain. Okay?"

This can't be good. But I nod. Not knowing something at all is worse than knowing and it being bad. I can't control or deal with what I don't know.

"Remember. Let me explain before you decide anything. Once I tell you this, if you decide you never want to see my face again, I'll walk right out that door. You'll never have to worry about me again." She says, pressing her lips together.

"Okay. I understand. But what are you talking about?" *Get on with it already.*

She pulls her hair over her shoulder. "First, we need to have a talk about Lucas."

I roll my eyes. "Hell, Erianne! What does Lucas have to do with this? Would you stop dragging this out and just tell me already?"

Her lips press into a firm line as she glares at me. "You need to know some things about him before you can understand anything else."

"Okay. Sorry." I grab one of my pillows and hug it against my chest.

She crosses her legs, wringing her hands together. "Lucas' full name is Lucas Danforth."

She stares at me as if that's supposed to mean something, but then sits upright. "You're telling me the name doesn't sound familiar to you?"

"No, Erianne. I'm saying Mathieu already told me about him. What the hell? Come on! You know that!" Laying backward on my bed, I send my pillow flying to the side of the room.

She clenches her jaw. "Patience!"

Sitting up again, I hold my hands up. "Okay, okay!"

I pretend to zip my lips together.

She glares. "Lucas' father is Dominick Vitale. Did he tell you that?"

Staring at her, silently I point to my lips, nodding.

Erianne scoffs. "What hasn't he told you?" She closes her eyes and takes a deep breath. "Never mind." Her lip quivers slightly. "My mother works for Dominick. She's his partner and almost as corrupt as him. They've been at this together since they were younger than you and me. Well before I was even born. That's how I know Lucas. I grew up with him after my mother moved us here from Ireland ten years ago to help Dominick build his business. Mathieu, too. Lucas has always had my back. So, I've always tried to look after him when I can. His father can be… difficult. When Lucas asks for my help with anything business related, I help. When my mother asks for my help, it's not really an option; it's an order. With Lucas, I have a choice. With my mother, not so much. You have to understand." Her eyes bore into me.

"Understand what, Erianne?" The shaking in my hands is back.

She closes her eyelids, squeezing them tightly shut. A single tear rolls down her cheek. "My mother ordered me to keep tabs on you. I lied to you when I told you I work at La Couronne because of tradition. It's true my mother wouldn't have me working anywhere else because she wanted me to work with you. To get close to you. She made sure you got the job there."

"What…" My chest heaves, struggling past the single word.

My face suddenly feels so cold. The sting from her words is like I've been slapped in the face. An emptiness, a darkness, boils in my gut.

Erianne's shoulders shake. "Please, Abigail. I didn't have a choice. Once I met you, I knew I couldn't do it. I risked everything and went behind my mother's back to go to Lucas for help. That's why he was at O'Kallaghan's. We were supposed to talk to you. We were going to tell you everything then, but I got so drunk I forgot to take you to meet with Lucas. Then when I went home, I got into it with my mother and I slipped up."

I want to be mad at her. I want to hate her. Everything tells me I should. She betrayed me, used me, and lied to me. I *should* hate her... But I can't. This isn't her fault. Still, I can't shake the knot in my throat.

I swallow hard. "What does that mean?"

She moves swiftly to sit next to me, gripping my hands. "I told my mother I didn't want to do it anymore. I refused. I disobeyed a direct order. Abigail, I spent the entire next day doing damage control. Lucas is pissed at me. He said his father found out that we went behind their backs, betrayed them. He was punished for my mistake and he might want payback. Which, until then, I didn't know why she even ordered me to keep tabs on you. I didn't know it was a favor for Lucas. I was worried about how he'd react when he saw me with you tonight, so I panicked."

Any trace of vibrance that usually lives within Erianne is gone, replaced by unmistakable dread. So many things, so many questions. It's all falling into place now. My head is spinning trying to put each piece of the puzzle together.

I got the job at La Couronne only because of Erianne's mother. Then, Erianne was forced by her mother to befriend me. She invited me for drinks, not to be nice, but to have me meet Lucas. When she got too drunk to remember she's a lying backstabber, she blabbed to her stalkerish mother. So, she never cared about me.

The job I got to get me out of the house, get through my mental health recovery, it isn't legit. None of it's been real. I thought everything has been getting better, that *I've* been getting better. I've just been getting played and lied to. All my progress with my mental health, it all feels so violated. Could my therapist be involved in this too?

"What about tonight? Was that all a setup too? Are you still pretending? Is this right now all just an act? How can I even trust you?" I jerk my hands back, standing up off my bed, far away from her.

"Abigail." She stands, taking a step forward.

I take another step away from her.

She stumbles backward. "Please. You... have to believe me. I'm putting my life on the line just to tell you all this. Dominick won't care if I'm the daughter of his partner! He'll kill me if he ever finds out you know anything!"

My head is pulsing like it's ready to explode. "What does he want with me? Why me?" Tears pool in my already puffy eyes.

She shakes her head. "I'm not sure. All I know is what Lucas told me. There's some man from America here. He's a friend of Dominick's and came asking a favor. That favor was you. Abigail, this man, whoever he is, wants you and your mother."

My heart sinks to the pit of my stomach, "...My mother? Why?"

Erianne tries to step forward, but I hold my hand up to stop her. "I don't know. Lucas said he bragged that he messed you up in the head and said he wanted payback for what your mother did to him. Does the name Sebastian sound familiar to you?"

It doesn't, but as soon as she says the name, it's almost as if a wall in my mind has been split; like a dam cracking from the pressure, ready to burst any moment. Something about that name. It sends a chill down my spine just thinking about it.

"No." Everything in me is screaming to protect that wall.

Erianne's shoulders droop. "I hoped it might, but that's okay. I think what happened tonight may have been related to this Sebastian guy. He said he made sure he hurt you so bad you'd never forget him."

That wall in my head is caving, the pressure against it building. "No, Erianne. I don't know what you're talking about. Honestly." Resting my face in my hands, I try not to focus on what's happening inside my head.

She shifts on her feet. "Well, earlier when you got out of the car, I saw Lucas. He saw you. We didn't exchange words, but I know he's going to help me protect you now. You just have to stay away from him. I don't care what he says or does, you have to stay away from him. The last thing you want to do is give anyone a reason to believe you know anything. We can't draw attention. Trust me on this."

My brows knit together. "What if I don't want to stay away from him?"

I don't actually want to be around him, especially knowing what I do now, but who does she think she is? She can't betray me, drop all this on me, and then try to order me around. What the shit? And I'm the basket case.

Erianne runs a hand through her hair. "Abigail. Dominick is not someone you want to ignore. He's dangerous."

"Well, that doesn't mean Lucas is dangerous. And you even said yourself that he's going to help you protect me! So, wouldn't I be safest around him?" I protest.

I still can't believe this. Every bit of safety I felt less than an hour ago has been ripped away.

She hesitates as if choosing her words carefully. "Abigail, listen to me. I've known Lucas since I was eight years old. For ten years now. He will protect you from afar, but it's not safe to be close to him. That's why you should let us do what we need to."

"I don't trust you." I admit.

She sits down on my bed, lowering her head. "I'm sorry."

She shakes her head as she smooths her dress out. Seeing her so hurt makes my heart ache.

She takes a deep breath. "Please listen to me when I say it's best to stay away from him. Let me deal with him. I'm already tied to all of this. I don't want you to be any more than you already are now."

"I will. And Erianne…"

She glances up at me, eyes tinged a hint of red. "Yes?"

Don't make me freaking regret this.

"I forgive you."

"Really?" Tears fall from her swollen emerald eyes as she wraps me into a deathly tight hug.

Erianne is as much a victim in all of this as I am. She's taken a risk to be honest with me. And if not her, who do I really have to help me?

"Okay. Need. To. Breathe," I say as she tightens her hug.

Erianne giggles. "Oh! Sorry."

Our laughter echoes off the walls of my bedroom, washing away all the earlier tension. Once she releases her grip, I grab the floral printed box of tissues off my desk.

"I think we both need these. Although, we do make a pretty hot pair of raccoons." I grab a few tissues and hand the box over to her.

She dabs underneath her eyes. "Thank you for understanding. And sorry for being such a cry baby." Her slight smile falters. "You really are a great person and I don't have many genuine people in my life."

I fall dramatically back on my bed, making the entire thing shake, and grin. "You can't get rid of me that easily."

Erianne rolls her eyes, the vibrance in her smile present again. "I'm sorry for screaming at you earlier. I just knew Lucas was pissed at me and he's been so unpredictable. I saw you walk out with him and the worst scenarios ran through my head."

"Hey. I already said I forgive you. That meant for everything." I purse my lips, pointing a finger at her. "And I'm fine. Just remind me never to piss you off."

She laughs. "I'm not that bad."

I raise my eyebrows at her.

She rolls her eyes. "Okay, so I'm incredibly terrifying."

I scoff. "I wouldn't go that far."

"I should get going. It's late. I picked up a shift at the restaurant, so I guess I'll see you at work." She kisses both of my cheeks.

"See you at work tomorrow," I say as she reaches for the door handle and walks out the door, shutting it behind her.

I immediately peel the high heels off my feet. The relief of having those things finally off is like a big fat slice of heaven. I still have to get up to switch off the light. Dragging myself out of my bed, I flip my light off. The moonlight casts a gentle glow into my room. Still not a single cloud in sight. Good.

What was *supposed* to be a girl's night out turned into a night of chaos and breakdowns. *Ah, hell.* I forgot Lucas still thinks I'm going to dinner with him. Boy, do I got news for him.

10

My shift at La Couronne is in full swing. The grills are sizzling, chefs are busy preparing five-star dishes, and I'm putting dazzling smiles on all the customer's faces.

Or maybe that's just the food.

The hours are passing like seconds, slowly creeping on and killing me just as slowly. Erianne is chatting with some guests, going over the breakfast specials. I don't think it's a great idea to tell her about Lucas showing up here later. It's not like I'm actually going with him. I'll march out there and tell him I'm not about to be his mafia princess or even his next conquest. Even though… *No. Bad, Abigail.*

I shake off the thought of Lucas being anyone's conquest, as hard as that is.

"Hey, Abby!" Erianne says as she rushes by me to grab a tray of food.

"Hey!" I blurt out a lot louder than I meant to.

My nerves are all flustered now as the image of 'conquest Lucas' floats through my brain. She doesn't seem to notice though because she's already serving the food. I've got to keep it together. Checking the clock, I realize it's break time. Finally. My last break of my shift. I put in an order of La Couronne's finest Pâtes a few minutes ago. It should be ready now.

Snatching up the plate from the kitchen, I head to the back room. Erianne storms in like a bat out of hell, fist clenched at her sides. I jolt forward, nearly dropping my Pâtes. *Oh, hell.* What now?

"Thank the heavens you're still here!" she exclaims as she sits next to me.

"What's wrong?"

"I need to leave. My little sister just got into town and needs to be picked up from the airport. I stupidly forgot, and now she's stuck waiting for me." Erianne shakes her head.

"I didn't know you had a sister," I say distractedly. The amount of relief that just flooded through me is more than words can speak. I didn't do anything wrong this time.

"Yeah. Not by choice, of course," Erianne smiles playfully, "but Delano won't let me leave unless I can get someone to cover my tables for the rest of the night. I know I'm asking a lot, but could you?"

"Of course! It's no problem." I hug her quickly.

"Thank you so much! My shift is over in an hour, so you would only be handling them until then." She releases me before getting her bag off the chair she usually leaves it on. "See you on Monday?"

"Yes, go." I shoo her off.

She blows a kiss. "You're a life saver, Abby. I owe you one!" she shouts, waving while walking down the hallway.

Well, I don't have to worry about her catching Lucas showing up, but now I have double the workload. Guess break time is over then.

I swear, one of these days I'll learn to ignore my curiosity and leave things be. It's what got me into this mess. I just *had* to know more about Lucas. My curiosity made me chase that enigmatic smile, panty-dropping charm, and deep sapphire eyes. I think I'm going to be the cat that curiosity kills... Or in this case, the one a mafia ring-leader kills. *Ugh.*

There's only fifteen minutes left to my shift. And I just have one table left to serve. Of course, it would be someone who could *not* possibly eat any slower. I could go now and let someone else handle clearing the customer's table. That would mean I would lose my tip, though. I mull it over... *Oh, to hell with that.*

I march over to her table. "Is there anything else I can get you, mademoiselle?" I ask, my customer service charm bordering over the top.

She looks up at me, taking a moment to eyeball my name tag, "Abigail, is it?" she asks before dabbing her mouth with her napkin.

I hesitate a moment, "Yes?"

I hope she isn't the type of customer that complains if you bother her while she's eating. That would make this *so* much better...

An eerie smile crawls over her lips as she stands. "I don't need anything else." She glances back at me a moment before walking toward the door.

"Are you sure I can't get anything else for you?" I call out as she pushes the door open.

She grins, her eyes shrinking to slits, "No. I have got all I need."

Uhm… o-kay. What the hell was that about? Oh well, at least I can leave on time now. All I have left to do is clear her table, and I'm done. As I begin, I notice something. No tip. I'm glad she left then.

"I can't stand people who come to a nice restaurant, pay for their meal that's been served to them on a silver platter, *literally,* and can't respect their server. If you can't tip, then stay home." I rant under my breath as I finish cleaning the tabletop.

Laying out the finishing touches to the place settings on the table, my pulse begins pounding in my temples. I don't know how Lucas is going to react when I tell him to take a hike. Erianne said to stay away from him. Maybe I should just avoid him altogether and let him take a hint. He doesn't really seem like the type to just say *'Okay. No problem. I totally understand!'*. No. It's more like *'I want. I bust kneecaps. I take. Grrr.'*

Chuckling at myself, I make my way outside quicker than usual. Just as I'm slipping my coat over my shoulders, a familiar black sedan rolls to a stop in front of La Couronne. This is it. Here goes nothing. The brute Lucas calls Jimmy steps out of the driver's side. As he walks around the car, a realization dawns on me. Jimmy is probably… no, *definitely* part of this mafia family. Hell.

With Jimmy holding the rear passenger door open, Lucas slides out. His cool confidence radiates like a heat wave. My breath hitches at the sight of him in his crimson button up. The ridges of his biceps flexes through the thin fabric. He catches me gawking and flashes a devilish grin, baring his teeth ever so slightly. An electric current blasts throughout my body, my gut twisting. *Ah, hell.* This is going to be a lot harder than I thought.

Closing my eyes, I take a few deep breaths to regain my composure. Maybe if I just keep my eyes closed while I'm talking to him, this will go just fine. Tsk. As if that's possible. *You can do this. You have to.* Masking my flustered nerves, I march over to him with clear precision.

"After you, Ms. Halsey." Lucas motions for me to get into the car.

My cheeks flush at the caress of his words. My mouth deceives me as it blooms, forming a bright smile. Shaking my head, I purse my lips together. "I can't go with you."

He chuckles. "Backing out of the challenge so quickly. I'm glad you admit I'm right."

You know what… maybe I should go. Maybe if I prove him wrong, that I'm not going to swoon over him or forget about Mathieu, he'll come down off that pedestal he's got himself on. I stand by what I said last night. Someone needs to knock his ego down a few notches.

I glare at him and climb into the car. The car door shutting resonates through my ears. All the warmth in my body is replaced by a cold, jarring panic. *Oh, my saints.* What did I just do? I need to get out. Frantically turning to open my door, a voice in my head is screaming for me to run. I reach for the handle. *Click.* All the locks activate, sealing my fate. I'm paralyzed as the car glides into motion, easing into traffic with Jimmy behind the wheel. Too late. There's no turning back now. So much for telling Lucas to take a hike. I'm so stupid.

My watch gleams 7:32PM. We've been driving for a long time. The tension burning through my head to my feet is suffocating. Where is he taking me?

"You seem nervous," Lucas says, glancing at my trembling hands.

I wring my hands together. "U-uhm. No. I'm okay."

The smile plastered on my face says *I'm totally okay with this.* But the trepidation gnawing away at my insides is screaming *I need to get the hell out of here.*

Lucas reaches to enclose my hands in his grasp. His fingers skim across the bandages on my palms. Furrowing his brow, he grabs my hands, turning them palm up.

"What happened?" Lucas' jaw flexes.

"It's nothing." I say, trying to pull my hands away, but Lucas' hold is firm.

His shoulders tense. "This is not nothing."

"It was an accident." Last night flits through my mind and my lip quivers. I bite it to keep it still.

Lucas gazes upon me a moment, his tension dissipating. "I understand."

"Where are we going?" My curiosity is my best friend right now.

"It's a surprise, but I promise you will enjoy it."

He gently pulls my hand to his lips, laying a gentle kiss on my palm all while keeping his eyes locked on me. I can't seem to tear my eyes from his lips as their soft, gentle touch caresses my skin. His mouth curves, forming a wolfish grin. My face flushes as I quickly pull my hand from his grasp, placing it safely back in my lap. I won't let him win that easily.

Lucas opens his mouth to speak but holds off as the car comes to a stop. Scanning the area outside, I haven't got a clue where we are and not really sure of what to make of the place either. Lucas steps out, exuding his gentlemanliness as he stands by the car door.

Taking in the restaurant, it's not hard to tell that it's classy. The castle behind it is a dead giveaway. 'Hermitage' is in cursive on the front of the restaurant building.

"Mon Cherie," Lucas says, gesturing for me to take his arm.

He seems like such a gentleman, so harmless. Makes me wonder even more what the hell Erianne was talking about when she said he's dangerous. Beaming at him, I loop my arm through his, allowing him to escort me inside.

Just like I thought, it's extravagant as hell in here. Golden candelabras are lit at every table draped with white satin cloths. Even the staff is dressed to the nines. Velvet, gold drapes hang from each window, flowing elegantly to the floor. I bet there's real gold in the threads.

We're greeted by a host standing behind a sleek podium, "Mr. Danforth, it is a pleasure to see you again. Where may I seat you?" he asks calmly.

He's completely unfazed by who Lucas is, talking to him like he's any other customer. Literally every single person I've seen come into close contact with Lucas cowers. Yet this guy acts like it's no big deal. Hmph. I'd like to ask *him* some questions.

"A table with a view for the lady." Lucas glances down at me, his expression filled with such admiration. But I know it's just a ploy to win me over.

"The best view in the house." The waiter says as Lucas pulls my chair out for me, "May I get you some wine while you look through the menu?"

"Bring me the bottle of Chateau Lafite Rothschild," Lucas responds.

"Of course, monsieur." The waiter bows to Lucas and leaves our table.

"I take it you come here a lot?" I'm sitting as patiently as I possibly can now.

"I own this restaurant."

Oh. He says that like it's not amazing. I'd love to own a place like this. I never really thought of him as the business owner type. At least not a legitimate business. What if this isn't a legitimate business though? Could I be in one of his mob workplaces? I doubt it. No way he'd take me anywhere like that.

I guess I better figure out what I want to eat. Picking up my menu, I scan it over. Yep. Good thing Mr. Richy-pants over here is paying. No way could I ever afford anything on here. A simple French Onion Soup is sixteen Francs. *Ugh.* My nerves are starting to get the best of me for so many reasons. For starters, I shouldn't even be here with him right now.

"Your wine, monsieur." The waiter displays the wine to Lucas.

"You may leave it." The sound of his voice brings my attention back to him.

"Certainly, monsieur. Have you found anything on the menu to your liking?" The waiter asks, but Lucas doesn't budge.

Frantically skimming my menu once more, I pick the first appetizing thing I read. "I'll take the Filet de Saumon with the Epinards a la Crème." A simple salmon filet with potatoes, red pepper coulis, and spinach in a garlic cream should be easy enough.

"I'll take the Bisque d'Homard with a Jarret d'Agneau Braise and a side of Fricassee de Champignons." Lucas orders with a silver tongue.

The waiter takes the menus as Lucas pours wine into our glasses. My patience is wavering as everything I've learned about him runs through my mind. I take a swig of my wine to keep from spewing all my questions at him at once.

Woah. It's like silk on my tongue. So soft. I would take this over that liquor Erianne had me trying any day. There's no burn, no bitter aftertaste. Instead, a gentle warmth slowly spreads over my taste buds, leaving behind a hint of berry floating in my mouth.

"This is good." I set my glass down.

"I would hope so. It's the best one we have in stock. This area is very well-known for its wine, particularly Bordeaux, but I prefer this gem." He swirls his glass, watching as the burgundy liquid spins. "I actually own a vineyard not far from here. I could show you some time?"

"Do you take a lot of girls there?" I ask, thinking back when he was surrounded by all those half-dressed women at La Luna.

Lucas sits forward, his eyes slanted as his teeth graze his lower lip. "I've never taken any girl there."

I press my lips firmly together, but it's no use. I burst into a fit of laughter. "I'm sorry." I take a deep breath and calm myself. "Does that really work on women? Come on, now. You'll have to do better than that." I grin.

He sits back, grinning. "Careful what you ask for."

I shake my head. "So, is this where you bring the girls you… entertain?"

He winks. "Maybe. Why? Jealous?"

"No." I chuckle, rolling my eyes. "When I first saw you at that club, you had women falling all over you. I just assumed that's a regular thing. And you *did* seem relaxed and carefree."

He shrugs. "What were you doing in a gentleman's club anyway?"

Huh? My face burns red-hot when I realize what he means. The women in lingerie, the woman dancing in that barred caged, and all the others in the less than modest clothes, or lack thereof... Erianne took me to a gentleman's club. How did I not notice before?

Lucas chuckles. "If that's your thing, or, your way, I won't judge. I'd be lying if I said I wouldn't be disappointed though." He presses his glass to his lips, taking a slow sip.

"N-no. I like men." I manage to stammer the words out of my mouth, "I didn't know it was...that type of place though."

His chuckling turns into pure, genuine laughter. "You mean to tell me Erianne took you there and didn't tell you?" He clutches his stomach. "That's rich. And just like her."

I sit silently, wishing I was as small as I feel. But Lucas carrying on laughing, his cheeks dimpling, distracts me from the anxiety crawling under my skin. A pale pink glow blooms on his face, and I can't help letting a mirroring smile reach my eyes as I stare at him.

"I didn't know you knew how to laugh," I say, admiring this unexpected sight.

Lucas grins. "I didn't know you liked to go to gentleman's clubs. Something we both didn't know about each other."

Okay. Time to change the subject.

"You never did answer my question when we were there by the way."

Lucas shakes his head. "Of course. That is why we came here, isn't it?" The boyish, carefree side of him has vanished.

"I asked why people seem to fear you." I prod, ignoring his change in demeanor.

He scoffs. "I'm sure you've heard the stories from Erianne."

"Erianne hasn't told me anything. Why else would I be asking you?" I snap back. That's not entirely true, but I don't want to get her in trouble. I think it's safer for everyone if I just play dumb with him.

A small smile plays at the corner of his mouth. "Abigail… Let's eat. Then you can ask me all the questions you want."

The pleading in his voice is like an arrow straight to my heart. I glimpse into his deep blue eyes as a hint of pain surfaces. My heart aches for him, but it only makes me want to know even more; to understand what this man has been through and to know his pain. It makes me want to hug him tight like my mother would me and tell him it will be alright. I can't imagine the things he's been through. Maybe that's why he acts like such an egotistical ass. It's either that, or he's just bad guy.

"Okay." I take a long, deliberate sip of my wine.

A suffocating silence takes over our table. The waiter brings our food, making me salivate as the savory, salty aroma of the salmon fills my nostrils. We eat, but the silence is nerve-wracking.

"Do you have family here?" Lucas asks without tearing his gaze from his plate.

I wipe my mouth with my gold cloth napkin. "No. It's just my mama and me."

"Your father?" He furrows his brow, sneaking a fleeting glance at me.

"I don't know him. He took off when I was younger. My mama doesn't talk about him. What about your family?"

His jaw flexes and a crease forms on his forehead. His family seems to be a touchy subject. I take a deep breath, trying to understand instead of getting annoyed with his mood swings. Setting my fork down, I wring my hands under the table. I study his face, finding myself wanting to see him smile again.

Lucas peers up, grinning as he catches me staring. "Do you like working at La Couronne?"

I shrug. "It's okay. My boss doesn't exactly make it the easiest job ever."

Lucas abruptly sets his silverware down, wiping the corners of his mouth with his napkin and leaning back in his seat. "What do you mean?" He takes a long sip out of his glass.

My brows knit together. "Well, he looks at me like I'm a walking steak. I'm constantly getting yelled at for something, even if it's not my fault. I think it's because I'm new. I guess he doesn't care much for new employees."

Lucas runs his hand through his hair, a low growl rumbling in his throat. "Let's see how he treats you after I have a chat with him."

Lucas grips the arms on his chair, causing the tips of his fingers to blanche. I realize my fork is mid-air in front of my mouth, a chunk of salmon hanging. I slowly take the bite, unsure of how to respond to his indirect threat.

Lucas empties his glass, gesturing to the waiter for more. "Is that how you met Erianne? Working there?"

"*Oui*. Well, kind of. We went to the same high school and I used to see her around. We never hung out with the same people though. But she's been pretty amazing. I'm really grateful for her." I smile as a warmth spreads through me from talking about her. She *is* my only friend.

He nods. "Good. How long have you lived in Rouen?"

"About three years now." I take the last bite of my Epinards and empty my wine glass.

"And how do you like it?" he asks.

"I have my differences with it." I sigh. So many questions about my life is making me feel like I'm back at Dr. Carrere's office for the first time. "How do you like living here?"

Lucas pulls his napkin off his lap, setting it on the table. "Will you take a walk across the grounds with me?"

He completely ignores my question. I'm starting to get irritated. And either he's oblivious or doesn't care. I'm going to go with the latter of the two.

"Okay." Maybe now I'll finally get some answers out of him. But, at this rate, I highly doubt it.

He leads me by the hand through the wooden door, outside, and up a gravel path toward the open scenery behind the restaurant. The same view that was visible through the window is now clear before me. Lush green rolling hills in the distance are all covered in the warm golden glow of the fading sunlight as it sets, painting the darkening blue sky shades of pink and orange.

"Its...beautiful." I stare in awe at the scenery.

"I'm glad you like it." He hesitates momentarily before turning to face me. "I haven't been completely honest with you Abigail."

My stomach turns at those words. William said that same thing to me before...No. I immediately push the thought back. I patiently gaze at him, allowing him to continue.

"I didn't bring you here just to let you barrage me with questions, as fun as that sounds." He smirks, reaching up and placing his hand over my cheek.

An ache blooms in my chest. I hope Erianne isn't right after all about me getting hurt if I asked too much. I should have left him alone, and I definitely should have never gotten in the car with him. The knot in my chest squeezes tighter, making it difficult to breathe.

"Why did you bring me here then?" I muster up enough courage to ask.

He removes his hand from my cheek, shoving both in his pockets. The absence of his touch leaves me with a hollow ache–one I didn't expect to have.

"Abigail..." He sighs. "I like you."

I stare at him open-mouthed. My brain can't process a response. This is probably just one of his tricks he uses on girls to get them to swoon over him. *He's good.* My body is definitely in full-on swoon mode.

His teeth graze his lower lip as he stares like he's trying to decipher a Rubik's Cube, "There's something about you." He reaches a hand up, running his thumb softly over my lower lip. "You're… You're so beautiful."

His usual calm, confident persona has dissipated. Looking lost in thought and unsure of himself, so vulnerable, it's every bit unlike a dangerous mob prince.

"Oh. You're good." I chuckle. "You almost had me."

He chuckles, rubbing the back of his neck. "Yeah."

A few more of those lines and I think it's possible I would have believed him. But I can't help wondering how many girls it took doing that to for him to get so good. It's kind of messed up when I think about it.

He takes my hand in his. "Let's walk. Besides, I'm a man of my word, and I think you have some questions for me now."

I smile broadly as we walk down the path. "I think you owe them to me now after I've told you almost everything about me."

He laughs. "So, what's your first question?"

"Well, why are people afraid of you?" This is the one thing I've wanted to know most. I'm sure it's because of his family and their 'business'. But I want to hear his answer.

He furrows his brow. "I'm sure you've heard about my father. People think because I'm his son that I'm just like him. I'm nothing like him though, and I'll never be like him either."

I nod. "Have you done things like your father has?"

His jaw clenches. "I did things I'm not proud of when my mother—" He stops himself and gazes out at the path before us.

"What happened to her?" I gently squeeze his hand to offer some comfort, but immediately want to kick myself for even asking. "I'm sorry. You don't have to answer that."

I swear. Sometimes I open my mouth and insert my big fat foot.

He flashes a quick, reassuring smile. "No, it's okay. My mother didn't ever want me to be like my father. She loved him but didn't agree with the path he took in life. I was closer to her than I've ever been to my father. After she was gone, I didn't know what to do. So, I asked my father if I could help or if he had any jobs for me. I was reckless and out of control, even with my father's direction. I'm not proud of it." His mouth turns down as he shakes his head.

"I understand." I nod. "What made you stop?"

A devilish grin creeps across his lips. "Who says I have?"

I stare at him horrified. Every time I start thinking he's not so bad, he says something like that.

He laughs, making the dimples in his cheeks visible. "I'm kidding, Abigail."

There's a good chance he's not kidding. Any chance is enough of a reason for me. I distance myself from him and he stops suddenly.

"Let's get you home. It's getting late." He says, clearly indicating the conversation is over.

Walking back to the car in total silence, it isn't as awkward as I thought it'd be. He maintains his gentleman-like manners, holding the car door open for me. Could he actually like me? No, this is just him trying to play me.

The drive back is just as long. My body is barely keeping up and all I want to do is sleep. I gave Jimmy my address so he could just take me straight home. As soon as I did though, it hit me how monumental of a mistake that probably is. A mob prince having my address. *Smart Abigail. Real smart.*

I peek over at Lucas in the seat next to me. He's staring thoughtfully out the window. Talking about his mother and family must have been a big deal for him. I can't imagine he talks to anyone about that stuff. Kind of like how I don't talk to anyone about William. I guess it's different though. William is still very much alive. Unfortunately. Lucas didn't just get his heart broke either. He lost his mother.

As the car pulls to the side in front of my flat neither men move from their seats.

"Monsieur, we have arrived," Jimmy says, glancing through the rearview mirror.

Lucas nods, breaking out of his reverie. "Of course. Wait here."

Lucas steps out of the car. Seconds later, he's standing on the sidewalk holding my door open for me. The night air hits me like a breath of life but doesn't help with how sleepy I am. The slight chill makes me shiver.

"Thank you for tonight. I had a lovely evening." Smiling graciously, I take a step back from him. "And for the record, I win." I beam.

Lucas' hands land on my waist, pulling me back toward him, but even closer. The gentle warmth of his palm greets my cheek, gliding over it in a light caress. His mouth slowly inches toward mine.

He scans my face, whispering, "What if I kissed you? Right here. Right now."

If I didn't already know this is just a ploy, I'd think he's serious. His eyes bore into mine as if his heart depends on my answer. But is this the best he's got? How do girls not see right through this? It's obvious this is rehearsed. I'll play his game.

I grin triumphantly. "It wouldn't make a bit of a difference."

His teeth graze his bottom lip. "Oh, really?"

I nod and not a second later, his lips press into mine. They're so soft and he's so gentle about it. Aside from being an overall ass of a guy, he's not a bad kisser. If the circumstances were different, I might actually enjoy this. Lucas pulls away, resting his forehead against mine.

I take a deep breath and gaze up at him. "See. Nothing."

"*Oui.* You were right. Nothing." He shrugs, dropping his hands and stepping back.

Who am I kidding? That was some kiss. My knees are wobbling and every nerve in my body is standing to attention. The air has grown thick, rigid with tension. My breathing is slower, deeper just thinking about his lips on mine. *Walk away*. I keep telling my feet to move, but they stay firmly planted.

"Goodnight, Abigail." He grins.

"Goodnight." I manage to choke the word out.

After fumbling with my keys, I rush inside. No way am I going to let him win that over one stupid kiss. I mean, he's Lucas Danforth. Womanizer, mob prince, and all-around bad guy. It's official. I've lost my damn mind. *Ugh*. Erianne is really going to kill me. I promised her I'd stay away from him. Not only is his father keeping tabs on me, I'd throw away any potential friendship with Erianne if I didn't stay away. So, obviously I'm going to. I made my point and hopefully took a chunk out of that ego of his.

11

"That's so exciting! I'm proud of you. You've exceeded my expectations with your fear ladder." Dr. Carrere beams from behind her glasses.

I sit back on her leather sofa, crossing my legs. "So, what other fear ladder do you think I should start?"

She pauses, pushing her glasses back up the bridge of her nose as her warm smile fades. She stares at me as if choosing her words carefully. My heart rate increases. Dr. Carrere never gets uneasy like this unless she's got bad news for me.

"What is it?" I sit upright, unsure if I really want her answer.

She sets her notepad and pen aside on the glass-top side table. "Well, what do you think about starting something called repressed memory therapy?"

My breath hitches at the mention of it.

She holds her hands up. "Now, hold on. Hear me out. I think, given your progress, this would be the next best step."

I shake my head and wring my trembling hands. "There's other fear ladders I can do. I'm still scared of stuff. Why can't we do those?"

She reaches over, placing a comforting hand over mine. "Abigail. We can do all the fear ladders in the world, but it won't make a difference unless we get to the root of the problem. These memories your subconscious has locked away is only going to continue to haunt you unless you face them head on. I can help you do that."

Swallowing the lump forming in my throat as my forehead grows damp, I stand from my seat, backing away from her. "What if I never want to face them? Would that be so bad?" I run a hand through my hair, shaking my head. "N-no. I... I won't. I can't."

Dr. Carrere stands, folding her hands. "It's okay. Remember your breathing steps. In. 5. 4. 3. 2. 1. And out." My heart gradually slows as I follow her directions. "Better?" I nod as she rubs her temple. "Why don't we end our session here. We can pick back up next Tuesday."

Forcing a smile, I quickly turn on my heel. My chest squeezes tighter and tighter by the second. This room is feeling smaller than normal. I need fresh air. Asap.

"Abigail." She calls.

I pause at the door.

"Would you at least look up the RMT? Consider it and think it over before our next session?"

I nod and rush out of her office. Her next patient is waiting in the lobby. I'd recognize him from anywhere. He's kind of hard to miss with the huge gauges in his ears and piercings all over his face. And if that's not enough, his arms are covered in tattoos. I kind of like the hair style he's got going on though. It's so weird, but adorable at the same time with the black leopard spots dyed in the shaved side of his head. The rest of his charcoal black hair is longer and swooped to one side, showing off his spots. He has this carefree vibe about him that lifts any tension in the atmosphere around him. I kind of admire that.

I smile politely as I pass him, just barely catching him waving a hello back. My hand greets the cool, smooth metal of the door handle and I fling it open. The humid summer air doesn't help much to soothe the burn that's settled into my lungs. I take a minute to calm down, but the sight of the tall, broad-shouldered man standing in front of a shop across the street sends my heart rate soaring. What the hell?

What is Lucas doing there? He's talking to someone and Jimmy is with him. The guy he's talking to looks scared out of his mind and keeps pressing his hands together, shaking them. It's like he's asking Lucas for forgiveness or something. *Oh, hell no*. I need to get out of here.

I turn down the street, heading for the intersection. All I need to do is reach *Rue De Buffon* and turn left. Then I'll be completely out of sight. Who knows what I just saw and I don't even want to try to guess. The last place I need to be is anywhere near that man.

"Hey! Abigail!" Lucas' voice slices through my ears, seizing all hopes of dodging him. His feet thudding against the sidewalk slows to a stop behind me as he grabs my arm. "Hey. I saw you walking. I was—uh… What are you doing out here?"

Pfft. Leave it to him to think I have to have a reason to be on a public sidewalk. What if I just wanted to go for a stroll? It's really none of his business. But I'm really not in the mood to get all confrontational, especially not with him. No way in hell can I tell him I just came from my therapy appointment though. Not that I care, but, again, it's none of his business. I quickly glance past him, scanning the street.

"I-I was having lunch over at Sci Le Flaubert." I force a smile.

"Really? That's one of my favorite places to eat. What did you have? Please tell me you tried their Gnocchi." He gushes, his face alight like a kid talking about his favorite toy.

Merde. I didn't expect him to ask me details. *Think. Think. Think.*

I step back, smiling politely. "I really should get going."

He reaches out for my arm again. "Wait." His smile fades as he rubs the back of his neck, shoving a hand in his pocket. "Sorry about last night. I got to thinking that maybe the kiss was going overboard. If you really like Mathieu, then you have my blessing."

I scoff. "I didn't need or want your blessing."

Lucas runs a hand through his hair. "Of course. Of course. Why don't you let me give you a ride home?"

I back further away. "No. That's okay."

A cold wet drop lands on my shoulder. Looking around, I notice the sidewalk speckling with little raindrops. *Oh, no, no, no.* I have to go. I'd already be home if it wasn't for Lucas holding me up. *Merde.* I can't get stuck in the rain. Or have a panic attack in front of him.

"Come on. It's starting to rain. What kind of man would I be if I let you walk in the rain?" He flashes his enigmatic smile.

Oh, give me a break. I roll my eyes and gesture for him to lead the way. His smile widens, making the dimples in his cheeks pop. I bounce on my heels as he beckons Jimmy to bring the car around. The rain picks up, each drop landing closer together. As soon as the car pulls up to the curb, I dash inside, not giving either men a chance to open the door for me. I'm not sure if I'm safer outside, getting stuck in a storm, or inside this car with Lucas. Maybe I should have just taken my chances with the rain…

I have never been in a more awkward situation in my life. Lucas is being so weird, so unlike his usual pompous self. We haven't said two words to each other. But thankfully we're pulling up to my place. But Erianne's car sitting out front diminishes all my relief.

"Could you drop me off at the corner?" I ask Jimmy directly.

He looks to Lucas through the rearview mirror. Lucas glances up, his eyes locking on Erianne's car, and nods his approval to Jimmy.

"You worried Mathieu will see you with me?" He smirks.

I'm not entertaining that smart remark. That would just lead to me denying it than him trying to prove he's right. I can't stand a guy who thinks he's always right. It really just highlights all his other unattractive qualities.

I jump out of the car as it rolls to a stop. "Thanks."

I start walking down my street as they pull off. Maybe I would have been better off going by myself. It didn't even really rain that bad. Pfft. That was pointless. As I reach my flat, Erianne and Mathieu climb out of the car.

Wait. How did Lucas know Mathieu was with her? Her windows are so tinted, you can't see a thing inside. So, there's no way Lucas saw him in the car. That's so weird.

"Hey you!" Erianne beams, her heels clicking as she saunters over to give me a hug. "So, how did it go?" She asks, holding me at arm's length.

I nod in Mathieu's direction as he approaches. "Can we talk about it later?"

She winks. "Sure."

"Hello, beautiful." Mathieu takes my hand and plants a kiss on my knuckles.

It's such a nice gesture. Mathieu is a great guy and we had a good date. It was kind of awkward, but we just need to get to know each other more. That's all.

"So, you going to invite us in?" Erianne chirps.

I nod and let them inside. Erianne immediately makes herself comfortable, flipping on the television. I gesture for Mathieu to take a seat. Erianne turns on one of our favorite shows. But I can't shake how weird is it Lucas knew Mathieu was with her.

How could he have known? What if he's helping his father? Maybe that's why Erianne wants me to stay away from him so bad. And maybe she just really can't tell me that. I'm more certain now than ever that I need to stay as far away from Lucas as possible.

12

Spending time with Erianne these last couple days—watching bad TV shows, binging on snacks, and hanging out with my mama—has been exactly what I need. It sounds so lame and boring, but it works for us. And my night terrors have been few and far. Mama has invited her over for dinner almost every night anyway. It's funny. She even pulls this stunt where she 'accidentally' cooks too much, so Erianne has no choice but to 'eat the extra so we don't waste food'.

She can be so transparent sometimes and usually I'd be annoyed with it. But Erianne doesn't mind. Plus, I know she means well. I just wish she'd cool it a little. Sometimes I have to get out of the house to get away from her smothering. Erianne has been a big help with that.

We went shopping a couple times. That's Erianne's first love. Surprisingly, I actually enjoyed shopping with her. Me. Plus shopping? I'd never have imagined it. I've always hated it before now. It helps that it keeps Erianne distracted from asking me a ton of questions too.

She's been constantly asking me what's bothering me. I haven't told her or Mama about Dr. Carrere suggesting the Repressed Memory Therapy. I can barely wrap my mind around the idea. Erianne assumes I've been acting strange because of my ex. Mama still insists on bringing him up. No harm in letting Erianne think that though. Keeps me from having to explain anything. I eventually will, but when I'm ready.

I reach into my locker and grab the purse Erianne convinced me to buy, then double check the break room for any more of my stuff. My shift is over and I'm more than ready to go home. I still can't believe Erianne talked me into getting a purse. I never liked carrying these things around, but now I can't leave the house without it.

"Hey, you!" Erianne, in all her peppiness, comes prancing into the break room. "You ready?"

I raise an eyebrow. "Ready for what?"

She rolls her eyes. "Please do not tell me you forgot!"

My eyes widen. I did forget. Everyone is getting together tonight at O'Kallaghan's to celebrate Bastille Day tomorrow. I haven't been there since I first met them.

"I didn't forget. I just didn't know what you were talking about." I try my best to sound convincing, failing miserably.

Erianne tosses her bag on her shoulder. "Abigail, *ma chérie*, you've never been a good liar." We laugh together. "What would you do without me?" She sighs overly exaggerated.

"Let's go." I smile, shaking my head at her. "Are we taking your car?"

"I was thinking we could walk, like last time. Besides a little girl talk couldn't hurt." Her familiar mischievous smile greets across her lips.

I can tell she's up to something, but every time she mentions that we need to talk about something, my nerves go haywire. What if she finds out about my dinner with Lucas? She still doesn't even know I went with him. Lying is exhausting. Hopefully, all of this will eventually stop. All this constant worrying and looking over my shoulder. I hate this stain of guilt I have for lying and I don't exactly like hiding things from her. I'm a horrible excuse for a friend. But, since she hasn't even asked, I guess I'm not *really* lying. I'm just not divulging that information.

"So, I was thinking. How do you feel about meeting someone?" Erianne peeks at me cautiously as we walk down the sidewalk.

I broke the news to Mathieu that we'd be better as friends. He took it well. Of course, I feel bad because he *is* a good guy. He's funny, smart, and seems to really have his life together. But he's just so… good. Too good and he's more like the friend type. He's not the guy for me.

I narrow my eyes. "…What do you mean?"

"Well… I may have, possibly, potentially, invited a guy to the pub for you to meet." She closes her eyes, bracing for my reaction.

"Erianne!" I playfully punch her arm. "Why in the hell would you go and do that?" The last thing I want is to meet another guy.

"What? You're practically a nun. You haven't even checked a guy out since Mathieu. I figured all you needed is a push, or shove, from a friend. AKA me." She beams as if that's getting her out of this.

I'm not ready for this and I can't do it—can I? Why am I thinking what Lucas would think of this? This feels like cheating which is weird. Who would I be cheating on? I only went on one date with Mathieu and haven't even talked to him since he was at my house with Erianne.

I take a deep breath. "Who is it?"

"Don't be mad, okay. I was just trying to help out. Besides, he is so hot. And he's in training to become an officer. If you are against it though, I can send him away."

I roll my eyes. "Alright…"

Erianne's face lights up as she clasps her hands together. "You'll meet him?"

"Yes, Erianne. I will meet him." I say flatly.

She practically bursts into cheers, bouncing on her heels. "Oh, thank god! I mean… good. I cannot wait for you to meet him. How long has it even been since you–"

"Erianne!" I gawk wide-eyed at her. She opens her mouth to speak again, but I put my hand up to silence her. "I will meet him, but I didn't say I would like him."

"Okay…But I know you will." She grins.

The scowl she gets from me only makes her laugh. Just as I'm about to grill her some more about her doing this, we stop in front of O'Kallaghan's. Erianne loses all possible patience and grabs my hand. She pulls me inside with her, immediately scanning the room. *Oh, hell.* What if Mathieu is here? Before I have the chance to even look for anyone, she's already pulling me toward a table.

"I told him that he could bring a friend along." Erianne shouts over the noise.

As we walk to the table, I immediately recognize Mathieu with a drink in hand. The sight of him sends my gut twisting in knots. I hope there's no hard feelings. The same girl that was daydreaming over America last time is here again too. Clarissa, with her bright red hair pinned into bouncy curls, is sitting next to the girl. Scanning the rest of the occupied seats at the table, two other men are drinking with everyone. One of them I don't recognize at all. I'm sure that's the one Erianne set me up with. Then, the man next to him draws my attention. He's facing away from me, so I can't see his face clearly, but something about him is familiar. Too familiar.

"Guys! Abby is here!" Erianne shouts, announcing my presence to everyone at the table the second we are within a few feet.

Both of the men turn around and the moment I lock eyes with them, the wind is sucked out of my lungs. The guy who seems a little too familiar, well, there's a particularly good reason why. I spent two years of my life with him, loving him, and only a few short moments watching it all get torn down. William.

13

William. How and why? Did she do this on purpose? Is this another one of her mother's orders?

Every ounce of happiness I've felt is knocked out of me as I'm filled with her betrayal. What is he doing here? I should have recognized that blonde-haired jackass from anywhere. My voice is caught in my throat. Hell, I can hardly think.

Shoving past Erianne with tears hot on my cheeks, I storm outside. The night air hits me like pins and needles all over my body. My heart races faster than my lungs can keep up with. I need to get out of here.

Without thinking, I force my feet forward. I have no idea where I'm going, but I need to get as far away from there—from William, Erianne, and everyone else—as possible. My lungs burn and my head throbs. Everything feels so small. *I* feel so small. My hands tremble at my sides. I have to move faster.

Taking off in a full sprint down the street, the need to escape takes over. Every ounce of panic sheds with each step I take. I can't start thinking about what he did to me. I can't go back to that place, that dark place I was in. I've come so far. I'm just starting to feel better, to feel normal again.

My breaths come in short, labored puffs. I try to take a deep breath, but the wind hits my face like bricks of ice, making it near impossible. I will my feet to slow down. Like a dam, the memories of William burst through, every single one, and all the pain it ended with. My cheeks dampen as tears sting my eyes.

A hand grips my arm firmly from behind. Startled, I jerk around, ready to punch whoever has the nerve to mess with me right now.

"Abigail?" Standing before me, staring at me like a lost puppy, is Lucas.

"What happened? Are you hurt?" He frantically scans my body as if he's checking for wounds.

The sight of him pulls at the deep ache in my chest. Dropping my shoulders, I stop holding back the tears and let it all out. Lucas' arms wrap around me, blanketing me in a safety net. I'd take being around a mob prince than William any day. His hand sweeps over my head as he holds me against him.

What am I thinking? I hardly know this guy and here I am crying all over him. I'm probably ruining his expensive shirt with my make-up running all over it. Attempting to pull myself together, I take a deep steadying breath. I probably look ten tons of crazy to him.

He loosens his hold on me, but only enough so he can reach up to wipe a stray tear from my cheek. Hesitantly peeking up through my lashes, I expect him to be gawking at me. But instead, he's staring with such admiration.

"Get me out of here…please." I croak the words out in a desperate plea.

Lucas remains silent. Keeping one arm firmly wrapped around my waist, he walks me to where his car is parked by the curb. The windows are so dark, they blend into the night. Jimmy stands by the back door, holding it open. I didn't even realize he was there. His reassuring smile is oddly comforting.

Lucas doesn't remove his hand from my body as he helps me in the car, even as he lowers himself in. I absently watch Jimmy climb into the driver seat. The throbbing in my feet draws my attention away. All that running was not the best idea. My feet are hating me for it.

"What happened?" Lucas asks softly.

I want to tell him because I just need to get it out. The moment I attempt to speak, tears pool at the corner of my eyes. I quickly look away.

Lucas squeezes my hand. "You don't have to hide your face from me, Abigail." He runs a hand through his hair. "I saw you running a block before I stopped you. Jimmy had a hard time keeping up with you."

"You saw me?" My cheeks enflame.

He nods. "I did. I had Jimmy stop the car as soon as you slowed down. Was someone following you?" His body tenses.

"No. I wasn't being followed." The words squeak past my lips.

He scoffs. "You could have fooled me. You looked like you were running from someone."

The worry laced in his voice fills me with gratitude, but why does he care so much? Aren't mafia princes supposed to not give a crap about anyone?

I mumble, "I was, but not like you think."

Lucas releases my hand, giving me the chance to place it safely back on my leg as he pulls a navy-blue blackberry out of his jacket pocket.

He shuts it off and takes a deep breath. "Are you hungry?"

My words failing me, I just shake my head. I don't have an appetite right now. Lucas lets out an exasperated sigh. I shouldn't have even gotten in the car with him. What was I thinking?

"Can you just take me home?" I ask, not wanting to burden him anymore.

Lucas' shoulders drop at my request like I've hurt him. He glances into the rearview mirror at Jimmy. I can't peel my eyes away as I witness this silent interaction between the two.

"Your address mademoiselle?" Jimmy asks as he continues looking straight ahead.

"Oh, it's 55 Rue Verte."

"Abigail, can you at least tell me if you're alright?" A pained expression clouds Lucas' face.

Leaning back into the seat, I stare at him. "I will be. Erianne just came up with this scheme to have me meet some guy."

His hands tighten into fist. "That girl… Did you not like the guy?" He forces the question through gritted teeth.

"Well, he happened to be my ex. I haven't seen my ex since we ended things." The sting of Erianne's betrayal makes my stomach churn all over again.

"I take it things didn't end well?" Lucas cautiously asks.

"If sleeping with my best friend counts as things not ending well, then no. They didn't. Two years of my life wasted." I shake my head as the beating of my heart returns to a normal pace. Sleep never sounded as good as it does right now. All that running really did me in.

"You deserve so much better than that," he says.

Ignoring his comment, I stare past him out the window. The sidewalks are near empty. Every store front is barely lit by nearby streetlamps and void of light inside. The street glistens, still damp from the rain earlier.

I watch the lines on the road passing by. "I just didn't expect to ever see him again. I was caught off guard, I guess. I got paranoid in the moment that Erianne had somehow set it all up, so I just took off. I needed to feel the air on my face, to feel my feet on the ground."

"I understand. As much as she can really irritate me, I still know her very well. She cares about you. I don't think she would have done that intentionally. She was probably just as confused as you when you took off," Lucas says.

"I know, now that I think about it, but I didn't in the moment. All I could think about was getting out of there. I still feel a little betrayed by her." Glimpsing at him, I notice the stain from my tears on his shirt. "I ruined your shirt." I point to where the make-up stain is.

Lucas takes my hand. "I don't mind."

"Monsieur, we have arrived." Jimmy interrupts.

Heat rises in my cheeks. I almost forgot he was there. Lucas, on the other hand, appears unfazed. Like this is totally normal. He steps out, taking my hand again.

"I'm glad you're okay." His lips just barely graze my knuckles.

"Monsieur." Jimmy's voice is laced with a sense of urgency.

Lucas gives my hand a squeeze before climbing back in the car and abruptly closes the door. Jimmy pulls off into the street without a moment's hesitation. What the hell was that about?

My head is spinning. So much is happening. My body feels so heavy as the rush dies down. My bed is calling my name. The silky satin sheets are begging to cocoon me in them. Turning to walk into my flat, a tall redhead is blocking the door. Erianne has a hand on her hip and she's glaring daggers. It dawns on me that she must have seen me get out of Lucas' car. I can only imagine what she's thinking.

Oh, god. She's going to hate me. I *cannot* handle this. This is too much. My head throbs. Gripping my forehead, I try to regain my balance as everything around me begins spinning. I didn't know Erianne had a twin. Maybe her sister came with her. I take a step toward her, but stumble. No. There's only one of her standing in front of me. All the light around me begins to fade. Gravity takes over my body as a faint cry from Erianne rings in my ears. Then, just silence. And darkness.

14

A blindingly harsh glow shines on the back of my eyelids, searing through and making my eyes burn. My hand is tingling underneath the warmth of someone's grasp. There's a steady obnoxious beeping noise next to me. I wish someone would shut it up. I'm overwhelmed by the throbbing pain in my head again. The last thing I remember is telling Lucas bye. I saw Erianne standing at my door, but then...nothing. What happened?

"Abby?" A weary, yet familiar voice is barely audible.

The grip on my hand tightens. Not able to stand the vice-like hold, I instinctively flex my fingers. A memory of being in the car with Lucas flashes through my mind.

A woman gasps through sobs, "Oh! Abby!"

I try as hard as I can to force my eyes open, but the heaviness in my whole body is making it hard. I struggle again to open them, blinking hard once I finally manage to.

"What's going on?" I croak.

Examining my surroundings, I realize I'm definitely not at home. Erianne is sitting next to me, sobbing louder. There are nurses walking through the hallways and a hospital gown where my clothes just were. Wait... I'm in a hospital. I can't remember how I ended up in a hospital. My head throbs even more as I try to process all of this.

"You're okay. You're gonna be okay. Oh, Abbs I am so sorry," Erianne says through stuttering breaths, relief flooding her voice.

"My head." I reach up with my other hand to rub it.

"Are you in pain?" Erianne asks alarmed, "Hold on. I'll get the doctor." She leaps from the chair, darting towards the nurse's station outside of my room.

What in the hell happened?

Erianne returns with not only the doctor, but Mama too. I could not be happier that she's here. The circles under her eyes are darker than normal and paired with bags. She probably hasn't slept at all. *Oh, Mama*. It breaks my heart to see her this way. Her eyes light up when they meet mine, and she rushes toward me. She gives me a once over before pulling me into a hug I gratefully return.

"My baby. My sweet girl," she cries on my shoulder.

"Mama, I'm okay. Really, I am. My head just hurts really bad." I rub her back, trying to reassure her even though I really have no clue why I'm here.

She releases me just enough to stare in my face. "Are you sure *chère*?"

"I'm sure." I smile to reassure her some more. "What happened anyway?"

I study the doctor as he walks up to the foot of my bed. Mama finally backs off a little, but ensures she isn't far. She scoots the chair next to my bed as close as she can possibly manage.

"You don't remember?" Erianne asks from the doorway.

The doctor flips a paper over on his clipboard. "It may take her some time to recall all the events leading up to the moment she fell unconscious."

Did he just say unconscious?

"Ms. Halsey, you suffered quite a blow to the head when you fell. You're lucky. Besides a minor concussion, you appear to check out. Head pain is to be expected. I will send a nurse in with some pain medication. Are you experiencing pain anywhere else?" The doctor glances up from his clipboard.

I do a quick mental check, "No, just my head."

"Doctor, do you know what could have caused her to faint like that?" Mama asks.

The doctor glances at Erianne. "From what her friend here told me, and after seeing for myself that she is perfectly healthy, I believe it was stress induced."

"Oh! My baby girl!" Mama exclaims and grabs my hand. Not that I don't appreciate the gesture, but I was just beginning to get the feeling back in that hand.

"She needs to take it easy and get some rest for the next couple days. She should be just fine. I do want to keep her overnight for observation, just to be sure. If there is anything you need, let me know. The nurse will be in shortly with some medication for your head." The doctor politely smiles before shaking my hand.

"Thank you so much," My mother says to the doctor.

He exits the room, leaving me with these two hovering over me. Erianne hasn't said much since the doctor came in. She's still standing in the doorway.

"Mama, could you get me something to drink please?" I ask, hopeful she says yes. I'm definitely thirsty, but I also need a couple minutes to talk to Erianne.

Mama stands. "Of course! What would you like? Name anything and I'll get it for you *chère!*"

"Some coffee would be great if you don't mind?" I would kill for a cup the way mama makes it right now.

"You got it. A cup of Mama's coffee coming right up!" She hugs me once more before leaving, looking like a woman on a mission. It makes me chuckle.

"What happened?" I ask once she's gone.

"I should be asking you that. One minute we're in the bar meeting the guys and the next you're bolting out the door. I came outside after you, but you were gone. So, I walked to your flat hoping to find you there." She throws her hands up. "God, Abby do you know how worried I was? When I saw you weren't home, I waited. I didn't know what else to do. Then you show up with Lucas," she seethes. "You had been with Lucas the entire time! How long has this been going on between you two? Have you been lying to me all along?"

It's not like I asked Lucas to be there. I'm glad he was, nevertheless. "I left for a reason, Erianne. When have I ever taken off like that?"

"Then tell me why you did. Abbs, tell me."

Sighing, I rub my temples as my head starts throbbing again. Maybe it is time I tell her about William and what happened with him.

"Ms. Halsey, I have your medicine." The nurse walks in the room, handing me two large white pills and a cup of water.

About time. I immediately pop them in my mouth. The quicker this pain in my head goes away, the better. The nurse takes the empty water cup and leaves the room.

"Sit," I tell Erianne.

She silently takes a seat in the chair next to me.

"I know the blonde jackass that was sitting at the table at O'Kallaghan's. His name is William. He's my ex."

Erianne sits forward, her hand flying up to cover her mouth. "Abigail, I had no idea! If I had known—"

I interrupt, "You couldn't have known. That's my fault."

"What happened between you two? It must have ended badly for you to run out like that." She shakes her head. "Never mind. You don't have to tell me that."

"It's okay. I was with William for two years. We broke up on my birthday last year. I used to think he was the perfect boyfriend. I was so in love with him, we made plans to go off to university together." I reminisce about when things in my life were normal.

"What happened?" Erianne asks cautiously.

"He threw me a birthday party." I take a minute to breath to keep myself from crying.

"Do you not like parties?" Erianne crinkles her brow.

I roll my eyes. "No, I love parties, but not that one. It's the day we split up. Everything was going fine at first. We met for breakfast that morning. He bought me a beautiful necklace and some roses. I even got a cute, cheesy card." A grin spreads across my face as I get swooped up in the memories. "He spent nearly the entire day treating me to a bunch of things for my birthday. After we watched a movie together, he told me he had a surprise for me." I swallow hard. "He walked me down to my best friend Monae's house. And the minute I walked through her door, over a dozen of our friends jumped out yelling surprise." Tears well up in my eyes.

"He seems sweet. All of that sounds really great." Erianne patiently waits for me to continue.

I take a deep breath. "It was great. Then it wasn't. I was hanging out with a couple friends while William was talking with his at the party. I got thirsty, so I went to get drinks. On my way over to the drink table, I heard Monae's voice. I wanted to thank her, so I started walking over toward her until William's voice followed hers."

"What were they saying?" Erianne asks.

"I overheard William saying I couldn't find out about something. At first, I just thought it was another surprise then Monae said," I mimic Monae's voice, "we're telling her today. You promised me, baby, you would tell her soon." I could never forget those words. "Then I watched as someone who had been my best friend kiss the guy I loved. Everything happened so fast after that. Monae saw me watching them. William broke up with me." A tear rolls down my cheek.

Erianne grabs my hand. "I can't believe those two. How could they do something like that?"

The weight that's been on my chest since December gets a little lighter, making it easier to breathe. Maybe what I needed this entire time was to tell someone, to get it off my chest. Beside my therapist, Erianne and Mama are the only people I've talked to about this.

"I completely understand why you ran out of the pub then." Erianne shakes her head.

I wonder if my so-called friends still remember. Knowing Monae though, I can guarantee they do. She wouldn't ever let me or anyone else forget. I've always wondered if they knew what was going on between William and Monae.

Erianne cocks her head to the side. "So, is that why your Mama hovers so much?"

"She got so worried about me because I withdrew my university application after that. I hardly came out of my room and it was a damn near miracle to her if I left the house." My eyes start to strain again.

If there is one thing Erianne has taught me since we have become friends, it's how to be strong. Erianne and my mother are the two toughest people I know. They have been my rock while I've been moping about all this. Now it's my turn to be theirs. No more crying.

"Abigail…" She hesitates.

"It's okay, really." I try to reassure her.

"I'm so sorry you had to go through that." She slumps in her seat and releases my hand. "And I'm sorry I got so angry with you."

"It's okay. I guess seeing William again brought up old feelings." I reach over and grab her hand.

I almost forgot what it felt like to have a best friend. To have someone who will be here for me no matter what, through anything. Someone I can talk to about these kinds of things. I missed it, that's for sure.

"As promised, Mama's coffee!" Mama proudly announces as she saunters into my room.

Erianne stands abruptly. "Ms. Halsey you can sit here." She scuffles her way back to the doorway.

"Oh no dear, you can sit next to Abigail. I got you a coffee, too." Mama hands Erianne a fresh, hot cup.

Erianne accepts it gratefully. "Thank you. I appreciate you being so generous, but I have to get to work anyway," she says before taking a sip.

"Well, be safe on your way to work." Mama gives Erianne a hug.

"Hey, Mama, why don't you head out too? You look like you haven't slept at all."

"I couldn't possibly leave you. No way." She takes a step back.

"Mama, I'm okay. The doctor even said I'm fine. Why don't you go with Erianne? You two can come back bright and early to pick me up." I give her my best reassuring smile, but I can tell she's struggling with the thought of leaving. "I promise. I'm just going to sleep anyway. I want you to get some sleep too."

Mama looks me over. She starts fidgeting with her hands; something I haven't seen her do in years. She's the person I got that habit from. Erianne notices my mama's reluctance about leaving me and reaches over to still her hands. I watch as a small smile plays across Erianne's lips and she gives me a knowing look.

"Ms. Halsey, I think she will be fine. Why don't I come by the house after work?" Erianne tries to ease my mama's worry.

"I-I suppose." My mother lowers her head.

I know she really wants to spend all night hovering over me, but I won't get any sleep that way. I outstretch my arms to silently request a hug. She instantly perks up a little and rushes over to embrace me.

"I love you, Abigail," she whispers.

I take a steadying breath. "I love you too, Mama." I hate seeing her worry about me so much. She's done enough of that.

"We better get going," Erianne says.

Mama reluctantly releases her hold on me. She glances back once more before leaving with Erianne. I'm so thankful to have such a good friend.

15

Frantically jolting upright in my hospital bed gasping for air, I grip the sheets as I come back to reality. I'd been dreaming about being chased by a twelve-foot gorilla during a thunderstorm. What kind of drugs did they give me? My astraphobia is clearly finding creative ways to torture me.

The clock on the table next to my bed is beaming 2:03AM. I scan the room, mentally checking my surroundings. Everything appears normal. I peer out the window in the corner of the room to find a clear night sky and lie back down in my bed. Pulling the cover over me, I roll over. My heart plummets when I register the shadow of a man sitting in the chair next to my bed.

"Ah!" I scream and reach for the remote on the table, hoping to grab it in time to press the nurse button. Just as my fingers glide across the red button, the man leaps from the chair. *No, no, no.* It's so dark in my room, I can hardly make out any of his facial features. He pins my hands to the table, leaving my fingers inches away from my call for help.

"Calm down. It's okay. I'll leave." His silky voice startles me.

I know that voice. Turning to survey the man, I find it's Lucas standing above me.

"Lucas?" My head is still spinning.

He scrunches his forehead. "Are you okay?"

"Wh-what are you doing here?" I ask as I sink back into my bed.

Knowing now that it's only him, I can relax. Oddly enough, I'm not worried one bit that it's him in my room this late. I'd rather it be him than a twelve-foot gorilla.

"I heard what happened. I just wanted to come check on you." He pauses, "I can see I've scared you though, so I'll leave." Lucas slowly releases my hands.

I watch as he walks toward the door, "Wait…Don't go."

Lucas glances at me. "You sure?"

I nod.

He reclaims his seat in the chair next to my bed. "What happened?"

"Well, after you left, I was greeted by Erianne. She wasn't all that happy with me. I guess it was too much at once and I fainted. The doctor said I'm okay though. I got a concussion because I hit my head when I fell. But I'm fine." I try to assure him.

He shakes his head. "I should have stayed to make sure you got inside safely."

"Why *did* you take off in such a hurry?"

Lucas grins. "As curious as ever, Abigail."

I laugh as he glances across my room. "I see you've already gotten flowers."

Following his gaze, I notice a bouquet of white roses setting on the meal cart. I didn't see any flowers here before.

"My mama or Erianne probably got them for me," I say, slightly distracted, wondering when those arrived.

"Where are they now?" Lucas asks, drawing my attention back to him.

"Oh, uh, they went home."

A knock at the door startles us. "Nurse. May I come in? I have your medicine."

Lucas abruptly stands as the nurse opens the door, not waiting for a response. The nurse sees Lucas and immediately stops in her tracks. "Mr. Danforth, visiting hours are over," she says sternly.

"That's okay. I was just leaving anyway." A devilish-grin spreads across his lips before he leans down, kissing my forehead. He inches down my face, closer to my ear, sending a delicious shiver down my spine. "I'll be seeing you soon."

16

After a long, really weird night in the hospital, I'm glad I get to finally go home. The doctor already brought discharge papers along with a clean bill of health. Of course, Mama is already here too. I can't stop thinking about how Lucas left last night. He'll be seeing me soon? I'm not sure how I feel about that.

"Hey Abs!" Erianne's voice, as perky as ever, echoes off the walls. I'm quickly enveloped in a hug.

I chuckle. "Hey. You're awfully happy."

"Well of course I am. My best friend is coming home from the hospital today," she says as she releases me.

I roll my eyes. "It's not like I was here for anything serious."

"Abby. If it requires a stay in the hospital, then it's serious." She points a finger in my face, but her attention is drawn to the meal cart behind me. "Who are the flowers from?" she asks, walking over to admire them.

I thought they were from her. "I'm not sure. I just noticed them last night when—" I immediately shut my mouth. No way can she know Lucas was here last night.

"When what?" She furrows her brow.

"Nothing!" I squeak. *Oh, no.* She's going to know something's up. I need to change the subject. "What does the card say?" I ask, nodding toward the flowers.

She skims through the roses. "There isn't one."

Okay…that's just weird. Who would have brought me flowers in the middle of the night and not left a card? Matter of fact, why would someone leave flowers in the middle of the night to begin with? I know it wasn't Lucas because I could tell he was agitated I got them.

"Are we ready to go?" Mama, who is also unusually perky this morning, asks as she walks into my room.

I can tell she got some sleep. I probably have Erianne to thank for that. Mama has been talking to the doctor since she got here. I've never seen her so neurotic. Normally, I'd be irritated with her for hovering so much, but I guess I can let it slide this time.

"You all set Abbs?" Erianne asks.

"Definitely." I smile as I grab my purse and hospital papers. Now to get the hell out of this hospital.

The drive home is silent, leaving me to my thoughts. Lucas seems like such a great guy from what I've seen for myself, but I can't ignore who he is. He's a mob prince for saint's sake. A ridiculously hot mob prince who visited me in the hospital last night. But he's dangerous as hell and has probably busted some kneecaps. Or worse. What am I even arguing with myself for?

Besides, I need to figure out who snuck into my room last night and left me flowers. My curiosity is piqued. For someone like me, that's like putting a bone in front of a dog and hoping it doesn't chase it. Curiosity should be my middle name. Abigail Karline-Curiosity Halsey.

"How does my Cassoulet sound for dinner?" My mama asks as we pull up in front of our flat.

A stew with duck, sausage, pork, and cannellini beans under a dark, rich crust all made by Mama? My mouth waters at the thought of it. *Mmm.* "Mama, do I even need to answer that question?"

Her laughter is a sweet sound as I climb out of the car.

But Cassoulet should be started the night before, which means she hasn't had any sleep. She's looking so rested and better than she did last night though. Only my mother would stay up all night preparing dinner for the next night while I was in the hospital. It honestly warms my heart knowing that I have a mother who does so much for me.

I notice her pulling something off the door to our flat before walking in. Something is wrong. She's frozen in place and her hands are trembling.

"What is it?" I rush to her.

She's holding a small square card. "The Vitale family has invited us to their masquerade ball," she says tight lipped.

Isn't Dominick Vitale Lucas' father? I snatch the invitation from her hands. The gold mask embossed at the top of the invitation is a nice touch, I guess.

> *Dominick Vitale cordially invites you to the annual masquerade ball at Chateau de Danforth.*

> *Party like Kings and Queens.*
> *Join us Saturday, August 16th for masked fun, drinks, and dancing. Wear your finest robes and costumes.*
> *We look forward to enjoying your company for what will be a night to remember.*

I read the invitation aloud and still can't believe it's real. Why would Lucas be inviting us to his father's ball at a castle? Fear lances through my body as I stare at the black paper embossed in gold. I can't think of a good reason Lucas' father would even want me there or Lucas for that matter. He can't think this is a good idea. This isn't happening. This isn't good at all. I face my mother who's staring off at nothing, her face void of expression.

"Mama… Did you hear?" I cautiously place my hand on her arm. I've never seen her like this.

She shakes her head. "We couldn't possibly go to that." She walks off into the kitchen like nothing happened and busies herself with making dinner.

"It might not be such a bad thing. I think it will be fun," I say, hoping to make light of it. I need to find out why Lucas sent this.

My mama abruptly stops what she's doing. "Abigail, *mon trésor*, we don't have money for the costumes," she says under her breath. She won't even look at me.

I force a smile, "That's alright, Mama. Maybe some other time."

No way do I believe her reason for saying no, but the last thing I want to do is upset her more. This has really gotten to her. It's pissing me off. Screw Lucas' dad. No one, and I mean *no one*, messes with my mama. I know if he sent this, there's no good intentions behind it. I don't think Lucas would be this stupid. So, I'm positive it wasn't him.

Glancing at my mother's café clock in the kitchen, I find it's still early in the day. Plenty of time to take care of this and be home in time for dinner. I'm going to find Lucas and figure out who sent that damn invitation.

"Hey Mama, I'm gonna head out for a little bit." I sling my purse on my shoulder and shove the invitation inside.

She sets her oven mitt down. "*Chère*, I don't think that's a good idea."

"I'll be fine. I promise." I force the most convincing smile I can muster up.

"Well… Okay, but make sure you're back in time for dinner sweetie," she says, her voice missing its usual warmth.

"I will. I'm probably just going to catch up with Erianne," I call out, heading for the door.

I don't like lying to her, but I can't tell her about this. I won't let my mama be brought into whatever Lucas' father wants from me.

Her smile barely meets her eyes. "Oh, alright. Invite her to dinner if you want." She's elbow deep in seasonings, putting the finishing touches on the duck for the Cassoulet.

"Sure thing." I stop at the door. "I love you, Mama."

"Love you too, *ma chérie*," she calls from the kitchen just as I'm stepping out the door.

Stepping out onto the sidewalk, it dawns on me that I have no clue where to even find Lucas. Maybe if I show Erianne the invitation and explain how upset it got Mama, she won't be so mad at me. I just hope Delano isn't at the restaurant because I really don't want to deal with him right now.

The bell above the door to La Couronne chimes as I enter. It's busy now that lunch is in full swing. Servers are rushing around balancing trays carefully organized with plates of food. There's a line forming outside while the staff rush to clear tables. Erianne is nowhere in sight. My frown deepens. She has to be in the back or the break room. No sign of Delano either. The coast is clear.

Trying to be as stealthy as possible, I tiptoe to the breakroom in the back of the restaurant. As I pass Delano's office, his voice booms through the door. Another voice yells louder, startling me. It sounds like an argument going on. Who could he possibly be arguing with? It's probably just him yelling at one of the employees. It could be Erianne though. Only one way to find out.

I press my ear against the door and do my best to remain out of sight from anyone passing by. I wouldn't put it pass any of my coworkers to tell Delano I was snooping.

Delano's voice blasts through my ear. "You think you're so damn better than everyone. This is my restaurant, damnit! If I want to fuck every bitch in here, you can't stop me! I can't help it she wants me." Delano spews.

"I'm not fucking with you!" a man shouts.

Delano scoffs. "You think I'm scared of you! I'm not 'Daddy's boy'."

A deafening thud makes me jump back. The crack of wood slamming into the walls resonates through Delano's office door.

"I'll show you what my father has taught me if you don't leave her the fuck alone! You're not scared of me? How scared will you be when you can't walk because I break both your legs? Or why don't I have one of my guys sew that smart mouth of yours shut? Huh? Fucking answer me!" the man screams.

I don't need my ear to the door to hear that. The entire restaurant probably heard it. Something is off though. I…know that voice. What the hell is Lucas doing?

"That tease would look good on my arm. What's it to you anyway?" Delano's laughter echoes off the walls. "You got a thing for her, don't you? You think a sweet girl like that would ever be with a thug like you? She may be a tease, but with a sweet ass like that she's d—" Delano's words cut off as the room behind the door erupts into chaos.

Things are definitely being broken in there. A series of choking and gagging noises are followed by a final '*crack*'. Delano's office door flies open. *Merde*. I stand frozen in place as my heart sinks to my stomach. Lucas is facing away from the door and Delano's office is trashed. No. Destroyed. Delano is lying on the floor sobbing, blood spewing from his face.

"That's my final warning. You keep your hands and eyes off Abigail Halsey. And keep your distance or you'll be getting a different view of the Seine." Lucas spits a last threat at Delano as he rocks on the floor, holding his face.

Oh, merde. Merde. Merde. Merde. Letting the latter of my fight or flight senses kick in, I run to the bathrooms. Once I'm safely inside, I lock the door behind me. Not a second later, the door to Delano's office slams shut. Lucas' footsteps fade as he exits the restaurant.

Why was he threatening Delano to stay from me? More importantly, why was Delano talking about me like that? Crap. I lean back against the door, trying to regain my composure. *Oh hell.* I completely forgot I need to talk to Lucas. That's the entire reason I came here. Maybe I can still catch him before he goes far.

Rushing out of the bathrooms, hoping I don't run into Delano, I keep my head down and exit the restaurant. I'll deal with him later. And I highly doubt he wants to see me right now. I search around the street and sidewalks. But there's absolutely no sign of Lucas. It's like the man disappeared. I need to get his attention somehow. My eyes alight. I know exactly what I can do to get Lucas' attention. They don't like when people ask questions about them so what better way to get their attention.

To hell with this.

I stop a woman as she walks past me, "Excuse me miss. Could you tell me if you know Lucas Danforth?" The feather-haired woman takes off down the sidewalk, hastening her steps.

If his father is keeping tabs on me, he's bound to have someone watching my every move now that Erianne has refused. They'll see me throwing their names around and alert Lucas. Hopefully, not his father.

Next up, an older gentleman walking the opposite direction, "Sir, who is Lucas Danforth?" He scowls at me as if I've lost my mind. "What about Dominick Vitale?" I shout as he rushes off.

A younger couple walking hand-in-hand eyes me warily. "Pardon me. I don't mean to bother you, but would you happen to know Lucas Danforth?"

The man pulls the woman closer to him. "Don't talk to her, darling," he whispers as he quickly pulls her along with him, watching me over his shoulder.

"Does anyone know Lucas Danforth?" I shout as loud as I possibly can. That has to get the goons attention. But what if there is no goon? What if I'm wrong and out here looking like a lunatic? I sit on the bench further down the sidewalk. This isn't going to work. It's a stupid plan, but what else can I do? I guess I could wait. Just in case.

Several moments have gone by and nothing. *Ah, hell*. What am I going to do now? This would be a lot easier if I had his number. I could just text him. Maybe Erianne will be at the restaurant later. She would at least be able to ask Lucas about the invite. I'll just go check the schedule.

Approaching the front of La Couronne, the hair on the back on my neck stands on end. I definitely got someone's attention, but not Lucas'. Mathieu is blocking the entrance and he's already locked his sights on me. He ends a call on his cell and slides it in his pocket.

"Hey, Mathieu," I say, giving my best poker face and trying to seem enthused. Who knows how he'll feel if he finds out I'm looking for Lucas. He's not fond of the guy and I'm not up for getting into that argument.

"Well hello, Abigail. Nice to see you're alive and well." A sly grin cracks across his face.

"Thanks." I force the corners of my mouth to form a smile. "So, this was great, but I should be getting to work."

He blocks my path. "You don't look like you're going in for a shift."

"Oh. I, uh, I have a uniform inside in my locker. It was supposed to rain earlier, and I didn't want to show up to work drenched."

He takes a step toward me, face inches from mine as his voice escapes his lips in a low sultry growl, "Why don't you skip work? Let's go spend some time together. Maybe at my place."

My heart thumps my chest. He's staring at me like I'm the dessert he can't wait to devour. Mustering up every last drop of composure I have left and speaking as obnoxiously loud as possible, "I'm sorry. I really don't have time to. Like I said, I have to get to work now. So, if you'll excuse me."

Mathieu takes a step back, his smile deflating as he surveys the customers around us. Several are watching intently. Perfect. Just what I wanted. He quickly plasters a charming smile any other bystander would be fooled by. I hurt his feelings. But I can't deal with this right now. Brushing past him, the chime of the front door to La Couronne opening has never been such a sweet and welcomed sound.

With my sights set on the breakroom, that suddenly seems so far away, my chest heaves as my lungs try to keep up with the ferocious beating in my chest. Breaking the threshold of the hallway, only a few more steps to go, I do a victory dance in my head. My arm is jerked backward. That celebration of freedom is brought to a skidding halt. *No, no, no.* The hand firmly gripping my arm is larger than Mathieu's. My skin crawls.

I twirl around. Lucas' stern icy blue eyes aren't as gentle as I've known them to be. If the iris were mood changing, his would be crimson right now. His jaw clenches as he presses his lips tighter together. Those broad shoulders are squared off. Poking his chest out while it rises and falls with each careful breath, his silence is deafening.

But I refuse to be afraid of him. Not now. Not ever. I just hope I don't learn my lesson about that the way Delano did.

"It took you long enough." I lower my eyes.

He squares his shoulders as his grip tightens, the pressure causing my arm to ache. Lucas' chest rises ever so slowly. Turning on his heel, he drags me behind him and out of the restaurant. As we pass the tables outside, I notice Mathieu is nowhere in sight. A familiar black sedan is parked by the street, but Lucas doesn't even glance at it. He keeps ahold of my arm as he guides me across the street, through the park, and under the portico connecting to the Church of St Joan of Arc entrance.

Just as I think he's done acting like Erianne, dragging me along everywhere, I'm pulled toward the entrance of the church. A chuckle escapes past my lips at the thought of Lucas taking me to church. He pulls me through a gated stone corridor next to the entrance. Once inside, he secures the lock on the wrought iron gate. The corridor is as dark as night aside from the rays of sunlight shining from each end through the gate doors. Staring off into the vast empty space before me, I formulate an escape place in my head. Just in case.

Lucas whips around and takes a step closer. With each move he makes toward me, I step away. The cold stone collides against my back. I try to sidestep out of his proximity, but his arms outstretch and block me in on either side, preventing my escape.

"Have you lost your damn mind?" Lucas shouts.

The cold, rough stone scrapes against my back through my blouse. I reach into my purse and yank the invitation to his father's masquerade ball out. I shove the paper against his chest.

"No. Have *you* lost *your* mind?" I shout back.

Lucas stares at me, raising his brow. He drops a hand from the wall to take the paper from me. As his eyes skim over the invitation, the intensity he's radiating dissipates. His eyes relax and his face blanches as if he's seen a ghost.

His tone is barely a whisper, "Where did you get this?" Staggering backward, he runs a hand through his hair.

"What do you mean 'where did I get this'? It was on my door this morning when I got home from the hospital." I throw my hands up.

"And you think I gave you this?" he shouts back, his tone pitched as if he's offended at my accusation.

I reaffirm my stance, not letting him scare me. "You said you'd be seeing me soon! How could you leave this on my doorstep for my mother to see? Being around you was a mistake. And this is crossing a line!"

Lucas reaches both hands out, enclosing my face within them. "Abigail, I didn't leave this on your doorstep." He runs his thumb over my lips to silence me. "But I promise you, I promise, I will find out who did."

My heart nearly leaps out of my chest at his touch. There's an unexpected fluttering deep in my gut. Stealing a glance into those dangerously sexy crystal blue eyes, my gut is telling me he's being honest. I'm taking a chance believing anything he says, but who else can I trust to take care of this?

"If you didn't, then why would someone leave this for me?" I ask.

He shakes his head, not meeting my gaze. "I don't know. But I will." His fingers brush against my skin as his hand finds its way to the nape of my neck. "No harm will come to you or your mother." The conviction in his words rings clear.

I know I shouldn't trust him. Every inch of my body is screaming for me not to. But I need all the help I can get. It's his father that's keeping tabs on me. What better ally to have than his own son.

"I have to get back to work…" I say, breaking the silence.

He abruptly backs away. "Go."

I hesitate before turning away from him. I don't know why, but a part of me doesn't want to leave. Having someone like him as an ally makes me feel a little safer. That all goes away the second he's not around. I'd never admit that. He's got a big enough ego as it is.

A small, satisfied smile plays across his lips. "I'll walk you back."

Lucas wraps an arm around my waist as I silently fall in step with him. His grip on my hip tightens ever so slightly. I shimmy out of his hold.

"Nice try." I playfully shove him.

He chuckles as we walk up to La Couronne. I immediately notice Jimmy standing by the rear passenger side of the black sedan. I wonder where he was earlier. Lucas doesn't release me as Jimmy holds the car door open.

"Can I give you a ride home when you're off?" Lucas asks.

"I think I'm just going to walk." I've risked enough being around him. I can only imagine what his father would do if he even thought for a second Lucas is helping me.

"Alright." He growls. "Be careful, Abigail. Please."

I nod and smile to reassure him. He climbs in the car. Jimmy tips his hat to me and walks around to the driver side. I watch as the car pulls off into the street. I wish I knew who in the hell put that invitation on my door. First the flowers and now this. What's next?

I turn around to walk home and instantly regret asking myself that.

All the blood drains from my face. Erianne towers over me, her fist clenched at her sides. She saw me with Lucas.

17

What have I just done?

Before I can answer my own internal question or defend myself to Erianne, she storms off inside La Couronne. I race to catch up with her.

"Erianne! Wait!" *No. No. No.* I follow her to the break room and watch her punch out. "Please. Erianne."

This is really bad. Erianne never leaves her shift early, especially not when she just got here.

She spins around. "No, Abigail. Please nothing. Are you out of your damn mind?" she seethes.

That happens to be the question of the day.

Erianne scoffs and grabs her bag. "You know what, just forget it. I'm not doing this." She bumps into me as she storms out of the break room.

Wordlessly, I watch as she walks through the restaurant and straight out the front door. I have to fix this. I can't lose her.

I run as fast as I can to catch up. "Erianne! Stop!" Breathless, I reach her just as she turns the corner onto Place De La Pucelle. "Just let me explain!" I call after her.

She whips around to face me. "Explain what, Abigail? How you can't seem to listen to reason? How you think this is all just one big game? For Saint's sake Abigail, after everything I told you? Are you trying to get yourself killed?" Erianne screams, startling a couple bystanders.

A tear rolls down my cheek. "No. Of course I'm not. I—"

Erianne cuts me off, "Well, that's exactly what you're going to do by involving yourself with him! I've told you this time and time again! You just don't listen," she shouts, pointing a finger at me. "You may want to dance with the devil, Abigail, but I sure as hell don't. So, you go chase after Lucas all you want. Don't expect me to be here when it all falls apart." She turns away and walks off down the sidewalk.

A knot swells in my throat. "Er-Erianne, please," I call out as she fades into the crowd of strangers walking along the sidewalk.

Erianne simply shakes her head and keeps walking. I'm frozen in place. My lungs burn as the space around me closes in. I'm outside, wide in the open, but it's like I'm trapped in a small box. No matter how much air I inhale, my lungs remain empty. *Breath in. Breath out. It's okay.*

But it's not okay. Nothing is okay. My only friend is gone. I ruined everything. This isn't happening. I was just getting used to not being alone. My mind is racing.

A single wet drop plops onto my arm as I'm standing on the sidewalk. *Oh, no. No, no, no.* I can't get stuck in a storm. Scanning the street, I try to get out of my head. Alcohol. I need alcohol. I mean, it solves everyone else's problems. Why can't it solve mine? Willing my feet to uproot themselves, another drop lands on my leg. *Move faster.* O'Kallaghan's here I come.

A sharp ache stabs at my chest. The last time I went there was with Erianne. *Merde.* I really screwed things up with her. She's been doing everything she can to protect me. She's been here for me and been a real friend. Hell, she put her life on the line for me. She has every right to be mad.

I've been so wrapped up in the vortex that's Lucas Danforth. He's toxic. He's like alcohol for an alcoholic. Speaking of alcohol…

I walk into the pub and the Irish music playing faintly in the background leaves a bittersweet ache. It's only about twelve o'clock in the afternoon, which explains why it's practically empty in here. I shuffle my feet forward to a seat at the bar top.

"Well, don't yer jist luk knackered." The bartender's thick Irish accent pulls me out of my thoughts.

I raise an eyebrow. "I'm not sure what that means…"

He laughs heartily. "Waaat 'ill yer 'av lassy?"

"I'll just take a beer." I rest my head in my hands.

"I thought that was you!" a squeal from behind me calls out.

I brush it off until a short, round woman with springy red curls sits on the bar stool next to me. She looks familiar, but I can't put the name to the face.

"You're Abigail, right? I'm Clarissa. I met you about a month ago when Erianne brought you here," she says, extending her hand.

I shake it as I try to remember what she's talking about. "I'm sorry. It's been a long day."

She smiles so big it makes her cheeks pop. "That's okay. Last time I saw you here Matt was talking about that cruise ship. It would be a dream to be able to travel on one," she gushes.

I remember her now. How could I forget? She was the one that was off in her own little world, daydreaming about going on that ship with the girl next to her. She hardly spoke the entire night. And when she did, it was about that trip to the Americas. Erianne told me about this girl, too. She didn't seem too thrilled.

"I remember you now. You sat next to Erianne." The bartender arrives with my beer and I quickly take a sip. "Sorry, like I said, it's been a long day."

Clarissa eyes my mug, smiling wider. As if her rosy pink cheeks could get any bigger. I can't tell if her cheeks are naturally that rosy or if it's just from her constant smiling. Either way, I wish she would take all this enthusiasm down a little.

"Oh, it's okay. I saw how you were staring at Mr. D all night." Clarissa gives me a penetrating stare.

I nearly spit my drink out. "Mr. D?"

She leans in and whispers, "You know. Lucas. *The* Lucas Danforth."

"I'm sorry I don't know—"

Clarissa holds her hand up, "Not another word. Your secret is safe with me," she says proudly while pretending to lock her mouth with an imaginary key.

I take a long drink of my beer, nearly downing the entire mug. "Look, Clarissa?"

"Yes." She beams.

"Clarissa. Thank you for being so nice, but I'm just not up to chatting right now," I politely tell her.

"Aw. What's going on? You can talk to me!" She rubs my arm gently.

At this point, she has Erianne beat when it comes to being perky. I'm beginning to see why Erianne doesn't particularly favor her. I stare at her. She's clearly not going anywhere, and I don't want to hurt her feelings either. As much I want her to just go away, if there's one thing I've learned recently, it's that sometimes talking to someone isn't a bad idea. What the hell. Why not?

"I just got into a fight with my best friend. Well ex-best friend. I guess. Maybe I shouldn't be this upset. It's not like we were in a relationship," I say.

"If you were in a relationship, that's okay. I won't judge. I firmly believe happiness is all that matters. Even if that happiness is between two girls. Or two guys. Or both," she trails off.

"Clarissa," I cut her off, "We weren't in a relationship."

"Okay." She winks at me.

I finish my beer in one last swig. I'm beginning to regret this already.

"So why did you get into it then?" Clarissa asks.

I rub my forehead as I try to sort through everything. "She thinks I've been seeing this guy, but I haven't. I just wish she would have let me explain. All he did was offer me a ride home. Which, I declined by the way. But that didn't matter to her. She saw me with him and that was proof enough. She yelled at me and pretty much told me we aren't friends anymore. I mean there are other times where she saw me with him, but I can count on one hand how many. She just assumed there was this long thing going on between the two of us."

My head is hurting trying to make sense of this crazy mess that's become my life. Too much is going on. I flag the bartender down and point for another drink.

"That doesn't seem very fair of her. She doesn't sound like a great friend to me." Clarissa's enthusiasm dies down. The corners of her mouth turn downward for the first time.

I shake my head. "No. She's a really good friend."

I gaze down into my drink. I can't help thinking of how much I've done wrong with Erianne. She deserves a better friend than me.

"Maybe she likes the guy and that's why she is so mad about you being around him," Clarissa says, her smile returning.

I burst into laughter. The thought of Lucas and Erianne. Together. It's insane. Clarissa has to be kidding. If only she knew what guy I was talking about. I'm not going to even go there with her though because I can only imagine where she would run with that.

"There. Isn't that better?" Clarissa asks with her smile as bright as ever again.

She's right. It does feel better to just laugh at something. Maybe talking to her wasn't such a bad idea after all.

"*Oui.* I guess so." I match her smile.

"Hey, do you want to grab a coffee or something to eat with me?" Clarissa asks.

The clock behind the bar says it's a little before one o'clock. Mama won't have dinner done until around seven, so I still have some time to kill.

"Sure, why not." I hop off the bar stool, grabbing my purse as I walk off.

Clarissa follows behind. "I know a really good place. If we hurry, we'll make it in time for lunch. Their fromage is literally to die for."

Clarissa isn't wrong. Their *fromage* is really good, but I'm not all that hungry. She's already ordered her appetizer and entree. I've had two cups of *café crème*—coffee with milk and cream—but nothing else until the *fromage* got served. Even still, I'm just barely picking at it. All I can think about is everything going on right now. Erianne isn't talking to me. Someone is sending anonymous flowers and ball invitations. And Lucas' father is having me watched.

Clarissa happily chews away at her array of cheeses. She smiles even when she's eating. I don't understand why she's being so nice to me.

"So, what do you think?" Clarissa asks in-between bites.

"Hm. Of what?" I ask, bringing my attention back to her.

"What do you think of the food and the place?" Clarissa asks as she shoves another piece of camembert cheese in her mouth. "You haven't eaten anything."

"I like it here. I just don't have much of an appetite."

I *do* like where she brought me. It's a quaint little restaurant closer to the Seine river. I think the name is *Minute et Mijoté*, but I'm not entirely sure. I haven't really been paying attention to much of anything since I fought with Erianne.

Clarissa finishes the last bit of the *fromage*. "Do you want dessert?" She wipes her mouth with the white linen napkin.

"No. I'm okay." I fidget with my hands in my lap.

Clarissa's smile falls abruptly. "*Oui*. Me too. I have to get to work anyway now." She pauses before draping her blue sweater back over her shoulders.

I've never understood why people do that. I know it's a fashion thing, but it doesn't make sense to me. Clarissa stands, smoothing out her white dress suit. I admire how easily she can pull off that form-fitting dress. She's a heavier set woman, about my size.

I stop her as she goes to leave. "Hey, I'm sorry I haven't been much company. I guess I'm just really distracted."

Clarissa's shining smile quickly returns. "I completely understand." She leans in to hug me.

Taken completely off guard, I half-heartedly return the hug. "Maybe we can get together another time."

She lets go and holds me at arm's length. "Oh, that would be great. Why don't we meet here tomorrow around twelve?"

"Sure." I smile politely at her. I wasn't expecting her to want to meet up again so soon.

"Fantastic!" Clarissa practically squeals before dropping her arms. "I'd better get going. You need a ride home?"

"No. I'm going to stay and finish my coffee. Thank you though." I don't think I can handle more of her energized enthusiasm today.

"See you tomorrow then! Same time! Byee!" Clarissa shouts as she leaves the restaurant.

I take a seat realizing that she was in a bit of a rush. I wonder what that was about. It's probably because of how I've been acting. I'm not much company to anyone right now. I sip my coffee as a waiter comes by the table to clear the food Clarissa ordered. She ordered some pricey items off the menu.

"Your check, mademoiselle." A brunette wearing a black apron over her white blouse hands me a small black envelope with a receipt hanging out of it.

I open it. "What the hell?" I nearly shout as my heart drops to the pit of my stomach. "Ninety-Six Francs?"

No wonder Clarissa bolted out of here like a bat out of hell. As if this day couldn't have gotten any worse.

"Is there a problem, mademoiselle?" The young petite waitress asks.

I take a few seconds to calm down. "No. Not at all." I force a smile on my face before handing her the ninety-six damn Francs.

This is unbelievable.

She hands me a receipt. "Here you go. Thank you for visiting *Minute et Mijoté.* We hope to see you again." She plasters a smile on her face as she walks away.

"That's it. I'm done," I mutter to myself.

Leaving the restaurant as quickly as I can, I just want to go home. As I'm walking, I remember Mama is busy cooking a Cassoulet. Despite not really having an appetite, I can never turn Mama's cooking down.

I speed walk down the sidewalk, more thankful for my flats than ever before. I don't know how far of a walk home I have ahead of me. I love that the thought of both my mother and her cooking can cheer me up, even if it's only a little bit.

I'm about to turn a corner but check the street for incoming traffic first. A black sedan parked on the corner looks just like the one Jimmy drives Lucas around in all day.

"Come on Abigail. *Mon Dieu*. Get it together. Not every black sedan you see is going to be Lucas," I mutter to myself.

Hastily crossing the street, I find myself wondering if Lucas actually owns that car or if it's Jimmy's. The distraction to think about for the next block is definitely welcome. I cross the street again and another black sedan rolls up, stopping just short of the cross walk. Maybe it's the same one. I shake my head at myself for even thinking so.

Just when I've convinced myself I'm nuts, the sedan pulls out onto the street, stopping next to me. The driver's door opens, but I don't look back. Nope. Nothing else today.

"Abigail!" a man's voice calls out.

The pounding of footsteps against the pavement is getting closer. This is what I was worried about. I keep my head down and hasten my pace. Maybe he'll just get the hint and go away. He's ruined enough already.

"Abigail! Hell. Would you wait a damn minute!" Lucas grabs my arm and stops me.

I roll my eyes. "What?" I shout as I turn around, "What do you want? For one day can't you just leave me alone?" I snap.

Lucas stares back at me dumbfounded. "What's wrong?" he asks cautiously and drops his hand to his side.

I rub my face. "Nothing."

"Why don't you let me drive you home?" Lucas reaches an arm around me to coerce me to walk with him.

I'm too exhausted to say no or give him a hard time. Today has been stressful enough. Plus, a storm is coming, and being with Lucas may help distract me from it until I get home.

Jimmy isn't standing by the car door when we get there. In fact, he's nowhere in sight. What's even more odd is Lucas getting in the front seat. My jaw drops at the sight. Where is Jimmy? And why in saint's name is Lucas driving?

Lucas starts the car, but tilts his head when he notices me just standing idly by the passenger door. His eyes shoot wide open and he quickly jumps back out of the car, rushing over to my side.

"Sorry. Jimmy usually does this," he says as he opens the door for me. His cheeks redden.

He must have thought I was standing here waiting for him to get the door. *Sorry to tell you Lucas, but I could have gotten my own door.* And did I really just witness *the* Lucas Danforth blush? This has got to go down in the history books. A mob prince blushing because he forgot to hold a car door open for a girl. I grin as Lucas shuts my door and hops back in the driver seat.

"So…you know how to drive?" I ask with an ear-splitting grin.

"Yes, Abigail. I do know how to operate a car." He rolls his eyes and shifts the gear into Drive. He's playful and seems so free, a far cry from the frightening thug on a warpath from earlier.

"I would have never known, since you have someone chauffeur you around all the time," I tease him.

A small smile forms at the corner of his mouth. "Jimmy only drives me when I have business to tend to. He's backup if it's necessary." His face falls and his shoulders tense at the mention of 'business'.

"Well I think he genuinely cares for you." I try to break this seriously awkward moment.

"*Oui.*" Lucas runs his hand through his hair. "I think I know who left that invitation for you."

My ears perk up.

"It could be one of two people, but I'll know after the masquerade ball." He peeks over at me.

"Okay." *Thanks for nothing.*

"By the way, I'd like you to attend it with me." Lucas flashes a smirk from the driver seat, his lips pressed together.

What did he just say? He wants me to do *what*? No way in hell. Not a chance am I attending a ball filled with criminals. And with *him* at that. Now, I know he's crazy. What's he thinking?

"I won't be able to know for sure who it is unless you're there." He watches for my reaction.

"Eyes on the road," I say, hoping to distract him.

"I'll put my eyes back on the road if you say yes." He grins mischievously.

I don't care who he thinks he is. This is insane. He's going to cause an accident. My heart slams into my ribcage as he presses down on the gas pedal. If the only way for him to find out who left me that invitation is for me to go, then what real choice do I have? I don't have enough time to really think this through. I *need* to think this through. The night Erianne pulled a stunt like this flashes in my head. As the car begins to pick up speed, the air leaves my lungs. I can't have an anxiety attack in front of him.

"Okay! Yes! Yes, I'll go with you!" I shout, squeezing my eyes shut as the car comes to a skidding halt at a red light.

Lucas burst into laughter. I open my eyes to witness yet another rare event from him. What has gotten into him today? His laughter bouncing off the confines of the car distracts me from how pissed I am at him. That stunt he just pulled makes me regret ever getting in the car with him. I don't care how funny he thinks this is. It's not. At. all.

"Have *you* lost your mind?" I ask while trying to calm my breathing, "Or have you been drinking. Or is it drugs?" I glare.

He grins wildly at me. "No. To all three."

"Good." I adjust my seat belt, tightening it in case he gets any more ideas. "By the way, you should continue to let Jimmy drive."

He chuckles just as we pull up outside my flat. I check the clock on his car radio. 5:45PM. Not bad timing.

Lucas puts the car in park. "I'll see you then."

"Not like you gave me much of a choice," I say as I open the car door.

He reaches over, grabbing my arm. "Look. I'm sorry if I scared you. I was just goofing off. I can get carried away sometimes. You don't have to go."

I clear my throat, "I'm going. But only to find out who sent the invite. Hopefully, we can put an end to all of this." I step out, but something dawns on me. I lean down. "Wait. I don't have anything to wear to the ball."

A sly grin outlines the corner of his mouth as he speeds off into traffic.

That doesn't help. I can't show up wearing nothing, and I definitely can't show up wearing anything I have. This is a ball. The invitation clearly said to wear your finest robes and suits. I don't just have an elegant ball gown lying around my bedroom or in my closet.

I wish I could go to Erianne.

The thought hangs heavy on my mind as I walk into my flat. At least Mama is home to keep me company. If there's one thing I have no doubt I can look forward to at the end of the day, it's my mama's cooking. And her, of course.

18

The savory aroma of Mama's Cassoulet still fills the house or maybe it's just me daydreaming about it. I'd kill for some leftovers right now, but Mama would lecture me into the middle of next week. She's strict about having certain mealtimes throughout the day. I'd usually get an earful for sleeping in. She hasn't said a word about it though. I think she's trying to give me a break. It really scared her when I passed out and ended up in the hospital.

It's almost twelve. Clarissa said she would meet me at the restaurant at twelve. If she shows up, I'm going to give her a piece of my mind. I slip on a blue t-shirt and my black jeans. Since I don't have work, I can wear my favorite Nike sneakers. They're so worn out, but that's what makes them so comfy.

Delano has been oddly nice. He texted to let me know he gave me today off. He insisted I didn't come into work until tomorrow. As much as I hope this doesn't have anything to do with Erianne, or Lucas for that matter, unfortunately, I think it might.

There's no sign of Clarissa when I get to the restaurant. Purposefully requesting the same table as yesterday, I've arrived just in time with only a few minutes to spare. All I can do now is sit and wait.

My mind drifts back to last night when Lucas drove me home. He's usually so tense, so intimidating. Last night, for whatever reason, he seemed so free. It's the opposite of what I feel like lately. What could his father possibly want with me and my mother? Why is he even looking into us? I don't get it. And how is he even getting any information about us? Maybe I can get some answers at the ball.

I tried talking to Mama about going, but she absolutely forbade me from it. I know it's dangerous for her to go, but I think it's more dangerous to leave her home alone while I'm there. Me being there is going to attract attention. I think she's safest being where I can keep an eye on her. I just don't know how I'm going to make it work. I'd better talk to Lucas about it first too.

The analog clock on the wall ticks until the hands line up at 12:20PM. I think I'm about to get stiffed again.

"Hey you!" A familiar squeaky voice calls out.

Standing from my chair, I do my best to match Clarissa's enthusiasm. "Hey! It's so great to see you!"

"Well, aren't you the happiest woman today," she says as she takes her seat at the table.

"I'm meeting here with you! How could I not be happy?" I feign ignorance.

She beams. "I'm so glad."

"I mean, how couldn't I be? What better way to confront you about sticking me with the bill yesterday?" I say just as she picks up her menu.

Clarissa drops her menu like a hot baguette fresh out of the oven and her hands fly up to cover her mouth. I didn't think her cheeks could get any redder than they already are, but guess I'm wrong. Her eyes are ready to pop out of her head. She looks absolutely mortified.

Maybe I jumped to conclusions. She did say she had to work…

"Abigail. I am *so* sorry. I-I don't know what must have come over me. I forgot about work and I was just so excited to make a new friend outside of work." She digs into her purse. "Here. Let me pay you back every coin."

Guilt for judging her so quickly tears away at me. "No. It's alright,"

"Nonsense. Here. Will one hundred Francs cover it?" Clarissa frantically holds out a one-hundred Franc banknote.

She seems to genuinely feel bad. "You keep it." I try to push her hand away.

"Oh, no! I couldn't possibly do that!" She shoves the banknote at me.

She isn't going to give this up.

I take the banknote from her and put it away in my purse. Seeing as I'm a total ass, I think it's best I just keep quiet. I've already put my foot in my mouth enough for today. My cheeks are burning. I guarantee they match Clarissa's natural rosy reds. While sitting in silence, I take a mental note that I officially owe her for this.

"How are things with your friend and the guy now?" Clarissa picks up her menu.

"Well, things are fairly the same." My thoughts drift back to yesterday. "Sort of."

"I know that look if I've ever seen it." Clarissa drops her menu. Her eyes pierce through me. "You saw him again, didn't you?" She's ready to jump out of her seat, gushing with giddiness.

"*Oui. Oui*, I did." I rest my head in my hands.

"Tell me all about it!" Clarissa gushes. As usual.

"Not much to tell. I got an invite to the Vitale masquerade ball and he asked me to go."

There isn't really much else I *can* tell without her finding out who 'he' is. Not only do I not even want to go into that with her, but I also can't take the chance of putting her in danger too. I think I've put enough people in danger already.

Clarissa gasps. "No way! If he asked you to go with him to that, he must really like you!" She's ready to burst at the seams.

I giggle. "You know about the Vitale ball?" Her enthusiasm is infectious.

Clarissa sits back wide-eyed. "You don't? I'm surprised. Typically, everyone in Normandy attends. They hold one every year in August around the Assumption of the Blessed Virgin Mary." She leans in closer, shielding her face with one hand from the nearby table and whispers, "But everyone knows the entire party is just a cover for Mr. Vitale's 'business' meeting with other criminals."

The waiter arrives to take our order and Clarissa straightens up quickly. Even she's afraid of that family.

She orders the veal sautéed with olives and a mint creme brulee with an orange zest fondant. All I have the appetite for is a coffee and a rum cake. Who could possibly go wrong with coffee and rum cake?

Thinking back on what she said, about why Lucas' father holds the masquerade ball in the first place, my stomach shifts uneasily. Not that I haven't already been a nervous wreck about going there. Finding out the entire thing is a cover up for criminal… stuff, doesn't exactly soothe those nerves. I'm getting in way over my head. Someone's going to get hurt.

The reasons I'm going to the ball aren't exactly the best either. And there's no doubt in my mind that Lucas' father has already heard about the little stunt I pulled yesterday. Here's hoping he'll be too occupied with 'business' to bother with me.

"Hey. I have an idea!" Clarissa says so loud I practically leap from my chair.

Scanning around the restaurant, no one seems to even notice. Maybe it wasn't loud at all. Maybe I'm just *that* distracted.

"What's your idea?" I ask, trying to focus my attention on her.

Her smile makes her cheeks pop. "Why don't we meet up at the ball? I know you're going with that guy so you won't be able to actually go with me, but we could hang out there." Her smile widens.

"I don't see why not. Sure." I smile back at her. Clarissa's never-ending optimism is growing on me.

She starts rambling on about dresses and masks for the ball. I haven't really thought about any of that because I have no clue how I'm even going to get it. Besides, I don't normally get all dressed up like that. The one time I did was when Erianne practically forced me to.

I miss Erianne.

Maybe once I find out who sent the invitation and flowers, I can talk to her about everything. She may not understand, but she'll have no choice but to forgive me.

Clarissa is still going on and on about the ball. I wish I had some of the energy she always does. Even as we're eating, it's all she's talking about. I'm jealous of her enthusiasm with life. She's filled with kindness, generosity, and humility. She's selfless to her core. I can't imagine her having a mean bone in her body. She reminds me a lot of my mama. Speaking of Mama, I have to convince her to let me attend the masquerade ball. But first, I need to talk to Lucas about it.

As I'm off in my own world thinking about the ball, something scratches at my memory. It's like I'm forgetting something. The clock on the wall reads 12:45PM. I'm not late for dinner. We haven't been here that long, but I can't shake the feeling like there's somewhere else I need to be…*Oh, merde.*

I interrupt Clarissa, "What day is it?"

"It's Tuesday. Why?" She smiles.

Oh, hell. "I have to go. I'm so sorry. I forgot about a doctor's appointment I have. I'll see you at the ball, no?"

She beams. "Of course."

I can't believe I almost forgot about my appointment with Dr. Carrere. I only have fifteen minutes to make it. I take of sprinting down the street. She's going to kill me if I'm late.

19

I make it to Dr. Carrere's office with one minute to spare. My lungs are on fire and I think I ran out of oxygen two blocks back, but I made it. The chairs in her waiting room are so uncomfortable. It's pieces of metal shaped into a thin frame and a paper-thin sad excuse for a cushion. My butt is already hating me for it.

The door to her office slowly opens. "I want to see you same time tomorrow. Okay?" she says to the patient as he walks out.

He nods and walks to the receptionist desk. Dr. Carrere notices me waiting.

"Hello, Ms. Halsey." She smiles. "Come in."

I wring my hands as I walk over the threshold into her office. There's no doubt in my mind that she's going to ask me about the repressed memory therapy. I haven't had any time to even do research on it. And I'm not sure I want to know what memories are lingering in my subconscious.

"How have things been since last week?" She asks, taking a seat in her usual leather chair.

"Okay. I guess." I flop down onto the black leather sofa.

"Anything new you want to share?" She grabs her pen and notepad.

As much as I want to, I can't tell her anything that's going on. It's not like it's normal everyday problems. I have a powerful criminal keeping tabs on me for god only knows what reason. My best friend is his bed mate's daughter. She's basically a mob princess. And I've been invited to the Vitale ball, which is really just a cover up to for them to conduct mob business. *Oui*, totally normal.

"Nope. Still having the nightmares, still scared of storms, and still a nervous nelly." I grin.

She sets the notepad in her lap. "Have you given any thought to RPT?"

I lay back on the sofa. "What is it exactly?"

She goes into some technical explanation of RPT that I can barely keep track of what half of it means. But from what I *am* understanding, it's going to make these memories come back. It *could* stop the nightmares, *could* put an end to my fear of storms, and *could* help ease my anxiety. All these uncertain promises of what it could possibly do makes me wonder if it's even going to be worth it.

It's up to me if I want to live the way I do, or if I want to change it. If I don't do it, I'm always going to wonder 'what if'. By doing it, I'd be at least trying something. Besides, what am I coming to therapy for if it's not to deal with this crap.

You know what, "Let's do it." I sit up.

She takes her glasses off. "Fantastic! We can start next week if that's okay. A friend of mine specializes in this. You'll love her."

I shake my head. "Wait a minute. I'm not going to be with you for it?"

"Don't worry. I'll be in the room assisting. I'm not going anywhere." She smiles.

I guess I'm going to find out what these memories are a lot sooner than later.

Mama should be coming home from work soon. She's not always in the best of moods after work, but I need to talk to her about the ball. Maybe if I start cleaning the house, it'll warm her over. Before I can talk myself out of the idea, I jump up off the sofa. The sitting room seems simple enough. All it needs is a little dusting and vacuuming.

Finishing with that, I get started on the kitchen. Just as I'm filling the sink with dish water, the jingling of keys echoes in the hall outside my flat. The front door makes the familiar '*click*' as Mama turns the handle.

"Abigail!" Mama calls out.

"In here, Mama!" I busy myself with loading the sink with dishes.

She gasps dramatically and places a hand over her chest. "*Ah bien*, as I live and breathe. Miracles do happen!"

I fling soap suds at her. "What? I can't help?"

She laughs and narrows her eyes. "Abigail, *chère*. You've been a part of my world for over seventeen years and in that time, you've never lifted a finger to a dish unless it was to eat."

"I cleaned the sitting room for you too," I proudly announce.

Mama places her hands on her hips. "That's it. What do you want?"

I roll my eyes. "Why do I have to want something in order to help you?"

Mama shoots me a cold glare. "Enough. Tell me. What is it?"

"Well…Now that you mention it," I bite my lip to suppress a grin and watch as a smile crosses her mouth, "About the masquerade ball…"

Her entire expression falls flat. "I thought we discussed this."

"We did. But Mama, I really would like to go to this." My hands are covered in dirty dish water and soap suds as I plead to her.

Her face stiffens, reddening. "My answer is final! You are not going to that ball, Abigail. Now I don't want to hear another word about it! I don't care if you're about to be an adult. If you want to live under my roof, then you must abide by my rules."

"Mama. What are you so worried about?" I cautiously attempt to sway her decision one last time.

She takes a deep breath and shakes her head. "You."

Me? If she doesn't want me to go because she's afraid I'll get into trouble, then she doesn't need to worry at all. I don't want to start trouble any more than she wants me to be in any.

"When was the last time you had fun?" I grin mischievously.

She furrows her brow. "Where are you going with this?"

"I was thinking…what if you come to the ball with me?"

She doesn't say yes, but she doesn't say no either. It's nearly impossible not to get my hopes up. I need her to come with me as much as I need to go myself. I just have to convince her. Hopefully this works.

"Abigail. We don't have anything to wear to that." She says the same excuse as before, but I know it's just that, an excuse. I'm starting to think she's hiding something.

"Erianne and I are going shopping for dresses tomorrow night so I can just pick one up for you." I lie with conviction.

Mama shakes her head. "I don't know."

"Come on, Mama! Enough with the excuses! Come to the ball with me! We'll have fun, and when was the last time you did that? We haven't had any mother daughter time lately either." Maybe pulling the 'mother, daughter' card will do the trick. "What do you think?" I patiently wait for her answer.

Her voice is barely audible, "Alright."

Jumping up and down, I rush over and wrap her up in a hug. She half-heartedly hugs me back. I can tell she's still on the fence about this, but she'll see. It's going to be fun. I can't remember the last time I've went out with my mama first of all and this way I'll be able to keep her safe. It's a win-win.

"So, since I have to be up early…I should probably get to bed. So, I'll uh… leave you to that." I point to the sink full of dishes.

She laughs and waves her hand at me. "Go on. Get to bed, but you owe me a clean house one of these days!"

I'm already at my bedroom door. "You got it, Mama!"

I kick my shoes off and sink into my bed. What a hell of a couple months it's been. Even though I'm tired as hell, my mind won't shut off. I scan my room, gazing from the papers and pictures along the walls, to the books on my desk in the corner, and up to the ceiling.

I like to stare at my ceiling when I can't sleep. So, a while ago, I put a poster up. It's a quote from the French poet, Victor Hugo.

"There is nothing like a dream to create the future."

It's the only quote that's stuck with me for so long. I first read it in middle school. I've spent most of my life thinking about the future. My future. I used to have it all planned out. I'd graduate lycée, go on to University, and get my degree in English. Things haven't been going exactly as planned.

20

I told my mama I'm meeting Erianne this morning to go dress shopping, so I have to get out of bed soon. If not, she's going to wonder what's going on. Lying is exhausting. Lucas is actually picking me up from La Couronne.

I reluctantly drag myself from under my warm duvet. The scent of fresh linens fills my nose as I spot the pile of folded clothes on my dresser. I sift through the pile until I find my favorite green blouse. I've had this thing since C.M. 1 year in middle school and I don't care how old I get. I'll always love it. It's comfortable and simple. I like things to be simple.

"Good morning sweetie." Mama stares down at her pager, her usual cup of coffee in hand.

"Morning. Everything okay?" I ask.

Her mouth presses into a firm line. "*Oui*. It's my boss again. I'm going to have to go into work early." She clips her pager back onto her belt.

Rapping on the front door makes me about jump out of my skin. I'm not expecting anyone. It would be perfect if it's Erianne. I can't get that lucky though. I need to stop being so jumpy or Mama is going to suspect something is up.

"Abigail, would you be a dear and get that for me?" Mama rushes into the kitchen.

"*Oui*, Mama." I glimpse out the peephole, my hands still.

Completely thrown off, I stare wordless at the tall dark-skinned man standing on my doorstep with his hands folded behind his back. It's definitely not Erianne. It's Jimmy, and I have no idea what he's doing here. *Oh, hell*. He cannot be here right now. I have to think of something quickly or Mama is going to freak out.

"Who is it, *chère*?" Mama shouts from the kitchen.

"It's just Erianne, Mama!" I shout back over my shoulder and open the door as the knocking starts again.

I whisper, "What are you doing here?"

"Mr. Danforth sent me," he says with the utmost professionalism.

"Oh, okay. Well, give me a minute and I'll come say hi to her before I leave." Mama shouts.

My eyes fly wide open. "Jimmy, can you please wait outside for me? Preferably inside the car. Please." I frantically plead with him.

"Of course, mademoiselle." He bows slightly and turns down the steps.

I quickly shut the door. Mama walks into the sitting room with her keys and purse in hand.

"Where's Erianne?" she asks as she scans the room.

"Uh. She couldn't stay. She wants to get going before all the good dresses are taken." I lie. Again.

"Oh, okay. I'll see her later. Aren't you going to get going dear?" She stares at me.

I grab my leather jacket off the arm of the sofa. *"Oui,* of course. I just forgot my coat and wanted to ask you if there's any particular color you'd want." I lie more.

My mother smiles tenderly. "Surprise me."

She gives me a hug and rushes out the door as her pager beeps again. I don't even need to guess who's paging her. The office hasn't even opened and he's already paging her.

Now that she's gone, I breathe a sigh of relief. That was close. *Merde.* I rush out the door and down the steps. I almost forgot about Jimmy waiting outside. What's he doing here anyway?

The driver side door of the black sedan parked on the curb opens as I reach the sidewalk. I'm fairly sure I know why he's getting out of the car, but it's really unnecessary. I ignore him and walk around the to open the passenger door myself. Jimmy grunts his disapproval as I climb in. He reaches to shut the door for me, but I beat him to it. What is it with him and Lucas? I have arms. I'm capable of operating a car door.

"So, what did Lucas send you here for?" I ask as Jimmy drives out onto my street.

"My orders were to pick you up and escort you to *Mère Caterina's.*" Jimmy glances at me through the rearview.

Caterina's is a dress shop in Rouen. It isn't just any dress shop though. It's fancy as hell and beyond expensive. I mean fancy as in you have to have a six-figure income just to be able to afford a thread off of one of the dresses there.

Lucas cannot be serious. He's doing too much. A small smile greets my lips at the thought of him. *Ugh.* I shouldn't even be here. After the ball, I need to cut all ties with him. He has to understand and if he doesn't, I'll just have to make him understand. Not only will I be safer that way, but so will everyone else. I'll never have a chance to fix things with Erianne if I don't.

The car pulls up to the dress shop, but Jimmy stays put in the front seat. For him, this is really weird because he's usually already jumping out to open my door. Maybe he took the hint. I take in the beauty that is *Mere Caterina*. And that's when I see it. Or rather, see *him*.

Lucas is standing tall in front of the dress shop with his suit jacket casually slung over his shoulder. The curves of his muscles stress the fabric of the light blue button up he's wearing. No tie and he's got a wicked grin plastered on his face. I'm suddenly more optimistic about this shopping trip as I watch his tousled black hair fall in a mess. I'm going to get the fun Lucas.

I hop out of the car as he approaches, making every attempt to not give him the satisfaction of knowing I'm sort of happy to see him. The sun damn near blinds me as it reflects off the gold letters of *Mere Caterina*.

Shielding my eyes, I walk right past Lucas into the store, but come to a skidding halt once my sights set on all the luxurious gowns hanging from racks and dressed on elegantly posed mannequins. It's overwhelming and impossible to keep myself from staring in awe.

"Which one do you like?" Lucas places his hand flat on my back.

"What are we doing here Lucas?" My mouth twists downward.

He smirks. "Well, Abigail. You're going to the masquerade ball, right?"

I eye him suspiciously. "...*Oui*."

"Then you'll need a dress." Lucas says simply. "Unless you'd rather go wearing nothing at all?" He shoots me a mischievous grin and walks off toward a rack of dresses.

Heat rises in my face. "No."

"No to going naked, or no to this dress?" He holds up a skimpy red dress. It really should just be a loin cloth because that's about how much material the dress consists of.

I narrow my eyes. "No to both."

I might as well see what they have here. It won't hurt to just take a little peek. This green and black one could work. Checking the price tag, I change my mind about that. He might be paying for all of this, but I'm not trying to rank up a six-digit bill. Nonchalantly putting it back on the rack, I catch a glimpse of a tall petite blonde in a black dress sauntering through the aisle, right over to me.

"May I help you?" A snide smirk crawls over her face.

"No. I'm good." Forcing a polite smile, I turn away from her.

She reaches for my arm, stopping me in place. I turn to face her. She wrinkles her nose as she takes in my outfit. Her mouth opens as if she's going to speak, but abruptly closes again. Her cheeks instantly turn redder than the dress Lucas showed me a second ago. I would have thought she would have some snarky remark to say.

Someone's arm grazes across my back, wrapping around my waist and gripping tightly. Peering up, I'm greeted by Lucas' reddened face. His lips set in a firm line. The woman drops my arm as if it's on fire. Lucas plants a swift kiss on my forehead then stares daggers at the platinum blonde bimbo.

"Jazelle. Show my dear Abigail here around, and help her with anything she needs," Lucas barks.

His 'dear Abigail'? What? He needs to stop right there. I'm not his 'dear' anything.

"Yes. Of course, Mr. Danforth. I was just offering my assistance to this lovely lady." She plasters the biggest fake smile over her face that I've ever seen.

"I'm sure you were," Lucas snaps.

"It's okay. I can show myself around." I wriggle free from Lucas and walk over to another rack of dresses.

As I'm sifting through a couple gowns, I peek up at Lucas. He's still talking to Jazelle. Veins are bulging in his neck, and his face is so red, it would explode if it could. She looks like she's ready to cry as she takes her apron off and storms away. Lucas unbuttons the top button of his shirt as he spins around, searching around the store until his gaze lands on me.

I quickly skim through the dresses, hoping he doesn't realize how nosey I'm being. What else does he expect from me, of all people, though?

"One of your women?" I ask curtly, not making eye contact with him.

"*Was* one of my employees," he says tight-lipped.

"Was?" I gape at him.

Lucas' smiles fondly at me, his tension melting. "My ever-curious Abigail. I fired her."

"You what? How did you fire her?" The man is taking his position of 'power' a little too far. "You can't just go around firing people from their jobs just because you're…" I stop myself.

I almost called him a mob prince to his face. Like that will really get me anywhere good.

Lucas grins and reaches up, lifting my chin. I stare into those intensely crystal blue eyes.

"I fired her because I own this place." His thumb skims across my bottom lip. "I named this place after my mother." A flash of pain surfaces in his eyes. Mentioning her takes him to a dark place.

"I think that's sweet." I run my hand across his arm, hoping to soothe him.

I find a cute blue ball gown with silver trim. "I like this one." I pull it tightly against my body to further distract him. His eyes darken as he takes a step closer to me. "I want to try it on." I turn away from him, sauntering across the store to where a sign in gold letters says, 'fitting rooms'.

Lucas stalks behind, like a lion to his prey. I hurry into the stall. That might have worked a little too well. I didn't even get a good look at the dress I grabbed. Hanging it up, what I thought was silver trim is actually diamonds. Like, real diamonds. The top of the bodice is lined with them and the diamonds sprinkle down like rain drops to the waist of the dress. More diamonds fade into the skirt of the navy-blue ball gown.

I'm not one for glitz and glam, but this... I could get used to something like this. Diamonds are supposed to be a girl's best friend, right? And I'm lacking in the bestie department. It's like this dress and I were made for each other. I run my hand down the outside layer of sheer fabric on the skirt. To think, there are people who wear things like this all the time.

"Do you need help in there?" Lucas calls in a low grumble from the other side of the door.

I roll my eyes. "No, *Mr. Danforth*. I do not."

The laugh that follows is good to hear. Playful Lucas is back.

The gown slips right up over my hips and hugs my waist. The thick, poofy skirt flares out and skims the floor. The skirt has the perfect amount of layers—not too thick and not too relaxed. I reach around trying to hook the clasp, but no luck.

"Lucas..." I'm dreading the torment I'm about to receive from him. "I need help with the clasp..."

The stall door flies open as Lucas slips inside. I watch in the mirror as my face burns crimson. I didn't expect him to walk right in. I thought maybe he would make some lude comments and get another woman to help me.

The other ninety-eight percent of me is mortified. This is a little too intimate. He won't even look down though. He's staring straight into my eyes. I'm genuinely surprised at how silent he's being too. I expected some kind of teasing. Yet, nothing.

He twirls his finger, gesturing for me to turn around. Staring at him through the mirror, his face is unreadable as he fastens the clasp on the back of the dress. So chivalrous. Another side of him I didn't think existed.

Lucas' eyes bore into mine as he rests his hands on my shoulders, "What is it?"

I grin. "Nothing."

Lucas kisses the top of my head. "I like this dress."

I stare at the dress snugging my body and smile admiringly. "I do too."

Lucas runs his hands down my arms. "Get dressed. There's somewhere I want to take you."

I nod my head in agreement and he leaves the fitting room. I'm not going to lie, taking this gown off is going to be depressing. It's so beautiful and I feel like a million bucks in it. I know I'll probably never see it again. So, I just want to soak this in for a little longer.

Lucas' phone rings as I'm getting changed. "I understand… No, I just think this can wait… Of course, I value the importance of this…" The tension in his voice, is thick. "I'm busy… I know business is important… Fine!" He growls.

He ends the call as I'm walking out of the stall. His hand is wound so tightly around the phone his knuckles are blooming ghostly white. That didn't sound good.

"Everything okay?" I cautiously ask.

Lucas runs a hand through his hair and sighs heavily. "Oui. Just business as usual."

Wringing my hands, I stare down at my feet. So much for carefree Lucas. I wonder who called and what it was about. It sounded pretty serious and almost like he was given an order about something. I think it was his father. Could he have found out Lucas is working against him to help me? Maybe I'm being paranoid.

Lucas exhales deeply. "I have to go. I'll give you a ride home."

I nod and fall in step with him. My plan was to talk to him about Mama going with me to the ball, but I don't know if this is the best time. So, I keep quiet on the ride to my house. Lucas is staring out his window, rubbing his chin. I can't help wondering what he's brooding about.

"I'll pick you up at seven the day of the ball." Lucas breaks the silence as we pull up to the sidewalk in front of my place. He won't even look at me.

Merde. "You can't. My mama is coming with me. She wouldn't let me come without her."

I hoped I'd be able to break this to him a little easier. And not when he's already in a bad mood. Lucas pinches the bridge of his nose, squeezing his eyes shut.

"Okay. I'll send Jimmy then. I won't have you, and now your mother," he glares at me, "arriving alone."

"Thank you." I nod. "She's going to need a dress too."

He sighs. "I'll handle it."

I reach over, grabbing his hand. "I'm sure whatever is going on, you'll handle it like the junior boss you are."

He chuckles and squeezes my hand gently. Something serious happened on that phone call to get him this mad. His shoulders relax and a lopsided, tight lipped smile greets his mouth.

"No. It's okay. I'll be seeing you." He says calmly.

I nod. "Until then."

21

Work is as trying as usual, but I haven't seen Erianne since our argument. Working with her right now is…difficult.

I miss her.

Nothing I can say will fix anything between us because I haven't stopped seeing Lucas. In fact, now that I think about it, I've seen him more. Again, though, none of it has been by my choosing. The man does what he wants. She should know that, seeing as she's the one that's grown up with the guy. None of that matters though. What matters is putting an end to all this at the ball, getting my best friend back, and not having to worry about anyone's safety.

I pin up an order sheet in the kitchen window. The customers at table six must really like fish. That's all everyone ordered. I grab the entrees for tables seven and two, balancing the four plates like a pro. It only took me a couple months to get the hang of this.

My stomach does a catapult as I stop dead in my tracks. The sight of Lucas casually sitting at a table throws my balancing skills to the test. I stumble and about drop everything. The food's presentation has definitely taken a hit. My heart is thumping wildly. What the hell is he doing here? And he's sitting in my section. *Oh, hell*. There's no way I can have anyone cover his table. The only person that possibly could is Erianne and she's not even talking to me. Great. I have to serve him.

I can do this. I take a deep breath and serve the entrees in my hand. With one last deep breath, I walk over to take his order. I catch him grinning at another server walking by. She giggles and waves at him. *Ugh.* Doesn't he have enough women falling all over him?

"Welcome to La Couronne. Can I get you started with a glass of wine?" I say professionally like I don't even know him.

Maybe if I keep it professional, short, and sweet, he'll get the hint. But he doesn't even realize I'm here. He's too busy checking out the other server and watching her as she's walking away. Oh, give me a break.

I obnoxiously clear my throat. "Excuse me. *Monsieur.* Could I get you a glass of wine?"

"Hm?" He grins as the server bends over to pick up her pin she dropped. "*Oui, bien sûr*" He waves me off.

I close my eyes and take a deep breath. I'm positive I'll get fired if I yell at him. So, can't do that. Let's try this one more time. I set the menu down on the table hard enough it makes a thud. Lucas breaks his gaze from the server to meet my eyes and gives me a wolfish grin.

"Hey, Abby. I didn't see you there."

Deep breaths. "Hm. Maybe because you were too busy gawking."

His grin widens. "Maybe." He furrows his brow. "What are you doing here?"

I sigh. "I work here. But you know that already. Now. Wine?"

He rubs his chin thoughtfully. "Maybe."

I throw my hands up. "That's it! When you decide what you would like to eat, I'll be back."

I turn and walk away despite him trying to call for me. I cannot talk to him like it's no big deal. That's the last thing I need Erianne to see. And being friendly with him isn't a good idea. I can be cordial and polite. Sure. But not friends. It's better that way since no one knows what his father wants with me.

As I'm grabbing food from the window to serve, the door to the entrance of the restaurant chimes. Great. More customers. They aren't exactly being mindful of the other people eating either. They're high pitched laughing and voices are making my ears ring. What's odd is the voices carrying across the restaurant are vaguely familiar. I walk over to greet them, and it hits me. I know exactly why they're so familiar.

Its William, Monae, and the rest of their friends.

What am I supposed to do? As much as I want to, I can't just run off like I did last time. All the air is leaving my lungs faster than I can fill them. I have to calm down. I'm at work this time. No doubt Delano is watching. I have to handle this professionally, calmly. Taking a deep breath, I waltz over to them.

"Welcome to La Couronne. If you will follow me, I will show you to your seats." Acting as if I have no clue who they are, I grab six menus.

"Abigail?" Monae snickers. "Oh, this is rich. It's great!" She starts whispering with her friends.

Whatever she said, the four of them are laughing together about it. I have no doubt it's at my expense. She hasn't changed one bit. Her cardboard flat brunette hair flares out around her face. Monae has always been in shape, having the right curves in the right places. None of that distracted attention from her gaping forehead though. Her brown eyes are staring, mocking me.

I clench my jaw, reminding myself, again, I'm at work. "Right this way."

Their whispering and laughing carries on as I walk them to their table. William is oddly silent. I can't muster up the courage to even look him in the face. I'm afraid if I do, I'll lose my composure. *Calm down. Calm down.*

I recognize the other guy with them. He's Erianne's friend. The same one she tried to introduce me to at O'Kallaghan's. The smirk on his face gives away how amused he is by this situation.

"How have you been Abigail?" The sound of William's voice sends a chill down my spine and makes my chest ache.

What's worse is that he's being nice. His question sounds genuine. Concerned almost. After being with him for two years, I can tell the littlest things about him.

I watch from my peripheral as Monae elbows him from her seat. "Why do you care?"

Doing everything I can to suppress the laugh daring to escape my mouth, I start handing out their menus. Anything that pisses her off makes me absolutely thrilled.

"Hey. How about that date?" The other guy chimes in. He starts laughing with the girls and nudges William. They couldn't possibly be more childish.

The sound of heels tapping against the wood floors stops next to me. I never thought I'd miss that exasperating sound so much. "Excuse me. Is there something I can help with?"

Peering at Erianne, I ignore William completely. She nods and smiles. Having her standing here backing me up, gives me some confidence. Since becoming friends with Erianne, my confidence has been through the roof. That's what friends are meant to do. They're meant to hold you up in time of weakness and show you what an ass you're being at times. Erianne reminded me of that. I'm not going to stand here and let Monae try to take that away again. I'm not a coward.

"*Oui*. I don't like our server. I think I'd like to speak to the manager." Monae says, puffing her chest.

I. Have. Had it!

"Monae. Shove it up your ass!" Everyone at the table stops talking and gawks at me.

Erianne's jaw drops. Heavy footsteps draw near until they stop completely on the other side of me. I glance up and catch Lucas' steely glare locked on the people at the table. The veins in his neck are bulging as he seethes. His fists are balled at his sides, knuckles blanched.

"Excuse me?" Monae snaps, bringing my attention back to her.

I stand my ground. "I believe you heard me. Shove. It. Up. Your. Ass." her friends gasp. "I am so sick of this pathetic act for attention. You've done this since we were kids. I'd get something new and you would either take it or complain about how bad it was. I'd get a new outfit and you would gripe about it being cheap. But then you'd end up with the same outfit. It's like you had to have everything I had, especially if anyone else showed the slightest bit of interest in it. Hell, you couldn't even get your own boyfriend. You went and slept with mine. I guess that just goes to show how cheap *you* are." I stare her down as a hundred-pound weight lifts off my shoulders.

Monae lurches from her chair. "You dirty little..."

Before her hand can connect with my face, Erianne grabs her by her wrist. "I think it's time for you to leave." Erianne's grip tightens as she glares at Monae.

Lucas steps forward. Erianne shakes her head at him and he backs off.

Monae looks between Erianne and Lucas, then yanks her hand from Erianne's grasp. "Come on. Let's go. This place is filled with trash anyway."

Monae snarls at me before grabbing her purse and walking toward the door with her nose in the air. The three girls follow in line behind her. Just like puppets.

"Come on, man. Let's get out of here." The other guy nudges William.

I grab onto the last bit of confidence in me and face William. His blonde hair is messy as it always was. The steely green eyes I used to be so fond of stare back at me with longing. But why? He chose everything he has. Looking at him now, I expect to be filled with the same longing. I expect to be filled with the grief of having lost him, the man I once loved, the man that once filled my every waking day.

But. I'm not. I'm...okay. This is throwing me off guard, but I feel so at peace. With him, I'm not sad. I don't feel like I've lost anything at all. All the heaviness that's been weighing on me since the breakup, lifts with the realization that I no longer love the man sitting in front of me. He can't hurt me anymore.

An ear-splitting grin spreads on my face. "Better get going. Wouldn't want to keep your girlfriend waiting."

He scoffs. "What happened to you?"

I beam at him, ready to answer that question, but Lucas intertwines his fingers with mine. "Leave. Now." He growls.

William glares. "Who are you?"

Lucas steps forward and tries to release my hand. I squeeze, not letting him go. He glances down at me and, without looking away, says, "Her boyfriend."

William sits back, stricken, but says nothing. His face pales and he leaves with the rest of his crowd, glancing at me once more on the way out.

Damn, that felt good!

I laugh, still reveling in what I just did. I peek up at Lucas, guilt eating at me for how I acted with him a minute ago. He nods and squeezes my hand gently. I forgot he's holding my hand but drop it like it's on fire as heat rises in my cheeks. He grins and silently walks away, back to his table like nothing happened.

"Way to handle that. Where has all that spunk been?" Erianne beams at me proudly.

"I guess I learned from the best." I grin. "Thanks for helping by the way." I almost forgot we aren't friends anymore.

She playfully nudges me. "I didn't do anything. Besides, that's what friends are for, right?"

"Friends?" I know she just helped me out, but I thought we weren't talking anymore.

Erianne rolls her eyes. "Of course, friends. You think because we had one fight, we aren't friends anymore? Can't get rid of me that easily, Abbs." She winks.

Hearing her call me 'Abbs' is something I never thought I'd miss so much.

"Abigail!" Delano's barks across the restaurant.

"You'd better go. We'll talk later," Erianne says, returning to her work.

Delano really does have the worst timing. I find him standing in front of his office door, just before the breakroom.

"My office. Now," he says through gritted teeth.

This can't be good. The lock on the door clicks behind me and my chest tighten. Why would he need to lock the door? Alarm bells blare in my head. Something isn't right. After what I heard him say to Lucas, I don't like this.

"Do you know why I've called you in here?" Delano asks as he takes a seat in the chair behind his desk.

"Not at all." Get to the point, Delano.

"I noticed you treated some of our guests poorly. Some very affluent guests." He folds his hands together.

I take a seat in the chair across from his desk. "Sir, I can explain."

"I don't want to hear it. You know the policy on how we are to treat our guests. The owners would be quick to let you go if I were to tell them about this." A dark, sardonic sneer creeps over his mouth.

My heart sinks as I realize I'm probably about to be fired. "Please, Delano, I need this job. I assure you. It won't happen again."

He holds his hands up. "I'm not going to tell them, but don't let this happen again. We value your employment here." His sneer grows wider.

Relief floods through me like a tidal wave. "Thank you. You have no idea how much I appreciate that." I sink into the chair.

Delano gets up from his chair, moving closer, sitting on the edge of his desk in front of me. His proximity is really unsettling. I lean back further in my chair to put even the slightest bit of distance between us.

"Now that we've settled that." He crosses his legs, peering down at me. "I'm sure you've heard of the Vitale ball that's tonight."

"...I have." Where is he going with this?

"Well, how would you like to accompany me there?" he asks smugly. As if I'm going to start gushing. As if him asking me is an honor or something.

I do my best not to roll my eyes at him. "I actually have a date, but thanks for the offer."

The fixed dark expression that etches over his face sends a chill through my whole body. "I'd better get back to work."

He doesn't move a muscle as I try to squeeze through the little space left between us, which only makes me more uncomfortable. Not trusting his reaction to me rejecting him, I hurry out of the office, letting the door slam behind me.

"What was that about?" Erianne scares the hell out of me as she pops around the corner.

"Erianne!" I shout.

"Why are you so jumpy? He didn't fire you, did he? Cause I'll kick his ass." She shoots a glare toward the office.

"No. He actually asked me to the masquerade ball tonight." I can hardly finish my sentence without laughing.

Erianne on the other hand has already burst out laughing. "He…what?"

"*Oui.* You can stop laughing now." I try to hide my own amusement with what just happened.

"I'm sorry, but that's just priceless." She grips her stomach trying to contain herself.

"Anyway…are you going to the ball?" I ask hopeful that this doesn't make the conversation take a turn for the worse.

"Yes. Aren't you going with Lucas?" She grins, still amused.

Oh, hell. "Uhm…" I stop myself because I don't want to lie to her, but I'm afraid the truth will cause another argument.

Erianne sighs. "Abigail, listen. I may not understand why you're doing what you are, but I'm your friend. It was wrong of me to just stop being here for you. If you want to see Lucas, then you have my support. Besides, I saw him the other day. He's seems alive again and happy. I haven't seen him this happy since before his Mama passed. All I want is you to be happy too, even if I don't agree with your choices."

Her words are like music to my ears. Thank god!

"I appreciate that. But I'm not going with Lucas." She lowers her eyes at me. "I am meeting him there, but I'm not going there with him. I actually convinced my mama to go," I say proudly.

Erianne's stares wide-eyed and unblinking. "How in the hell did you manage that?"

I grin. "She apparently thinks that I won't get into any trouble if she comes along."

"Yeah. Tell her I said good luck with that!" Erianne scoffs.

"Whatever!" I smack her playfully.

Laughing with her makes everything feel better. Finally, things feel somewhat normal again. She gets back to work, and I'm left wondering if I should repay Lucas for coming to my defense like that. William backed down as soon as he said he's my boyfriend. It's obviously not true, but William doesn't know that. I have to at least tell him thank you. I grab a menu and waltz over to Lucas table.

"Hey, babe!" He calls, catching me off guard. Hearing him say that makes me stop abruptly. My chest tightens and grows lighter.

I take a breath. "For one, I'm not your girlfriend." I hold my hand up as he's about to speak. "Two. Thank you. I...really appreciate what you did." I chuckle. "Exes, am I right?'

Lucas smile falters, but he plasters it right back on. "You can take me to dinner tonight to say thanks."

I suppress a smile. "Nice try."

He drapes his arm over the back of the chair. "Come on. I heard Erianne. She doesn't care if we're friends. Two friends can go to dinner especially after one just rode in on his white horse."

I laugh and playfully smack his arm with the menu.

He chuckles and narrows his eyes. "Besides, I'm your best possible ally against my father."

He's got a point there. I've thought that since I found out about all of this. What better ally to have in my line of defense than my enemy's own son? And he even said as friends. So, no harm in it.

"As friends?" I ask.

He nods. "Friends."

"Be here at 8. We can go after my shift."

I hope Lucas doesn't get all snobby with me about what I have planned. It's not like this is a date. It's just a thank you from one friend to another. I grab the to-go boxes from the kitchen window after clocking out. Erianne is closing tonight. So, she'll be here until almost midnight. I wave to her as I'm walking out the door. She beams and waves back. My heart has never felt so full. I got my best friend back. There's no tension and I've made one hell of an ally in this thing against Lucas' father. Speaking of Lucas, he's standing by his car, hands in the pockets of his dress slacks.

I smile warmly. "You ready?"

He opens the car door. "Always."

"Actually, I thought we could walk."

He shuts the door and nods. "Lead the way."

He follows as I walk through the park across from the restaurant. I don't want to be visible from there. So, I find a table at the furthest end and set up the food in the to-go boxes. Filet of beef for him and salmon for me. It's the only thing I know for sure he likes because he ate it when we went to L'Hermitage. And it's only right I get the same thing too.

"I brought dinner to us." I beam.

He nods in appreciation. "I like it."

"You do?" I tilt my head.

He chuckles. "Did you think I wouldn't?"

I wring my hands. "Maybe. You don't seem to like simple things."

He takes a seat at the wooden table with me. "There's a lot you don't know about me." He reaches over and grabs the beef entree. "Like how I love picnics in the park with beautiful girls."

I roll my eyes. Of course, he can't go long without putting on that charm, even though he knows it doesn't work on me. A couple walks by, not noticing us as they talk amongst themselves. I can't shake the thought in the back of my mind. What if Lucas and I hanging out gets back to his father? The person responsible for keeping tabs on me, now that Erianne walked away, could be watching as we speak. My smile turns downward, and I fidget with my hands, scanning the park.

"Hey. Maybe we should go somewhere else." I suggest.

He furrows his brow. "Why? What's wrong?"

I glance down at my hands. "I…just… What if your father finds out?"

Lucas reaches across the table. "Give me your hand." I tilt my hand and he waggles his fingers. "Hand." I slowly place my hand on his and he encloses it gently. "I'm the one in charge of keeping tabs on you. You left work twenty minutes ago on schedule and right now you're at home. You turned out all the lights and went to bed. Right now, you're sound asleep. Do you understand?"

Wait a minute. So…he's the one filling in for Erianne? I thought it's been some random goon. All this time, it's been him. I don't know how to feel about this.

My heart beats faster. "Does Erianne know?"

Lucas nods. I stand and back away. So, her 'giving her blessing' or whatever, is only because he's already keeping tabs on me anyway. It's not because she's seen how happy he is. I can't believe this. Can I trust anyone? I shake my head and walk away from the table. I need a second to myself. Staring up at the clear night sky is peaceful. There's no dark clouds hanging around and the stars are sparkling like tiny lights. A hand rest on my shoulder as I'm gazing up.

"Hey. What's going through your mind." Lucas asks, staring up.

I shake my head. "How can I know who to trust? Everyone seems to be a part of this thing your father has against me. What does he even want with me?"

Lucas shoves his hands in his pockets. "Let's not talk about that."

I face him. "Why not? Why can't anyone tell me what the hell is really going on?"

He takes my hand in his. "Walk with me?"

He steps forward and lightly tugs on my hand. I sigh, giving in. Walking with him isn't awkward at all. It's just comfortable. There's no expectation of me to fill the silence, no expectations between us either. I can relax and take a minute to just breathe.

"How is Mathieu?" Lucas asks as we walk along the church.

I chuckle. That's the last question I'd ever expect him to ask me.

"Well?" He playfully nudges me.

I smile. "Well, nothing. I told him we would be better off as friends."

"Ha! So, I won our bet. That's called 'game'." He brushes his shoulders.

Okay. Now he's just being goofy. I laugh. "Sorry to burst your bubble, but I told him on the first and only date we went on. So, technically, I won. *He* never thought of *me* again. Not the other way around. And also, you have no *game*."

He scoffs. "I have game. And panty-dropping charm." He flashes that devious smile of his. "Any of my girlfriends would agree."

My chest lightens with each laugh. "It's a good thing you're not my boyfriend then."

Lucas raises a brow, then quickly wraps his arms around my waist, step by step backing me up until my back presses against the cool, rough surface of the church wall. His finger gently lifts my chin.

His voice deepens and is barely a whisper, "What if I want to be your boyfriend?" His mouth moves just centimeters away from my ear. "What if I want you? All to myself."

My breath hitches. Every nerve in my body is on high alert. An ache blossoms in my gut. The tickle of his fingertips traces down from my shoulder all the way to my wrist. He pulls my hand up to his mouth. The contact of his lips on my skin sends a delicious shiver down my spine. His lips linger a little longer on my knuckles, deepening the ache in my gut. I stare and watch intently until he drops my hand. He backs away, a full-blown megawatt smile slowly creeping across his mouth, eyes alight.

My jaw drops. "No way! Were you just teasing me?"

He laughs, nearly doubling over.

I punch his arm. "Not cool! You don't get to tease me like that!"

He waggles his eyebrows. "Who says I wasn't serious about what I said? Maybe I was?"

After Lucas is done teasing me, he takes me home. Ants got to our food while we were talking, which sucks. I was looking forward to that. I can't get what he said out of my mind. Was he joking or being serious? If he was being serious, could I really picture myself with him? I wouldn't have to worry about Erianne being mad about it. But there's still the fact he's a freaking mob prince. And how could I ever trust that he wouldn't, or isn't, just helping his father? I don't know who I can trust anymore.

With all the things I don't know yet, there *is* one thing I'm absolutely certain of: despite everything going on, there's this happiness that's been awaken deep within me. And I'm craving more of it.

22

August 16th could not have crept up any slower since I got that invitation to the Vitale ball. It's the day of the ball and as much as I'd like to attend this thing and have the time of my life, that's not what I'm going for. Lucas needs me there to find out who sent the invitation in the first place. I'm not going to have fun. It's time to put an end to all this craziness.

I've been bursting with a newfound lightness. Erianne is talking to me again. I faced Monae and William. Ever since I did and felt absolutely nothing, I feel free. Like there's a space in my heart that's been cleared for better things. Better blue-eyed, tall, devilishly sexy things. What Erianne said about Lucas being happier than he's been in a while is bugging me. I'm not sure if she meant it or if her being okay with me being around him has something to do with his father.

Lucas helps me forget everything going on when we hang out. He's constantly goofing off. When I first met him, I never would have thought he had a carefree bone in his body. It didn't help that all I heard was bad things about him: He's dangerous, no good, and his heart is ice cold, void of any emotions.

Okay, so maybe that last one isn't true, but that's pretty much the message I got. Then I ran into him at La Luna and everything changed after I gave him the benefit of the doubt. Past his rigid…well-built but rigid exterior, there's a good guy, and I might want to get to know him. I need to make up my mind. Either I'm going to stop talking to him after tonight or tell him how I'm feeling. I have to really think this through. He might end up being a good guy, but there's no ignoring he's a mob prince.

I still can't believe Delano really asked me to go to the ball with him. Lucas is going to get a kick out of that…on second thought, that might not be such a good idea. After what Lucas already did to him, the saints only know how he's going to react this time. I think I have a rather good idea though.

Climbing the steps to my flat, a large black box on the stoop grabs my attention. A silk crimson ribbon is wrapped around it and tied into a bow. More anonymous stuff? I'm not sure if I should be worried or excited. I brace myself as I approach the box and pull a small white envelope off the top. It's blank, but there's a card inside. Breaking the seal, I read the card.

Tonight at 7.

- Lucas

That's all that's written inside the black and white card. Subtle Lucas.

I pick the box up, allowing myself to welcome the ear-splitting grin forcing its way on my face. Now that I know Lucas sent this, there's nothing to worry about. The box is kind of heavy. It's hard to juggle it while I'm trying to get my front door open. It's got to be my dress.

"What's that dear?" Mama asks as she sees me walking inside, holding the large box.

I quickly hide the card. "I'm not sure. I think Erianne might have dropped our dresses off for me." *Lies, Abigail. All lies.* I wish I could be honest with her.

"Oh. Well, let's see them, then." Mama takes a seat on the sofa, patiently waiting for me to open the box.

Here goes nothing.

I carefully unravel the bow and slowly slide the lid off. The familiar navy-blue gown lays inside. The gown I tried on when I went to Caterina's with Lucas. It's really here, lying in front of me. A knot forms in my throat. It's like it got even more beautiful just from officially being mine.

The diamonds along the bodice sparkle under the lamp's glow as I pull the gown out. I hold it up to myself and sway side to side, listening to the skirt swish back and forth. This is so different from just trying it on at the store. Stealing a glance at Mama, her bottom lip is trembling.

"It's absolutely beautiful, Abigail!"

"Thank you, Mama." I smile and set my dress aside, eager to find out what else is in the box.

On top of a layer of navy-blue fabric lies another black and white card.

For your mother.

Pulling the dress out, I can already tell it matches mine. He picked out a sleek evening gown for her in the same navy-blue fabric. Holding it up, I notice the sheer cape connected to the lace trim at the top of the bodice. It drapes down the back of the dress. I think it suits her. It's modest, but elegant.

"This one is yours." I explain.

Her eyes light up. "I love it!" She takes the dress out of my hands. "Abigail. There's other boxes inside here." Mama removes three small crimson boxes.

Huh? I didn't know there was anything in there besides the dresses. I open one of the red rectangular boxes to find a pair of silver heels, each strap lined with diamonds to match my dress. *Woah.* It's so many diamonds.

"*Mon trésor*, look!" Mama holds out a pair of velvet black heels. "That Erianne. She is such a sweetheart." I almost forgot she thinks this is all from Erianne. "Well, don't just stand there! Open the last one," she rushes me.

A grin creases at the corner of my mouth. I've never seen her this excited about something. I grab the last red one and open it. Lying inside are two masks. One is black, silver, and navy with *more* diamonds. I don't know if I can handle much more with all these diamonds. It's a little over the top for me. The other mask is a black velvet with a navy-blue sheer rose attached on the side. I have to say the man really has taste. These outfits are incredible.

"I don't know about you, but I think I'm going to go get ready now." Mama says.

With her dress draped over her arm, she casually snatches up her mask and rushes upstairs. I burst into fits of laughter. I can't help it. It's nice seeing her relax so much. Guess I'd better start getting ready too, seeing as the ball is in three hours.

It takes me a little over an hour to apply some makeup and fix my hair before slipping into my ball gown. Almost ready. Just need to get my shoes on. Pulling the heels out, I notice a small black velvet case lying underneath. I didn't see this earlier. Popping it open, my jaw hits the floor. *More* diamonds. A set of diamond earrings are resting next to a silver necklace with a small diamond pendant dangling. It's overwhelming. A note is printed on the inside of the jewelry case.

For my dear Abigail

Now he's really outdone himself. This whole thing is just to put a stop to the people sending me stuff. But I'd be lying if I said a part of me doesn't want it to be more. And I still think being closer to him would only make me and everyone around me a lot safer. He can protect us. He's a mob prince for saint's sake.

"Abigail, how is it coming along in there? You almost ready?" Mama asks from outside of my room.

I slam the case shut. "I'm almost ready. I just have to get my mask and shoes on." I slip my feet into the straps of my shoes.

"Let me help with your mask." She waltzes in.

I freeze at the sight of her. That's my mama, standing in an elegant gown cascading down to the floor. Her hair is up in an array of loose ringlets. The navy flower on her mask lays vibrantly against her chocolate-brown hair. She looks beautiful all the time, but right now she is absolutely glowing.

"Mama…You look amazing." I stare in awe.

"Thank you, *chère*." She grins. "Here." She grabs the mask off my desk as I finish fastening my shoe.

I curled my hair and left it down to flow freely. Erianne showed me how to curl it the same way she did when we went to La Luna's. There's a sudden hollow echo of rapping on the door to our flat just as Mama finishes tying my mask.

"Is that Erianne?" she asks.

"Uh, no, I think that might be the driver. Erianne had other plans, so she sent a car to bring us there." I almost forgot about Jimmy picking us up.

"Oh. Alright. Well, we had better get going then." She leaves my room.

I let her go ahead so I can put my earrings and necklace on. I have to hide the box. She can't find out Lucas has anything to do with all of this. Necklace on. Earrings fastened. Time to go to a masquerade ball.

I have no idea what this night is going to have in store for me, but one thing I'm sure of is this *is* definitely going to be a night to remember.

23

The drive to the castle is long and agonizing. As we cruise up the drive to Chateau de Danforth the lights illuminating the grounds brings everything into focus. A lot of other guests have already arrived, and more are just pulling up.

Once we get past the front gate, I search for Lucas. No sign of him anywhere. I have to remember why I'm here—to find out who invited me in the first place. But first, I need to find Lucas.

"Are you ready?" I ask Mama.

"Yes, dear." Her eyes twinkle as she stares up at the castle.

Mama is always happy, but tonight, she's gushing. I could get used to seeing her like this. It's the least she deserves. She's taken care of me by herself since I was two years old, when my dad died. I mean, she's never even been on a date. I definitely wouldn't be able to stay single for fifteen years. The willpower in her alone is admirable as hell.

Jimmy pulls the car around front. A guy standing by the drive in a black and red tux opens the rear passenger door. The cool crisp air sends chills crawling over my arms and legs. Mama and I climb out, taking in the overwhelming size of the chateau. The lawn stretches for acres as far as I can see. The walls are built with stones of varying shapes and sizes, but each unique. From far away, it was flat grey. Being up close now, it's a mixture of modest rocks no one would give a second glance if they laid alone. But together they make up this breathtaking castle, the trophy of the landscape.

The moonlight shines down on the uneven, dilapidated rooftop. The turrets, crumbling in places, casts shadows over the walls. Moss clings onto the stones nearest to the ground. Flaming torches line the perimeter, warming the surrounding area despite the unsympathetic cold of the mid-August night.

"There you are!" Erianne shouts from across the lawn.

She rushes over with arms outstretched. Her bright red hair, illuminated by the soft glow of the flaming torches, is pinned up on the top of her head and wrapped in the string from her white lace mask. I'm suffocated in a hug from her before I have a chance to refuse or speak.

"Let me look at you!" She's more vibrant than usual. "Abbs, you look amazing. And Carla! Your dress is stunning!" She rushes to give Mama a hug.

"Thank you, sweetheart. I've missed your company at the house." Mama returns her embrace.

As Erianne backs away, I get a better look at her ball gown. She would be daring enough to wear a corset ball gown. I love the black and white design she went with. It's definitely her style. The white corset lined in black sheer fabric snugs her waist, showing off her curves. A single layer of sheer black fabric lines the white skirt.

"Why don't we get inside?" Erianne motions for us to follow her.

Before I have the chance to make it through the tall, looming wooden double doors, someone shouts my name. I'd recognize that high-pitched squeak from anywhere.

"Abigail! Finally, I found you!" Clarissa shouts.

I catch Mama's and Erianne's matching raised eyebrows and crinkling of their foreheads at the sight of Clarissa running toward us.

"Hey, Clarissa." I politely pat her back as she hugs me.

She backs up, pressing her palms together and bouncing on her heels.

Her eyes bore into mine as if it's a matter of life or death. "So. Where is the g—"

"I almost forgot!" I quickly cut her off, "Clarissa. Meet my mother. I came to the ball with her." I shoot Erianne a knowing look, hoping like hell she catches on.

This is not the time for Mama to find out. Not while we're at his father's masquerade ball…in their castle.

"Hello, Abigail's mother. It's nice to meet you." Clarissa fervently shakes Mama's hand.

"You too," she says, a bewildered expression clouding her face.

"Clarissa you've been to one of these before, right?" I ask, hoping to get her to stop shaking Mama's hand.

Clarissa nods enthusiastically. "Yes, plenty of times."

"Would you mind showing my mother inside. I'll be right behind you. I just need to talk to Erianne for a minute."

Mama scowls. I think she feels the same way about Clarissa as I do. Good person, but so much enthusiasm. So. Much.

"Oh. Sure thing!" She intertwines her arms with Mama's and drags her along inside.

"Why did you just do that to your poor mother?" Erianne asks.

I laugh. "Mama doesn't know anything about Lucas. She doesn't even know that I know him."

Erianne puts a hand on her hip. "And let me guess. You want me to help you lie to your Mama?"

"No. I need your help explaining it to her," I playfully pout.

Erianne furrows her brow. "Really?"

Her lack of trust in me is well deserved.

I nod. "Yes. Really. I'm tired of lying about all of it. I tried to keep the truth from you and look at what that got me."

She smiles proudly. "I'm proud of you, Abbs. About damn time."

I playfully nudge her. "Just let me talk to Lucas first, okay?"

Erianne grabs my arm. "I can deal with that." She doesn't waste any more time and drags me along inside with her.

Walking into the ballroom, I'm taken back. Two six-foot crystal chandeliers hang from each sides of the ceiling. The room is lined with intricately placed table settings surrounding the massive dance floor. All of the different dresses and robes and masks are impressive.

One woman is dressed from head to toe in gold. A pure gold mask covers half of her face. Gold satin gloves cover her arms up to her elbows, and a layered gold ball gown claims a foot of space around her. Even her jewelry is gold. I wouldn't be surprised if her shoes and hair are lined in gold.

As I'm admiring the dedication this woman put into her outfit, I notice Lucas in the middle of the crowd. He's standing around, searching for something. Guests dance all around him, but he doesn't care. He's focused, his eyes darting through the crowd.

Most of the men I've seen tonight are wearing black and white tuxedos. He, on the other hand, is wearing all black, aside from the navy-blue tie and handkerchief sticking out of his jacket pocket. His jet-black hair is pushed back and lying underneath the tie of his intricately designed black mask.

His ice-cold blue eyes warm over once they recognize me. A smirk crosses over his mouth, and he glides directly toward me. My heart picks up pace with each step closer. A tight, suffocating sensation throbs in my chest. Fluttering in the pit of my stomach makes me queasy.

Everything around me fades. It's just him, me, and this vast distance between us closing in. I break my stare, glancing at my side where Erianne has been this entire time. I almost forgot about her being here.

She's beaming, looking from Lucas and back to me. Her smile warms my heart. Over her shoulder, I spot Mama and Clarissa making their way toward us. Erianne tilts her head slightly, noticing the pained expression on my face. She turns around, following my gaze.

"I'll take care of it. Go get him," she says with steely determination.

Every bit of worry and panic coursing through my body washes away. Turning to meet Lucas halfway, I collide into a firm surface. He's already standing in front of me. And I just ran into him. Nice.

His hand glides to my waist. "If you wanted to get close to me, all you had to do was ask," he teases.

Heat rushes to my cheeks. Realizing I've been gripping his biceps, I drop my arms and step away. He wraps an arm around my waist and gently pulls me back to him. My breath hitches.

He tilts my head up by my chin. "You look so beautiful, Abigail."

"You don't look too bad yourself." I smile.

He plants the usual kiss on my forehead, but catches me off guard when he leans down, placing a soft kiss on my cheek.

"Dance with me?" Lucas asks.

I nod. He smiles as he entwines his fingers with mine, leading me out onto the dance floor. He's as graceful and smooth as ever as he takes the lead, twirling me around. Despite being surrounded by hundreds of other couples, the space around us isn't restricting. In fact, it's opening up the more we dance. Scanning the room as he spins me around, I notice everyone else has stopped dancing. Their eyes follow our every move. A crowd has formed around us, watching as if it's a spectacle. I catch a few casting glances at me as they whisper to each other.

I whisper, "Lucas… Everyone is staring." My legs are failing me as they grow unsteady.

Lucas wraps an arm around my waist, steadying me. He presses my body firmly against his. My breath hisses past my lips as his hand grips the small of my back. He lifts me off the ground and I quickly grip his shoulders. *Merde. Please don't drop me.* Effortlessly holding my body up, he spins me around. I feel like I'm flying. Like I'm free.

An unfamiliar calm takes over my nerves. I've never felt so at ease, so safe. He isn't going to drop me. Staring down into his eyes, the few short seconds he's spent twirling me in the air pass like minutes. A realization dawns on me. He's never made me feel unsafe or unprotected. Any time I've been around him, I had no doubt I'm protected. He'd never let anything happen to me or anyone I love. I know what I want now. And I know what I'm going to say to him.

Lucas lowers me easily down. My feet connect with the solid wooden surface of the dance floor, grounding me. He holds me, standing still in place as the room erupts into applause.

Gaping at the crowd, I ask, "What just happened?"

Lucas grins. "You just joined me for the first dance of the night. It's tradition that either I or my father perform the first dance to kick off the whole ball."

I stare at him slack-jawed while everyone else disperses. "But…"

Lucas places a finger over my lips to silence me, "No buts. Unless it's yours. Then I'll have to reconsider," he teases, winking.

I playfully smack his arm. His laughter is soothing. I need to get everything off my chest. Now or never. My chest tightens.

"So… I wanted to talk to you about something." I wring my hands.

His hand skims down my spine, stopping at the small of my back. "What is it?"

"We've spent a lot of time together. I know it's only because of this thing with your father. And you're just following his orders." Staring down at my hands, I force the question out. "But I was wondering if it meant more than that to you. If…*I* meant more than that to you."

Lucas lifts my head with a single finger under my chin. His smile meets his eyes. "My dear, ever-curious Abigail—"

"Excuse me, monsieur." A short man wearing no mask interrupts him.

"What is it, Lenny?" Lucas glares daggers at the man standing next to us.

I turn my glare on the man. I'm just as mad. He hardly looks like he should be here. He's not even wearing a tux. Or dress clothes of any kind for that matter. I don't care who he is. Lucas and I were having a moment and he just ruined it. Lucas was about to tell me if he felt anything. *Hell.*

The man clears his throat as his hands tremble. "I apologize for intruding, monsieur. Your father has requested your presence in the meeting hall," Lenny's voice quakes.

Not only is he not dressed right for the ball, he's really skittish for a guy who works for a criminal. It's not hard to put two and two together that he works for them.

The muscles in Lucas' jaw flex. "I'll be right back." Lucas reaches for my hand, briefly kissing the top of it. He shadows behind Lenny.

I had just started allowing myself to enjoy his company. Really enjoy it. Without holding back. I might not get another chance the rest of the night. He's with his father now and I have no intentions of running into that man. This doesn't put a damper on my night at all…

I need Erianne.

I push my way through the crowd until I catch a glimpse of her and my mother. Clarissa isn't with them anymore. As bad as it sounds, I'm sort of relieved about that.

"Well, hello," Erianne says. My mother is standing next to her expectantly.

"Hey." I wave. "Where did Clarissa go?"

Erianne lowers her eyes at the sound of Clarissa's name. She grunts. "She went to join some friends I guess."

I chuckle. "I used to think your peppiness was over the top, but she has you beat."

"*Chère*, who was that you were dancing with?" Mama asks, smiling from ear to ear.

I glimpse expectantly at Erianne. I need to tell my mother about Lucas. No time like the present.

"I'm going to go get drinks. I'll be right back Abbs." Erianne rushes off, taking the hint.

"Mama…I have something I need to tell you." Taking a deep breath, I muster up all my courage.

"What is it, dear?" She reaches for my hand.

Her smile fades slightly. She can tell something is up. This isn't exactly good news. All of a sudden, I'm not all that eager to tell her. I know it's going to upset her and tonight, she's been the happiest I've ever seen her. I don't want to ruin her night. I can't.

"May I have this dance?" A husky man with a full-face mask approaches my mother.

Mama's cheeks blanche. Her gaze darts between us.

"Go ahead. We can talk later." I force a smile.

She gives my hand a reassuring squeeze and lets the man escort her to the dance floor. I have to tell her before the night is over. I can't take the chance of her finding out from someone else. This has to come from me. But she deserves one carefree night. One night where she doesn't have to worry about me. Maybe I should wait until tomorrow. Now isn't the right time.

"I see you've moved on," a man's voice breaks me out of my thoughts.

I turn to find William behind me. The blonde, ruffled hair and steely green eyes scowling back at me easily give him away, even from behind a mask. Three months ago, I'd have fallen apart at the sight of him. Now, I hold my ground, confidence bursting through me.

"Don't you have a girlfriend to tend to?" I snap.

William reaches up, snatching his mask off. "No. I left her."

I laugh half-heartedly. "What, did you get bored with her too?"

He flinches at my brashness. "When did you get so brave?" He mocks.

I think I hurt his little ego. Good. Serves him right. I shake my head. "What are you even still doing here William? I thought you went off to University."

"I've been on holiday break. I go back tomorrow," William pauses and steps closer, "I miss you Abb."

I used to love when he called me that. No one else did. Now, it's void of any meaning.

I scoff, shaking my head. "I guess you should have thought of that before you slept with my best friend then. On my birthday." I roll my eyes. "William. You're an idiot."

I don't even care what he has to say. I wouldn't take him back even if Joan of Arc herself told me to. I shove past him, not wanting to give him another second of my time.

He whips around, yanking me back by my arm. "You really got brave. I left because you held back on me. A man has needs Abb." He snarls. "Didn't you like the flowers I left for you in your hospital room?"

William brings his face inches from mine. His breath is like a bourbon-scented heat wave over my face. My arm stings where he's digging his fingers in. I try to wriggle free from his grasp just as a tall dark figure moves swiftly in front of me, shoving William back.

"I suggest you keep your hands to yourself," Lucas roars.

My shoulders sag. My hero. I rub my arm where William had ahold of me. A dark purple bruise has already begun to form. Lucas whips around, scanning me over and silently checking if I'm okay. His eyes fixate on my arm, zeroing in on the bruise. An unwavering darkness clouds his expression. His jaw tightens as the veins in his neck pop. This is *not* good. May the saints be with William right now. I've never seen Lucas so pissed.

"What the hell!" William shouts, his voice resonating off the high ceiling.

Within seconds, men in black and crimson tuxedos come from all directions, swarming the three of us. I recognize Jimmy amongst them.

Lucas whips around, snatching William up by his collar. "You ever think about laying a hand on Abigail again and I'll end you," he growls.

The menacing threat in his words causes me to flinch. Everyone is staring. He needs to calm down. Reaching forward, I cautiously grasp his hand. Squeezing it slightly, I hope to offer him some solace. Lucas releases him, gently squeezing my hand back.

Jimmy pushes past all the men in suits and grabs ahold of William. I nod my head in thanks to Jimmy. I'm not sure Lucas would have kept his cool much longer, especially if William kept talking.

"Let me go! Are you out of your mind?" William resists, but it's no use. Jimmy's got a tight hold on him.

"I'll handle him, monsieur." Jimmy nods to Lucas.

A couple of other men in matching black and crimson suits make their way through the crowd. Jimmy whispers something in their ear, but I can't make out the words. They turn to leave, towing

William along with them. He struggles and tries to break free. One of the men leans down, putting an arm over him. To any other person, it just looks like a couple of friends. I know better once the man pulls his red silk handkerchief from his suit pocket, covering William's mouth. He falls silent and his body sags against Jimmy's hold. I stare absently as Jimmy, William, and the other men fade out of sight and out the doors, disappearing into the chill of the night.

Lucas turns to face me, his shoulders relaxing when his eyes meet mine. His mouth sets into a firm line. He reaches up, gently removing my hand from my arm to examine the mark. His eyes squeeze shut, the muscles in his jaw tightening. He pulls me close, bringing my hand to his lips.

Losing myself, I yank my hand away and throw my arms around him. The sense of security he brings is magnified as soon as his arms wrap fiercely around me. He presses my head against his chest, encasing me protectively, as if I'm his prized possession he doesn't want to share. I welcome all the emotions that follow with his touch. No more holding back. No more doubts in my mind. I want him.

24

"Thank you." I take a step back, wringing my hands as the heat rises in my cheeks.

Lucas shakes his head. "He's a worthless excuse of a man. You don't need to thank me. He deserves it," he snarls.

The image of Jimmy holding William against his will and saying he'd 'take care of him' is seared into my memory. This is normal for Lucas. This kind of stuff happens all the time. Wanting Lucas means wanting all of that. Could I really accept this? This is the reason I wanted to end all of this. I didn't want anyone else getting hurt because of me. Now that's exactly what is about to happen.

"Lucas…They aren't going to…" I try to ask the question but can't form the words.

"Unfortunately, no. It's not my place to make that decision, but he will pay for laying his hand on you." He casts a fleeting glance behind me, his mouth pressing into a firm line. "I have to go for a minute. Are you going to be okay? Should I leave someone with you?" he asks, eyes boring into mine.

The casual way he talks like that is unsettling. This is normal for him though. Just another part of his life. I don't know how I feel about that.

"I'm okay." I force a smile.

He runs a hand through his hair. "I'm really sorry, Abigail. I promise I'll make this up to you." He plants a swift kiss on my forehead and walks across the room.

Lenny is standing with arms folded behind his back near a set of doors. Lucas brushes past, disappearing into the room behind him. This is not how I pictured the night going. I could really use a hug from my mama right now.

Searching the crowd, I find her amongst a cluster of people on the dance floor. She's laughing and smiling brighter than I've seen in a long time. She's having the time of her life. Seeing her so carefree is possibly the best thing about this night. I should leave her alone.

Walking away quickly, I notice Erianne talking with a man in a black and crimson suit. That's one of Dominick's men. They're the only ones wearing those colors. It's like a uniform or something. Erianne works for them though. Maybe I shouldn't disturb her. But what if she's in trouble?

Before I can change my mind, I storm over to her. I'm like a walking beacon of protection. Lucas gets one word of anyone harming me and it's over for them.

I can't believe I just thought that. Who knows what happened to William. But Erianne might be in trouble. That matters more. She grins vibrantly when she notices me approaching.

"I saw that," she says, staring me up and down.

"Saw what?" the man asks, before turning around noticing me standing here. "Oh. Abigail," he says through gritted teeth.

"Do I know you?" I ask, ready to make a scene in case I'm in danger.

Erianne chuckles, disarming my defenses. "Abigail, it's Mathieu."

Mathieu? But why is he dressed like Jimmy and the other goons? Glimpsing the details of his suit, it doesn't just look similar to theirs. It's exactly the same. The dark crimson tie and vest over his black dress shirt. Everything impeccably dressed under the black suit jacket. It's all identical—all the way down to his shined black dress shoes. This doesn't sit right with me.

Maybe I'm overreacting though. It's just a suit. They're just colors. *Get a grip Abigail*. And Mathieu did grow up with Lucas just like Erianne did. His family could be tied to Lucas' too.

"I'm sorry Mathieu. I didn't recognize you under that mask." I smile.

"That's alright. I have to get going anyway. It was nice seeing you ladies." He raises his glass, draining it in one swoop and stalks off.

"So. How did it feel to be the star of the night?" Erianne asks, grinning from ear to ear.

I grab a drink from a passing waiter. "I'm not sure. Being with Lucas was great, but you know how I am with being the center of attention."

"I never did understand that about you. Still don't." She smiles, her eyes crinkling at the corners.

Erianne is the type that loves being the center of attention and fully embraces it when she's given the opportunity. I love that about her though. It's one of her more admirable traits. She's always so confident, as confident as I wish I was. But I guess she's rubbing off on me. I stood my ground with William twice now. And I went for it with Lucas, even though we were interrupted before he could shoot me down.

"William was here," I say casually.

Erianne spits out her drink. "What? When? What happened?" She scowls and scans the room.

"He's gone now. He told me he misses me and didn't like my response. Decided to grab my arm, but Lucas took care of him." I shrug. Nearly choking on my drink, I stare wide-eyed, realizing what I just said. *Merde.*

Erianne's face pales. "Abigail. What do you mean?"

"No! I mean he had him kicked out!" I quickly reassure her.

She breathes a sigh of relief. "You can't say things like that Abby."

I take a long swig of my drink, nearly finishing the entire glass. "I'm sorry," I groan.

I didn't realize how that would come across. If I decide to keep associating with Lucas, I'll have to get used to it. Not sure I like that...

"By the way, how are you and Clarissa close all of a sudden?" She wrinkles her nose in disgust.

I chuckle. "How do you get Clarissa from the thought of someone being 'taken care of'?"

"That girl is terrifying." Her eyes widen as the corners of her mouth turn downward.

I laugh. "I ran into her after we got into that argument. She can be really persistent."

Erianne glares at me sideways. "So, she was pretty much my place holder?"

I furrow my brows. "No. I mean, yes. But no. She's a good person underneath all that positivity she's got going on."

"Yeah, well I'm back so you don't need her. Besides her 'positivity' is horrifying. Who is seriously that happy all the time anyway?" Erianne jokes.

"Is that really how you feel?" Alarms blare in my head as the shrill voice directly behind me reverberates.

I know Erianne was just joking around. She meant absolutely nothing she said, but there's no way Clarissa will see it that way. All the blood drains from mine and Erianne's faces.

"We never meant anything by—" I try to defend us.

Clarissa holds her hand up, "Don't even worry about lying to me. I take it this is the 'friend' you were talking about? You could have told me it was Erianne. Like I said, she doesn't seem like much of a friend." Her eyes redden, tears pooling at the corners. All color leaves her face. I've never seen her so pale.

"Excuse me?" Erianne snaps.

"I'll excuse myself." Clarissa storms off, wiping her face with the back of her hand.

I should go after her. She might not even hear me out though. While I'm debating it, an older man glides past her, catching my attention. He straightens his black suit jacket as he saunters our way. I can't seem to catch a break.

A bleak, pained expression clouds Erianne's face. "A-Ab-Abig-gail…" She croaks. "That's Lucas' father. That's Dominick Vitale. *Merde*. Dominick Vitale is coming over here." Her cheeks pale until they're almost sickly. Her hands tremble uncontrollably at her sides.

"What?" I frantically glimpse back and forth from him to Erianne.

No, it's not. No. *Oh, shit. What the hell?* It can't be. There's no good reason for him coming over here. Did I get Erianne in trouble? I shouldn't have come here. This was such a bad idea.

"Abigail. You don't understand. He hasn't shown his face at one of these in over a decade. This isn't good. *Merde*." Erianne quickly sets her glass down. "I need to get Lucas." She turns to walk away.

I grab her arm. "You can't leave me!"

She stares intently back. "He won't let me stand here anyway. I have to go. Lucas can help."

I reluctantly release her. She races through the ball room, disappearing into the doorway Lenny took Lucas through earlier. A sly, arrogant grin spreads across Mr. Vitale's face as he stops in front of me.

"So, you're the one causing all the commotion at my ball." He raises a brow, staring me up and down.

I'm completely lost on how I'm supposed to speak to him right now. What exactly is the proper way to address a 'mob king'? Thinking about exactly what he does only worsens the fear coursing through my veins. The things he's done to be 'successful'…

"Abigail Halsey. Right?" He says curtly.

"Yes, monsieur." My voice quakes.

Dominick shakes his head, laughing. "I hear my son has gained quite the fascination with you."

"He has?" I hope this isn't about that dance.

"Don't play dumb with me girl," he scolds. His moods shift rapidly before my eyes. "You seem like a good girl. If it weren't for my son already being engaged, I'd allow this situation to continue."

The world falls from under my feet as the impact of his words collide with my heart. Did he just say *engaged*?

"Lucas is not engaged. He would have told me about that." I'm not sure who I'm trying to convince.

Despite what I just said, I can't shake the knot forming in my throat and the swirling in my stomach. The word 'engaged' hangs over me like a dark cloud. Every heartbeat is accompanied by a crippling sharpness, my lungs burning. This can't be true. I didn't think I cared this much about him. I'm not even sure why this has me so upset. It's not like we were together or anything. But then, why does this hurt so much?

He scoffs. "You really believe that? My son was having his cake and eating it too. Makes a father proud." He beams. "But he's allowed it to interfere with more important things. Now I have to step in and put an end to this. His wedding is four days away, so this thing between you and my boy stops here. Now," he growls, "My son means more to me than anything. I won't let you take him away." He straightens his jacket and narrows his eyes.

"Believe me, that won't be a problem." I squeeze the words past the growing lump in my throat, choking back tears.

All the debating over whether I should end whatever has been going on between Lucas and I has been for nothing. There has never been anything to end apparently. His father helped make that decision for me.

"Ah. There his fiancé is now. Elizah. Come over here, dear." Dominick calls to a woman passing by.

As if this couldn't have gotten worse. The woman's outfit I had been gawking at when I got here is the same woman Lucas is engaged to. That's just perfect. The irony isn't lost on me. Covered head to toe in gold, she approaches Dominick, kissing each of his cheeks.

"Dominick." Elizah bows.

I know her. I know that voice. My memory pulls me back to the day Lucas took me to dinner at L'Hermitage. I was waiting on one customer at the restaurant to leave so I could clock out for the day. The customer who made a point to know my name…was Elizah. Wait a minute. It's no coincidence that the very same woman Lucas is engaged to came to my work the same day we went to dinner for the first time. Elizah had to have found out. Is that why he took me so far out of town? Lucas was hiding me...I can feel the tears trying to escape but swallow hard, I shove them down.

"You came into La Couronne a while back. I remember you." I pull at every strand of composure I can muster up, holding on with a death grip.

I won't give either of them the satisfaction of seeing me cry.

A cold sneer crawls over Elizah's lips. "It was a lovely meal. I told Dominick here all about it. Isn't that right?" She places a hand on Dominick's bicep.

"Yes. It seems like a lovely place. I'll have to visit it myself to be sure. You'll be working won't you, Ms. Halsey?" Dominick is all too pleased with himself.

I don't miss the hidden threat laced within his words. "Most likely, monsieur." Pressing my palms firmly together, I try to stop the shake starting in them.

"It was...interesting meeting Abigail there. She was a wonderful server, really knew her place." Elizah peers up at Mr. Vitale as they share knowing glances.

"I'll leave you two to chat." Dominick nods to Elizah before crossing the room. His silhouette is still visible out of my peripheral.

"Just who do you think you are?" Elizah's snaps, snarling and catching me off guard.

"I'm sorry?" Staring back at her absently, a darkness creeps over me, inside my heart.

"No, you aren't. You've enjoyed your little trips with Lucas. Did you really think someone like you could ever actually be with him?" She curls her lip.

"No, I didn't." The truth behind my lie twist at the knife in my heart. I was starting to believe it was a possibility, but I would never fit into his world.

Elizah laughs as a tear rolls down my cheek. "That's just pathetic. Lucas has duties to fulfill and responsibilities that you couldn't possibly imagine on your worst days. You could never handle his life."

"And you can?" I spit back.

Elizah steps nose to nose with me. "You're sticking your nose in business that doesn't concern you, in a world that doesn't have room for you." She snarls through her gold mask. "I don't know what you're trying to pull or whether it's money you want, but I suggest you leave. And stay away from Lucas if you know what's best for you." She shoves past me, but the pain of her shoulder slamming against mine isn't there.

My body is cold and numb. Everything from William comes swimming back as if it had never left. How could I have been so stupid? I should've known better than to let myself get close to him. I need to get out of here. I just want my mama.

Desperately searching the ball room for her, I wipe a stray tear from my cheek. My heart drops once I find her. She's dancing with Dominick Vitale. *Shit.* Dominick Vitale is dancing with my mother.

No. Not my mother. You will *not* mess with my mother. He's made his point.

I storm past a few couples dancing. Dominick dips her low as the song comes to a close and watches with a cold sneer as I stride up to them.

"Mama. We should go." I grab her hand the second she's in reach, but he doesn't relinquish his hold on her.

"Carla! There you are! I've been looking everywhere for you." Erianne's voice rings through my ears like a melody.

"What is it dear?" Mama asks empathetically, completely oblivious to what's really going on right now.

"I'm about as dumb as a broom. I left my purse in the car. Would you mind walking outside with me?" Erianne pulls my mother from Dominick. "I'm sure this nice gentleman won't make a whole cheese about it." Erianne purses her lips.

"Of course not! Thank you for the dance, Carla. I'll remember you." He bows, kissing my mama's hand before relinquishing his grasp.

Despite the ache in my heart, a hint of relief sparks once my mother and Erianne are safely outside.

"What a lovely mother you have. Tell me, Ms. Halsey, what would you do for your mother? I would hate to see something happen to her." Dominick's unnerving dark expression bores through me. And just like that, the relief is gone.

"You wouldn't!" My jaw drops. After what happened to Lucas' mother, he would do this?

"You have no idea what I would do, child. I won't let you fill my son's head with ideas of leaving. You screw with my business *and* my son, that will be the final thing you do," he growls, taking a menacing step closer to me.

No! My mind pulls me to the nightmare that haunts me. *The man stepping toward me, ready to continue his assaults. My vision blurred by the swollen skin surrounding my eyes.* My chest is rising and falling, but no air will fill my lungs. The memories continue to flash in my mind. I need to escape.

A hand grips my elbow, pulling me back. I'm at the ball. Everything is okay. The vast room suddenly feels so small as it closes in on me.

"Father." Lucas stands toe to toe with Dominick.

"Ah, there's my boy. How did it go with Elizah's father?" Dominick asks the question proudly.

Lucas jerks, turning to face me. His face pales and tells me all I need to know. I can't handle any more of this. Pulling my arm free of his hold, the only thought repeating like a mantra in my head is *I need to get out of here*. I need to escape. My head is spinning. Dominick's satisfied grin creeping at the corners of his mouth deepens the hollow ache ebbing away at the pit of my stomach. I'm going to be sick.

I shove past Lucas and anyone else in my way. My cheeks dampen as the tears cascade down freely. The look on Lucas' face, like he knew he'd done something wrong, like he'd been caught in a lie. I didn't need to ask at that point.

"Abigail." Mathieu blocks my path, grabbing my arm forcefully. "Hurry. In here."

"I'm okay. I just need to go outside." I try to break free from his hold, but it tightens painfully.

He drags me through a set of large double doors and flings me into the room. My back smacks against a piece of furniture. A searing pain rips through me. I catch a glimpse of Lucas through the doorway. He's barreling through the crowd, rushing to me. But Mathieu slams the doors shut, securing the lock. The room is lit by a single lamp in the corner, making it hard to see much of anything.

"What's going on Mathieu? What are you doing?" I ask as the situation gets a little too familiar.

My nightmares start to mix with reality as I frantically scoot backward. Mathieu takes one menacing step after the other toward me. *No, no, no. The bad thing is going to happen.* The infantile thought floats in my head and I don't know where it came from. *He's getting closer. I'm getting smaller. Mama is banging on the door, trying to get in, trying to stop him. She always tries, but she never makes it.* The banging and rattling of the doors echoes throughout the room. My heart is slamming against my chest.

"Stop!" I scream past the suffocating lump in my throat.

Mathieu freezes, his expression shifting from confident to uncertain.

I meet his sunken grey eyes, my face soaked with tears. "If this is about our date—"

He cuts me off, "You think I really liked you? I could never like a low-class slut like you. The only reason I even pretended to like you was because Dominick ordered me to. You just wouldn't back off Lucas and let things be!" He swiftly crosses the room.

His foot connects with my abdomen. All the air escapes my lungs as if exiting out a one-way door. I'm suffocating. I need air. The ceiling shrinks and the walls start to cave in. I wrap my arms around my knees as my body shakes uncontrollably. Tremors run through me as sweat beads along my hairline. A throbbing pain takes over my head.

"Now, I have to handle this." Mathieu reaches inside his jacket, pulling out a silver object.

He holds it skillfully, aiming at my head. *No!* The wall in my head bursts. Memories escape through. My father, a drunk, constantly hitting my mother. Then, laying in on me until he was too tired. Blow after blow, he'd break bones, leave bruises. School days missed with no good reason except he didn't want them to see the marks. Mama pleading in an American accent that shoots through my heart with a bittersweet ache, like it's something I've missed hearing for so long.

One by one, every memory of my childhood—the good and the bad—I had locked away from before I was ten years old floods into my mind. Mama singing an American nursey rhyme about a mockingbird, *"If that mockingbird don't sing, momma's gonna buy you a diamond ring. And If that diamond ring turns brass, momma's gonna buy you a looking glass..."*

Merde. I remember. Everything.

25

The wooden doors fracture then crash open with a deafening crack as splinters fly into the air. Lucas and Jimmy barrel inside. Mathieu whips around, aiming his gun at them.

"Make one more move, and I'll kill all of you!" He shouts, his hands trembling.

Lucas freezes, fists balled at his sides. I have no doubt in my mind both of those men are armed, but neither can get to their weapons. It's up to me. I'm not that scared little girl anymore. I won't cower down. My father beat me down most of my life. I won't let anyone make me feel so small, so weak and helpless ever again.

Remembering the strength my mama raised me with, my lungs slowly fill, and I revel in the deep breaths moving through me. With my hands quaking, I push myself up off the floor.

Lucas watches, his expression switching to horror as he realizes what I'm about to do. I channel all my strength and, despite my unsteady legs, charge at Mathieu as he whirls around. The cool metal presses against my stomach, grazing my side as a thunderous shot echoes out. I can't hear anything past the ear-piercing ringing as the weight of his body crushes mine.

The gun clatters to the ground next to me as a puddle of red liquid seeps across the floor. *Oh, my saints. Is he dead? Am I shot?* A million thoughts race through my mind at the sight. My stomach hurts and I don't know if it's from him kicking me or that I've been shot. My vision blurs. I frantically shove him off and shuffle away, wincing at the dull white-hot pain. Lucas rushes to my side, his hand wound tightly around a gun.

"Please. Please tell you're okay. I'll fucking kill him if he hurt you." Lucas lifts me up, scanning every inch of my body.

A crimson stain has seeped into the fabric of my dress. The beautiful bodice is ruined. "L-Lucas. I'm s-shot. He shot me." I weep as tears stream down my face.

His hand cups my chin. "No, no. *Ma moite*. Look." He grasps my hand, pulling it to my stomach. "Feel. No bullet wound. This is his blood. You're okay. *Mon cher*, Abigail, you're okay."

I feel around, relief exploding through me. "I'm…fine?"

"Fucking stupid move you pulled. But damn, it was so brave. And kind of sexy to see you handle yourself like that." Lucas' teeth graze his lower lip as his eyes darken, locking on my lips.

He sets me down on my feet, taking off his suit jacket and gingerly putting it on me. With expert fingers, he fastens the buttons. "There. Don't want anyone seeing the blood." His voice is raspy as his eyes find my lips again. I want to kiss him. A need gnaws at my insides. But then I remember everything that happened before Mathieu tried to kill me. Lucas lied to me.

I shake him off. "I-I just need to go outside." I say, shoving past him and out the doors.

"Abigail!" Lucas shouts but I ignore his plea as my body meets the cold chill of the night. "Abigail!" His voice is getting closer.

No. I can't turn around. Between what happened earlier and just now, I need to get out of here. If I turn around and see those sorrowful crystalline eyes, I might not be so sure of that. My stomach churns. I jog as fast as I can in these heels through the crowd that's formed outside.

I reach the car where Mama and Erianne are waiting. "Can we leave please?"

Mama furrows her brows. "Yes, of course, *mon trésor*." Mama doesn't hesitate. Erianne opens the car door for her as she rushes in. "What's happened? Abigail, are you okay?" She asks frantically.

"Abigail! Stop!" Lucas calls just as I set one foot in.

"No!" I shout, swinging my head around, not holding back the rage seething in me as I continue to climb in the car.

The warmth of Lucas hand connects with my skin. "Abigail. Talk to me." Lucas asks, his words a desperate plea.

I step out to face him. Erianne takes a step toward me, ready to 'handle' Lucas, but I hold my hand up to stop her.

"What happened? What happened is you failed to tell me you're engaged! You know, for a second there, I thought everything you said actually meant something. I thought everything everyone said about you was wrong. I guess that's my fault though, huh? What just happened in there is crazy." The tears escape, flowing uncontrollably.

Lucas drops my arm, stepping back as if my words are a blow to his heart. "Abigail, what do you mean?" He runs his hands through his hair, his usual collected, graceful nature gone.

"What do I mean? I mean I'm done with you Lucas! I never want to see your face again. I don't give a damn. I mean—"

Lucas abruptly grabs my face in his hands, startling me. I stare wide-eyed and frozen in place as he closes any possible distance between us, instantly silencing me with the contact of his lips. My eyes drift closed. The touch is soft and tender. But his need comes through loud and clear as his hands grip my face like his life depends on it. A mix of cedar and lavender fills my nostrils. My mind is telling me to push him away, but any thought of actually doing so is drowned out. It's like a need deep in my gut is being fed. I need this. I need *him*.

I give in and allow myself to get lost with him. Wrapping my arms around his neck, I pull him closer. Lucas grabs my waist, pressing my body tightly against his. He entwines a hand in my hair. There's no space between us, but I still want him closer. A different kind of need blossoms deep in my gut. Each kiss is like medicine to my wound, soothing all the aches eating away at me. Lucas reluctantly pulls his lips away.

He whispers, "I've wanted to do that for so long now."

Stealing a glance up, he rests his forehead against mine, holding me in place. I'm brought back down to earth as the whispers from the other guests around us fills my ears.

I pry his hands from my skin. "It doesn't change anything Lucas." Saying the words drives the knife deeper into my heart. I cautiously step away from him.

"No!" Lucas shouts. His glazed blue eyes stare back at me fiercely. A tear escapes the corner of his eye, gutting me.

"You have to, Lucas. I don't belong," I croak.

"Merde! Abigail, please." His cheeks dampen from the tears flowing down them.

"I have to go." Shaking my head, my lip quivers. I turn away from him to get in the car.

"Let me drive you home!" he blurts and grabs my arm, stopping me again, "We can talk. I'll explain everything. Anything you want to know." His frantic plea chips away at my strength.

I don't know what to do right now. I need to let him go. His father will never leave me or the people I love alone. We will never be safe as long as this continues. Erianne would know what to do. Breaking my gaze from Lucas' reddened face, I peer up at Erianne, silently seeking guidance.

She nods her head. "Go."

Bringing myself to stare into Lucas' strained blue eyes, I say, "okay."

Lucas releases my arm, running both hands through his hair. I lean down into the car to tell Mama I'll meet her at home, but I don't have to. Her disapproving scowl tells me all I need to know.

"We will talk at home," Mama says and turns away from me.

I stagger backward. She's never been so cold with me before. Erianne smiles apologetically.

"Go with her please."

"Of course." Erianne gets in the car with my mother.

I watch wordlessly as the car fades away into the night.

26

Lucas drives away from the castle, leaving all the chaos behind with it. Thinking back to his kiss, I gently touch my now swollen lips. He promised me answers and I agreed to let him explain.

"What's going on, Lucas?" I ask.

"You want the truth? And before you answer really think about what you're asking." I watch his chest slowly rise and fall.

"Yes."

I need answers.

"Alright." Lucas takes a deep breath. "But just tell me to stop if you don't want to hear anymore." Lucas glances sideways.

I nod. "Okay."

"The engagement between me and Elizah is an arrangement. Do you understand? It's a business arrangement."

I crinkle my nose, not understanding what he means.

He shakes his head. "My father arranged for me to marry Elizah because her father is Antonio Salvatore." He scans my face, waiting for any sign that I understand.

"I'm sorry. I don't know what you're trying to say." I wring my hands as the words echo in my head: "*I don't belong in his world.*"

Lucas sighs. "Antonio Salvatore is the reason we moved here to begin with. He offered a business arrangement with my father. Antonio needed someone to test out Normandy to see if it was logical to conduct business here. With the help of Erianne's mother, my father did just that. But after their feud that cost my mother her life, they came to a truce by arranging the marriage to merge our families. And by merging the families—"

"Your father gains more power." I finish Lucas' sentence.

A smirk spreads at the corner of Lucas' mouth. "Yes. You're getting it. Not bad. You catch on quick."

"Why would you go through with something like that?" I can't help being just as curious as I am angry.

Lucas shakes his head. "I'm not. I met with Elizah's father earlier tonight to tell him I don't want this. Hell, Antonio was more understanding and accepting than my own father. We shook hands and that was the end of that. I'm not marrying her."

I bite my lip to suppress the grin breaking free. Running all of this through my head, Elizah's words echo into my thoughts. "*...I suggest you leave and stay away from Lucas if you know what's best for you.*"

My curiosity piques. "Why does Elizah seem like she wants the marriage then?"

Lucas scrunches his forehead. "I don't know. Elizah grew up being groomed for this life. If it weren't for my mother, I may have turned out just like her. Elizah probably sees the business advantage to it and the peace it would create."

"Isn't there already peace?" I ask.

Lucas runs a hand through his hair. "I shouldn't be telling you any of this."

I reach over and grasp his hand. His jaw relaxes as the tension melts away.

"You can tell me. I can handle it," I reassure him.

Lucas keeps his eyes on the road. "The peace between the families is only temporary. There was a point when my father and I were going to lose everything. That meant our lives."

"Why? What happened?" The thought of someone wanting to take his life sends a chill down my spine. Not him.

His hands tighten around the steering wheel. "When my mother passed, my father lost control. He had been fighting Antonio for power. Elizah's mother lost her life as well during the feud. Every day I went out, I never knew if I was going to make it back. Then, Antonio suggested the truce. My father accepted without even consulting me."

"What happened to her mother?" I swallow hard, not sure if I want to hear this.

"My father had her killed the same way my mother was. She was run off the road late at night." A twinge of anger flashes on Lucas' face.

"Why would he do that?" I caress the back of Lucas' hand with my thumb. "I-I just don't understand." You would think the man would have learned what actions like that cause.

"Because my father isn't happy unless he's in control. Of his business and even me." His knuckles bloom ghastly white as his grip on the steering wheel tightens. "I think he felt guilty about what happened to her. But in his eyes, nothing was going to be good until Antonio knew the pain of losing the woman you love." He keeps his eyes steady on the road.

"So, why in the world did your dad come to the decision to have an arranged marriage?" I'm so confused.

Elizah's words ring through my thoughts again: "*You're sticking your nose in business that doesn't concern you, in a world that doesn't have room for you.*" Maybe she was right. This 'world' is already hard for me to comprehend and I've only just dipped my toe in.

"My father saw an opportunity for more power and couldn't resist. Hell, I found out he sent you the invitation to the ball." He shakes his head.

At least we know who sent the invite. But I don't feel any better.

"What are you going to do? Your father clearly isn't going to just let it go. He threatened my mother and went through a lot of trouble to try to scare me off tonight. He and Elizah warned me to stay away from you." I patiently wait for his solution.

Lucas pulls my hand to his lips. "I will never let anything happen to you or your mother. I'll overthrow my father before I ever let that happen. I already discussed this with Antonio. I'm prepared for the fallout of this. You have my word, Abigail."

"I don't know, Lucas. This is a lot to take in. It's not just me involved anymore. What we decide will affect everyone I love." I stare at him, more uncertain than ever.

"Abigail, just tell me what it is you want me to do? I'll walk away from all of it if I have to. I want you in my life. No matter what the cost is," Lucas pleads.

Watching his smile falter, I cave. "Let's just take everything one day at a time."

I have a feeling I'm going to regret this.

"Okay, but you're a terrible kisser. We should work on that," he says with a cocky grin as he parks the car along the curb in front of my place.

"Is that what you think?" I pretend to be offended.

"No. That's what I know. But practice makes perfect." He winks.

I grin. "You know you could have just done that to begin with."

Lucas smirks proudly. "Are you teasing *me* now?"

"I learned from the best." I bat my eyelashes.

Lucas grabs my hand, pulling me over the center console. His lips press against mine, desperate for the connection. He groans as I pull away from him. I climb out of the car, grinning like a fool.

"Goodnight." I beam.

"Goodnight, my dear Abigail."

27

My dress feels like a ton of bricks as I climb the steps to my flat. Everything that happened tonight is weighing on me more than ever. I still have to face Mama. Despite all that's happened, I can't ignore the sinking feeling it's only going to get worse.

I cautiously open the front door. Instead of being greeted by Mama, Erianne is pacing back and forth in the front room.

I whisper, "Hey, how is she?"

Erianne about jumps out of her skin. "My saints, Abbs. You scared the hell out of me!"

"Sorry." I quietly shut the door.

"She's in the kitchen waiting for you." Erianne smiles apologetically. She knows how pissed Mama is with me right now. "I have to get going. Unless you need me here."

"No. It's okay. I need to talk to her." I reassure Erianne, giving her a hug. "I'll catch up with you at work tomorrow."

"Okay, but if you need me tonight, I'll be at O'Kallaghan's. I need a drink. *Imedíat!*" She hugs me quickly and quietly leaves.

Now it's just me and my mama. Taking a deep breath, I make my way into the kitchen.

Mama is sitting at the table with her hands folded. "Sit," she snaps. I know better than to argue with her right now. "Is it true? Are you seeing that man?" Her voice is scary quiet.

"Yes." My lip quivers.

"And you've been lying to me this entire time? About where you've been, who you've been with?" The sullen expression on her face causes tears to well up in my eyes again.

"Yes." I swallow hard, forcing the tears back.

"Abigail Karline Halsey, how could you? Have you lost your mind? Do you know who he is? He's dangerous and an awful man! How dare you disrespect me in my own home! How dare you lie to my face! I didn't raise you this way. That man is no man at all with the things he's done. He's an ill-mannered, disgrace of a man. I won't allow you to see him. Do you hear me, Abigail? You are not to see that man under any circumstances!" She shouts, her voice resonating off the ceiling of our small flat.

I clench my fists at my sides. "To hell with this being your house! This is my house, too! I live here too! You can't...no, you *won't* stop me from seeing him! I'll see him if I damn well want to!" I shout back instantly regretting the words, but unable to stop them as they pour out, "You didn't complain when you were dancing with his father!" I jump from my seat, shoving the chair backward. "You know what? Forget it! I'll save you the trouble in *your house* and leave!" I storm off to my room to quickly change.

Mama is still sitting at the kitchen table when I come back downstairs. She must think I'm not really leaving. Well, I've got news for her. I grab my purse and throw my leather jacket on. The front door clicks as I open it. The kitchen chair scrapes across the floor as she leaps from it.

"Abigail. What are you doing?" Mama rushes out the door after me. I stop myself from looking back and force my feet to keep moving forward down the sidewalk. "Abigail, get back here! Now!" she calls out, but my mind is set. I'm leaving. "Abigail!" The cringing echo of my mama sobbing pierces through my heart.

I want to stop, to turn around and tell her how sorry I am, but I just can't. I need to walk. I need to clear my head of everything.

Hours later, I've done nothing besides walk around aimlessly. As my nervousness and anger starts to die down, the cold of the night air becomes harsh. Each time the wind blows, it's like pins stinging all over my skin. My shoulder is numbing from carrying my purse around all night. I haven't the slightest clue what time it is. This was such a bad idea. I shouldn't have gotten into an argument with Mama like I did. She has every reason to be worried. I'm such an ass for treating her like that. She's my mama. Putting my hood over my head, I walk home as fast as I can.

The closer I get to my flat, all I can think about is the mass amount of regret and guilt breaking me apart, eating away at me. I *cannot* believe I treated her like that. She deserves better. So much better. As much as I hate it, I have to go back to face her. I have to apologize. If she wants to kick me out for real this time, I'll understand. I have no right to be mad at her for anything, not after how I just acted.

As I walk down my street, I stare aimlessly at the other buildings and houses. All lights are off in the houses besides a porch light here and there. Not a single glimmer of light is on in the buildings. All flats facing the street are as dark as the night sky. Well, all but one.

Mine.

I reach the porch of my flat but stop in place, dropping my head. I'm so ashamed of myself. I don't know if I'll even be able to look her in the face. Here goes nothing.

Keeping my head lowered, I turn the doorknob. Inching inside, Mama lurches from the spot on the sofa she's been sitting on, but stops in place. I can tell she's trying to gauge my mood. I can't take this. Without waiting another minute, I rush over, throwing my arms around her.

"Oh, my sweet girl. Mon trésor." Mama sobs as she folds me tightly in her arms.

I let the tears pour out as the comfort of my mother's warm embrace soothes away all the aches in my heart.

"It's okay. Everything is okay. Mama is here. Mama is always here." She runs her hand down my head over and over as I cling to her.

"I'm so sorry, Mama. I didn't mean anything I said. If you want to really put me out, I understand. I'm just so, so sorry." My shoulders shake as the tears continue to fall.

She holds me out at arm's length. "No darling. I would never put you out. Come. Sit." I wipe my face as she pulls me to sit on the sofa with her. "We need to talk."

"Okay," I croak, trying my best to calm myself.

"Abigail. I haven't been completely honest with you either." She grasps both of my hands.

This time I'm not sure if it's to comfort me as usual or to keep me from leaving again. She doesn't lie to me. If she did, it'd be for something serious. Life or death serious.

"What are you talking about?" My heart is beating harder and harder the more I consider the reasons my mama would lie to me.

She exhales deeply. "Do you remember how I told you your father passed away when you were little?"

"*Oui*…" My stomach twists in knots as the newly resurfaced memories flash through my mind at the mention of him. Where is she going with this?

"Well…that wasn't exactly true. I left him." Her lower lip quivers as her eyes lose their vibrance.

"He's alive?" I can't believe I'm even asking that question. I stare back at her. "Why have you lied to me all these years?" Clenching my jaw, I do my best to hold back the rage building inside me. I don't want him to be alive. Not after what he did to us.

She clasps my hands within hers. "Abigail, I did it for our safety. Your father was far from a kind man. He was a drinker and when he had too much…" Her voice trails off as a single tear rolls down her cheek. "He would get violent. I tried to protect you from him, but I never could. The memories you've been having, the dreams, those are of him. I'm so sorry, *ma chérie*. I never meant for any of that to happen." Sobs wrack her body.

She squeezes my hand, soothing my rattled nerves. This '*man*' hurt my mother. To hell with what he did to me. He hurt my mother. Lucas. One word to Lucas and he'd get what he deserves. A sly grin creeps over my lips, but my mouth turns downward the second I realize how crazy I sound. No one will get hurt because of me. Even my not-dead abusive father.

"So, where is he now? How did you get away? I swear Mama, if I ever run into him, I'll kick his ass!" I seethe.

Mama grips my hands. "No! You can never go anywhere near him! He's a dangerous man. It took me years to be free of him. He has friends in all the wrong places. I don't want you ever going anywhere near him. Do I make myself clear?"

I nod. "Yes."

She leans back against the sofa. "The only reason I even managed to escape was because he left for a business trip. I happened to be extremely sick and the doctor ordered me to stay rested. So, he went without me. I knew he wouldn't be back for a few days and knew that was my only chance to leave. I already had our bags packed and hidden."

"I drained our bank account, bought two tickets for the next cruise out on the Royal Princess. Such a beautiful ship. You wouldn't stop screaming how 'oober ginormous' it was." She chuckles. "We left New York that night, headed straight for Le Havre here in France."

"Wait…what?" I sit back, away from her. She can't be saying what I think she's saying. She can't.

She looks away from me. "…Abigail. You're not from France. You weren't born here. You're…American."

My whole world falls from underneath me. So, basically everything I know my life to be…just isn't? My father is an abusive psychotic criminal, my mother is from America. *I'm* from America.

I'm American …I'm American? What… I open my mouth, wanting to speak, to ask the millions of questions overloading my brain right now, but the words fail me.

"What?" I manage to force the single word out. My body is as light as a feather, my skin tingling all over. The room is spinning.

"Chère, you never wondered why you and I talk so differently from most of the people here? Aside from tourists." Mama places a hand on my shoulder, helping to ground me.

Different? I talk normal. Not everyone here fluently speaks French or has a strong accent. I meet tons of people at the restaurant who speak English and French. This has to be a joke.

"I never paid attention. I guess I thought this is normal." I sit back against the sofa. I'm having a hard time taking all this in right now. My head is pulsing, the pounding only getting worse.

"I'm sorry I never told you before, but it just never came up. And tonight, when I saw you with Lucas, it scared me. I've heard nothing but awful things about him, and I guess it reminded me of how your father used to be." She wrings her hands tightly together.

"That man is not my father. He hurt you. He hit you and me. How long did this go on? You knew what the dreams I've been having were about? This entire time." I stare at her in disbelief.

I don't even recognize the woman sitting in from of me anymore. Dr. Carrere is going to have a field day with this Tuesday. I don't even know how to tell her everything. I barely understand what's going on right now. Nothing in my life has been real. I've been living a lie created by my mother. But how can I be mad at her? She did it to possibly save our lives.

She shakes her head. "Let's not focus on that, mon trésor. It's long in the past now. When you ran off, I sat here thinking. Lucas isn't your father. He's a young man whom you love. I shouldn't cast judgement on him over my bias against men."

Wide-eyed, I stare at her. "I don't love him. I hardly know him."

She pats my hand, grinning. "Abigail, I have watched the light come back in your eyes, your smile, and your entire self these past few months. I thought it had to do with Erianne, but if Lucas has anything to do with that...then you have my blessing."

I freeze, stock still trying to reign myself in. *Oh, to hell with this.* I quickly sit up and wrap Mama in the tightest hug I can manage.

"Thank you, Mama! Thank you!" I squeeze her tighter.

"You're hurting me darling," she squeaks as she pushes me gently off.

"Oh. Sorry." I let go, setting back against the sofa.

"You want to tell me about him?" She winks, grinning ear to ear.

I chuckle and spill everything. Well, everything besides the part about Lucas being a mafia prince. Best not to even bring it up.

This night has been a roller coaster enough as it is. I have a lot to be worried about, but a lot to be thankful for.

28

It might be a stupid decision, or it might prove to be the best one. Either way, I'm going down to the police station to file a report on Mathieu. Someone needs to do something. All this sitting around waiting for Dominick to hurt someone is driving me crazy. At the very least, I could get police protection around my house for Mama.

I don't think this is something you call emergency services about. So, I've waited until the station is open. Here I am, on Monday at 8:57am, standing outside like a lost puppy. I'll probably get ticketed for loitering if I stand here much longer. *I got this.* I shake out my hands at my sides like it will shake out all the nervousness coursing through my body. I steady my breathing and walk inside. An older woman with streaks of grey highlighting her black hair smiles warmly as I approach her desk. It's sitting cozy behind a barrier of bullet proof glass.

"May I help you?" she asks.

Taking a deep breath, I nod. "I'd like to speak with a detective please. It's an emergency."

She furrows her brows. "What kind of an emergency?"

"I'd like to tell that to the detective. If you don't mind." I force a polite smile, hoping she doesn't give me a hard way to go.

She stares thoughtfully at me a minute. "Okay. What's your name?"

My heart skips a beat. I stammer, "I-I'd rather r-remain anonymous. Please." Sweat beads on my temple. I don't want my name on any official records. Maybe I'm being paranoid, but it doesn't seem like the best idea.

She narrows her eyes. "Please have a seat. I'll have someone come speak with you." She picks up her phone and presses three numbers then the pound button. "There's a young lady that would like to speak with a detective." She covers the mouthpiece and whispers, "Please have a seat."

I nod and scurry over to a chair in the open stale white lobby. The chairs remind me of the ones at Dr. Carrere's offices. They're so stiff and uncomfortable. Waiting is agonizing. Maybe I shouldn't do this. I can't just sit back and do nothing anymore though. To hell with my anxiety. To hell with my astraphobia. And to hell with the not-so-repressed memories. Someone has threatened my mother's life and then tried to kill me. They need thrown in prison, locked away forever.

The solid wooden door next to the glass barrier clicks as it opens, echoing throughout the lobby. A husky man in a long sleeve green button-up and brown dress slacks walks out. The fluorescent lights reflect onto his shiny scalp. He runs a hand over it as if it were a habit from his hair days.

"Miss," he calls out, "Right this way."

I leap from my seat like an eager soldier and follow him into a long narrow hallway. He leads the way into a tiny cramped square room. I've seen rooms like this on TV shows. A rectangular pane of glass on one wall is so dark it's practically a mirror. A metal table the size of a coffee table but taller is sitting in the center of the room, a single chair on opposite sides. Why does he have me in an interrogation room?

"I'm Detective Croww. You can have a seat." He gestures for me to sit in the chair facing the glass as he sets his phone down on the middle of the table, just inches from me.

I stare at the glass, wondering if someone is on the other side watching me. A shiver runs through my body at the thought of Dominick or one of his goons knowing I'm here. There's no way they could though. I didn't tell anyone I was coming here, not even Lucas or Erianne.

"So, what's your name young lady?" he asks, leaning back in his chair.

I squeeze my hands together. "Can it be kept off record?"

The detective leans forward. "Why don't you tell me what's going on first? Then we'll worry about that."

I nod. "Someone tried to kill me last night."

His mouth presses into a firm line. "Did you get a good look at this person? Know who they are?"

I take a deep breath. "Yes. His name is Mathieu Donbas. He has brown hair and—"

He holds his hand up, "You can stop right there. I know who you're talking about."

Hope blossom within me. "You do?"

His jaw clenches. "Yes, and you shouldn't be making false accusations about someone. Do you know I could put you in jail for this?"

His words are like a blow to my stomach. "B-but. I'm not making this up! I was at the Vitale ball a few nights ago and he pointed a gun at my head. He would have pulled the trigger if—" I stop myself. I can't tell a police officer that Lucas shot someone.

"Until what?" the detective snaps.

I stare down at my hands. "Nothing. I tackled him to the ground and ran out."

He laughs, but the echo behind it is cynical, holding no kindness. "So, you mean to tell me, the guy pointed his gun at you and you're calling that attempted murder? Did he say he was going to kill you?"

I shake my head. "Not exactly."

"I think I've heard enough." He stands from his chair. "You want to know what I think happened? I think you got turned down by Mr. Donbas and thought you could come in here to get a little payback. Is that why you came here, Ms. Halsey?"

My skin crawls. How does he know my name? I specifically made sure I didn't give anyone my name. *Merde.* The detective's phone vibrates on the table and the screen lights up. A calendar reminder flashes on the screen.

Meeting with D.V.
Tonight, August 18th, 09:00pm

All the air leaves my lungs like I've just been hit by a freight train. There's no doubt in my mind that D.V. stands for Dominick Vitale. I need to get the hell out of here. This was a colossal mistake. I quickly stand from my chair. The detective catches me staring at his phone and snatches it up.

"Y-you know what? You're right. I shouldn't have come here." I keep my head down and rush past him, flinging the door open.

As soon as I'm in the hallway, I take off in a full sprint, not stopping until I'm outside of the station. I should have figured he'd have the police in his pocket. How else would he get away with all the crap he does? I'm so stupid. There's no way this isn't going to get back to Dominick either. *Merde.* I have to warn Erianne and Lucas.

29

I couldn't sleep at all last night. There's no way for me to get ahold of Erianne and no way in hell am I going to try to contact Lucas. So, I just have to wait until she shows up for work. I checked the schedule and she's supposed to come in for a shift at 11:00am. My watch flips to 10:58AM and the click clack of heels against the pavement sings through my ears. I look up and Erianne tilts her head.

"Abby? What are you doing here? Did you pick up a shift?" She asks, greeting me with a hug.

"No. I, uhm, I need to talk to you." I pull her away as one of our coworkers walks up.

She grins. "Yeah, you do. What happened with your mother?"

I forgot. She has no idea I'm American and I haven't told her what happened with Mathieu. He's one of her best friends. I don't know how she's to take it and even worse, I don't even know what happened to him after I left.

"Erianne. Lucas shot Mathieu." I place my hand on her arm.

She swats the air. "Oh, I already know about that."

My jaw drops. "You do?"

She chuckles. "Yeah. Lucas told me. So, what happened with your mama?"

I stare at her, gob smacked. I can't believe she's acting like Mathieu trying to kill me and Lucas shooting him is no big deal. "Erianne, this is a big deal. I went to the police."

Her eyes widen and she grabs my arm. "Please tell me you're joking." I shake my head and she throws her hands up. "Great! This is just…great," she says through gritted teeth, rubbing her forehead. "I'll handle it. Just come to me with this stuff first from here on out. Okay?" She sighs heavily.

"Okay." I wring my hands.

"Anything else happen that you want to tell me about?" She glares and presses her mouth into a firm line.

"Well. Mama told me I'm American." I force a smile, hoping this news will lighten the tension, but still reeling at how nonchalant she's acting about what Mathieu did.

Erianne blinks a few times then burst into a fit of laughter.

"Okay. *N'importe quoi!* Laugh all you want." I shake my head.

She wipes a tear from her cheek. "Don't 'whatever' me. And I'm sorry. It's just, the irony in that. You hate Americans and come to find out, you are one." A few more laughs escape her mouth.

I scoff. "I'm glad you can laugh about this. I have a mad man trying to kill me, threatening my mother, and to top it off I find I'm American. This isn't some joke. This is my life. What if something happens to my mother?"

"Hey," she places her hands on my shoulders, "It's going to be okay. You have me and Lucas. We aren't going to let anything happen to you *or* your mother. Trust us."

Easy for her to say. I don't know who I can trust anymore. Her, Lucas, and even my mama have been keeping secrets and lied to me. Every time I think my life is getting back to normal, something monumentally bad happens. I don't want any of this and I definitely didn't ask for it. I wish I could hit the reset button and go back to the day mama asked me if I would like to live in Rouen. I'd tell her no and pick the place farthest away. Maybe convince her to pick up and move to New Zealand. It's beautiful there.

But that's not possible. I'm stuck here and I can't run from my problems. I have to face them head-on.

30

What better place to start with learning how to face my problems than Dr. Carrere's office? It's Tuesday and like any other Tuesday, I have an appointment with my therapist. But this one is different. I'm starting the repressed memory therapy. I keep telling myself this is a good thing, but I can't shake the foreboding gnawing at my gut. I'm going to still do it because I don't really know if I got *all* my memories back.

Deep breaths.

She's taking a long time to come out of her office. My appointment started thirty minutes ago, and she still hasn't come out to get me. I didn't see any other patients leaving either. Maybe she lost track of time talking to the colleague she told me about. But her receptionist isn't here either. *Oh, crap.* Did I get my days mixed up? Nope. The calendar on Heather's desk says it's Tuesday. Something's wrong.

I knock on her office door. "Hey. It's your favorite patient. You know, Abby." I wait, but no one responds. I knock again. "Uhm, so, did you fall asleep in there or something? Dr. Carrere?"

I turn the knob. It's unlocked. She always locks it when she's in session, which means she's not with a patient. That's good, but I hope she doesn't get mad at me for just walking in. I peek my head inside. Her office is trashed. Papers are strung everywhere. Picture frames are shattered and the chair she usually sits in is flipped on its side. The hairs on the back of my neck stand up as a cold chill runs through my spine.

I rush inside, shutting the door behind me and frantically searching. "Dr. Carrere? Are you in here? It's Abby."

Silence. A shoe is lying on the floor next to her desk. Wait a minute…that's her foot. My heart thumps wildly as I dash across the office, stepping on scattered debris along the way. She's lying unconscious behind her desk and her ivory skin is so pale. My knees give out on and I drop to the floor next to her. *Please, no. Don't be gone.* My heartbeat thumps in my ears, overtaking the silence.

I shake her gently. "Dr. Carrere. W-wake up." My throat is as dry as cotton.

No. She can't be. I squeeze my eyes shut as I struggle to breathe. Tears cascade down my cheeks. She can't be gone. I have to do something.

My mind races as I try to think of *what* to do. I need to call the police. Who would do this to her? I stand and scurry for her desk phone, picking up the receiver.

Her officer door crashes open. Splinters of wood spray outward. "Police! Put your hands where I can see them!" An officer screams, pointing his gun at me.

I put my trembling hands up and drop the receiver. Officers file in one by one, all aiming their pistols at me like I'm a criminal. I didn't do this.

One officer steps forward. "Get down on the ground! Hands on your head! Do it, now!"

I drop to the ground, putting my hands on my head like he instructed. *Merde.* The officer sprints over, forcefully yanking my wrist and bending my arms behind my back. I wince as he snaps the cuffs on too tight.

Something catches my eye as he starts to yank me off the ground. There's something taped to the underside of Dr. Carrere's desk. It's a brown folder. A name is on the outer tab, but I can't make it out in time before I'm lifted to my feet. Why would she tape a folder to her desk like that?

The officer escorts me into the lobby. The detective I spoke with yesterday is leaning against the receptionist desk, a smug grin plastered on his face. *No way.* I've got a really bad feeling about this. Is Dr. Carrere dead because of me? Because I just had to run to the police? I opened my big mouth and now someone is dead. It's all my fault.

I'm starting to hate interrogation rooms. The detective had me put in here and is probably on the other side of the glass watching me. I've been in here forever. Why aren't they out there trying to find her killer? Someone did this to her. I've got a pretty good idea who that someone is. My blood boils.

The metal door rattles and opens. Detective Croww walks in, sealing the door shut behind him. He silently stalks to the corner of the room and reaches for the camera, unplugging it.

"We received an anonymous tip about a murder. Want to tell me what you were doing there?" He leans against the wall.

I narrow my eyes. "She's my therapist. I found her like that. Why aren't you out there finding out who did this?" I shout.

He chuckles. "Haven't you learned yet to stop asking questions?"

His words are like a slap to my face. I know without a doubt he has something to do with this. But I can't do anything about it. Dominick could have this whole department in his pocket. There's no telling what would happen if I tried to go to another officer. I sit back in my seat, drooping my head.

"Besides, I think we have the murderer right here." He grins.

My eyes frantically meet his as my blood boils. "I didn't do this, and you know I didn't."

He scoffs. "You may not have pulled the trigger, but this is still your fault. All you had to do was mind your business and keep your nose out of shit. She's dead because of you."

His words slam into me like I've just been hit by a car going 100km/h. He's right. It's all my fault. I should have minded my business.

"Hmph. You know, I think you're telling the truth. You can go." He removes the cuffs and stands back.

I scurry to the door, wanting more than ever to be out of this seemingly smaller room.

"One more thing!" he says, "Have you ever heard the saying curiosity killed the cat?" He cackles as I sprint out of the interrogation room, not stopping until the crisp autumn air stings my face. This is so much worse than I thought. What was I thinking?

Carrere Therapy Solutions LLC

Patient: Lucas T. Danforth

Start of service: 04/02/2017

The words on the top of the paper are there, but I can't believe it. I went back to Dr, Carrere's office to grab the brown folder. It wasn't the easiest thing I've ever had to do. A police nationale officer was standing by the door to her office. I took a gamble on calling in a report of a man streaking in front of the office building, hoping he'd be dispatched. Sure enough, he got the call on his radio as I listened in around the corner. It gave me just enough time to slip past the bright yellow caution tape and snatch the folder.

It's a patient file like I thought, but I didn't expect Lucas' name to be on the tab. He's been seeing the same therapist. How is this even possible? Out of all the therapists in France, he somehow end up at the same one as me. Sure, it could be possible. It must be a coincidence. But I don't know what to do with this information. It's getting hard to tell what's coincidence and what's part of Dominick's psychotic plan. I need to confront Lucas.

Thank the saints for Erianne's unrelenting need to pick up as many extra shifts she can. I still don't get why she works there. Her mama is Dominick's partner and the epitome of rich. Erianne has all the money she could ever want. She drives a Bugatti for saint's sake.

I'd bet it's to shove it to her mama, knowing Erianne. Either way, I'm thankful I always know where to find her. She paged Lucas for me and told him to meet me in the park.

His black sedan rolls to a stop in front of the park entrance. I jog over and climb inside. I'd rather do this where I know no one can hear us. The last thing I need is to make all of this even worse than it already is.

Lucas grasp my hand and his lips brush against my knuckles. "What's going on?"

I hand him the file. He opens it, realizing what he's holding. His jaw flexes as his eyes skim the pages. "Where did you get this?"

I fill him in on everything that's happened within the course of this one day. Of course, he gets overprotective. And I think Dr. Carrere's murder is bothering him more than he's letting on. I could have sworn I saw his eyes water like he wanted to cry. I've only been working with her for less than a year and she means everything to me. I've never seen him look so genuinely hurt. But I still can't shake the feeling that something isn't right about all of this.

"How and why do we have the same therapist?" I ask.

He shakes his head. "I don't know. Do you think I set this up?" His forehead scrunches.

I sigh. "Maybe. With everything else going on, I don't know what to think anymore."

He encloses my hand within his. "That's understandable. But I didn't have anything to do with any of this. I didn't even know you were in therapy until just now, let alone that we have—had the same therapist."

I pull my hand away and stare out the window as a tear streaks my face. "I can't believe she's gone."

Lucas runs a hand through his hair. "I know."

I take a deep breath. "It does seem crazy to think you'd go out of your way to get the same therapist as me. It's not like you're a stalker." I chuckle.

He grasp my hand, pulling me closer to him and pressing his lips firmly into mine. This kiss is different than before, rougher, like a desperate grab. It's absent of the passion from our first kiss. I pull away from him, squeezing his hand gently.

"Thank you for meeting me. I should probably get going." I force a small smile, ignoring the doubts swarming in my head.

I quickly get out of the car, waving as he pulls off into traffic and leave it at that.

32

I can't believe it's November 1st already. In one month and two days, I'll be an adult. I'll be a free woman. Mama hasn't said another word about my father. Lucas has been more overprotective than usual after what happened to Dr. Carrere. He wanted to confront his father, but, with Erianne's help, I convinced him not to. I'm sticking to what I said. No one else will get hurt because of me.

Lucas wants to keep me away from his world. So, we aren't able to be in public together anymore. If the wrong person sees us, it could get back to Dominick. His father made it clear he didn't want us together. So, for now, Lucas is going along with the arranged marriage. But he asked that they postpone it to give him some time. It makes me wonder how being with me can be worth it to him. We're playing with fire just by being together. One of us is going to get burned and it's not going to be pretty.

Everyone seems safer this way though. Things have been quiet. Peaceful even. I keep waiting for the other shoe to drop, but it hasn't happened. Erianne and my mama are the only two people that know about Lucas. Thank the saints Clarissa never found out. I don't even want to think about the number of people she would have blabbed to. I wonder what happened to her. I haven't seen her since the ball. At the very least, I wish I had a chance to apologize for what happened.

Besides Lucas and Erianne picking on me constantly about being American, things have been perfect. I have the best mama anyone could ask for. Erianne has become like a big sister to me. And Lucas. I don't know what I'd do without him.

Ever since I got all my memories back, my fear of thunderstorms hasn't been as bad. I think not knowing where it came from is what triggered most of the panic attacks surrounding it. It's been a little easier to be outside *and* in the rain. I guess I owe part of that to Dr. Carrere's fear ladders. I'm still working through my anxiety and not sure I'm ready for a new therapist yet. But maybe one day.

For now, I'm looking forward to seeing Lucas. Mama has welcomed him with open arms. She actually invited him over for dinner tonight after the All Saint's Day commemoration the Church of St Joan of Arc is hosting.

All Saint's Day is today. So, the catholic church organized a commemoration after service in Place Du Vieux Marche, the Old Market Place in the city centre. The entire *Place* is going to be filled with hundreds of people from church. There's going to be music playing all afternoon until dark. And if I read the program announcement correctly, food is being catered across the street from La Couronne. It's nice some people volunteered to work for this event. The church has never done this before, but the priest said it's important to celebrate the lives our loved ones carried out.

I cannot wait. Every business is closed today in honor of the holiday. Families spend the time cleaning their loved ones graves and paying their respects. I've never had a family. It's always just been me and Mama. So, this day is awkward for me, which is why I'm glad the church organized the commemoration. It's something I can actually join in on because, even though I don't know them, I have family in America.

But, before I get to enjoy the commemoration, I first get to enjoy some alone time with Lucas. Mama is letting me miss church service this year. Lucas arranged the whole morning for us. No matter how much I press him for information, he refuses to tell me where he's taking me. He did say to dress comfortably, though. My favorite green blouse, a nice pair of jeans, and my comfy black flats should suffice. I still can't believe we *finally* get to go on a real date. It's even far enough away that no one will recognize him. Which means we get to be just like a normal couple, even if it's only for a day.

"Abigail! Lucas is here!" Mama calls from the bottom of the steps.

"I'll be right down!" I shout back.

I can't get down the steps quick enough to see his devilishly handsome face. He's respectfully waiting by the door for me, with his hands folded behind his back. Always such a gentleman. He won't move from the front door unless Mama invites him to. Seems kind of ridiculous if you ask me.

The floor creaks under my foot when I reach the bottom of the steps. Lucas is like a bee to honey.

"There's my girl." He grins and envelopes me in his arms, kissing the top of my head briefly.

He's always respectful around Mama, never kissing me in front of her unless it's just on my forehead or the top of my head. Mama said she thinks it's sweet. I'm just happy she doesn't give me a hard time about seeing him.

"Make sure you two are back in time for the commemoration," Mama says, pointing at Lucas.

"We will be mademoiselle," Lucas says, respectful as ever.

Mama beams. "Oh, call me Carla, dear. You two get going and have fun. Be safe."

She doesn't have to tell me twice. I pull Lucas out the door with me and shoo him into the car. I want to know where we're going already.

As we're driving, I drink in the sight of casual, carefree Lucas. A plain t-shirt hugs his torso, and he's even wearing jeans. Who would have thought the man even owned a pair? It's a sight to behold compared to his usual suit and tie.

"No suit?" I ask.

He grins sideways at me. "Not today."

I glance out my window. "Where are you taking me, anyway?"

He chuckles. "You know, one of these days that curiosity of yours is going to bite you in the ass." A sly grin spreads at the corner of his mouth. "Or maybe I will."

I smack him playfully. "Stop kidding, Lucas! Really, where are we going?"

"You'll see in about five seconds." His grin widens into a full mischievous smile.

Ugh. We've been driving for over an hour. I want to know where we're going. And why it's such a big deal he couldn't tell me. A faded, dingy white sign on the side of the road catches my attention. "Bienvenue à Paris" is written in bold letters.

"Paris?" I ask, pressing my palms together in my lap.

"Paris," he says, clearly proud of himself.

The vast, enormous buildings are scattered around all the people bustling around. Not a single shop in sight is open. The people walking aren't rushing to get anywhere. They're so relaxed, just enjoying the day. I spot a couple flower shops along the way that have all assorted colors of Chrysanthemes on display for the holiday. The city is so serene and full of life at the same time.

I gape around in awe the further we drive in. I want to jump out of this car right now. All my time living in France and I've never been to Paris. And the person to take me is Lucas. It's perfect. My throat tightens. I want to cry. This couldn't get any more perfect. We've barely driven into the city and I'm already in love with it.

"It's amazing Lucas." I stare out the window, gawking like a child. "Is that? Are you really?" I ask, bursting at the seams as he drives toward the Eiffel Tower.

"You've lived in France all this time and have never seen the Tour Eiffel. I thought I'd be the one to show it to you." He reaches across my lap for my hand. "I want to show you the world, Abigail. Let's start here. With Paris." Pulling my hand to his mouth, the delicious contact of his lips brushing against my skin sends a chill down my spine.

All my excitement pops like a balloon, dwindling away at the sight of the sign out front stating, "*Closed*". That's weird. It's never closed.

"Why is it closed?" I ask, leaning forward, trying to see what's wrong.

He ignores me completely, throwing the car in park, and walking around to open my door. I take the hand he's extended and step out of the car. Lucas tows me along to the gated entrance of the Eiffel Tower. A man in a work uniform walks out from behind the gate, opening it without hesitation once Lucas walks up.

He glimpses at his watch and gestures for me to enter first. "I reserved it just for us today."

"How did you manage *that*?" I ask, following him up the stairs of the tower.

A sly grin forms. "I have my ways."

My feet connecting with the steel of this masterpiece is so overwhelming. *No crying.* After taking two different lifts up three flights, we finally reach the top. The view is breathtaking. The setting sun is painting the sky various shades of pink, blue, and yellow. Cars, the size of an ant from up here, drive by, in a hurry to get through their day and completely oblivious to the masterpiece they're a part of. I can see the whole city from up here.

Lucas walks over, standing behind me as he cocoons me in his arms. I've never been more at peace, seeing one of the greatest landmarks in France while in his arms.

Lucas trails agonizingly slow, feather light kisses from my temples down to the base of my neck. My knees grow weak and fluttering in my stomach mixes with a deep ache. I twirl around, wrapping my arms over his shoulders and running my fingers through his hair, giving in to the need gnawing at my insides. His hands move to grip my hips fiercely as our lips meet. I inhale the scent of his cologne, one of my favorite smells. Our tongues entwine and I match the passion in each kiss with him. A fire ignites within me. My cheeks burn hot despite the crisp air outside.

Lucas nibbles my lower lip, his hands skimming up my back. "You hungry?" he asks, leaning his head back.

"For you." I grin.

He laughs. "I'm rubbing off on you too much. That or the air is too thin up here for you and you've lost a screw up there." He pokes my head.

I laugh. "Hey!"

He checks his watch again. "Come on. I have one more place to take you." His smile is warm, tender.

Lucas escorts me down the Eiffel Tower. Each step closer to the ground is heartbreaking. I would stay up there forever if I could. Walking hand-in-hand across the empty stone courtyard, he stops in front of a restaurant on the waterfront of the Seine River. 'Le Restaurant Parisien' is in black cursive letters on the sign above the door. I furrow my brows as he checks his watch for the third time. What is he waiting for?

"Isn't this closed for All Saint's Day?" I ask as he waltzes up to the entrance.

"Yes. Except I asked a couple employees to serve us. Don't worry though. I paid the restaurant well to cover it." He casually blows it off as he opens the door for me.

First, he takes me to Paris. Then he manages to get the Eiffel Tower reserved just for us and takes me all the way to the top. Now he's taking me to a waterfront restaurant where he's personally requested the staff to be available for us. I'm speechless as we walk inside.

It's a cute, chic little place. There's nothing too obscene or fancy about it, which is unusual for Lucas. Mr. Richy-Pants is always throwing his money around carelessly. I would too if I was as loaded as he is though.

There's only about a dozen tables throughout the small space. Everything is done in wood, from the walls and floors to the furniture. Except one wall is made entirely of glass, the one facing the river. It really makes it feel more open in here and the view is beautiful.

A waiter asks if we have any seating preferences. Lucas chose a table outside to get an unobstructed view of the tower. In all the time I've spent with him these last couple months he's never done anything like this. He's gone over the top this time. And it's all for me.

"Lucas?" A woman's voice calls from across the courtyard.

Both Lucas and I turn. My heart drops to the pit of my stomach the second I recognize the woman gawking at us. Why? Why is she here right now? I want to scream. This can't be happening. Is this what Lucas was waiting for?

"What is Elizah doing all the way out here? Did you plan this?" I ask Lucas, my blood boiling as she prances over to our table.

He opens his mouth to answer but closes it as Elizah stands before us.

"I thought you needed time to think about your position right now?" She snaps at Lucas. "And what the hell do you think you're doing?" She growls, directing her glare at me.

Lucas lurches from his seat. "Back off, Elizah."

"Why are you even here?" I ask, trying to back Lucas up.

She scoffs. "This is my family's city. And that," Elizah points to Le Restaurant Parisien, "is my father's restaurant. I should be asking *you* what you're doing here. Was my warning not clear enough?"

"I said back off!" Lucas' voice booms, but Elizah doesn't appear fazed by him at all. She doesn't even flinch. Why is she so comfortable with him?

"Your father will hear about this. Get your priorities straight, Lucas. And you." She snarls and points at me. "You were warned."

Without another word, Elizah takes off, walking briskly down the courtyard like nothing ever happened.

He did not really bring me to the city where Elizah lives and to the restaurant her father owns. Why would he even take this chance? Who knows what's going to happen now. Elizah is, without a doubt, going to run right back to his father. She even said so. He, of all people, should have known better. But maybe that's exactly what he wants…

"We need to leave. Right now," Lucas says, interlacing his fingers with mine.

He leads me back to the car, gripping the steering wheel as if his life depends on it as he drives away from the Eiffel Tower. His chest heaves. The veins in his neck haven't receded.

All this time I've been waiting for the other shoe to drop. Well, it just did, and it's Lucas' fault. He did this on purpose. I have no doubts about that. A small place in my heart breaks at the thought of how he just used me as some ploy. Every worse possible scenario plays in my head, like the thought of him doing this to make Elizah jealous.

Lucas reaches over, resting his hand on my thigh. Normally, I'd welcome the contact, but all I want to do is be as far away from him as possible. I'm not just mad about what this means for our relationship. This could put my mama in danger.

I notice his eyes are tinged red as he abruptly pulls the car over, parking on the side of the road in front of a flower shop.

"What are we doing?" I ask, frantically checking our surroundings.

He takes the keys out of the ignition. "I need to get flowers."

Lucas opens his door, but I stay seated, not moving an inch.

He runs a hand through his hair, his mouth setting into a firm line. "Abigail. Please, I am sorry. I didn't intend for any of—"

I hold my hand up, cutting him off, "Don't. Do not sit there and lie to me. I *know* you did this on purpose. You've been checking your watch this whole like you knew what time she'd show up there. You used me, Lucas. And now you're trying to lie to me?' A tear streaks my face.

Lucas shakes his head, covering his face with his hands. "Abby...I'm tired of hiding. Don't you understand? I only did this so we could never have to hide again. And I did really also just want to be the one you experienced your first time seeing the Tour Eiffel with. I wanted to make it special for you. That wasn't a part of any of this. It was just for you, *mon chérie*."

His hand caresses my cheek. Despite how mad I am, I can't deny I'm tired of hiding too.

I silently get out of the car, an ache lingering in my chest. I ignore it and walk up to the flower shop with him, admiring the wide array of flowers—Chrysanthemes in blue, red, orange, purple, and some are even multi-colored. I pick a pot of the multi-colored ones for Erianne. I promised her I'd grab a pot for her.

With the pot in hand, I search for Lucas. I find him talking with an older woman. Her hair is almost as white as one of the flowers. Expertly balancing the pot in one arm, I glide over to him.

"Abigail, this is Ms. Amelia. She owns this flower shop," Lucas says, glancing down at the pot in my hand. "Let me help you with that." He rushes over, relieving me of the pot.

"Lucas was just telling me how you've never seen the Eiffel Tower until now." The older woman beams, her smile warm and tender like a grandmother's.

"He was?" I ask, tilting my head slightly. Why would he be telling some random shopkeeper about that?

"Yes dear, he was." Amelia watches Lucas walk to the car. "I haven't seen that young man in such a long time. You know, his mother used to come to get flowers here every single year on All Saint's Day."

I furrow my brow. "She did?"

I guess this isn't just some random shop then. And Amelia isn't some random shopkeeper. Lucas has never talked about his mother. I hardly know a single thing about her.

"Oh, why yes. Caterina was such a beautiful, lively young woman. It still troubles me what happened to her. The last time I saw Lucas was at her funeral. He was never the same after that day." Amelia quickly grasps my hand. "Thank you, sweet girl."

What could she be thanking me for?

I stare at her, frozen in place. "I'm sorry, I don't understand what you're thankful for."

Her smile widens. "Because I've known Lucas since he was a bright young boy. His mother, long before that. In all that time, I've never seen him so vibrant and alive. His life is filled with so much darkness. It's you that has brought the light back into his life dear girl. Bless you," Amelia gushes. A twinkle surfaces in her eyes.

"Dare I ask what you've been telling my girl?" Lucas says playfully as he joins me at my side.

"Oh, don't worry yourself with it." She swats the air, smiling vibrantly at him.

"It was good seeing you Ms. Amelia." Lucas smiles tenderly. He hugs her and kisses each of her cheeks.

"You too dear. Don't be a stranger anymore. And you bring this lovely young lady with you next time," she says, pointing a finger at him.

Lucas laughs. "Yes, mademoiselle."

"It was nice meeting you," I say politely.

"And it has been an honor to meet you." Amelia nods, smiling as Lucas walks me back to the car.

"I'll be right back. I forgot something," Lucas says, holding the car door open for me as I climb into the passenger seat.

He shuts the door and jogs back over to Amelia. They're talking, but I can't make out what they're saying. I still can't believe everything she said. And if it's true, this place must mean a lot to him. This is a lot to absorb at once. I thought he just took me to some shop. I didn't know it means so much to him.

Lucas walks back to the car, a flowerpot overflowing with white Chrysanthemes in hand. As we drive off, Amelia waves until we're out of sight. She seems nice. And reminds me a little of Mama.

I reach over to entwine my fingers with Lucas', caressing the back of his hand with my thumb. Lucas glances away from the road, over at me. There's no stopping what's about to happen with his father now. But, no matter what, he and I will survive this. There's nothing we can't handle together. So, if it's a fight his father wants, we will fight back. I'll protect my mother at all costs, even is that cost is my life.

33

"There you two are! I was beginning to worry you weren't coming!" Erianne pecks both of my cheeks. "Your mother was going to kill Lucas if you two were late." I laugh with Erianne as she steps away.

"I'm sorry we're a little behind. I took Abigail to pick up flowers," Lucas says, greeting my mother with a hug.

He never hugs Mama… Okay, now I'm being paranoid. He's probably just trying to be considerate now that he knows she's American.

"So, where did he take you?" Mama asks. Her smile broadens, crinkling her eyes at the corners.

"To the Eiffel Tower," I gush.

Erianne swats his arm. "Look at you Lucas, pulling out all the stops. I'm impressed."

I was wrong earlier when I said being atop the Eiffel Tower is the most at peace I've ever been. Right here and now, with my mama whom I love more than my own life, my best friend who's been here unconditionally, and the man I honestly believe will fill many more years of my future, this is the pure definition of being at peace. I'm surrounded by people that care infinitely for me. My heart is so full.

Nighttime is approaching fast. With only a few more minutes left, the commemoration is almost over. A couple people have already started saying their goodbyes. As I dance with Lucas to the final song of the night, the crisp night air cools my face. All this dancing is a workout. It's been so much fun though. A goofy, lopsided grin forms over my mouth the more I think about it.

"What is it?" Lucas shouts over the music, cupping my face in his hand as he smirks.

"I'm just so happy." I shout over the music.

Lucas gently lifts my chin with his finger and places a soft kiss on my lips. "Let's go."

Lucas takes it upon himself to bring the two pots of Chrysanthemes over. He won't let anyone help him. I shake my head, smirking. He's so stubborn.

"I'll take this one." Erianne takes the multi-colored pot out of Lucas' hands. She stares at it, her trembling hands making the flowers shake. Her voice quakes, "I'm not looking forward to this." Erianne's cousin passed away a few months before we met. So, I can't imagine how hard this is for her.

Lucas steps forward. "I can go with you."

Erianne smiles weakly. "No. I know you want to visit your mother's grave."

Oh, hell. I can't believe I didn't remember that. On the day dedicated to loved ones who have passed away, it slipped my mind Lucas is paying his respects to his mother today. I'm a terrible girlfriend. And I was so hard on him earlier. I didn't even stop to think what today means to him. He hardly talks about his Mama, but this is something I should've remembered.

Mama encloses one of Erianne's hand within hers, smiling warmly. "Well, I was just going to head back home, but I can come along with you."

A tear streaks Erianne's face. "Thank you, Carla."

"It's no trouble dear. We better get going before it gets dark." Mama leads Erianne toward the cemetery.

Lucas holds his flowers with one arm as he laces his fingers with mine. "Would you like to come with me? It's been awhile since I've done this and I'm not sure I can do it without you."

I nod, not really knowing the right thing to say, but wanting to be here for him.

Walking alongside Lucas, we cross through the gate into the cemetery. Erianne is slowly walking toward her family crypt with Mama's arm draped over her as she holds onto a rosary, praying. Erianne's shoulders shake as sobs wrack her body. Lucas stops in front of a small pathway leading further into the cemetery.

"I can't do this." He turns to walk away.

I grab his hand, stopping him. "You *can*. I'm here for you."

He grips onto my hand, a small smile brightening his face, and nods before continuing ahead. He leads me down the pathway and through the graveyard, stopping in front of a large statue of an angel. The stone wings are outstretched, spanning at least a foot each. The angel's hair cascades past her shoulders. She's so… life-like. Lucas stares at it. His mouth turns downward, and any traces of happiness evaporate. His shoulders sag as he slowly walks up to the marble tombstone underneath the angel.

Cautiously, as if the stone will shatter from his touch, he crouches and places the flowers down. His fingers glide over the inscription on the headstone, tracing the outlines of each letter.

Caterina Réabeck Danforth

April 6th, 1977 - April 5th, 2013

Beloved Wife and Mother

My throat tightens. I wish I had a way to ease his pain. To make this hurt less.

He stands and silently walks to the marble stone bench positioned in front of her grave. Tearing my gaze from him, I approach his mother's headstone. Such a finite resting place. My heart strains, as if a ton of weights are pressing on it.

I kneel next to Lucas' blooming white Chrysanthemes, whispering, "I wish I'd have gotten the honor of meeting you. Lucas cherishes you and loves you like a son should love a mother as great as you were. Thank you, Mrs. Danforth, for the incredible man you brought into this world. I promise to take care of him and to always be good to him. Rest in peace. And may the saints grant you eternal paradise."

A tear trickles from the corner of my eye and down my cheek as I join Lucas on the bench. Lucas' reddened damp face and swollen eyes squeeze my heart. I wrap my arm around him to offer him some solace. He rests his head against my shoulder.

"Thank you for that," he croaks. "I know if she was listening, she would have loved to hear you say all that." He wipes his face, taking a steadying breath.

I regard his mother's resting place with admiration. "I think she's always with you. And always listening."

Lucas hesitantly stands. "Let's head back."

"We can stay longer if you'd like." I peer up at him from my seat on the bench.

His smile doesn't quite reach his eyes. "That's alright. It's getting late and your mother went through all the trouble of making dinner for everyone."

As I stand, my hands graze over small divots in the bench. I hadn't noticed earlier, but there's something engraved on it.

I will always be with you, even in your darkest days.

I wonder what the meaning behind it is.

"She always used to say that to me." Lucas regards the engraving, his frown deepening.

"It's beautiful, Lucas." I join him at his side.

He takes my hand, leading me out of the graveyard. "It was actually my father who had the bench placed there. He said it was so we could sit with my mother when we came to visit her resting place. I asked for that to be engraved on it though."

I didn't expect that. To think his father could be sentimental enough to have a bench carved for his departed wife is odd. It's such a loving notion. And *so* unlike the heartless, cruel man I met that carelessly threatened my mama. I'm surprised Dominick didn't show up here tonight then. If he cared so much, he should have been here.

Maybe all these years dealing with her death has hardened his heart. He obviously used to have some amount of warmth in there, but I think recent events can attest his heart has grown cold. I wonder what living with him through the years has been like for Lucas. Peeking up at him, his swollen eyes, tinged red, are narrowed as he stares straight ahead.

He snarls. "Will you give me a moment? I need to take care of something."

Following his fixed stare, I realize he's laser focused on Mathieu standing outside the cemetery gates. Why is he here? My stomach does somersaults at the sight of him.

Nodding at Lucas, I give his hand a gentle squeeze and walk away down the paved path. Not too far, though. Just enough to give them distance, but to where I can still hear what they're saying.

I want to be respectful of Lucas' privacy, especially if this is 'business'. But after Lucas' stunt, I want to know what Mathieu has to say to him. I *have* to know. And Lucas would never tell me himself no matter how many times I ask.

"You've got some nerve showing your face here," Lucas seethes, standing with his fists clenched at his sides just a few feet away from Mathieu.

Mathieu throws his hands up. "Orders are orders. You know that. I didn't mean any disrespect, but your father said to keep tabs on the girl."

"I don't give a damn what my father said, and to hell with his orders! I trusted you! Erianne trusted you!" Lucas growls.

Mathieu scans the area, his eyes frantically darting from person to person. "Quiet down. The last thing we need is to draw attention. Especially right now." He smirks, a deep cackle escaping past his thin lips.

Mathieu's gleaming eyes full of sickening pride meet mine. Lucas glimpses over his shoulder, following Mathieu's beady daggers. The muscles in Lucas' jaw tighten, his mouth pressing tightly into a firm line. His knuckles bloom a ghastly white. In one swift motion, Lucas whirls around and grabs him up by his collar. Mathieu gags, gasping for air.

Lucas roars, "What are you talking about? What have you done?"

Instinctively, I take a step toward Lucas to calm him.

Lucas glances to the side. "Abigail. Stay!" His voice booms.

I stop dead in my tracks. This isn't about me right now. I need to let Lucas handle this because saint only knows what Mathieu has done. Wringing my hands, I try to keep steady as my head swims with the possibilities.

"You think I'd live to see tomorrow if I didn't tell your father you took her to the graveyard?" Mathieu spits back.

All the blood rushes to his face, his cheeks burning crimson. His eyes tell me he'd murder Mathieu right where he stands if it weren't such a public area.

He tightens his grip on Mathieu's collar, his voice a low grumble. "You may not live to see tomorrow anyway."

The veins in Mathieu's neck pop as he chokes, clawing at his throat and Lucas' fist blocking his airway. Lucas squeezes harder, lifting him in the air until his feet dangle off the ground. Mathieu's skin fades into a sickly grey and gradually blooms a mix of blue and purple. His feet kick and kick hopelessly, frantically, as he tries desperately to fill his lungs.

Oh, my saints. Lucas *is* going to kill him. I have to stop him. My body won't obey what my mind is telling it though. The sight of Lucas with someone's life in his hands, ready to strip that life away so carelessly, shakes me to my core. I can't move. I can't will my feet forward. The vast open space of the graveyard caves in on me. A gust of wind smacks my face. As if I've just been knocked in the gut, all the air is sucked from my lungs. The wind howls in my ears. *No. No. No.* Not a storm. I haven't had a panic attack in so long. Now, it's like all that time is catching up with me and crashing down on me at once. I stumble backward, losing my footing.

Lucas breaks his focus on Mathieu and stares wide-eyed at me, as if just now realizing what he's doing. He drops Mathieu.

"Get the hell out of here," Lucas snarls.

Mathieu gasps for air and takes off running down the street. Lucas rushes to my side. In the distance, the faint echo of Erianne's laughter slices through my panic. A small drop of calm, but not enough. The trees and headstones swirl in my vision. Lucas grabs my face in his hands, but my body is numb. His touch is absent to me.

"Abigail. I'm so sorry, *mon chérie*. I'm here. You're okay." He leans his forehead against mine.

A chaste kiss greets my lips, the contact acting as an anchor. Blinking rapidly, I gaze up into his hooded eyes full of need. He kisses me again and again. The panic attack subdues. I place my hands over his as they grip my face, deepening the next kiss. I need him. As if he understands this need, he doesn't break contact with my lips.

He drops his hands from my face and grabs my waist, lifting me off the ground just enough to carry me out of the cemetery. I wrap my arms around his neck as he presses me against the outside wall surrounding the graveyard. My back collides with the rough surface of the brick. A moan escapes past my lips. I need him. I need this, to be lost with him. He pulls his face away from mine, planting a final swift kiss on my now swollen lips. Our breathing is ragged.

Seeing him so violent, so angry, set off something in my mind. I've never really grasped the full extent of who he is and what he does. I've never witnessed that side of him either. Seeing it with my own eyes is a world of difference from just hearing about it. Normal people would walk away. Hell. They'd run for the hills. But… I'm not normal.

I want more. More of him. More of his life. The good, the bad, the ugly, even the most terrifying parts. It's all a part of who this magnificent man is, and I want all of it with him.

I love him.

34

"Ahem." Mama clears her throat, standing just a few feet away from Lucas and me.

I jump back and try to step away from him as my cheeks enflame. He doesn't let me free of his arms though. I rest my hands on his biceps.

"Get a room!" Erianne rolls her eyes, playfully hitting Lucas in the arm.

His muscles tense under my fingertips. Squeezing his eyes shut, I can tell he's concentrating on shoving his natural reaction down. Deep down. Slowly and deliberately, I graze my hands down his biceps to his forearms, allowing my fingertips to brush against his wrist. Like fire to gasoline, his hands melt into mine.

Lucas' eyes blink open, fixating on my face. As I gently squeeze his hands, his muscles gradually relax. A crooked grin just barely dimples his cheek as he pulls one of my hands to his lips.

Erianne doesn't seem to notice at all what just happened. What felt like an eternity between Lucas and I, really has only been a few fleeting seconds. Mama is glowing, staring at us with admiration. Erianne won't stop bouncing on her heels.

I giggle. "What are you so excited about?"

She staggers backward, placing a hand over her chest. "How can you not be excited when we're only minutes from having your Mama's cooking in our stomachs?" She smirks.

I shake my head, laughing as she leads the way to my place.

Mama opens the door to our flat and the salivating savory aroma of lamb hits us before we even step inside and fills our nostrils.

"Carla, what is that?" Erianne's eyes alight as she sniffs the air like a hound dog.

Mama chuckles. "Follow me and you'll find out."

Erianne doesn't hesitate, trailing behind Mama inside, practically panting along the way. The lamb has been roasting in the oven since earlier this morning, so the house is swarming from the floor to the roof with the mix of aromas from lamb, spices, and trimmings. Enough for a small meal together to end the night.

I can't shake the looming warning screaming in my gut. Things with Lucas' father are about to get bad. There's no telling what he's going to do now that he knows Lucas betrayed him. A father betrayed by his own son…

I don't want to think about all that right now though. All I want to do is enjoy this time with my family. I may not live past the new year. A lump forms in my throat at the thought. All of this is a lot to deal with and I'm trying so hard to be strong for everyone else.

These moments—Lucas and Erianne teasing each other, bickering like brother and sister while Mama fixes the plates—these little moments are the most important.

Lucas reaches across the table for a slice of baguette and Mama's hand cracks across his. Anticipating the same reaction as earlier when Erianne hit him, I rest my hand on his knee to soothe him. But he just flashes me a boyish grin.

"We pray before we touch anything." My mother scolds him.

"Yes, mademoiselle." Lucas pouts, sticking his lower lip out.

Erianne snickers. Mama scowls at her and she quickly zips her lips. It's like I'm sitting at the table with a couple of kids. Mama holds her hands out. Erianne and Lucas each take one, bowing their heads in unison. Reaching to place one hand in Erianne's and the other in Lucas', I bask in the overwhelming sense of family as Mama prays.

"Father, All-Powerful and ever-living god,
who dost enkindle the flame of Thy love in the hearts of the *saints*,
Today we rejoice in the *holy* men and women,
mothers and fathers, brothers and sisters,
and all kin of every living time and place
Grant unto us the same faith and power of love;
That as we rejoice in their triumphs, we may *learn from their examples*
May their own prayers bring us your *forgiveness* and love.
Amen."

35

Yesterday was possibly the best All Saint's Day ever. Not that all the other ones I've spent with Mama haven't been great. It's just nice to know what it feels like to have family. My mama, Erianne, and Lucas are the closest thing I have to one.

Being that it's the day after All Saint's Day, everything is slowly starting to return to the usual mundane routines. The shops, restaurants, and other businesses are opening up. Delano has me working a double shift. I'm hardly four hours in and already want to go home.

I finish clearing a table, stacking all the dirty dishes together. Erianne saunters out of the kitchen carrying a tray of food as I'm balancing the tower of soiled dishes. A wicked grin takes shape on her mouth just as she bumps her hip into me.

"Merde!" I blurt out, every dish nearly crashing to the floor.

Thankfully I'm quick on my feet. I'm able to balance everything back, but my stack has turned into the leaning tower of dishes. If she wants to play, then we can play. I set the dishes next to the kitchen sink. After checking that Erianne isn't watching, I swap two of her order receipts and place them with different trays. Now to sit back and watch. She's going to give the wrong orders to two separate tables. That's going to be a royal mess.

She waltzes over picking up the trays without even checking the receipts. I watch, narrowing my eyes, as she serves the food to all the right people, at the right tables.

Erianne saunters back over behind the counter. "You gotta try harder than that Abbs." She laughs.

Delano is staying confined to his office. Thank the saints. I've been avoiding him as much as possible since he asked me to the ball. It's just too awkward. And Lucas already wants to wring his neck. Again. Not that any of that has stopped Delano from making vulgar comments or violating the sexual harassment policy in new ways every day. He's a creep, but a harmless one. So, I don't bother with any of it.

Erianne and I spend most of the remainder of our shift trying to sabotage each other. I mix up the bills for her tables, but she masterfully corrects it within seconds. She locks the cash drawer and pockets the key right as I'm about to cash a customer out. But all I successfully manage to do is break the thing trying to get it open. Oh, and I scared the customer. Needless to say, I did *not* get a tip for that. Every time I try to one up Erianne, she diverts the problem effortlessly. But when she does the same to me, it ends in disaster. Entertainment for her, maybe, but disaster for me.

The hallow booming of church bells sounds off from every direction as the clock strikes six in the afternoon. I run up to Erianne, dropping my pen and notepad not so subtly on the counter.

"I call a truce. You are the better server." I bow, giving up entirely.

She laughs. "Abby, I've been working here for years. It was almost five years ago when I first walked in that front door for this job." The familiar chime of the door to the restaurant rings in my ear. "Speaking of. You've got customers. Better get to it," Erianne sneers, chuckling as she gets back to balancing the register.

I pout as I walk over to greet the customer but stop dead in my tracks once I realize just who the customer is. Swallowing past my tightening throat, my lungs deflate instantaneously, making me choke for air. My heart stops. A cringing, stomach-turning knot is already growing, my lunch threatening to make an appearance.

At a loss for words, I gape at the two men in black and crimson suits shadowing a tall, husky man. His suit is almost entirely crimson, except for the tie that's black as night. The colors are a dead giveaway, but I don't need to see the colors in his suit to know it's Dominick Vitale, with his black hair streaked in gray, standing in front of me. I stagger backward, barely able to maintain my balance.

A dark, cold grin crawls over his mouth. "Well? Are you going to seat us or are we going to stand here staring at each other all night?"

"Right this way." I lower my head as I walk them to their table.

Peeking sideways behind the counter, Erianne is standing stock still. All the color drains from her face as she watches Dominick take a seat. I know this isn't good.

"What's good here?' Dominick casually picks up a menu off the table.

Does he really expect me to serve him and act like he's just some regular customer? Whatever then.

"Well, I've been told the Saumon a la crème—" I shut my mouth as he holds his hand up.

I guess not.

"On second thought, I'll just take a bottle of one of your reds." He hands over the menu. I cautiously take it from him, not sure exactly what's going on here.

We have hundreds of different red wines. The last thing I want to do is make the mistake of bringing one he doesn't like.

"Which—" I squeak.

Dominick cuts me off. "Why don't you just take a seat?" An unnerving dark smirk creeps over his face.

I should have just brought him the wine.

I don't understand why he wants me to sit. As I hesitate, the two men with him scoot their chairs back like they're about to make me sit. Choosing the latter, I take a seat using my own free will—what little bit of it I have right now.

"I thought you might see it my way." Dominick rubs his chin. "You see, Abigail. I'm a man of my word. I tell someone I'm going to be on time for a meeting, then I'm on time, if not early. I tell a man I'm going to shatter his rib cage if he doesn't pay up, then I'm going to personally shatter his rib cage. So, when I tell you to stay away from my boy or else, and you don't listen, what do you think I'm going to do?"

Dominick patiently waits for my answer. How in the hell does he expect me to answer that question? My head throbs. I have to say something though.

I twist my hands, pressing them together in my lap. "I haven't seen Lucas." I try to lie.

The lump in my throat threatens to suffocate me. My heart is beating a million miles a minute. Dominick straightens up in his chair as the men with him slowly rise from theirs. The room sways. I think I'm going to be sick. What are they going to do to me?

"Winnow. Pogrom. Close up shop," he orders to the men in black suits.

Both men walk around the restaurant, escorting all the customers out—some willingly and some by force. I watch as these innocent people are dragged from their seats to the door if they refuse to leave. These men are acting like soldiers, the way they follow their orders without question or cause to do so. Just not the kind you'd trust with your life.

Casting a quick glimpse at Erianne, she's toying with something in her hand. Her fingers fumble the small rectangular black object as they shake violently. Squinting, I watch her without making it obvious, trying to figure out what in her hand is so important.

It's her phone. She's typing on her phone. A sliver of hope sparks within me. Please be sending a distress signal to the military, coast guard, anti-mafia group. *Something.* I don't care who she's texting as long as it's someone that can help. I have no idea what Dominick is up to, but it's far from good.

"You can stay. Maybe you can talk some sense into this girl," Dominick says to Erianne as the other two men lock the doors.

She jolts her head forward, stealthily tucking her cellphone away. A bead of sweat rolls past her temple.

Dominick grunts. "Now. Back to our conversation. I'm going to give you one chance to think about what you just said to me."

"I'm sorry. I saw him once, the day before All Saint's Day. I swear that was the only time and I haven't seen him since!" I plead, sitting forward.

That's an absolute lie, but what am I supposed to do? Admit that we never stopped seeing each other in the first place? Uh, no. I like my kneecaps in place and intact.

Dominick cackles. "Elizah did bring that to my attention. Unfortunately for you, I saw you at my dear Caterina's grave." His eyes darken, an eerie grin pressing onto his mouth. "Tell me. What right do you think you have to go anywhere near there?" His voice booms, echoing off the ceiling and making me cringe.

So, he did go there that night. Maybe he does have something left of that cold, dark heart of his. But knowing that isn't going to help me.

"I meant no disrespect. I only—" My words get caught in my throat as I frantically try to fix this, but I know it's beyond repair. I've not only just pissed off a crime lord, but I've offended him, too. May the saints be with me.

He leans forward in his chair, resting an arm on the table dangerously close to me. "You sat there lying to me, little girl." The way he relaxes so easily is unsettling. "I could easily squeeze the truth out of you, but that's not why I'm here. You see, I don't like it when people disobey me. Lucas is being reprimanded as we speak. So, now all I have left to deal with is you." A sly grin crawls over his mouth as he sits back in his chair, folding his hands together.

What does he mean 'Lucas is being reprimanded? *No.*

"What have you done to Lucas?" I shout, sitting forward.

Dominick ignores my question and snaps his fingers, keeping eye contact with me. A thunderous crash makes my heart skip a beat and my breath catch in my throat. The men are tearing the restaurant apart. Tables and chairs are being thrown everywhere, glasses shattered, cabinets turned over, and everything one by one is getting destroyed.

I watch mindlessly as a crippling fear overtakes my whole body. I can't move despite how badly I want to. The sadistic sneer plastered on Dominick's face shakes me to my core. What is he doing? I want to scream for them to stop, but I can't force my mouth to form the words. Erianne makes a run for it toward the hallway just as Delano's office door rips open.

Delano barges out. "What the hell?" he shouts.

He gawks around at the chaos unfolding in front of him. One of the men grabs Delano, restraining him.

"Get your hands off me, you buffoon!" Delano shouts.

Dominick's face reddens as any sign of amusement wilts. He stands and faces Delano and instantaneously Delano deflates, compliantly bowing his head.

"Winnow. Pogrom." Dominick calls and directs his attention back to me. "Now you know what happens when you agitate me. I warned you and now you get to find out what happens when you cross me." He spits the twisted words out and signals for the men to follow him.

His goon releases Delano and the other throws a chair down, shattering it to pieces. I can't process anything right now. I can't believe this just happened. All I keep replaying in my head over and over are the words he last said "...*now you get to find out what happens when you cross me.*"

The terror coursing through my veins is weighing my whole body down. Blinking my eyes, I try to focus. Erianne isn't crying like I thought she might be. Instead, she rushes from the hallway, kneeling in front of me. She grabs my arm, but I don't feel the contact of her touch.

"Abigail! Are you okay? Please tell me you're okay. Don't faint on me again, okay?" Erianne firmly grips my shoulders as she hysterically checks me over.

My legs are there, but there's no sensation coming from them. Shaking my head, I meet Erianne's worry filled emerald eyes.

"I'm…okay." I force the words out of my mouth still not able to accept what just happened.

"No! No! No! The owners are going to kill me!" Delano screams, gripping his face with both hands.

Erianne acts as my temporary anchor, bringing me back down and out of this haze. With a bittersweet ache, I use the breathing technique Dr. Carrere taught me. Inspecting the room, I can hardly see the floor through all the debris.

"I-I'm sorry Delano," I croak.

"To hell with you and your sorry. Clean this shit up! Now!" He bellows, throwing his hands up in the air.

He kicks a broken chair leg to the side as he walks back to his office. I wince as the deafening thud of the door slamming echoes through the now empty restaurant. Everything on the walls has even been torn down. All that history…just ripped away like it means nothing.

"Come on, *chère*. Let's get you home," Erianne says and pulls me up from the chair I've sunken into.

I plant my feet firmly. "I don't want to go home right now. I need to make sure Lucas is okay." His father's words repeat over and over in my head like a broken record. *"Lucas is being reprimanded as we speak."*

"Abby, he isn't going to be coming any time soon. He didn't answer my page. You and I both know he would've already been here if he could be." Erianne tries to easily let me down.

Nothing about what she just said is easy to digest though. How far is his father willing to go to make his point? What's he doing to *mon amour*, my Lucas? A tear streaks down my cheek.

This is all my fault.

I can't think clearly, but one thing I'm certain about is that I'm not going home right now. I refuse to scare Mama or worry her. Even slightly.

I shake my head. "My mama can't see me like this."

"Okay. We can go back to my place." Erianne tugs on me again.

"No. Let's just clean all this up," I say and mindlessly begin collecting broken furniture pieces.

"Abigail." Erianne cautiously approaches me.

All the self-control I'm using to hold myself together gives out. "Erianne! I can't help Lucas right now and I can't go home to my mother. I can't do anything right now to help anyone. So, the one thing I can do is clean this mess. Dominick did this because of me. All this because I fell in love with Lucas."

My face strains as a few stray tears escape the corner of my eyes. Despite my best efforts.

Erianne nods. "Okay." She walks to the back room, returning with a broom in hand. "We will clean then."

36

I'm starting to feel a little better, calmer now. But nothing is going to take away the fear lingering throughout my body. I doubt even Lucas will be able to make me feel better. All this because I kept letting my curiosity get the better of me. I knew being with him was going to be dangerous, but I stupidly thought he could protect every last one of us. I should've walked away when I had the chance.

It's been hours since we started, and we've made some real progress. The sun is setting behind the Church of St Joan of Arc across the street. Small rays of sunshine glare through the windows, blinding me when I lean the wrong way. Both Erianne and I are sweating like crazy by the time we finish sweeping up the broken glass.

Erianne scoffs. "You think Delano is going to stay in his office all night? Or do you think he might actually get up off his ass and help us?"

"What are you little tarts talking about?" A husky, slurred voice barks behind us.

We practically jump out of our skin. I definitely didn't hear anyone come in. Following the voice, I roll my eyes at Delano leaning against the back wall, a glass in hand. He lifts the glass to his mouth, taking a long swig of the mahogany brown liquid inside. The foul, bitter stench from his glass wafts around the room.

He's drunk.

Erianne rolls her eyes. "Delano, go away." She goes back to sweeping.

Delano's face twist and melts bright red. "Listen here, you trashy little slut!" He crosses the room too quickly, yanking her up by her burgundy blouse.

Erianne grasps his hands and attempts to pull them off, but she can't get free. He lifts her in the air. I have to stop him. He needs to get his grubby paws the hell off of my best friend. After everything I've been through and the people I've faced, Delano doesn't scare me.

"Get your hands off her!" I growl, clenching my fist, and charge at him.

But I'm not fast enough.

Delano tosses Erianne to the ground, her head slamming against the hardwood with a crack. The sound startles me out of my intent to attack him. Standing no more than a few feet away, he whisks around. The back of his hand slams against my cheek, jarring my head to the side. I stumble backward at the sudden, hard contact. Losing my balance, my feet catch on a broken piece of furniture. I barely catch myself as my body collides with the wooden floor as my blood boils.

"Abigail!" Erianne's scream pierces my ears.

Delano crosses the room. "Shut it, bitch!" His voice booms as he slowly turns back to me, taking one menacing step after another. "All of this is your fault. I was fine staring at your sweet little asses all day, but then you had to go and fuck with that criminal! None of this would have happened if you picked me. Now look at what you've done." His tongue glides across his lips, dampening them.

Frantically, I search for something to use as a weapon. A sharpness splinters through my head and more memories flood in like water bursting through an already broken dam.

A man hovering over me, readying his fist for another blow. His face, usually blacked out, is clearer than ever. Every detail–down to the creases around his mouth from a time when joy once filled that cold, darkened soul–is crystal clear. The nightmares, the memories that have been haunting me. My father caused those. I knew that. But…reliving it so vividly… My vision swirls.

Delano's footsteps thump the floor inches in front of me, his eyes raking up and down my body. I restrain from gagging as his teeth graze his lower lip. My heart stops. No matter how much I choke for air, I can't breathe. An uncontrollable quake overcomes my body. I always knew he's a disgusting excuse for a man. No way am I letting his filthy hands touch my skin. No one will *ever* put their hands on me again.

He reaches down and I kick his hand to the side as hard as I can. Pushing past the panic attack trying to take control, I grab a nearby broken chair leg and swing it. It connects with Delano's knee and he buckles, wincing in pain. Readying the chair leg above my head, I swing it down hard, prepared to crash it right into that thick American skull of his. But he catches it in his hands, yanks it from my grip, and slings the chair leg across the room.

Erianne's ear-splitting cry pierces my ears. "Leave her alone!"

Delano's feet scrape the wood as he stands and whips around. "Didn't I tell you to shut the—"

A deafening crack resonates throughout the room, followed by a final thud. I peek past my hand just as Delano's head bounces off the floor. Lucas is looming tall over his unconscious body, rolling his broad-shoulders. He steps over Delano like he's just a pile of trash on the floor, stopping in front of me.

"Jimmy. Check on Erianne," he orders before cautiously leaning down, "Abigail, baby, it's me."

His voice washes over my body like a protective blanket. I want to leap into his arms, but as he scoots an inch closer, the light gleaming in from the window illuminates his face, shining on a bright purple bruise decorating his cheek.

Reality slams down on me. I choke as the warm liquid puddles in my eyes and burst through uncontrollably. My lungs fill with oxygen only to quickly empty again with each sob leaving my body.

"I-I'm so…sorry," I croak.

Lucas swoops me into his arms. "No. No, baby, listen to me. Do not apologize. Shh, now. I'm here. Everything is okay." He sits on the floor and rocks me gently in his arms.

His hand glides over my cheek. Instead of being filled with the warmth of his touch, I instantly wince, jumping back at the unexpected sharp, burning pain. My hand instinctively shoots up to protect my face. I don't need to protect myself from Lucas though. Ashamed of my reaction, I bury my head in his chest, wanting nothing more than to escape. Escape all of this with him.

Lucas grunts, exhaling deeply. He silently and gingerly peels my hand from my face. His finger twirls, gesturing for me to turn my head. I do as he asks, and his hand grips the back of my shirt firmly as he examines my cheek.

"That scumbag cut you! I'll kill him!" he roars. He leans forward to set me down.

I desperately grip his shirt. "No! Don't! You can't leave..." I tighten my hold on his shirt.

He plants a kiss on the top of my head and wraps his arms underneath me, holding on as he stands up. "I've got you, *mon amour*."

Jimmy helps Erianne into the car, draping his suit jacket over her shoulders while Lucas carries me out the door. I squeeze my eyes shut, soaking in the satisfying warmth of his embrace. The oak scented cologne he usually wears fills my nostrils and acts as an herbal medicine for my soul.

"Take care of this son of a bitch." Lucas snarls the order to Jimmy.

Jimmy quickly makes a phone call.

"Lucas, no," Erianne calls from inside the car.

"Not now, Erianne," Lucas snaps. He presses me tighter against him, his voice softening. "Let's get you home."

Home. Home sounds good.

37

Lucas holds me tightly in his lap the entire way to my place. Erianne stares out at the window, pulling Jimmy's jacket tightly against her.

"Are you okay?" Lucas tilts my head up.

He's all the comfort I need.

"*Oui*. I'm alright." I smile. "What did you tell Jimmy to do with Delano?"

Lucas presses his lips together. "You don't have to worry about that."

I can tell he isn't going to tell me and I'm too exhausted to try to get it out of him anyway. Jimmy drives past a nearby streetlamp, its warm fluorescent glow casting light into the car and outlining Lucas' face. The bruise on his cheek is worse than I thought. It stretches from the tip of his cheekbone down to his chin. The sight of it sends an arrow straight to my chest, piercing my heart. *What have they done to him?*

Lucas wipes a stray tear from my face. "What's wrong?"

"What did your father do to you?" I ask as I stare at the purple spot on his face.

Lucas closes his eyes, shaking his head. "Nothing." He points to his cheek. "This is from his bodyguard. My father told me he was coming to La Couronne after you. I tried to stop him." He gently caresses my cheek. "I'm sorry I didn't make it sooner."

I place my hand over his. "You made it. That's all that matters."

Lucas runs his finger along my face, being careful to stray from the cut Delano left. "Everything is going to be okay now."

He kisses my temple. Jimmy puts the car in park. I glance out the window. We're in front of my flat. Home sweet home. I have no idea how I'm going to explain this to my mama. She's definitely going to want to know how I got a cut on my face.

"Sir." Jimmy's voice quakes.

Why does he sound upset? Jimmy is always so professional. His composure never wavers. Lucas jerks his head forward, squinting into the rearview mirror. Jimmy nods toward my place. Lucas quickly looks up then back to me, grasping my chin.

"Stay here, Abigail." Lucas gently sets me on the seat next to him. "Erianne." His mouth sets into a firm line.

She nods silently as if she completely understands what's going on. He and Jimmy silently get out of the car.

"Lucas, what's happening?" I ask, my heartrate accelerating. "Erianne, what's going on?" I frantically ask her.

The grave, pained expression that forms on her face sends chills down my spine. Tears pool in her swollen emerald eyes. She won't answer me. Turning in my seat, I watch as Jimmy and Lucas climb the steps. My front door catches my attention. It's been busted open and is barely hanging onto the frame.

No… *Mama.*

I fling the car door open, frantically climbing out as limb by limb my body goes numb.

"Abigail! Stop! Don't!" Erianne's cries fade away as I reach the steps.

Jimmy grabs ahold of me, stopping me in my tracks. Lucas is standing in my doorway with his hand cupped over his mouth. Tears are streaming freely down his face. He never cries. It must be bad…really bad.

No. No. No.

I shove Jimmy, breaking free from his grip and race to the doorway. Lucas quickly turns around, grabbing me and trying to hold me back. But not before I see the inside of my home.

My entire world comes crashing down as I see the puddle of red liquid. "No! Mama! Oh my god! Mama! Mommy!" Tears flow uncontrollably down my face as I fight Lucas, trying to break away.

Lucas' grip weakens just enough that I'm able to slip past him. I make it just inside the doorway and my entire being is overtaken by a crippling grief. My mother is on the floor, underneath the red liquid. She isn't moving. Why isn't she moving?

No. No. No.

I crumple to the floor next to her. "Mommy. Mommy, please wake up. Please." I beg through my sobs. She doesn't move. "Someone help me! We have to wake her up!" I scream.

Lucas and Jimmy are just standing in the doorway. Why won't they help? Can't they see she needs help? Erianne rushes to the door but comes to a skidding halt. She collapses in the doorway, her shoulders shaking. She'll help me. I need to wake my mama up. She has to wake up.

Lucas won't stop staring wide-eyed, his face paler than I've ever seen it. Erianne pulls herself up, her heels clicking against the hardwood floor as she stumbles over next to me. She's going to help.

"Abigail, you have to get up." She tries to pull me to my feet.

"No!" I shout at her, yanking away, "Mommy. Mommy. Please. I'm so sorry." She isn't waking up. The red liquid smears onto my hands and knees as I pull her into my lap. "Please come back to me. Please." I weep over my mama's lifeless body.

I move a stray hair from her face as I rock back and forth with her in my arms. The warmth in her that usually makes all my worries go away with one simple hug…isn't here. She's cold as ice. There's no twinkle in her loving brown eyes anymore. They're void of any emotion, of any sign of life. My mommy, my dear sweet mama. Not you. You don't deserve this. Why won't you come back to me?

This is punishment for what I've done. Everything around me drowns away as I grip her tightly in my arms.

This is all because of me.

38

I was wrong when I said I'm going to be the cat curiosity kills. No.

My curiosity got my own mother killed. I'm the reason this happened.

"Abigail. The police need to take her now," Erianne says, trying to move me.

"No!" I shout, "My mama needs me. I have to stay with her." I wrap Mama tighter in my arms.

Erianne's cries are muffled out by the thoughts swarming in my head. There are people in uniforms of all kinds in my home right now. This is mine and my mama's home. I want them to get out. Erianne should have never called them. I don't care what Lucas told her. Why isn't he here right now? He should be here…

The grip of someone's hand grabbing my arm startles me. I jolt my head upward to find Mathieu standing behind me, holding my arm. *No.* He shouldn't be here. Why is *he* here?

He yanks on my arm. "Abigail. Come on, you have to get up. Get. Up!"

I fight him with every bit of strength I have, but it's not enough. A man wearing sterile blue gloves pulls Mama away as Mathieu lifts me off the floor. *No. My mama. I can't leave her.*

"Let me go! You son of a bitch! Let go of me! She needs me! Don't you understand? She needs me!" I scream, hitting Mathieu in his chest as hard as I can over and over.

Mathieu wraps his arms tightly around my body. I try and try to break free, but he won't budge. Another man with glasses carries a long black bag inside and lays it next to Mama. No, they can't put her in that. She doesn't belong there. I thrash in Mathieu's arms. They can't take her.

"Let's take her up to her room," Erianne says to Mathieu.

I'm right here and I don't want to go to my room. I want to stay with my mama. She needs me. Why isn't anyone listening to me? The men in suits lift Mama into the bag.

"She can't go…" I croak as they pull the zipper closed, concealing her face.

My legs give out. Mathieu lifts my feet off the floor, carrying me in his arms. I don't have any fuel left in me to fight back anymore. Collapsing, I drown everything else out. Erianne's crying, the commotion of all the people in my home, the clanking of the gurney as it carries Mama outside. Nothing matters anymore.

A cold, wet drop plops onto my cheek as Mathieu lays me in my bed. He's crying? Why? I shut my eyes, not wanting to see or hear or feel anything.

"It's okay. You can go. I've got her," Erianne whispers.

"What's he even doing here?" I snap.

"I called him." She runs her hand down my head over and over again. My mother does exactly this to me when I get upset. I grip my pillow as the aching all over my body becomes unbearable. I welcome the darkness as it overcomes my body.

39

A week has passed since my world was filled with a dark void. Erianne has been a leech on my side, but I'm thankful for that. I don't know what I'd have done without her here. Lucas disappeared as if I never existed. As if *he* never existed. I don't care either. This is more his fault than it will ever be mine. I don't ever want to see him again.

Mama's funeral was one of the hardest things I've had to make it through in my entire life. Nothing can describe the crippling pain that runs through you as your mother's casket is lowered into the ground. The sky shone bright that day for her though.

An anonymous donor paid for everything. I normally would've turned it down, but I don't think I'd have been able to pay for any of it anyway. Erianne took care of all the arrangements. Mama would have liked the pink Chrysanthemes that surrounded the funeral home. Our flat is so quiet and empty now. I'll never hear the clinking of dishes, get a whiff of her famous *cassoulet,* or feel the warmth of her protective embrace when my anxiety gets the best of me.

The front door downstairs clicks. *Mama?*

"Abbs, hey, it's me." Erianne's voice echoes throughout my flat as she walks inside.

No, not Mama. I don't feel like talking right now. Her heels tap against each step as she makes her way upstairs and into my bedroom. I crinkle my sheet under my hand as I'm reminded of my mother once again. All I want to do is wake up from this nightmare.

"Come on. Why don't you come out with me today?" The bed shifts to her weight as she sits next to me.

"I don't want to go anywhere," my voice cracks.

She runs her hand down my hair. "You can't stay in this bed forever."

That's a novel idea. I roll away from her.

"Alright. That's it. Get up." She shoves me out of my bed.

"What are you doing?" I growl as she yanks me up and forces me to stand.

"I am getting you out of this house. Now, get in the shower. I'll set your clothes out for you. Meet me downstairs in twenty minutes or I'm coming back up here after you!" Her eyes bore into mine.

I lower my head. She isn't going to give up. Silently staggering my way to the shower, Erianne follows behind, turning the water on for me. She is so pushy, so bossy. But so strong… I wish I could be strong like her. She's put her entire life on hold to care for me like this. It warms a small corner of my heart.

I shower and get dressed. Erianne drags me out to shop for outfits for Armistice Day. I had no idea the holiday is just a few days away. Usually Mama and I celebrate every single one together. Not this year…

"What do you think of this?" Erianne holds up a bright yellow top.

"It's cute," I say flatly.

I don't have the energy for any of this. I know she's only trying to help, but shopping isn't going to make the hollow ache in my chest go away. None of this is going to bring my mama back. None of this is going to change the truth: the reason she's gone is because I couldn't keep away from *'the oh so famous Lucas Danforth'*.

"Yeah. You're right. It's not really for me." Erianne examines my face. "Why don't we grab something to eat?"

"That's fine." I shrug.

"I just have to pay for these earrings first," Erianne says and loops her arm around mine.

As usual, I'm being dragged along by her with no choice in the matter. But I've just accepted it as part of being her friend.

We approach the register, but the cashier is reading a newspaper. The popping of her gum as she chomps on it like a mad cow is ear-splitting. Erianne narrows her eyes and clears her throat.

"Oh! I am so sorry, mademoiselle!" The cashier quickly sets the newspaper on the counter. "What can I do for you?" She beams at Erianne.

"Just these earrings." Erianne politely smiles back and hands the sparkling silver earrings to the cashier.

Glancing down at the newspaper, one of the headlines catches my eye: *"Rouen resident victim of neighborhood robbery."* I haven't heard of any robbery. Rouen is usually really good about keeping the crime under wraps. If there was a robbery, I'd have definitely heard about it. I lean in closer to read more.

"*Thirty-two-year-old Carla Emeline Halsey, of Rouen, was enjoying a normal afternoon in her home following Toussaints. That Sunday, around 9:00pm, two assailants entered her home. Police Nationale Officer Croww stated Mrs. Halsey was shot multiple times. Her death is being ruled a homicide. No suspects have been named at this time…*"

What the hell did I just read? My heart sinks. Blood rises to my head. That was no robbery. How can they talk about my mother so callously? Who the hell do these people think they are?

"*J'en ai ral le cul.* This is *putain de connerie*!" I shout, not giving a damn who hears me.

Erianne rushes over. "What is it, Abby?"

"Who the hell does he think he is?" My voice booms, carrying throughout the store.

"Who?" Erianne asks cautiously.

"That scumbag Dominick Vitale!" I scream.

The cashier's eyes shoot open and her jaw drops. Erianne tries to pull me away from the counter.

She whispers, "Abby, quiet down!"

"Screw that!" I yank away from her. "Why aren't the police doing something about it? My mother wasn't a victim of a robbery! That worthless man thinks he can murder my mother in cold blood and just get away with it? Fuck this!" My rage builds and builds, consuming me. I can't control it anymore.

I storm off down the street. And I don't care if Erianne follows me. That man is not getting away with this. My mother's death will not be lied about like that. I know why that man has so much 'power'. It's because all the people of Normandy give it to him by fearing him, working with him, and even acknowledging his name.

"Abigail! What the hell are you doing?" Erianne shouts.

"I'm going to deal with this man once and for all!" I call over my shoulder.

I don't bother turning back. I know what I need to do.

Her long slender fingers wrap tightly around my arm, stopping me from taking another step. "You need to stop and think Abigail!"

"Think? Are you kidding me?" I try to yank my arm away, but she's stronger than she looks. "All I've done is think! Think about how my mother was killed because I couldn't stay away from Lucas Danforth. Think about how she felt so cold when I held her in my arms. Think about how I will never...*never* hear her voice again because some sick sadistic man thinks he runs this city!" I savor every shallow breath I'm able to inhale.

Erianne's eyes gloss over as a tear rolls down her cheek. "Abigail. I know you're hurting, but whatever it is that you think you're about to do...just stop. This isn't the way to handle this. Please. Just come with me," she desperately pleads.

"No." I glare. "I'm going to confront Dominick Vitale."

40

"You're what?" Erianne's face drains of all its vibrance.

Her fingers loosen around my arm enough that I'm able to pull free. "You heard me. I'm done talking about this."

"Abigail! Stop right now!" she orders.

"No, Erianne! I'm going whether you like it or not!" I shout.

Before she's able to change my mind, I turn away from her and storm off down the sidewalk. I need to do this. I need to confront him and to know why he would do this to my mother. And I need to know what my father has to do with any of this. They need to be stopped. I may not have experience in their lifestyle, but I won't let this go.

A glossy black Bugatti with a single crimson stripe down the side pulls up along the sidewalk as I reach the corner. I look over as the passenger side window rolls down.

"Get in!" Erianne calls from the driver seat.

"No! I'm going!" I keep walking.

The car moves forward to keep up with me. "Then at least let me be the one to take you!"

As soon as the words register in my ears, I immediately halt. "What did you just say?"

She throws her hands up. "Damn it, Abby. You're so stubborn! You're going to go whether I let you or not. So at least let me take you! I know where their manor is, and I've been there before. I grew up with Lucas, remember? You'll never get past the front gate without me!"

I squint. "You promise that's where we are going?"

"Yes! Abby, get in the car!" she yells.

I hope she knows I'm not kidding. I get in the car and don't relax until I'm sure we're driving away from home. I lean back into the seat once I see unfamiliar signs and we drive down roads I've never really seen before. The more we go along our route, the less buildings there are around us. I can tell we're close because there are no houses, buildings, shops, or really anything besides the grass and trees for miles. A family like theirs would be the type to live isolated from everything. I guess it makes sense when you're a criminal

"You're sure you want to do this. Just say the words and I'll turn back." Erianne stops the car in front of a long, paved driveway.

Staring down the path, I can see the smallest glimpse of the Vitale manor. The rage boiling within me only magnifies at the sight of it.

I nod. "Just go."

Erianne drives down the driveway and up to a wrought iron gated entrance where two men are standing on either side. One of the men nod at Erianne, she returns the nod, and the gates open. Erianne continues through the entrance

The manor that was barely visible a few short seconds ago now towers over us. It's so dark and unsettling despite that it's the middle of the day. Shaking off the unease, I hop out of the car.

"Follow me," Erianne calls back as she walks up to more men in black suits blocking the two doors leading into the manor. Same as before, when Erianne nods at them, they allow her past them without hesitation. But my path is immediately blocked by the shorter of the men.

"Where do you think you're going?" The man stares me down.

To any other person, possibly even myself at any other time, he would be intimidating. Right now, though, he does not scare me one bit. I know what I'm here to do. If I let this man deter me, then there's no way I'll be able to face Dominick.

"I'm with her." I maintain eye contact.

Erianne's eyes fly wide open. She steps forward. "She's okay. She's with me."

"Mr. Vitale won't be happy you brought her here." The taller man growls.

"I'm here to see Dominick." I bark right back.

Erianne locks eyes with me, mouthing '*Shut up!*'

The two men blocking my path chuckle. "Looks like you'll be going to two funerals in one week." The shorter man bellows, staring at Erianne.

My cheeks blaze as I ball my fist. Erianne shoves past them, pulling me inside before I do something to make all this worse. She doesn't let go as we rush through the foyer and into the main hall. The creaking of the front doors echo off the lofty ceilings as the men shut them behind us.

Erianne keeps her hold on me as we step into an office. My head spins, but I'm focused. My chest aches, but I'm determined. My legs and body are numb, but I've never felt more alive. This is for my mother. She isn't here because of him.

Dominick is sitting at a desk positioned in the center of the room, a familiar smug grin plastered on his face. He thinks he's being clever or instilling fear in me, but he's only making me more and more pissed by the second.

"How can I help you Ms. Halsey?" he asks.

I scoff. "How can you help me? You murder my mother and you want to know *how you can help me?*" I can't manage to hide the rage in each word that spills out of my mouth.

He laughs. "I did no such thing. My hands are clean." He waves his hands in the air to taunt me further.

My blood boils over. "How dare you deny it! You're sick! You won't get away with this!"

His grin widens. "Did you read the paper? Was it your mother that was the victim of that neighborhood robbery? I'm so sorry to hear that." The mocking tone in his voice is only fueling the rage coursing through my veins.

I squeeze my fist tighter. "You know damn well she wasn't a victim of a robbery! What did you do, pay off the police?"

"Didn't I tell you that you'd find out what happens when you cross me, little girl?" He spews the words out so callously.

That's it. I cannot and will not take this anymore. I charge toward him, not holding back. His goon blocks my way as he cackles.

No. I shove the man with the red tie back hard enough that he stumbles and continue after Dominick. The man is quick to regain his grasp, stopping me from reaching him.

"Abigail!" Erianne's shrill cry from behind me barely registers in my ears.

I glimpse behind me to find another man has Erianne held with a gun to her side. The shiny, black metal reflects off the sunlight peeking through the curtains. *No. Not Erianne.* I remain stock still, unsure of what this man is about to do to my best friend. I shoot a cold stare back at Dominick.

Dominick holds his hand up. "I have a proposal for you, Abigail." He smirks.

I glance at Erianne, then back to him. "I'm listening."

"I thought you might see it my way again. I hope you know to take me seriously when I ask something of you now." He rubs his chin thoughtfully. "It's obvious as long as you're here, you'll never leave my boy alone. With that being said, I've arranged transportation for you to travel to the Americas."

I blink my eyes rapidly. Did I just hear him correctly?

"You did what?" I stare at him, dumbfounded.

"You're from America so why not explore the states? Start over. Start fresh. Go. Explore! Meet someone who can make you happy because my son won't be that person. And, if you go, I'll leave Erianne here alone. I'll let her go, and you can live your life without any more intervention from me or my employees." Dominick folds his hands together.

An unnerving silence darkens the room as I consider my options.

"Abigail, don't do it!" Erianne screams. "Ouch! Stop!"

I glance back. The man digs his gun further into her side. I don't have a choice right now. I won't let what happened to Mama happen to Erianne. I can't, and if me leaving for good means she'll be safe, then what other choice do I have?

"You give me your word that Erianne will be safe? You won't interfere with her life either?" I face Dominick, my mind made up.

Dominick holds both hands in the air. "You have my word."

I look back to Erianne. As I stare at her, all I can do is think back to the day we met. She was there for me in the simplest way, being so kind, so generous when she barely knew me. The pleading, grave expression clouding her face makes my chest ache. I have to make this decision. For her.

"Abigail don't trust him. He'll hurt me regardless of what you do! Don't do this! Remember, the night at O'Kallaghan's when you told me Rouen is your home! Abigail do not do this. Please." Tears stream down her face. "Think about Lucas!" She screams a final plea.

"Yes, do think about Lucas," Dominick says.

He signals something to the man holding Erianne. In the same instance, the man shoves Erianne down to her knees and puts the gun at her back. *No, no, no.* He places his finger on the trigger.

"Stop!" I scream as loud as I can, "I'll do it!"

"I'm sorry, but what was that?" Dominick cups his ear.

"I said, I'll do it. I'll leave. I'll go to America," I yell at him.

"No, Abigail!" Erianne screams, her voice cracks.

"You can let her up," Dominick orders coolly to the man holding Erianne. "I knew you would do the right thing." His grin widens, baring his teeth.

"Like you would know anything about doing the right thing," I spit.

Dominick laughs. "That may be true. However, your travel arrangements are set. You'll take a plane from the local airport to New York. I'll provide you with enough cash to get you started."

"No," I snap.

"Excuse me?" He straightens in his seat, his smug grin turning downward.

"No. I won't take a plane." Straightening my stance, reaffirming my confidence, I glare back at him.

"What do you suggest then?" The amusement in his voice has diminished.

I think back to the conversation with my mother about how we came to America to begin with. I remember every detail. She said that we came over on a ship called the Royal Princess. It seems only fitting I go back to the Americas the same way I originally came here. Besides, it's going to be the only piece of my mother I'll be able to take with me.

"If I'm going to do this, then I'll only leave on the Royal Princess cruise ship," I say.

Dominick rubs his chin. "I know the ship well. I can work with that." An eerie grin creeps over his mouth. "It's settled then. The ship ports in Le Havre December 3rd. I'll make the arrangements." Dominick returns to being overly pleased with himself. "It was a pleasure doing business with you ladies! Dubois, see these two out." He orders the man with the crimson tie.

Great. On my birthday. Happy birthday to me…I don't like how he agreed so easily. Something doesn't seem right about that. Erianne and I are forcefully removed from the room. The man isn't even giving me a chance to walk on my own. Any other time I may have been scared. But now, it's as if my body is present and my mind has checked out. What did I just do?

The doormen from before are waiting with the doors to the manor wide open. Both men grin while Erianne and I are shoved out. The man with the red tie releases me as soon as we reach the bottom of the front steps.

Their laughter reverberates through my ears. Erianne and I rush into her car. I haven't even got the door shut all the way and she's already squealing out of the drive. Watching her hands shake as she grips the wheel to turn onto the street, I can't help thinking of how all of this has affected her. Her life was just fine before I came into it.

"You're out of your damn mind! What is wrong with you? Why would you agree to that?" Erianne yells through the tears still cascading down her face.

"What are you talking about? He was going to hurt you!" I squeal.

I won't lose anyone else and I *cannot* believe she thinks that was an option.

"You don't understand, Abigail. He will not stop now until you're gone. Do you even comprehend what you just did?" She starts to relax as we drive further and further away from the Vitale Manor.

She must think I don't intend to follow through on my word. By leaving, I'm ensuring Lucas' safety, Erianne's safety, and the safety of everyone else involved. As much as I love Rouen, it just doesn't feel the same anymore without my mama. It's like there's a hole in my life now, a deep emptiness I can't ignore. I love Erianne, but nothing is the same.

"Abigail, say something!" Erianne shouts, breaking me from my thoughts.

Shaking my head, I stare absently out the window. "I have to do this Erianne. Everyone will be better off. All of your lives can go back to normal once I leave. You'll see."

I resist the urge to look at her. I know if I do, I won't be able to hold myself together.

"You don't know what you're saying, Abigail." She weeps.

The knot in my chest tightens. I open my mouth to speak, but tears threaten to break through. I *cannot* start crying or I won't stop. As we pass La Couronne, I realize we aren't far from my flat anyway.

Erianne continues softly crying in the driver's seat as she pulls the car up to the front of my place. Staring up, it hits me that in just a few weeks I'll never see this place again. I'll never see the woman sitting next to me that has become such an important part of my life. Everything I've ever known, as far as I can remember, will be gone forever. It hits me that in just a few short weeks it will be time to say my final goodbyes to everything I've known since I was ten years old.

41

The moonlight shines in through my bedroom window as I lay cocooned in my blanket. My bed probably has the perfect impression from my body with how much time I've spent in it, comfortably drowning everything out.

I can't believe I really agreed to leave. I don't remember any part of my life from when I was in America. I was only ten and I'm still trying to get all my memories back. If Mama was here, she would know what to say, what to do. I bury my head further in my pillow.

It's been almost two weeks since she's been gone, but it feels like years. Every second with her gone, is another second I wish she would've taken me with her. I hope she knows how much I miss her. I hope more than anything that she knows how sorry I am. Despite my best efforts, a tear streaks down my cheek onto the plush, pale pink pillow. Swallowing hard, I close my eyes, shoving the tears back. I have to focus on the happy moments, the good memories.

She was always so full of life when she'd cook or bake. I'll never forget the way her face lit up when she successfully made a cider lamb for the first time. The entire house was filled with the savory scent of the lamb, the sweet hint of cider, and a lingering stench of burnt meat. She burned the first one and it stunk *so* bad.

She made so much food for All Saint's Day. The fridge is still packed full of the leftovers. My stomach rumbles as my mouth salivates. I'd really love some of her cooking right now too. Even though the darkness is creeping around the corner, I can't handle crying anymore.

Hopping out of bed, I head downstairs and straight for the kitchen. The lamb should still be good. Lifting the cover of the dish it's resting in, the familiar savory, sweet aroma fills my nostrils. It definitely doesn't smell like it's gone bad.

Just as I pop the container in the microwave, a loud rapping on the front door about scares me half to death. I drop my shoulders, sighing loudly. It's probably just Erianne trying to talk me out of leaving again.

The rapping continues, more frantically this time. I wait, hoping she just decides to go away. More frantic, even louder knocks on the door make it clear that isn't going to happen. Shuffling my feet, I go to open it. Instead of being greeted by an over-exuberant redhead, my breath gets caught in my throat at the sight of glacier blue eyes staring back at me.

"Have you lost your fucking mind?" Lucas yells, barreling into my flat, making me scramble backward. "What are you thinking, Abigail?" Lucas asks, lowering his voice just enough that it isn't ringing in my ears.

"What are you talking about?" I keep my voice quiet because I don't have the energy to poke the bear tonight.

He takes a deep breath, pinching the bridge of his nose. "Don't play dumb with me. Why were you at my home? Why the hell did you make a deal with my father? You know, just when I think you'd learn about prying into things, you find a new way to prove me wrong." He growls.

I'm sure him finding out is partially Erianne's doing. Who does he think he is, though? Barging into my home like this after disappearing like he did. He has no right to yell like this. Let alone even being mad with me.

"*Ouais, enfin*, just when I think you're not who everyone says you are, you go and find a way to prove *me* wrong!" I spit back.

Lucas staggers slightly. "What is that supposed to mean?"

I scoff. "Where have you been, Lucas?"

"Abigail, I..." Lucas runs his hands through his hair, his anger dissipating with my one simple question.

"You know, I thought everyone was wrong about you. That maybe no one took the time to get to know you, but I was wrong! I should've listened when I was warned to stay away from you!" I scream back, my chest lightening with every deep, steadying breath.

His voice is barely audible, "You don't mean that..."

"I mean every word! And you know what? I'm starting to think us having the same therapist and then her dying wasn't a coincidence. So, tell me the truth, Lucas. Did you find out I went there and start going too?" I shout as the thoughts swirling around in my head leave my lips without a filter.

He steps back, shaking his head. "No. I—"

I narrow my eyes. "Don't you dare lie to me."

His shoulders droop. "I did."

"What?" I ask, backing away from him as a cold tremor runs through my body.

"Please understand, I know it sounds crazy, but I didn't mean for all of this to happen. I didn't think it would go this far." He rushes to me, but I quickly move away.

I hold my hand up to keep him at a distance. "What are you saying?"

"All I did was ask Erianne to find out a little about you." He runs a hand through his hair.

I step back. My chest feels like it's just been smacked with a baseball at 70KPH. "Did your father ever order anyone to watch me?"

He shakes his head. "My father found out about you when I told him I didn't want to go along with the marriage anymore."

"So, you're telling me you set this in motion? That my mother is dead, Dr. Carrere is dead, all because *you*?" Unable to swallow away the tears, I let them flow as my blood boils. Lucas' silence pisses me off even more. "Get out!" I shove him as hard as I can.

He doesn't move and just stares down at me with sullen blue eyes. I try to shove him again, but he swiftly grabs my wrists before my hands can make contact with his chest.

"Stop this!" he says softly, his voice trembling.

I try to yank free from his hold, but he grips my wrists tighter. "Let me go! Get your hands off me!" I scream until all the air leaves my lungs, forcing me to catch my breath. "I. Don't. *Ever*. Want to see your face again."

Lucas drops my hands and staggers backward. His face blanches as he gawks at me, stepping backward toward the door. He runs a hand through his hair, his hand trembling violently.

I scurry backward, my back connecting with the wall. The house phone above my head is knocked loose. Falling off the mounted base, it dangles by the wiry cord. I quickly grab the receiver.

"If you don't leave, I'm going to call Erianne." I swallow hard. Calling the police isn't an option.

Tears streak his cheeks. "You think I'm going to hurt you?"

Lucas shakes his head, covering his face with his hands. My heart shatters seeing him like this. I know, deep down, *I know*, he didn't mean anything by what he did. But how can I not blame him? My mama and Dr. Carrere died because of Lucas. I'm so pissed at him, every inch of my body aches. Leaving will be easier if he thinks I don't love him anyway.

He turns around and opens the front door. "Maybe it's better this way. I'm no good for you."

His shoulders shake as he walks out, slamming it shut behind him without even looking back at me. The thud echoes throughout the room, making me wince.

My stomach churns. I cover my mouth and run to the bathroom, sliding to the floor and hovering my face over the toilet just in time. My stomach heaves and heaves until I'm my head spins. Dizzy, sweat beading along my hairline, I grab some toilet paper with my trembling hands to wipe my mouth. Collapsing to the bathroom floor, I pull my knees tight against my chest, sobbing uncontrollably.

He came here to change my mind, but only made me more certain I should go.

42

Only one more day left before I leave, and I'm pulling a shift at La Couronne. Normally, I'd be dreading it. However, things have changed since Delano disappeared. The owners of the restaurant have stepped in as management. They're saying he mailed a letter of resignation that said he wanted to move across country…

Being back at work with Erianne gives me a sense of calm, but the bittersweet ache has been gnawing at me all day. This is the last day I'll ever work with her. The owners were kind enough to give her the day off tomorrow to spend with me. Delano definitely would've never done that.

After he left, the owner's found out about Erianne's mother. Turns out Delano appointed her the financial liaison for the restaurant. They'd been filtering profits and stealing from the company. *Pfft.* She's even the one that made up the stupid dress code. Something about everyone wearing the Vitale family colors out of respect. The owners had no idea what had been going on. They announced they're buckling down on security, but so far, the only 'security' that's been put in place are the shiny new padlocks on our lockers.

"Hey, you ready to go?" Erianne shuts her locker door just as I enter the break room.

"*Oui*." Forcing a smile, I slide my jacket over my shoulders.

"Oh! I almost forgot!" she blurts.

She turns to open her locker again, pulling out a large package wrapped in bright orange, glossy paper. A poofy red bow sits on top, bouncing with her movement.

"What's that?" I ask, furrowing my brow at the bright wrapping.

Erianne's cheeks flush a light shade of pink. "Just something small I wanted to get you." She shoves it at me. "Open it!"

Grabbing the package, I'm surprised by its weight. Careful not to tear the masterpiece of Erianne's wrapping, I remove the paper. Inside the box rests a ruby red pea coat. I pull it out, and the large black buttons reflect the light. Tears pool in my eyes as I stare at the gift.

"I don't know about the weather in America, but I heard it's really cold over there. I just figured you could use it," Erianne croaks.

I lower my coat to find tears rolling down her cheeks. She's making it incredibly difficult not to cry, too. I rush over, wrapping my arms tightly around her. "Thank you." As she squeezes her arms around me, the tickle of tears meets my own cheeks.

She releases me, chuckling slightly. "Look at me getting all emotional."

I laugh with her as I place the coat in my locker. "I'll wear it tomorrow."

She smiles. "We better get going. Everyone is probably waiting for us."

Linking my arm with hers, we stroll outside. "I still can't believe this is going to be the last time we go to O'Kallaghan's together. Or at all, really. For me at least."

"I know, but that's exactly why we're going to make it a night to remember!" she says as she pulls me along with her down Place De La Pucelle.

The last time I heard that was when I got that invite to the Vitale masquerade ball. It was for sure a night to remember and not in a good way. But I know this is entirely different.

As we approach the front step of the Irish pub, a wave of nostalgia hits me. I don't have long to think about it though because Erianne has already grabbed ahold of my arm. Matching the grin growing across her face, I let her drag me inside just as she did the first time we came here.

These little things have so much meaning to me now. The stale odor of beer oddly deepens the ache wallowing at the pit of my stomach. Not able to contain myself anymore, I hug her as tightly as I possibly can.

"Enough of that. We're here to have fun." Erianne's voice cracks despite her efforts to hold the tears at bay. "Let's go get drunk and forget about all of that for a while!"

This is my last night here in Rouen. I don't know what tomorrow has in store for me, but I do know I'm going to miss her. She's become part of every thread of my life. I wish things were different. They aren't though and I made this decision. I need to stay strong because there's no backing out of it now. All I can do is enjoy the time with everyone while I can.

Tomorrow will come.

43

Today is the day. The day I leave everything behind. When I imagined my future, I never thought it would include me leaving this place. Rouen is my home. I went through so much convincing Mama to stay here. I've always thought of it as a great place with rich history.

It still is, but now that I know about Dominick's influence, I also know Rouen has a dark history. That dark history seeps into every corner of the town. Meeting Lucas has been life changing, to say the least. I used to have my life all planned out. One look at him and all of that got derailed.

Some people would call what I'm doing now *brave*, taking a ship over to the Americas, but it's for selfish reasons. I need to get away from here and start my life over.

Erianne wouldn't let me go alone today, so she drove me to the docks at Le Havre. By wearing the red pea coat she got me and tugging Mama's red suitcase, I get to bring a piece of home with me. The wind is abnormally harsh today, adding to the mountain of nerves crawling through me. The image of going through a storm on a ship in the middle of the ocean sends a shiver down my spine.

"*Now boarding! All aboard the Royal Princess!*" A raspy voice announces over the speakers by the dock, pulling me out of my thoughts.

"It's time." The knot in my throat is suffocating as I stare up at Erianne.

"Oh, wait!" She digs into her bag, pulling out a small red book with a tiny bow on top. "I saw this in a shop window last night on my way home. It made me think of you. Now you can write about all your adventures over there and your time on the ship. Don't think that gets you out of writing me to tell me all about it though!" she says as her cheeks flush. Her emerald eyes shimmer as tears pool in them.

"Thank you! I love it!" I quickly wrap her in my arms. "I'm going to write you every single day!"

Erianne returns my embrace, breaking the dam for our tears and turning us both into sobbing messes. "Don't go turning American over there on me and forgetting all about us here. I don't care what anyone says or where you were born." Her arms wrap tighter and tighter around me.

"Erianne, I could never forget you! You would hunt me down anyway if I even thought about it." I giggle.

"*Last call for the Royal Princess! Departing Le Havre to New York City in America!*" The voice echoes from the speakers again.

"You better go." She reluctantly releases me.

I nod but can't seem to will my feet to move. I don't want to do this right now. Maybe I shouldn't. Maybe there's a way to fight back against Dominick. "Erianne. I'm not going." I drop my suitcase.

"What?" She pulls me to the side.

My lower lip quivers. "I can't leave you like this."

Tears pool in her eyes. "Oh, Abby. I wasn't supposed to tell you this, but…Lucas left town last night. You have to go. Dominick is going on a warpath."

My jaw drops. "He did *what*? Why?" Fear lances through my body.

She shakes her head. "All I know is he told his father he wants nothing to do with the business anymore and he left."

All the air evaporates from my lungs. "Erianne. Dominick only made that deal with me to keep Lucas here. What if…" I wring my hands. "Erianne I can't leave now. He's going to come after me. He might hurt you! I can't let that happen!"

She quickly wraps me in a hug. "It's going to be okay. I promise. I'll handle this. You just need to worry about getting yourself on that boat." She holds me at arms-length, her voice cracking, "You hear me? You get on that boat and you don't look back. No matter…" Her eyes squeeze shut. "No matter what happens, you *don't* look back. Okay?"

With my shoulders shaking, I nod. Erianne can fix this. Her mother can keep her safe now and there's nothing I can do. Even if I went to Dominick, he may not even believe me. Erianne knows what's best. This is the last time I'm going to see my best friend for a long time. We need to leave with happy memories. I have to trust her. Taking a deep, steadying breath, I pick up my mama's suitcase, packed with everything I could possibly fit into it. It's kind of hard to pack your entire life away into one tiny suitcase though. As my feet step onto the boardwalk leading up to the ship, I steal one last glance back at Erianne.

She's running toward me. I step toward her, my body trembling with fear. Something's wrong. She stops in front of me, breathless with a wicked gleam in her eye.

"Screw… this. I'm coming with you."

I drop my suitcase. "You're… what? But…" I can't find the right words. I'm so damn happy. Is this real? This is really happening? Maybe I'm hallucinating.

"Abby, there's nothing left for me here. What would I really be staying for? To get in the middle of some stupid feud. Nope. Let's go travel America." Her familiar mischievous grin warms my heart as she lifts up my suitcase, extending it to me.

What the hell. I grab the suitcase, smiling and swallowing past the knot in my throat. She links her arm with mine and tows me along onto the deck of the ship. A part of me wants to turn around and run back home to the flat I shared with mama. But the other part knows I have to keep moving forward. It's like I've reached the finish line. The end of my old life and beginning of a whole new journey. Erianne and I squeeze our way through the crowd to lean against the railing.

"*Now departing!*" The raspy voice makes the final boarding call as the boardwalk is stowed away.

"Oh!" Erianne squeals. "Your surprise is here!"

I try to spin around to see what the hell she's talking about, but she roughly twist me back around to face the dock as it slowly fades away.

"No peeking!" She shouts.

I chuckle. "This must be a really big surprise."

"Well. I'd like to think it is." A familiar smooth voice says from behind me.

The knot in my throat expands. I drop my suitcase and turn to face him. My hands fly up to cover my mouth as tears streak my cheeks.

"Lucas?" I choke.

He opens his mouth to respond, but he rakes a hand through his hair. "I'm sorry. I know we have a lot to talk about. I... know you might not even want to see me."

That's right. We didn't exactly leave things on the best of terms. I want to run to him, but remembering how I got here, how he played a part in all of this stops me. I squeeze my eyes shut. Stupid, stupid, stupid. Him or me. I don't know. Maybe both.

"How?" I keep calm, breathing through the desire to run into his arms. "How are you here and—" My voice cracks. If I keep talking, I'll cry. I don't want to cry in front of him right now.

"To hell with this." Lucas blurts and closes the distance between us, wrapping his arms tightly around me.

I tense, but as the comforting scent of lavender and cedar fills my senses, I relax slowly into his touch. I never thought I'd miss this smell so much. And now I'm the one who sounds like a creep. Burying my head into his chest, I revel in the warmth of his embrace. This. This is what I've needed. His hand runs soothingly down my hair.

He pulls away, swiftly kissing my forehead. The gesture is polite to him, but it's so foreign. Like we're back to where we first started, keeping each other at arm's length.

Lucas takes a step backward, away from me. "I'm so sorry. I swear to you. I didn't mean for any of this to—"

I grip his t-shirt like he's going to slip away if I don't hold on tight enough. Pulling him back to me, I throw my arms around his neck, pressing my lips to his desperately. My stomach tightens as I rake shaking hands through his hair, pulling him closer, pressing my lips harder to his. His fingertips snake onto my waist, gripping tightly.

Erianne coughs loudly. "Idiots. I'm still here."

I leap away from Lucas as my cheeks burn. He keeps his hold on my waist, pulling me back against him with a wolfish grin.

"I knew you missed me." He winks.

I playfully smack his chest and roll my eyes. Leave it to him to hang onto that stupid ego of his even after everything. But it's kind of growing on me. I'd never admit that to him. Not a chance in hell.

I shake my head. "This doesn't get you off the hook. That was just… a hello kiss. You know, because… it's been so long. And it doesn't mean we're back together," I stammer, wringing my hands, "We still need to talk."

He nods. "I know."

Erianne chuckles and leans against the railing, staring as the docks shrink to a tiny spec in the distance. I wriggle free from Lucas' arms to watch with her. All of this is so surreal. Staring out at the enormous ocean, a bittersweet ache fills my chest. I'm leaving behind everything I've known for so long.

Erianne used to be a stranger to me; an old schoolmate I was thankful to work with because she never made me feel alone. Lucas is still the arrogant boy who can't see past his ego, but I fell in love with his playful boyish charm. I don't know what's going to happen with us. Maybe we can find a way to be friends.

No matter what we decide though, I couldn't imagine my life without *either* of them. And now here we are, cruising to America together to start a whole new one. Despite how much I've lost, having these two at my side makes me feel like there's still hope left after all.

"To die is nothing; But it is terrible not to live."

- Victor Hugo

Note to the reader – *You*!

Thank you for taking the time to read *Death 2 My Past.* I genuinely hope you enjoyed it! Don't worry if you cried. I did too. But alas, wipe those tears! Abigail's story isn't over yet…

Yep. That's right! Abigail's story continues in *Death 2 My Present*. Follow her through a string of gut-wrenching twists and turns that take her (and you) across the ocean in a transatlantic cruise to America aboard *The Royal Princess*.

Some unexpected familiar faces boarded the ship, but now Abigail has the fierce love of her friends, new and old, behind her. So, what's stopping her from taking them all down the same way her mother was cut down? Careless, swift, and without recourse. Will Abigail fight fire with fire? Or will her intensifying depression continue to eat away at her until it consumes her will to fight?

Death 2 My Present

Coming soon…

Lightning Source UK Ltd.
Milton Keynes UK
UKHW010633160720
366640UK00002B/451